THE FANGS OF THE FEN SNAKE

Act One

Copyright © 2022 Howard Sargent

All rights reserved.

ISBN: 97984394261329

THE FANGS OF THE FEN SNAKE

ACT ONE : THE HUNT

For Helen

ACT ONE : THE HUNT

THE FANGS OF THE FEN SNAKE

The Fangs of the Fen Snake

Prasiak, "Shak"; the leader
Crastanik, "Stan"; the muscle
Gremmick, "Stauncher"; the healer
Kalinaga, "Dead Eyes"; the scout
Randali, "Dormouse"; the novice

Lord Prasiak Mazuras, Shak to his friends, commands a warband specialising in raids and sabotage behind the lines of the enemy. He fights for the country of Arshuma, whose ten-year conflict with their rivals of Tanaren has left a vast area of the latter country a wasteland, home to wolves, bears, and other beasts too terrifying to comprehend. His latest mission is a little unusual, to kidnap an heiress enroute to her wedding, and to deliver her for ransom. At first, the operation goes like clockwork, within two days they should all be safe and sound, counting their hard-earned coin and making plans to return home, possibly for good.

Then though things start to go horribly wrong.

Their horses gone they have no one to guide them save an eccentric hermit with a questionable grip on sanity. Together, they are forced into a long march through the wilderness; wandering amongst trackless forest, scaling high cliff faces, journeying over water, and both above and below snow-capped mountains, battling an array of monsters as they go. And all the time they are being pursued; firstly by knights, whose number includes the brother of the kidnapped girl, secondly by assassins, one of whom appears to hold a long-standing grudge with his quarry, and finally by a local army patrol rife with internal tensions. As hunters and hunted prepare for their explosive final showdown, all are disturbingly aware that at least some of their comrades have already seen home for the last time.

This novel is an account of an incident that took place in the war between the countries of Tanaren in the west and Arshuma (the invader) in the east. A fuller account of this war is given in the novel, "The Forgotten War", by the same author.

ACT ONE : THE HUNT

THE FANGS OF THE FEN SNAKE
CONTENTS

1. A LETTER FROM A BELEAGURED GENERAL   PAGE 10

2. THE GODS OF THE ARTORAN CHURCH   PAGE 14

3. ACT ONE: THE HUNT   PAGE 18

ACT ONE : THE HUNT

THE FANGS OF THE FEN SNAKE

A letter from a beleaguered general

To Grand Duke Leontius, Ruler of Tanaren, commander of its armies, bulwark against the Arshuman invader, I hope this letter finds you safe and well.

As you are by now undoubtedly aware our army has suffered a catastrophic defeat in battle, at a place known locally as Wolf Plain. Our general, Baron Lukas Felmere, is dead and the city of Grest has fallen back into enemy hands. This letter attempts to clarify the political situation here, in lands where things could be best described as "volatile".

One of the most important frontiers at the time of writing is the river Whiterush. Broad and swift it serves as a barrier as impenetrable as any fifty-foot wall and the only bridge, close to the city of Grest, is under Arshuman control. Suffice it to say that all lands east of the Whiterush are now Arshuman territory. This includes every city, town, village, hamlet, and border fort constructed by Tanarese hands and populated mostly by Tanarese people. Tis a grievous occupation and all of those of our blood that live under the yoke there cry out to be free once more. Yet liberation might be hard for us to deliver, and for one simple reason,: treachery.

For our defeat at Wolf Plain would have been a great victory had not one of our own turned his banner Arshuman yellow and charged his former allies in the rear, precipitating our defeat. I refer of course to Baron Fenchard Aarlen of Haslan Falls, or, as he is now styling himself, "King" Fenchard of West Arshuma. "West" Arshuma is the name he has given to the lands west of the Whiterush that lie between that river and the river Vinoyen. He claims it all as his personal fiefdom, his reward for betraying his country for Arshuman gold. Yet the situation is not nearly as clear cut as he claims.

That is because this "West" Arshuma is still very much disputed territory. Fenchard does not have the men to either control or administer such a large expanse of land. Furthermore, I have heard from those that have deserted from him and returned to us that there is much dissension in his ranks, that many are still loyal to Tanaren and to you and are only being kept in check by threats, violence, and the mercenaries that Fenchard has bought with Arshuman coin.

Even more importantly though, the greatest city and fortress in this disputed territory remains in Tanarese hands. I refer of course to Felmere city itself. The blue and white flag of Tanaren still flies from its battlements and every day its army swells as those scattered at Wolf Plain return, and deserters from Fenchard's army seek sanctuary here.

We will not cede this city, this country, without a fight. Arshuma seeks to strengthen Fenchard's cause by deploying their own raiders and bandits in our lands, seeking to harry and disrupt our resistance to their barbarism; but they will not

ACT ONE : THE HUNT

succeed.

We hear from our spies that Fenchard plans to assault Felmere city soon, that his general, Trask, is building siege engines for this purpose. They will find us obdurate and unyielding, for every one of us who gives his life's blood for the cause we will send two of them into the furnace. Our cause would be greatly aided though if you could send a force north from Tanaren city, to threaten Fenchard on two fronts, to keep him constantly looking over his shoulder.

In conclusion my Lord, I ask for aid. We are still here, we are still fighting, and we will turn every blade of grass red in order to purge ourselves of the traitor baron and the Arshuman menace from whose strings he so willingly dangles. I am a humble man, relatively unlearned, yet I was charged in Baron Felmere's will with the responsibility of leading the resistance, and to, Gods willing, finally send the Arshumans back to their swamps and their wastelands and leave us free men once more. We can do it; of that I am confident, but any assistance rendered by the capital city and by your honourable self can only hasten our deliverance. All glory will be yours, and the chroniclers of our nation will speak your name with the same reverence afforded to your ancestors, Typhon the Nation Builder and Evan the Founder.

For Tanaren! for freedom! For Leontius the Liberator!

Dictated by Protector Baron Morgan of Glaivedon, Chief Prosecutor of the war in the east and defender of Felmere city.

THE FANGS OF THE FEN SNAKE

ACT ONE : THE HUNT

THE FANGS OF THE FEN SNAKE

The Gods of the Artoran church

Like many northern nations the people of Tanaren and Arshuma follow the polytheistic Artoran faith. Originating in the cities of Chira, Anmir and Codona it was carried westward, northward, and southward as the Chiran empire expanded over the years to the extent that it is now the dominant religion in half of the known world. Every village has a house of Artorus, where any of the Gods can be worshipped and larger towns and cities often have houses devoted to one specific god, several houses in one town. The principal gods and goddesses in the pantheon are as follows though the total number of gods that constitute the entire pantheon number over a hundred.

ARTORUS- The father and leader of the Gods. Often depicted as bearded and wielding either an axe or hammer he is responsible for order in the world, for the movement of sun and moon and is seen as the protector of those that worship him.

CAMILLE- The consort of Artorus. Depicted as a humbly dressed woman with short, cropped hair she is said to embody both wisdom and mercy. Those who wish for peace in this world often invoke her name.

ELISSA- Daughter of Artorus and Camille, Elissa is a much more popular goddess in Tanaren than her mother. Depicted as a long haired, voluptuous figure she is the goddess of motherhood and the embodiment of all that is feminine.

LUCAN- The God of magic. He is a shapeshifter constantly taking on the physical attributes of the various magical disciplines, frost, lightning, fire, earth etc. Common folk fear Lucan almost as much as the gods of the damned though he is their protector just as much as his brother, Artorus.

MYTHA- The God of war. Depicted as either bear or bull he is one of the most secretive of the gods. Who his priests are is unknown, all that is known is that they are warriors and that before battle they perform the rites of blood and sacrifice upon those seeking victory on the field of conflict.

UTTU- The God of storms and extreme weather. Depicted as a giant smiting the skies with his double headed axe of lightning it is his intemperate nature that causes thunder, howling winds and raging seas.

HYTHA- The God or Goddess of the seas. Male or female depending on which part of the world you hail from it is Hytha that steers ships to a safe

ACT ONE : THE HUNT

harbour and the eye of Hytha that is painted on the keel or prow of every boat or ship that follows the faith.

SARASTA- Goddess of the harvest. Depicted as a tall woman carrying a basket and wearing a wide brimmed hat Sarasta makes fields bountiful and orchards fruitful. Every farming community reveres Sarasta as much as they do Artorus.

MERIEL- Goddess of healing. Houses of Meriel are both places of worship and hospitals, they are where children are born and where the elderly make their final journey to the next world, where plagues are treated and wounds are dressed, everybody needs a house of Meriel at least once in their lifetime.

UBA- The God of fools. The mad, the stupid, even the intelligent who have lapses of reason or concentration are said to be touched by Uba. A colourfully dressed, spindly fellow it is Uba that controls games of chance, all gamblers are therefore beholden to him.

JHUNA- Goddess of nature. Only the most remote areas of the world worship Jhuna and her priestesses are the most secretive of all. Their rites and ceremonies are jealously protected, all that is known is that they take place in fields and sacred groves, often at night and that sacrifice is involved. What is actually sacrificed though is known only to very few.

HUAGA- God of slaughter. Not really part of the pantheon he is a god imported from the far south by unhinged mercenaries and soldiers who are no longer able to wipe the smell of battle from their nostrils. Worshippers believe that every life they take increases the god's potency and their own standing in his eyes. No god inspires so much terror in civilised parts.

KETH- God of the damned. The brother of Artorus and his would be usurper. Banished to the underworld after his defeat he constructed the furnace upon which the souls of the condemned labour ceaselessly creating the demons of fire that he hopes will retake the seat of the gods and return him to power. He is a dark figure always depicted as being wreathed in flame, to serve Keth is to be damned for eternity.

XHENAFA- Harbinger of the dead. The withered one. The one tasked with guiding the living into the world of the dead, with transporting their souls to stand before the gods to be judged. The only god that the living ever sees and then it is only for the last moment of their life. Skeletal, cold, Xhenafa is the only god never to appear in depictions of the pantheon, for to paint him is to invite death into the world.

THE FANGS OF THE FEN SNAKE

ACT ONE : THE HUNT

The Fangs of The Fen Snake

Act One

The Hunt

1

No one could deny that she was beautiful. She lay, face turned up to the sky, flaxen gold hair spread about her shoulders, arms folded over her chest, hands resting on a linen shift embroidered with images of birds on the wing, their carmine and turquoise feathers fluttering in an imaginary breeze. Ordinarily, there would be a bloom about her, full berry-red lips opened in laughter, her laughter a song to shame the minstrels as she ran barefoot over lush grass. But that was an image from the past for now she was abed, and her lips were grey as ash, and her bed was one of wood and oil, and her bloom was with the Gods. For Lady Mazuras was lying in the peace of death, long before her time.

And her murderer lay next to her, on the same pyre, and this murderer was bound head to foot in pristine swaddling clothes, an infant stillborn, its only purpose in creation being to claim the life of its mother. So together they lay, side by side, waiting for the touch of flame that would consign body and soul to the Gods.

The pyre sat on a small bare hillock next to which lay a silent, dark mere, its waters still and mournful. Across the mere were the gates, towers and walls of a city, grey stone spattered with lichen, flags flying from the towers, black flags and flags of sunflower yellow bearing the heron emblem. The towers were high and watchful, shutters open, sentries patrolling, yet even the bustle of the city seemed strangely subdued. To the west of the city lay a long stretch of marsh, lime green in colour, a thin, washed out green reflecting the glare of still water and silent pools, and to its south, shimmering in the half light of the dawn was the ocean, waters barely moving, the few ships resting on it silhouetted by a sun that was by now starting to peek nervously over the distant mountains in the east.

A crowd had gathered around the hillock, a well-dressed crowd, velvet, silk, damask, boots of leather, buckles of brass and gold, brooches

ACT ONE : THE HUNT

studded with gems, cloaks embroidered in gold thread. It seemed the finest citizens of the city were gathered to watch and sing and pray, yet one figure amongst them stood out.

And he stood out probably because he wasn't amongst them. The torch bearing priests surrounded the pyre, the mourners stood a respectable distance back yet one of them was defiant, planting his knee length black leather boots on the bare strip of ground twixt priests and watchers. He was a tall man, rangy, long legged and spare of frame though most of his body was swathed by a thick cloak of purple velvet. His hair was black, thick as wire and streaked with grey, cut to the length of his collar. He had shaved recently but despite that stubble was showing around his chin, the skin of his face being brown and weathered. He wore a moustache in which the grey was more prominent than in his hair, it had been clipped carefully so that it did not exceed the width of his thin, bloodless lips. His nose was high bridged and characterful; it would have dominated his narrow face if it hadn't been for his eyes. Large and deep brown but flecked with amber they stared resolutely outward and expressed …. nothing. It could be seen that they had the depth of a castle well and that they could convey laughter, joy, and sorrow to a degree of which an actor would be proud, they were sensitive eyes, even caring eyes, but they were not now, now they were as blank as the city walls. Lord Prasiak Mazuras had extensive experience of concealing his emotions when he had to.

He did not join in the singing, concentrating solely on staring at the pyre and the figures resting atop it. Nearly everybody else did sing, their fulsome, lusty voices carrying over the marsh and startling the white wading birds into indignant flight. At the very back of the crowd though were two other men and they also had declined the call to song. Young they were, yet to make their mark on the world, they were both wearing cloaks fastened with brooches girt with rubies and carried swords that hung casually from their belts in scabbards finished in silver. One, fair haired, sporting a poor attempt at a beard stood half a foot taller than his fellow, a man with a full face which had not yet banished the chubbiness of youth. His hair was brown and unkempt and though his clothing matched the others in terms of richness, it looked far shabbier as it fought his tubby frame.

And they were not singing because they wanted to talk, craning their lips to the others ear they spoke in whispers loud enough to defy the description of that word. And it was the fair man that spoke first.

"It is a terrible morning, is it not? We only arrived at last evening's prayers and the whole city seems to be in shock. There are black flags in the streets, everywhere stinks of holy incense; how has your family been, especially your poor uncle?" He nodded towards the man next to the pyre.

"Uncle Prasiak?" the podgy man shook his head. "He has barely spoken since her death. Four children, none of them lasting the week and the fourth one took auntie Elspeth too. They were devoted, Shak and Elspeth, how devoted we only found out this morning when he spoke to all the family just before the funeral procession. Things will be changing in Mazuras now; you can be sure of that."

The fair man's eyes widened in surprise. "What do you mean Garazar? Isn't your uncle going to remarry? It is one of the reasons my sister came with us, father is keen to discuss arrangements when he can."

Garazar shrugged his shoulders. "No idea Banacides, normally I would say it was a certainty, the Mazurans and the Cressenids have been the closest of allies for centuries. And the most intermarried." He sniggered. "But if there is going to be a marriage it will have to happen pretty sharpish, Uncle Shak will not be living here much longer, that was what he told us this morning."

"Not living here?" Banacides frowned. "You speak in riddles friend."

"Well we are all confused at the moment, my uncle's words still haven't sunk in properly."

"But how can he consider leaving?" Banacides persisted. "His father is ailing, when he dies Prasiak will be the ruler of the city, head of one of the founding families, he cannot go anywhere at a time like this."

Garazar gave him a sly smirk. "But he is, he told us as much and one thing Shak is, is a man of his word. He is renouncing his inheritance and crossing the belt, going north to fight the Tanarese in that poxy Agana war. My father wishes him well seeing as he will now be next in line, and of course when father is gathered by the Gods the burden of heading the family and ruling the city will fall upon..."

"You." Banacides practically croaked.

"Me." Garazar gave him a fat smile redolent with smug contentment.

"Wait." Banacides ran his hand through his hair where strands of it caught the breeze and blew away freely. "Why? Why go north to fight for the cursed Agana family? Aren't there enough conflicts here in the south? Bect is fighting Zatalia, Crathobek is fighting Lungmus, there are family feuds in the east. No one wants to fight for the usurper king, we send the minimum number of troops north and always the worst quality and Mazuras has been at

ACT ONE : THE HUNT

the forefront of this resistance. Your uncle would surrender the city, his wealth, his birthright, for that?"

"I fear," Garazar made an attempt at gravitas that he was sadly ill equipped to achieve, "that the God of fools has driven sense and reason from my uncle's mind. He was emphatic when he spoke this morning, that it would be Ilasko Mazuras that will command on the death of lord Ragun, and that when Ilasko is gathered unto the Gods it will be Garazar Mazuras that will rule. Perhaps your sister should be looking at me as a future husband. I seem to have far better prospects than Uncle Shak at the moment."

Banacides looked sceptical. "I am sure your uncle will come to his senses soon enough."

"I have not your certainty. Remember, I was there when he spoke to the whole family," Garazar was now betraying the faintest hint of triumph as he spoke. "Do you want to know what I think? I think my uncle wants to cross the belt, to fight in a war no one here cares about because he no longer cares if he lives or dies. This city is poison to him now, his inheritance means nothing, he wants to never see the place again. All he wants is death, and a death in battle is the best ending for a warrior is it not? I will wager you a thousand kopits that once my uncle leaves the city, he will never return again."

The singing had stopped hushing them both into silence. The head priest made the final eulogies then recited the prayer of Xhenafa before nodding to his acolytes and stepping well back.

One by one the torches were thrust into the piles of kindling that supported the pyre. Soon, helped by the breeze that blew westwards across the fens, tongues of flame started to set the wood to crackling. It would only take minutes before the oil turned the pyre, and the dead upon it into a torch that could be seen for miles across the drear flats, by the peat diggers and shellfish harvesters punting their flat boats over the narrow watercourses. It would be seen from the city, by the populace starting to crowd the city walls, it would be seen from the ocean, by the seamen hoisting the sails or gathering in nets or anchors, and it would be seen by the folks of the mountains to the east, mountains whose snow-capped heights were now blushing cerise under the glow of the strengthening sun.

But there was one man who had no desire to see the full power of the conflagration, no interest in seeing the flesh of the dead crisp and blacken till only the charred bones remained. Lord Prasiak Mazuras turned and made his way through the watchers, who parted in silence as he approached. Down the hill he went, not changing expression, not looking back. Seeing him draw close though, his nephew Garazar Mazuras went up to him as though to offer him words of condolence. He had not the skill of masking his feelings like his uncle though, insincerity crawled across his face like nettle rash. He opened his mouth to speak and at that moment, for the first time, Prasiak saw him, and the falseness that he embodied.

They bumped, arm to shoulder and the younger man was almost sent toppling. Prasiak did not open his mouth, did not bother to see his nephews scowl, he just carried on along the road to the gates as behind him the pyre started to collapse into cinders.

ACT ONE : THE HUNT

2

It had felt like an awful long time since he had been in such a city. It wasn't even a city in truth, just a provincial town, but to a man more used to wilderness these days it seemed like a bustling metropolis, more akin to his home city of Mazuras than what it actually was, a surly, resentful little backwater that had been living under occupation for a long time.

Occupied or not though, it still had to do business, money still had to be made, people still needed to eat and for that purpose Arshuman coin was as welcome as Tanarese to the traders in the market street. Shak was walking amongst them now, boots leaving imprints in the soft mud, looking left and right, taking in the smells, sights, and sounds, remembering at last what to mingle with humanity meant. He felt its coarseness, its laughter, its shouting and cajoling, its heckling and berating, its complaining and its gossip, it felt to Shak like meeting a friend one had not seen in years. His nostrils were full of the scents of mud, leather, and sweat, of wood smoke and coals, of damp and of ordure, and of food, hot food that was not salted meat, dried fruit, hard bread, or something that had to be tracked for hours on end, killed, skinned and consumed raw. He stopped at one of the food stalls, a long trestle that sat under an awning stained black by wind and rain. He checked himself for a moment, surprised that the man working behind it was a burly fellow in his late thirties sporting an impressive ginger beard. Most of the stallholders, indeed most of the people of the city were women, with the majority of the men being very old or very young. Few men of fighting age remained in such places, they were either in the Tanarese army out west, or they were taking coin as turncoats in the Arshuman army, or they were dead. Or in this case crippled, for at last he noticed that the man had only one leg and supported himself with a stick, leaning upon it heavily.

"You want something?" the man asked gruffly. It was the voice of a Tanarese man addressing a hated Arshuman, Shak knew straight away he would have to pay over the odds for anything here.

But the food did smell good. He spotted tagli, spicy meat or fish parcels cooked in pastry. It was an Arshuman speciality, so the man may have resented his conquering overlords, yet he was pragmatic enough to cater for their tastes. Elsewhere he spotted cheese in batter and fish and pepper

ACT ONE : THE HUNT

skewers, both Tanarese favourites. Shak liked them all, his culinary preferences were not determined by nationality but by the more visceral responses of his nose and stomach, and they were both in full approval right now.

He bought two of each and, with juices from the tagli running down his chin continued on his way. Exiting market street, he turned and headed for the city walls, where the first stop in his double rendezvous lay. The city walls were maybe eight feet high, augmented by sharpened wooden stakes fixed on top of the badly mortared stone. The gate towers were originally built of stone too, small and unprepossessing they had been strengthened and greatly enlarged by the addition of two high wooden towers, that had been built both over, and next to the stone ones. Protected by hides and stakes they could each accommodate some twenty to thirty men and were one of the main bases the Arshumans used to exert authority over the town.

The south tower's narrow doorway was guarded, two men in leather and mail, spears bearing a yellow pennant. Shak was going to hail them when through the door stepped an amiable looking fellow with a stained yellow cloak fastened tightly by a silver buckle in the form of a rearing lion. He wore a broad smile that sat easily over his heavy jowls and under his fair, pencil thin moustache. On seeing Shak, he gesticulated ostentatiously, beckoning him in through the door whilst hailing him in a voice of which a lion would indeed be proud. "Shak! Earlier than expected! But times are auspicious are they not? Come on through, we have much to discuss."

Wordlessly Shak followed the man into the tower, it was a sturdy structure, walls and ceilings supported by tarred crossbeams, and was some four storeys high. As he climbed the ladders up to each floor he passed bedrolls and weapons, men playing dice or scooping food from wooden bowls. It was a cramped life, guard duty, for Shak the months stuck in the wilderness had suddenly regained their appeal.

The yellow cloaked man led him up to the third floor and into the only private space in the tower, a room partitioned by linen screens barely large enough for the two men to fit inside together. The man kicked his bedroll into a corner then placed a table covered in charts and letters (mostly still sealed) next to it. After gesturing for Shak to sit on the rooms only stool he disappeared outside for a moment before returning with a stool for himself, perching himself upon it with all the grace of a drunken bullock.

"I lost a man Ogun." Shak saw the man looking at his food with

THE FANGS OF THE FEN SNAKE

lascivious eyes and so offered him one of the fish skewers, an offer that was greedily accepted. "I never lose men needlessly, not till now, Red's death was avoidable and that is something I shall not forget or forgive easily."

Ogun chomped on his food, almost devouring the skewer too. "You have lost men before Shak, " he glibly pointed out.

"Oh, I accept that I cannot keep everybody alive forever." Shak's voice had a deep, rich, timbre that almost set the wooden tower to shaking. "But Red was run down by horsemen I had not planned for, that we had not planned for. The intelligence we had was bad and I only compounded the error by not setting a watch, we had been told there would be no guards after all. My people are a tight knit team, we go into enemy territory, hit them hard and get out before they can respond. It went wrong this time, if it goes wrong again I will be back here seeking answers. Understand?"

"As clear as an Artoran bell my friend." The fish had been eaten; Ogun was now waving the skewer around like some sort of conversational aid. "But we have a new man here for you, and another job, a job for the best of us, a job for the Fen Snake, a job for you."

"You know I hate that name." Shak ate his final cheese in batter and reluctantly handed the final tagli over to Ogun, who popped it into his mouth without looking at it. As he tasted it though his eyes rolled upward in inexpressible pleasure.

"Ah, tagli, they do not make it hot enough here, but it still tastes like home."

"So what is this job then?" Shak asked bluntly. "It had better be quick, and easy, the winter snows are not far away, and I have no intention of spending days up to my neck in the stuff."

Ogun wiped his fingers on his cloak, eased himself onto his feet and trod the cramped space, floorboards creaking underfoot. "Maybe quick, but probably not easy, but then, Gods take you for a fool, it is your choice to be here after all, you can hardly get sniffy about orders from the generals. If you are that unhappy you can always go back to the fens of Mazuras and claim the city off your brother, sorry, I mean your nephew now your brother is dead. How many years have you been out here now?"

"Nearly five." Shak replied tersely.

"Five since you lost your wi…"

Shak nodded. "Been out here that long. Swore never to go back…"

"But you are head of one of the founding families!" Ogun protested.

ACT ONE : THE HUNT

"You could have any command you wanted out here, you could be king Aganosticlan's right hand…"

Shak cut him off sharply. "Neither I, nor my family ever want to be associated with the usurper king! No southern noble ever would be. It is why I am out here, raiding supply lines, intercepting their scouts, staying well away from the hierarchy of "command" …"

"I am a southerner," Ogun pointed out. "Yet I am out here."

"Because it is in your interest to be so. For southern nobility this war is toxic, an attempt by the usurper to swell his prestige at the expense of ours. But for you, for merchant's sons, for those who are not the wealthiest yet not the poorest, coming out here is a good way to increase your families' standings. You are the governor of the town of Tantala for Artorus sake, it is a rank and a status that you could never achieve at home. When this war is over, if we keep the land we have gained, you will have wealth you would never attain selling burlap to the provinces."

Ogun gave him an unctuous smile. "And the war couldn't be going better, the key town of Grest is back in our hands, some Tanarese barons have defected to our side, we are holding more territory now than we have since the first months of the war. Ambassadors have been sent out, the Tanarese Grand Duke must surely be keen on suing for peace, and I hope to do very well out of that peace. We will surely keep this town in any political settlement. I have the word of the king no less, the king saw me and praised me just days ago, on the way back to his palace."

"But Felmere has not fallen," Shak pointed out. "And until it does all our gains mean nothing."

"But their baron is dead, and the city is surrounded, it is only a matter of time before they surrender, one harsh winter is all that it will take."

Shak smiled for the first time. "Then it seems I am not needed anymore, perhaps I shall return home after all…."

"Ah!" Ogun lifted the small flap of hide that concealed the tiny window in his ad hoc office and stared at the bustle of the streets below. "When you came out here it was as a man of integrity grieving for his wife and trying to put a life behind him that was all bad memories. Yet you still remarried the day before you left. A strange thing to do, as many people said, for somebody who wanted to sever all ties with his past."

Shak stood then and joined Ogun next to the window, a stiff and cold breeze shivered through it causing him to blink to moisten his eyes. "Let me tell you a tale," he said, his thin lips pale as the cool sun outside. "As I stood there and saw my wife prepared for burning I had made my mind up; my home was a curse for me, I was going never to return. My father was dying, I had already made my peace with him so my brother could have the city, plunge himself into the struggle of maintaining Mazuras pre-eminence in the far south of Arshuma. I had had enough of it. Then though, as my wife and child burned and I walked back through the crowd I saw my brother, he could barely stop himself from smiling, it was a good day for him, he had as much excess of ambition as he had an absence of talent. And then I brushed past his boy, and he was exactly the same. And I knew that neither of them had the capability to run the city properly. I still wanted to leave, but at that point I was no longer sure that I would never want to return, especially if the two of them run the place into the ground. So yes, I decided to keep by options open; the day before I left I married Naressie, of the Cressenid family. I spent one night with her, giving me claim on any child she might have and allowed her to return to her family in their city. If one day I do need to recapture Mazuras, I now have allies I can call upon. Head always ends up ruling heart with me, which is the way it should be in those born to rule, and I am sure it is a lesson you yourself have long learned in this place."

Ogun returned to his stool. "Long learned indeed. You know, you should sire a bastard while you are out here, always handy to have an heir to back up your claim."

Shak did not look at the other man; he was still staring out the window. A soldier was relieving himself against the stone tower opposite, a couple of cavalry men were riding into the city, kicking splashes of mud over the protesting locals. "I do not get many opportunities, spending nearly all my time out in the wilderness."

"The Tanarese baron of this city fled long ago, but he left a couple of his daughters behind. They are kept hostage in the manor house, but I could hand one over to you if you wanted, you being of noble stock and all that."

"What are they like?"

"Middling. In looks and brains. Their sister had ten children though so if you want to sire a bastard they are of fertile…"

"I shall think about it after I complete this task you have for me."

Ogun didn't appear to have heard him. "Stock. But then you have a girl in your war band. Perhaps you could…"

Shak laughed uproariously at that. "Dead Eyes? Are you mad? Firstly,

ACT ONE : THE HUNT

she is an elf, or a Wych as they call them out here. Secondly a man tried to force himself on her once. Before he died she made him watch as she draped his severed genitals over his nose. Now, what orders are you trying to give me? Bear in mind I will probably say no to them."

Ogun watched patiently as Shak returned to his stool. Then he went to the table of papers and after ferreting around a little while handed Shak a crumpled sheet on which the seal had been broken. "The Agana seal?" Shak noted. An order from the top then?"

"The intelligence was first received when the king was spending a few days in the reconquered city of Grest," Ogun tried to clarify things. "I am not sure how much you know but our victory at Wolf Plain has changed things. All lands east of Grest and the Whiterush river are ours, all lands west of Grest up to the Vinoyen river and beyond belongs to Fenchard the turncoat. He is calling it West Arshuma but in truth his control over the territory is limited. Our men are there, southern slavers are there, mercenaries and brigands are taking what they can off the locals, and Tanarese resistance is still strong in places. It will take a long time to establish order in the area, a long time. And that is where your quarry is located..."

"A Tanarese heiress?" Shak raised an eyebrow as he read the missive before him.

"Yes. She has been stranded there. She was on her way south to marry one of their barons, but Fenchard holds the south now, so her route is blocked. And returning to her home means travelling through a land chock full of brigands. She is stuck, and ripe for plucking."

"Won't Fenchard get to her before we can?"

Ogun shook his head. "No, he knows nothing about her... yet. It was our scouts that spotted her and her small retinue holed up in some Gods' forsaken village, isolated and wondering what to do next. One of the scouts, a man called Siras, will take you there, he has horses waiting, you can leave in the morning because speed is essential here. We want her taken and brought here before Fenchard becomes aware of her."

"And you want to keep her away from him because..."

"Her name is Eleanor Lasgaart. The Lasgaarts are a major Tanarese family out here, you know, you have fought them often enough. If Fenchard gets hold of her and things start to go badly for him, there is nothing to stop him keeping all the money we have given him, marrying her himself and declaring for Tanaren again. She would give him legitimacy in Tanarese eyes, but we obviously want to keep him as beholden to us as possible; if he marries, it will be to an Arshuman girl. So you go out there, snatch her and bring her back to us. We can keep her and ransom her back to the Tanarese when the occasion suits us."

"And how large is her retinue?" Shak growled, shaking his head and giving the impression that he was very unhappy with what was being presented to him.

"People were deserting as the scouts watched them. Siras can tell you more, my guess is that there will be a dozen fighting men at most when you arrive."

"Four of us, five including this scout, Siras, against twelve." Shak put his hands behind his head and stretched. "I have faced better odds, and worse."

"Six," Ogun pointed out. "It will be six. We have a new man for you remember."

"I pick my own people," Shak's eyes glittered in the half light of the tower. "This is dangerous work, work for an elite, for people used to moving quickly, living off the land and killing swiftly and silently. To have one man present who is not up to it is to doom us all."

Ogun set his chin as firmly as he could, Shak could be a very intimidating presence, no one crossed him voluntarily. "He will not slow you down," was all he could manage by way of reply.

To his surprise Shak laughed, he clasped his hands behind his head and laughed. "It is some nobleman's whelp isn't it. A fourth or fifth son, not an heir, not an equestrian, not a priest, someone his father has no use for, so he is gambling on death or glory for him. And if it is death who is going to care anyway? A boy that won't be missed by anyone of note. If not a fourth son it is a bastard. Good armour, finely crafted sword powered by an arm that has never lifted anything heavier than a lady's skirts. Come on then, tell me I'm right, or shall we lay odds instead? Ten kopits enough for you?"

Ogun shifted on his stool, briefly wondering if he should donate it to the city torturers. "No odds, you are not entirely correct, but you are still too close to the mark."

Shak got up and went to look through the window again. "The whelp stays here, or I am not taking the job. Give it to some younger blades eager to prove themselves. As I said earlier, perhaps I shall go home after all."

Ogun picked his nose, rubbing the extracted mucus on the leg of the stool.

"You know this is a job for you and no one else. I would say that doing it would increase your standing with the king, but I know you would say...."

"I couldn't give a rat's carcass for my standing with the king."

"Exactly. So I am asking you to do it as a favour. For me. We have helped each other out many times in the past so I am asking for just one more such favour. Just take this boy. I don't care if you gag him and tie him to the saddle, just so long as he can say he went out with you. And you are right, if he dies he dies, it will be an honourable death at least."

"There is no such thing as an honourable death." Shak was looking at the nearby streets. A man was selling some scarves on one of the main thoroughfares. The scarves were cheap, badly dyed, they would run like a river once they tasted rain. A couple of Arshuman soldiers were trying to move him on but he was waving his arms and resisting. A crowd had gathered and were shouting at the soldiers in the man's defence. "Arshuman cock!" he heard a woman berating them. Other, pithier epithets soon followed as the crowds' anger grew, this was yet another incident started over the most trivial of matters, more hatred fomented, the cycle truly was endless. He turned away from the window.

"We will never take this place," he told Ogun. "We have won so few locals over. Using the sword and nothing but the sword has gained us nothing. As to your proposal, well it has set me to wondering why I am here at all. You see I quite like the Tanarese people; they have spirit, to still resist so fiercely after all that has been done to them is admirable. I take no pleasure in killing them, I only do it when I must. So what am I doing, talking to you, so far from home? Truth is I am here because the challenges are the greatest, the odds the slightest, the enemy the fiercest. And I have never kidnapped an heiress before. So yes, I will do this for you. It may well be my last mission up here so why not end things doing something... memorable. I will see my people, and this scout, and we shall prepare to leave at first light."

Ogun, evidently relieved, stood and shook the other man's hand. "Gods grant you swift success my friend. Now I need to get to the manor house to send your new recruit over to meet you. Where are you headed next?"

"To meet and brief my people. They are staying at the Crippled Beggar tavern. Send him over there. What does he look like?"

"Nondescript, but he knows of you and your appearance, he will seek you out. I only wish you had chosen a different inn that is all."

Shak had noticed Ogun's face falling. "Why? Is the beer bad?"

"Fine, to my knowledge. It is just that the inn has a reputation as a hangout for Tanarese loyalists. My men rarely go there and those that do often come out with their nose greatly altered in shape."

Shak released Ogun's hand and patted him on the back. "Do not be so crestfallen my friend, my people are expert at keeping a low profile. They won't even be noticed."

Ogun continued to shake his head. "Artorus make it true, I would hate you to lose your team in such…. inglorious circumstances."

Shak gave him a reassuring smile. "Do not worry, my people are the best, they will have no intention of tasting a tavern floor."

ACT ONE : THE HUNT

3

Crastanik Bectalis had tasted many tavern floors in his lifetime but this one was possibly the most noisome he had encountered so far. He was proud of his name, Crastanik was an archaic moniker from Arshuma's distant past, before the days of exile. It meant, "the mighty one", which made it all the more irksome when he was called Stan. Everybody called him Stan come to think of it, there was a time he would have turned the culprit upside down and dunked his head into the nearest horse trough but now it happened so often he supposed he had become inured to it. Stan he was and Stan he would be until his heart stopped beating. And speaking of beatings, he was currently having his arse handed to him.

He had just been tipped over a table, it had upended sending ale, pewter plates and spilt potage flying in all directions, a lot of it landing on him. With a world weary groan he eased himself back on to his feet and wiped some tepid soup off his weathered jerkin. It always took him a while to stand, being such a tall, stocky man meant that he had never been built for speed; strength though, now that was another matter.

He put his large, doughy hand to his neck, easing out a crick and looked down on his tormentors with dark, beady eyes. He was an almost bald man, his only hair being a small ring of steely grey that sat on his pate like a wreath. He had a wide, flared nose, a wider, generous mouth with lips as thick as an eel and a dimpled chin to which clung strands of thick wiry beard, for he was never an attentive shaver and often missed a clump here and there. He beamed at his enemies, his teeth large and white, though about one in four of them were missing.

He had three opponents, all wiry men a good head shorter than he was. Their leader was a fair haired fellow in his thirties, his companions being somewhat younger. Why they were not at war was anybody's guess, deserters maybe, bandits probably, suddenly discovering a surge of ale fuelled patriotism ten years after it was really needed. It didn't matter really, all that did matter was that they needed to be taught a lesson.

He looked over at the table where he had been enjoying an amiable meal and drink before his urge to chance his arm at dice had got the better of him, and into this little spat. His two companions were still drinking and eating

ACT ONE : THE HUNT

and regarding him with a certain wry amusement borne of the confidence that he was in nowhere near the degree of trouble that he appeared to be. Stauncher had got ale foam on to his thick, auburn moustache. He was grinning from ear to ear, pox scars cratering his sallow cheeks, gold teeth glinting in the lantern light, shapeless felt hat sitting on his head like a somnolent cat. Next to him, petite and delicate, peridot eyes full of laughter was the paradoxically named Dead Eyes. She had a round face for a Wych, blue black hair cut short, sharp ears fully displayed as though daring anybody to comment on them, that scarlet tattoo of a flying bird with its wings spread covering her forehead. She dressed in tight fitting green leather looking every inch the tracker that she was. If he was in trouble they would be at his side in a moment, that was the camaraderie that four years serving together in this guerrilla war had bred in them. But they had judged that he wasn't in trouble, they had seen him laugh off far worse scrapes than this. Still, there were three of them facing him, one lapse in concentration could have nasty consequences. And the day had started so well for him too...

****

She was in bed with him, counting the scars on his chest, looking for new ones as though he acquired them purposefully, just to intrigue her, just to give her a new game to play every time he returned to her. Like him her hair was shot through with grey and her breasts these days reminded him of pendulous pig skins, filled to the brim with water but it mattered not. She was still his Aureline, always there for him when he needed her, though the price was ever the same, a verbal searing from that scalding tongue of hers.

"Do you know what today is?" She asked him.

He shook his head.

"Eighteen years since we first met, back in Bect, when you picked up all that linen for the soldiers."

"Is it really?" His voice betrayed an abject lack of interest.

"Really," she nodded. "We hooked up almost immediately. Lived in that place near the cliffs. Till the war started and we came north, firstly to Kitev and then to here. Do you remember why we moved?"

"Because I am a soldier?"

"Partly. But mainly because I listened to a block headed ox and believed him. "There is a war on in the north, let us move there, I could make a fortune fighting in it." So we moved to Kitev. Then it was "We are winning the war, let's go west, towards the frontier, I could make a fortune fighting out there." So we did. And, after eighteen years do you want me to sum up the results of these moves and your quest for wealth beyond our most feverish dreams?"

"Sum away."

"Well, I swapped a one room flea infested hovel in Bect, for a one room flea infested hovel in Kitev, for, and I hope you can contain your excitement, a two room flea infested hovel in Tantala. And this fortune you have supposedly accumulated, what exactly have I got here that bears witness to the piles of gold you have made in your travels? Anything at all?"

"Er..."he shifted uneasily under the sheet, "a new brooch?"

"Precisely," she said in triumph. "A new brooch. Eighteen years for a new brooch, with a sapphire in it, which you can just about see on sunny days if you hold it up to the light. Do you know something Stan? I am beginning to believe that all your promises and your sweet assurances of love might actually be, let's see, what is the word...."

He braced himself. "The genuine sentiments of an honest man?"

"No," she purred. "Not quite, I was rather thinking that you have, over your entire life, done nothing but talk complete and utter bullshit!" The last word was spoken with such vehemence Stan had to open his eyes. Aureline slid out of bed and started lacing up her dress, her face red and puffy as she vented her spleen. "When will you accept that this," she waved her arms at the small room. "Is no longer acceptable to me."

"Erm, it is not that bad really, at least you have a view." He said sheepishly.

"Because we are on the third floor of a slum! One window, very well, let me see what this "view" is exactly." She made an exaggerated pretence of looking through it. "Ah yes, there is the large pile of refuse by the wall, oh and it looks like it has been recently enhanced by somebody who has thrown a dead dog onto it! Obviously as a garnish for the heap of rotten cabbage that has been there for days. Only the rats get fat in this place! And there is the sewage trench behind it and lo, what timing I have, a small boy is crapping in it as I look! If only the wind would change so we could get the smells as well as the sights. And tonight, if you are here tonight, directly underneath us you just might see a couple of soldiers rutting with the local whores!"

"Well, it is a colourful area, lots of local character...."

"Enough!" Aureline raised her arms to the heavens. "Stan, I put up

ACT ONE : THE HUNT

with this in years gone by because I believed it was just a stepping stone to something better. But it isn't is it? This is the something better, with the life we are living we can hope for nothing more than this. Problem is, we are both getting old, and you cannot keep cracking heads forever. Soon all of the men you face will be younger, fitter and stronger than you and then where will you be?"

She had a point. He rested his chin in the palm of his shovel like hand. "It is all I can do love. I fight, I am a fighting man. I know nothing else."

"Well," she said sharply. "You will have to learn something new if you want to keep me. I am moving back home, back to Bect and I am taking the kids with me."

He sat up at that, back straight as a spear. "What do you mean? What will you do, how will you eat?"

"I will wash and darn clothes, work in the fields, brew and sell ale, there are a thousand ways to make a living if you but knew it. I want a house Stan, just a small house with a cottage garden where I can grow things. A house with a well and an apple tree, where I can hear the birds singing instead of the drunks. I have worked hard all my life and I think I am not being unfair when I say I deserve it. It would be easier for me if you joined me in this, but it is your choice, I am going home regardless, whether you like it or not."

Her chin was set firm, yet again he felt himself feeling pride at having the loyalty of such a woman. She was trying to give him an ultimatum, but he knew that she would never abandon him. Even so, he had to at least sound like he was compromising. "I suppose I could turn my hand at something else, let me speak to Shak. I used to do a bit of smithing in my youth, I can dig, put up fences, anything that requires a bit of muscle. Perhaps it is time for a change, I should see more of the kids I suppose, I am sorry I wasn't here when little Ergenie..."

"I do not blame you for that, she slipped away quickly, there was nothing anybody could do about it, you being here would have made little difference...."

"But I could have held her hand."

She shook her head dismissively, her face set hard, eyes staring fixedly ahead of her. "The Gods will what they will. Now is not the time for blame, I have cried enough over it. Anyway I still have five other mouths to feed..."

"I have seen them all except Monyzas, is he avoiding me or something?"

THE FANGS OF THE FEN SNAKE

Her smile returned, she started to tie her hair back. "He is nearly sixteen, he spends most of the time with his friends. You know he wants to join the army don't you..."

"A fine young man. His father's son." Stan beamed effusively.

"The Tanarese army that is."

"What!" He choked then started to cough, it took him a minute before he could speak again. "Why in the name of Keth would he want to join the enemy? Does he hanker for bad food and worse teeth? Does he fancy the idea of never having to wash again?"

She gave his shoulder a playful slap. "I have been in this town for four years. He was eleven when he came here, he has grown into manhood here. All his friends are from Tanaren, he speaks like a local, he calls himself Morran because it sounds more Tanarese..."

Stan raised his right hand. "All right, all right! You have made your point. Artorus beard, I never thought he was my boy anyway."

"Why would you say that?" She managed to affect affronted indignance whilst tying a cloth over her head.

He shrugged his shoulders. "Because nine months before he was born I was garrisoning the forts around the belt, didn't see you for months, plenty of opportunity for you to find alternatives."

"You are wrong," she said matter of factly. "You were with me; you didn't move to the garrison until seven months before his birth. Definitely."

"You sure?"

"Of course."

He eased himself out of the bed and started pulling on his clothes. "Oh well, I never could count up to nine."

She was adjusting her dress now, tightening her laces. "Mind you, Aliata and Merisite are nothing to do with you, their father was a Kitev wool merchant."

He shrugged his shoulders, apparently completely unsurprised. If anything he seemed to take a perverse pleasure in her words. "Ah, now that is no shock to me at all."

"It isn't?" She looked disappointed. "Why?"

He pulled on his leather jerkin and started fastening the straps. "Oh come on," he said, inviting her to stare at his torso, though in truth it was struggling slightly to fit into its leather sheath. "Could a bull like me ever be capable of fathering mere girls?"

ACT ONE : THE HUNT

****

Stan was back on his feet. He stretched out his right hand and started to click the bones in his fingers. It was a good sign to someone who knew him well and Stauncher was just such a man. He could see that Stan was preparing a response, the next few minutes were going to be interesting.

Stauncher was of course not his real name, Gremmick Prasticas was too much of a mouthful for desperate troops in the heat of battle and, as he had a basic knowledge of field medicine and the staunching of wounds, his name had come to him by default. He hailed from the small port town of Prast. Sitting just north of Harshafan's belt, that narrow band of land that marked the division of Arshuma between north and south, it was the only real port in North Arshuma and compared extremely unfavourably to the great ports of the south like Mazuras. The main reason for this was that it was built into a gorge in the cliffs and so was unable to expand to any degree, it would always be an insignificant little place with few prospects for a man wanting to get rich. So, after spending his early years as a fisherman there he had joined the army just as soon as the muster had been called concerning the then surprise invasion of Tanaren. He had somehow become involved in applying field dressings on wounded men after the only man in the unit with such knowledge had been fatally injured. Since then he had acquired fragments of knowledge on healing from various sources, an old warrior here, a wise woman there, but nobody had been as helpful or forthcoming in that respect as the people he had visited earlier on this very day.

The house of healing run by the Sisters of Meriel was instantly recognisable from the sign of the red heart and blood drop painted on the door. He pushed it open and walked into a small room which served as a shrine to the Goddess. A statue of her stood in an alcove illuminated by candle flame and, placed carefully in smaller alcoves around it people had left their prayers and offerings, exhorting the goddess to heal them or a loved one, ensure a smooth pregnancy, protect against plague, set a lame leg, anything that needed the touch of the healing Goddess warranted a prayer of some sort. Through the next set of doors lay the beds on which the sick were housed but Stauncher didn't need to go that far for in the room of offerings stood just the person he wanted to meet.

"Sister Gladys, may the Gods bless you this finest of fine days, I hope and trust that I find both you and your fellow sisters in the rudest of health

THE FANGS OF THE FEN SNAKE

and that your devotion to your duties remains as fervid as ever."

"You mean," Sister Gladys replied through pursed lips; "have we got the herbs and salves that you ordered."

"That as well." Stauncher kept his smile up. "But it would be impolite not to enquire as to your well-being first."

Sister Gladys, a woman of middle years with a thin face lined by stress and hard work finally returned his smile, indeed how could she not as he was straining so hard to maintain his own. "I am well master Gremmick, as I hope you are too."

"I improve whenever I walk in here, the smells of herbs and incense and of course the company, that alone can set many a broken body to healing itself."

"You have the money?"

"You mean the offering for the Goddess?" He held out his opened palm on which sat a variety of glinting silver coins. Sister Gladys whipped them off him with some aplomb before scrutinising each of them in turn, almost as though she didn't wholly trust the man that gave them to her.

"A Kudreyan spenit?" She arched her eyebrow. "Really?"

"Worth ten times its face value, Kudreyans mint few coins, that one is a rarity. Oh and it is often used as a token to buy favours from those of, shall we say, more questionable moral fibre than your good self. Find the right dealer, turn a blind eye, and you could do very well with it indeed."

"And do you know who the right dealer might be? I hope you are not talking about gangsters."

"I can give you a couple of names. Just don't ask too many questions, that is all."

She shook her head, weary at the corruption of the world.

"Very well. Wait here. I will bring you what you ordered."

With a swish of her white and red trimmed robe she vanished through the door leading to the main part of the hospital. Stauncher remained standing where he was, but his ears were good enough to hear a man's voice in there, a patient, and he appeared to be complaining. Within a minute though Sister Gladys returned carrying a full satchel. "Check it by all means master Gremmick, I am sure that in your line of "work" you will have need of it all at some point."

"I will that." Stauncher opened the satchel, scanning its contents with a practised eye. "I often wonder sister, how you feel about handing over your

ACT ONE : THE HUNT

hard grown, hard prepared balms to an Arshuman, who will use them to aid his fellow Arshumans, all of whom are fighting your own people."

A fleeting look of distaste passed over Gladys features. "The Goddess has no concept of nationhood. To her mankind is a commonality, our duty is to everybody, we do not distinguish by place of birth. A person in need of healing is a person in need of healing, wherever he or she might be from."

"And with those words," Stauncher slung the satchel over his shoulder, "you prove yourself a far greater person than I could ever be. I thank you and wish you well in your future endeavours."

He turned to go but at that moment the disgruntled man next door started to raise his voice so that he was now screaming at the hapless sisters around him.

"What is his problem?" Stauncher asked.

"A dislocated shoulder. Very painful but he is refusing to let us touch him. He obviously feels that verbally abusing us will cure him summarily."

Stauncher removed the satchel, handed it to Gladys and made for the door to the hospital. "Just give me a moment sister."

He disappeared through the door. Gladys sighed, put the satchel down and started to tidy the offerings in the alcoves by the shrine. Suddenly there came a piercing shriek from behind the door, followed by a piteous sob and then a whoop of delight. Shortly after Stauncher returned and picked up his satchel. "He won't be bothering you again."

"Is the shoulder reset?" Gladys enquired.

"Oh yes. He is happy now, but I made the cure as painful as I could. I cannot abide a man that shouts at a woman."

"And will there be a fee for your services?"

Stauncher stopped at that, rubbing his chin and looking thoughtful. As he did Gladys flicked a coin at him which he caught with one hand. It was the spenit.

"You are always polite master Gremmick, but your words often reveal a man uncomfortable with the concept of truth. A spenit is a valuable rarity in some parts of the world but here its only use is to fill in a hole in a shoe. You will have more use of it than we ever will."

He came over to her, gently prised open her palm and returned the coin.

"Cleythorn, on Candlemakers street, tell him I sent you. He knows a few less than er...salubrious people who will pay over the odds for it. He does a good line in torinbalm, it will send your patients into next week for a while, but it works fast, and kills pain like nothing else. I am a rogue and a liar to all but the sisters." He pointed to his scarred and mottled face. "They kept me alive when I had this and a favour done to me is a favour never forgotten. Gods keep all of you, I will be back in a few weeks with another order."

He planted a gentle kiss on both cheeks, Arshuman style, and was gone, behind him Gladys shook her head, looked at the coin, and smiled.

****

Stauncher and Dead Eyes exchanged a knowing glance. Stan had finished clicking the knuckles on both hands and now moved past the upturned table to face his attackers on the open floor with maybe just ten feet separating them.

"Well," he said, his voice commanding the attention of all present. "I come in here for a quiet game of dice and this happens. Not only am I accused of cheating, but I have also been referred to as an Arshuman snail sucker. Now really, is that called for? Is that what passes for manners out here? A friendly afternoon of gaming and banter disrupted by such a distasteful lack of decorum, it is a pain to my delicate heart. Now, before I respond to such an unprovoked assault on my person perhaps I should explain to you who exactly I am."

He took a step closer to his attackers, they warily took a step back.

"My name," he boomed, "is Crastanik Bectalis. I hail from the south of Arshuma where gold falls like rain, the poor folk dress in silks and even the beggars feast on white bread every day. I came to this mud pile to make war upon the milk white, soft sinewed men of this land and believe me, war I have made. I crashed through the shield walls at Roshythe and Hibalkun, I took the heads of your captains Marik, Bregan, and Barko and I wear their teeth on this necklace about my chest. I split your baron Lorimar from scalp to cock and use both halves of his skull to drink the finest Arshuman mead. You three, whose idea of combat is mugging single men in the dark, you feeble, womanish dolts, so infirm in spirit that not even the Tanarese army will take you. You three, whose kind I have faced in battle a hundred times before, prepare to have your arms snapped and your spines cracked, I will use your kneecaps to eat my potage off, your finger bones to clean wax out of my ear, prepare to face me! And prepare to know pain!"

His words had the desired effect. The three men leaped at him

ACT ONE : THE HUNT

simultaneously as Stan set about them expertly with his fists. Soon the brawl had spread and the entire tavern, save Stauncher and his companion, were rolling, punching, and kicking they knew not who as the war between Tanaren and Arshuma was being played out on the floor of the Crippled Beggar tavern.

****

Stauncher loosened his dagger in its scabbard, just in case, and next to him Dead Eyes eased a thin stiletto free from a concealed pocket in her tight jerkin. Then she moved her bowl of food off her table and set her short bow down upon it, checking to see how it was strung. Unlike Stan and Stauncher, who had their own rooms in the town, she had nowhere to stay here, relying on Shak to secure her a tiny servant's room in the local manor house. For Dead Eyes was not from Tanaren, she was not from Arshuma, technically she was Chiran, from the great empire to the east, though if you applied that term to either her or her people, the response would likely be an arrow in the eye or a knife in the belly.

Since her arrival in this town she had spent her time in virtual silence. She had moved around the fetid streets with her hood up, unwilling to attract the attention her ears undoubtedly would bring, looking for a suitable place, a place to sit and think.

Human cities were always confusing locales, too many unwashed bodies, too many overpowering smells. Her senses were more acute, more finely attuned than a humans, to turn a corner and be confronted by a putrid dung heap would be enough to make her younger self faint. But then her younger self was more naïve, more guileless, and far more optimistic than her current persona.

She passed the food stalls and purchased some of those spicy meat things that were quite agreeable to her palate, then she went down this winding street, then that winding street, past gaggles of playing children and packs of skinny dogs rooting through rubbish until she found a step ladder, one that led to a section of the city wall that had a walkway. With a practised grace she climbed it, stood upon the wall, and looked at the country lying about her.

It would have been all trees here once she thought, but centuries of human occupation now meant that the landscape was mixed, the lowlands were mainly fields or fallow plains, the many hills remained forested, the few villages dotted here and there were mainly ruined and abandoned. Behind her, to the east of the city ran a silent, winding river and to her right, in the distance, were the array of spiky blue mountains that ran both east and west for hundreds of miles. She knew that on the other side of those mountains was a forest that her people called home. She never felt the need to visit though, same people maybe, but they were from different tribes, probably hostile tribes, it was really not worth the effort.

She too came from a land of mountains, higher mountains than the ones here, mountains whose crowns were constantly tipped with snow. Through this range ancient glaciers had carved deep, forgotten valleys pock marked with cold crystal lakes, that in turn were enclosed by taciturn, gloomy forests. The humans called those mountains the Hagasus but their true name, the name given by her people were Ometosefel, the Mountains of Dawn. Today, far away from those mountains, in the world of humans she was constantly teased by her close companions every time she exhibited a trait they deemed as too "elfy". A love of trees and nature, a propensity to sing to herself, a proficiency in archery, she had been teased for them all, albeit affectionately. But she could not forget or deny her past, the way she was, the way life had shaped her personality. She looked at the blue peaks of the Derannen mountains from her vantage point in this city, but she remembered the Hagasus and the shadowy mountain valleys that she still called home.

And now, in her mind, she was back there again, sitting in the high branches of one of the great trees fringing the wide lake in which the pristine white peaks of the mountains were reflected. Across the lake, a journey of some hours if one deigned to row it, stood the human settlement, one that she had once thought was a city but which in truth was a town half the size of the one she now inhabited. The elves hid in the thickest trees, in the darkest cloud forest, living amongst the woods and the caves. The humans lived in the town, and they had the lake which they fished and the mountainside where they grazed their sheep and their goats. That way the humans and the elves would never meet. As long as they kept to their own worlds they were safe, there would be isolation, not conflict. Little did she know then of the greed, the avarice, and the rapacity of the hairy ones, the humans, those people whose world she now inhabited utterly.

A thin, icy breeze keened over the top of the city wall, pulling her hood down, teasing her close cropped silk soft hair, bringing her back to the present. She pulled her cloak tightly around her, showing how slim she was, how vulnerable she appeared in the teeth of the west wind. She truly was the

ACT ONE : THE HUNT

unlikeliest of warriors.

Dead Eyes, or more accurately, Kalinaga of the Vavanaskal tribe, shut her intelligent jade eyes and inhaled deeply, dragging the cold into her lungs. Then she opened them and spoke quietly, to no one else but herself.

"How in the name of the God and the spirits did I end up here?" She mused before pulling up her hood, checking her bow and quiver were in place, and gliding down the ladder. Once down she was soon absorbed into the teeming streets, heading towards her meeting at the tavern.

****

Shak had bought some more tagli to share with his companions but, as he opened the door to the Crippled Beggar he almost lost them all as a figure was hurled bodily past him to land with a thud and a groan into the soft mud of the street. He peered into the gloom to witness a scene of unmitigated chaos, flailing limbs, and falling bodies wedded to a cacophony of grunts, swearing, shouting, knuckles hitting bare flesh and fists smacking against leather and bone.

Shak rolled his eyes and took a couple of steps inside, light from the street silhouetting his tall, imposing frame. As his eyes got used to the shadowy darkness he saw Stauncher making his way towards him, pushing bodies to one side as he did so and sometimes assisting them on their way with a well-timed smack from his cudgel.

"Stan ingratiating himself with the locals?" Shak asked him.

"Oh yes, he is over there somewhere." Stauncher indicated the thick of the fight where Shak finally saw the big man laying about with his fists, laughing as he did so.

"Oh, tagli," Stauncher said, eyeing Shak's purchases greedily. Stauncher was always hungry and took the food as soon as it was proffered.

"Any news?" Dead Eyes had materialised at Shak's side like a ghost. She too took a piece of tagli, nibbling it fastidiously.

"Yes," Shak said. "We have a job. A challenging job. We need to go somewhere quieter to talk."

With a great roar Stan floored two of his assailants, brushing past others with barely a glance. "Shak!" he called out. "I am bored already. Have you got me any real work?"

"I have," Shak nodded. "But not here. Say goodbye to your friends first."

THE FANGS OF THE FEN SNAKE

"Of course. Fare thee well my Tanarese imps, thanks for the entertainment!" Stan aimed his final punch at one of his original attackers, the older man of the three. It hit him full in the face and Stan's final view of the inn as he strolled into the bright street outside was of the man collapsing into a weary heap on the floor.

Shak looked around to check that his companions were both with him and relatively undamaged. "Plenty of room in the manor house," he said. "We can plan there. We will be leaving in the morning if the Gods are with us."

As he spoke he noticed the man that had flown past him earlier, the one who had almost knocked his food out of his hand, get to his feet with a groan. He was a young man, well dressed, his jacket was of velvet, dyed in a deep and rich blue. Shak noted that on the left breast was an emblem stitched in gold thread, a rearing lion, the symbol of the house of Agana. The only people who wore such an emblem belonged to the family of the king...

And then Shak realised, and slapped his forehead with his palm. The man, who was probably still in his teens, seemed to recognise him for he made a bee line towards him, sandy hair half covering his blue eyes, split lip spattering blood on to a yellow neck scarf. Yellow was the colour of Arshuma. This boy had walked into a tavern known for its Tanarese sympathies wearing a kerchief proclaiming himself as Arshuman. The boy was either courageous in the extreme or duller than unpolished lead, and Shak could guess into which category he fitted.

"Lord Mazuras?" the boy enquired; his breathing still ragged from his fight. He was a good looking lad, a bit puny but there was plenty of time for him to fill out. "I am Randali Aganistlan, fourth or fifth great nephew of king Aganosticlan. I am so excited at the prospect of working with you. I will do my utmost not to disappoint."

He held out his hand, which Shak took with a groan. He knew exactly what his people were thinking, and he guessed word for word what they would say next.

"You have got to be kidding." Stauncher sounded half strangled.

"Is the boy drunk? Should we take him home?" Dead Eyes suggested.

Stan looked at Shak and saw his fears confirmed there. He stepped forward and slapped the boy's shoulder with a mighty hand, almost sending him flying again. "Welcome boy!" he said effusively. "You are now part of the greatest fighting unit in the country, one of the fangs of Shak, the Fen Snake. Come to the manor house with us where we can introduce ourselves

ACT ONE : THE HUNT

properly."

Enthused the boy started to half walk, half run to where the manor house stood on its low hill. As he did so Stan took a step or two backwards, leaned over and whispered into Shak's ear.

"I give him a week."

THE FANGS OF THE FEN SNAKE

4

The manor house in the city of Tantala had long ceased to be a relatively luxurious dwelling for its baron. Controlled by the Arshuman invader for most of the last ten years it was now partly a barracks, partly a command and administrative centre, and partly a prison. Its encircling wall had been built up so that it was now six feet high, peppered by guard towers, and entirely enclosed the hill in the city centre where the house was located.

Its windows were all glazed (well, except for the servants' area but that hardly mattered) and that was a luxury that could not be underestimated as winter began to bare its teeth. And garrison commander Ogun liked his luxury. He had long since requisitioned the former baron's private bedroom as his office and now sat in his favourite leather bound chair staring out of the window and crunching a ripe, juicy apple. One thing Tanaren did well was apples, he would commission an orchard of apple trees to be grown outside the city walls next spring; for Arshumans only of course, Tanarese apple thieves would be hung from the branches they were stealing off, a good way to show the locals who was master here.

A burning log shifted in the fire, sending sparks up the chimney flue, a second later the door behind him softly clicked open and the firm tread of heavy boots set the floorboards to creaking, Ogun did not look behind him for he knew already who the interloper was.

"They left at first light," he said. "They already have half a morning on you."

"They can have the whole day," came the reply. "They will be caught soon enough."

Ogun always found his companions voice unsettling. It was not a powerful voice, nor a particularly deep one, it was rather soft in truth, almost a whisper, a corpse wind hissing over a barren, mist covered moor, a sibilant purr redolent with barely suppressed menace. Ogun still did not look round, there was little point, the man always kept much of his face cloaked with a black scarf, all save the eyes, and Ogun did not want to look at the eyes.

"I am...uncomfortable with all of this," Ogun said. "Prasiak is a friend and ally of long standing, it feels...remiss of me to do this to him."

"Coin can ease many a guilty conscience," came the hiss, "as can

ACT ONE : THE HUNT

power, and you stand to gain both by doing this. This scout of yours will leave a trail for us?"

"He will. Whatever you have to do, do it a long way from here. No traces, understand?"

"It is bandit country," the voice pointed out. "People die forgotten all the time out there, they will be food for wolves soon enough."

"Soon enough," Ogun sounded thoughtful. "Let them get the girl first mind, then bring her to me."

"Mightn't she talk?"

"Gag her, she is a prisoner of Arshuma. I will keep her here and she will talk only to me or those that I trust. She will have no idea about the power struggles between the founding cities anyway."

"If you are happy with that then so be it. She is not my priority anyway; the Fen Snake is."

"And your master…"

"My employer. I serve no man. Since the death of his father…"

"A death you seem to know an awful lot about…"

"A riding accident, no more, it is nobody's fault if a man cannot ride a horse properly. Anyway, since the death of his father young Garazar is eager to consolidate his position as ruler of Mazuras, so, to further that end all other claimants to the Heron crown need to be…"

"Eliminated."

"Persuaded as to the futility of any challenge."

"Eliminated."

"Your word, not mine."

"Whatever words are chosen; the outcome is usually the same. Will you be doing this alone?"

"No, I will have two associates, any more than that you need not know."

Ogun threw the apple core into the fire. "Any more than that I do not want to know. Your expenses are on the table."

There was a clink of coin as money was pocketed, Ogun heard footsteps as his visitor made for the door." Oh, and Doul," he called to him.

The man named Doul stopped.

"Part of me hopes that it is Shak that returns with the girl, not you, I hope you understand that."

"More than part of you I suspect." Doul's whisper was never more

THE FANGS OF THE FEN SNAKE

threatening. "If you did not stand to gain from his demise then you would be wholly on his side. It will be interesting for you, will it not, trying to guess who will be riding the path to your gates in a few days' time."

"I will be watching carefully," Ogun said. "Hopefully by then I would have shaken off the notion that I have made a deal with Keth of the underworld."

The strangest sound came from behind the other man's scarf. Hoarse and rasping, it sounded like scree sliding off a mountainside and falling uncountable fathoms into empty space, or maybe sand blasted by gale force winds stripping leaves and bark off wraithlike trees, Doul was laughing.

"A deal with Keth? Oh, I very much doubt that you would have shaken off that notion garrison keeper, I very much doubt it indeed."

****

"I push my nails through my throbbing head,
I open my eyes and can only see red,
The words form on my lips, yet remain unsaid,
Unknowable fear still surrounds me

Sun shines through the glass so I shy away,
Crave the cloak of mid night on this endless day,
Need a corner to hide, a dark place to stay,
Unspeakable fear still enfolds me

I remember the time when joy filled my heart,
When I took pleasure in song, and in dance, and in art
Alas now my love has been pricked with a dart
Unbreakable fear has enclosed me

The portrait close by I have fervently kissed,
No letter of goodbye, will it ever be missed,
As I open the skin surrounding my wrist,
Intractable fear has consumed me."

By Eleanor Lasgaart, Lady of Bearnside manor, Protectress of Bear valley.

ACT ONE : THE HUNT

"And I really cannot write poetry," she said with a heavy sigh.

She pushed back her chair and, in the softly dancing light of the oil lamp next to her, gazed tentatively at the polished silver mirror in her hand and at her own face reflected within.

She used to be obsessed with her appearance; in fact, "used to be" was an erroneous assertion for she was as obsessed with it now as much as she had ever been, and even more so after Baron Vinoyen's visit a year or so ago. He was of course visiting her uncle to talk interminably of war and strategy. She had endured it, sitting as sweetly and politely in their company as she could, but it had eventually become too much for her and she had made her excuses and left. Then, as the door shut behind her she had stood and listened as the baron had talked, not of war, but of her.

"She is an interesting creature, that niece of yours. She is so close to being that kind of beauty that would light up the Grand Duke's court. Yet everything about her is slightly skewed; her chin is slightly too broad, her cheekbones slightly too high, her nose slightly too prominent, her lips just the wrong side of delicacy. Her eyes are neither green nor blue, but an unsatisfying mix of both shades and her hair may be close to being a cascade of golden corn if it were not tainted by another shade, that of straw that has stood too long in a stable and has been stained by water and piss."

She had left after that, thoroughly mortified and close to tears. Not only had she been described by a near stranger like some kind of farmyard animal, but he had also been close to intimating that she was actually ugly. Ugly! Her! A Lasgaart of marriageable age condescended to by a Vinoyen, the old rivals of her family! She had wished all the fires of the underworld upon him that day and for many days afterwards and, so it seemed, that wish had come horribly true for now the baron was dead, killed in the recent battle at Wolf Plain, and her uncle was nowhere to be found as his men had been scattered by the triumphant enemy.

And it was that battle that had marooned her here, in this small town in a land that was now surrounded by foes. And it seemed Baron Fenchard had been unmasked as a traitor, an Arshuman sympathiser, and was claiming this territory as his own! It was an eventuality that no one had predicted, no one, Fenchard a traitor, a filthy traitor, a man who would sell his country for a patch of ground and a bag of gold. She had been promised to him once, as a child of five or six but then she had been promised to a lot of people over the years. And now, just at the wrong time, her nuptials had finally been confirmed and she had been travelling south to fulfil them, a journey that had been unexpectedly curtailed by events. The lucky man was one Ralf Spalforth, he was a year older than her, and she had never met him. The Spalforth family were one of the most powerful south of the Marassan hills, a sparsely populated area riddled by marshes and lakes but a key one in this endless war. And now it seemed likely that this marriage would never take place.

She looked around her, around the chief guest room in what was laughably called the manor house here. Night pressed hard on the windows, the fire glowed and sputtered, all was shadow and silence. She looked at the chests next to her bed, the ones holding all her beautiful dresses, her silver and golden head dresses, her brooches, her diamond pins, her rings, and her necklaces, all the wealth a minor noblewoman brought to a marriage. It was all there and she had no way of protecting it from thieves. They had been just four days into the journey south when this disastrous battle had taken place in the foulest of weather. Outriders had reported that Fenchard's men were blocking the roads ahead, and most of the roads behind. She was stuck, they had been in this village for over a week and unless they moved soon the enemy would be on them, and what a prize hostage she would be. As her maidservant Iris had told her, if Fenchard got his hands on her he might forcibly marry her against the wishes of her family and her own personal honour. Added to that Eleanor, who had seen him often, had always found him slimy and insincere, it was a truism that she should never trust a man who spent more time on his hair than on martial training and Fenchard spent more time on his hair than she did.

"My Lady?" The door had opened, it was Iris, her entry presaging a smattering of rain on the window glass.

"Is it time?" Eleanor asked her.

"Yes my lady, the men will be loading your things shortly so that we can move out at dawn."

"And this particular road back is definitely clear? Fenchard's men have abandoned it?"

"So the outriders say my lady."

"Those that haven't deserted me."

"People are frightened my lady; their first thoughts are for their families."

"Rather than the person who pays them to feed those very families,"

ACT ONE : THE HUNT

Eleanor said tartly.

"With all due respect my lady, your uncle has disappeared, the family treasury has an uncertain future, nobody knows when their next coin is coming from."

"That last statement," Eleanor spoke in bitter tones, "applies to me also."

"I know my lady. Shall I dress you now? I have been told that you should wear only green and browns, no colours that might attract attention."

"Yes you may Iris, and if the Gods are willing in a few days we will be back at Bearnside, just over the rivers where, Artorus willing, we will be safe."

"And your brother is coming my lady, he should be joining us soon after we leave here."

Eleanor made the sign of Artorus over her breast, she was still looking in the mirror, apparently the latest Tanarese fashion was for a couple of curled ringlets to hang down around the ears, would she look good with ringlets? "If only he had been with us when we left home, at least I would have had some loyalty off people with him around."

"I am still loyal my lady."

"Yes you are." Eleanor slid off the chair. "Now you can demonstrate your loyalty by dressing me, for we have a dangerous journey ahead, green velvet dress, silver fillet and veil, if that dog Fenchard gets his filthy paws on me I will at least look respectable when I defy him."

****

Night in the wilderness was not something that Randali Aganistlan was overly familiar with. Randali, or to give him his new name, Dormouse, lay on his back on his bedroll staring up at what he had hoped would be an array of brilliant stars but, because of the patchy, intermittent rain, was just a blanket of smothering darkness. The moon was obscured, the stars invisible, and the air was chill, even under his blanket. Above them the broad boughs of a protective oak sheltered them, its branches sighing under the wind, its remaining leaves rustling under the feet of an unseen arboreal creature. Surrounding them were the bushes and grasses of the wilds, bowing under the rain, soggy and heavy with moisture. The wet earth was pungent, sodden soil and stones slippery with moss, the foliage was fresh, revivified by the persistent soft drizzle. A thousand scents, bitter, clean, cloying, decaying, pure, and fragrant fought each other constantly, an olfactory confusion never to be

THE FANGS OF THE FEN SNAKE

satisfactorily resolved. And the quiet, outside of the dripping water little stirred here, just the timorous voles and the owls hunting them with velvet lethality. The silence of nature was the most natural thing in the world, so how did it feel so unnatural?

The last four and a half days, that is the period of time elapsed since joining up with Shak and the others had been an education for him. The four full days had been spent riding across country, from Tantala to the bridge at the hill town of Grest, over that and into the territory disputed between Lord Fenchard and the new, Tanarese, protector baron of Felmere. Fenchard's captured town of Tetha Vinoyen was some miles to the west and south, but they weren't heading there next, their route led north and west, to a ravine close to the Vinoyen river, all they were waiting for now was the signal to move out, and dawn was not far away.

But it was the first half day with his new companions that he remembered the most, where he acquired his new nickname, in the downstairs room at the manor house, next to the blazing fire. Shak had left them kicking their heels briefly while he went to speak with the scout that would be leading them on their mission. When he did re-join them it was with a giant loaf of rough bread fresh from the kitchens and a full wineskin which he took no time at all in dispensing to those present.

That done he eased himself into a chair, tore off a hunk of bread and eyed his newest recruit quizzically.

"All right then young Randali, now you have met all of us I have only one thing to ask you."

"Just the one sir?" Randali drank the wine and reached for the bread, this was the sort of wine that would need a lot of absorbing.

"Just the one." Shak rarely raised his voice, people usually listened when he spoke. "And there is no need for the "sir"."

"None of us call him "sir"," Stauncher told the young man. He still had his hat on, even in this overly warm room. "Actually "my lord" would probably be more accurate but we don't call him that either."

"I see," Randali said. "So what is the question er.... Shak."

"Why?" Shak said.

"Why what?"

"Not what," Shak said quietly. "Just why. Why are you here? Why ask to join us? Why use your family's influence to join us, and don't pretend that you haven't because nobody leaves Kitev and travels hundreds of miles out

ACT ONE : THE HUNT

here just to be told to get lost. You know that you are probably in the deepest water of your life here and are as like to drown as not. So why? I am extremely interested in finding out. And then I might just make you an offer, one that you would be wise to take up."

Stan inched forward in his chair and planted both elbows on the table, Stauncher sipped his wine quietly, staining his moustache but his eyes never left Randali once. Dead Eyes, the Wych girl, was not at the table, preferring rather to sit on a stout bag of meal stacked against the wall, curling up on it like a contented cat, they were all waiting for him to speak.

"Well," he said, clearing his throat awkwardly. "I told you earlier that I am related to the king and indeed I am. Everyone in my circle knows of my lineage so I am treated as king's family when it comes to parties and balls and other things that mean little to me and yet when it comes to advancement at court, then I am suddenly too distant a relative to be given any position of responsibility at all. I am stuck in some sort of nowhere, in some respects I am important, in others I am a nobody. And I have had enough of it."

"Then join the army, ride with the knights, it is what most of the aristocracy at your level do," Shak frowned at him.

"And they just sit on their arses never seeing the hint of a battle in their lives," Randali protested. "Even when there is a war next to their front door they are kept well away. People like me are marriage stock, kept in hand until the right match comes up, it cannot be done that we are needlessly killed in the pursuit of glory, that is what poorer people are for."

"So you are bored," Shak said. "You are here because you are bored."

"Well you won't be for long," Stan added.

"Not bored," Randali answered firmly. "I want to make something of myself."

"And if you die?" Shak slowly sipped from his goblet.

"Then that is the will of the Gods."

"But," Stan spluttered, "but this life you are running from, it is wealthy I imagine, with lots of women ready to…"

Randali looked up at the ceiling. "Oh women…," he sighed, "hundreds of them, I have no idea how many I have been promised to over the years."

Stan shook his head with incomprehension. "And you are running away from all that? Don't you like women?"

"Well enough," Randali admitted.

"Then why? why?"

THE FANGS OF THE FEN SNAKE

Dead Eyes eased herself off her improvised seat to sit at the table right next to the young man. She gently turned his head to face her, green eyes smiling as she did so. "So what is her name then?"

He blushed a little, squirming under her close scrutiny. "Her name?"

"Yes." Shak nodded at Dead Eyes, the two of them understanding at last. "Let me guess, you are to marry somebody…"

"But it is another that has captured your heart!" Stauncher blurted out in triumph.

"Well," Randali grimaced. "It is a little more complicated than that…"

"But we have hit on a grain of truth," Shak said.

Randali nodded. There was much roaring and drinking and spilling of wine at the admission.

"So you are running away." Shak spoke once the noise had died down.

"No," Randali's expression was stubbornness incarnate. "I need to raise myself above my peers so that she…so that I am recognised as a man of honour and of courage."

"Then you may be able to choose the lady you really want," Dead Eyes breathed softly.

Randali nodded. Stan clapped him on the shoulder, an impact the younger man was finally getting used to. "Bet you any coin you care to name she will be married by the time you get back to her. Woman cannot wait when their menfolk are at war."

"She will wait." Randali asserted.

"Unless her family decides otherwise." Shak shook his head, seeing the scowl on the man opposite. "Women have no say in these things."

"And neither have men," Randali asserted. "My wedding date, that is the day I don the shackles and wed the woman I do not love, is set three months from now. I prevailed upon my uncle the king to let me come out here and show what I can do. If I return in glory, then my bride might just be mine to choose, if I return in ignominy, then…"

"But we do not seek glory in battle." Shak pointed out to him.

"But you are the best. The palace is well aware of your exploits, any that serve with you are feted by default. If I serve with you for two months and return alive, that should suffice in itself."

"We are well known?" Stan sounded surprised. "I could leave here and return in glory?"

"Yes," Randali admitted. "But it would assist you further if you were of

56

ACT ONE : THE HUNT

noble birth."

"Well," Stan thought and rubbed his chin. "My great, great uncle on my mother's side did clean the latrines at Bect palace…"

Randali shook his head.

"Oh well, worth a try, no money and no glory for the foot soldiers, it was ever thus." Stan pushed his chair back a little and stretched out his arms. "For a while, you know, when things were quiet I did some prize fighting in the Kitev slums, you know, Kitev has a lot of slums, you probably have never seen them. I had my nose broken, my ear chewed and my shoulder put out of joint and I only ever made copper pennies out of it. Yet it was still safer and better paid work than what we are doing in this place."

"Listen to the man," Shak told Randali. "He speaks the truth. You come here seeking glory? Then you will find little to sate you out here. We have been on raids where we have been ordered not to leave any witnesses alive. If you had been with us then and if you had seen that the witnesses included women and children, what would you do? It is the job of the junior member to silence those we need to; you have the knife, and a woman with a babe in her arms is kneeling before you begging for her life, and the life of her child. Would you have the mettle to do what you must? Would you revel in the "glory" acquired in such an act? Well?"

Randali's mouth had gaped a little as Shak spoke to him. He swallowed hard and shook his head. "You are testing me; I do not believe any of you would do such a thing."

The three other men in the room exchanged glances before Shak spoke again. "Now I will make you the offer I promised earlier. Get drunk with us tonight and sleep a heavy sleep, the heaviest and happiest sleep of your life. Then, at dawn get on your horse and ride east. Ride back to Kitev, ride all the way home, do not stop for any reason, just ride away from all of this chaos and misery. Then when you get home, join the knights, abduct this woman of yours and wed her in secret, the anger of her family is but little price to pay compared with the one that faces you here. This will be the best offer you have ever had in your young life. Accept it now and be free, with no loss of honour. Refuse it and when dawn arises we will wake you and take you with us, but remember, whatever happens to you in the days to come has happened by your own volition, not ours."

Stauncher had said little of late but as Shak was speaking his eyes had welled up. Randali could not be sure, but it seemed that they held a weight of suffering and regret fit to overburden any man. What exactly was he remembering? "Listen to the chief young fellow," he said softly. "They are wise words, ignore the offer and bear the consequences."

Randali paled a little, he swallowed and was silent for a moment, then his eyes hardened, he clasped his hands together till his knuckles whitened. "Then I will refuse the offer," he said firmly. "I came out here to prove myself and that is exactly what I shall do."

Dead Eyes shook her head and returned to her sack of meal. Shak though seemed to relax a little, he threw Randali a hunk of bread before starting to refill everybody's drink. "Very well, welcome to the party young man, you do have courage, we can all see that, I hope it will avail you in our days together. Now, I suppose I had better brief you all regarding the task to come."

"Yes," Stauncher said, "this scout that is joining us, what do you make of him?"

"Taciturn, a man of few words, I had to prise what I needed to know out of him."

"Really! Fewer words than you? That must have been a conversation to behold!"

"Indeed," Stan laughed, causing wine to spill over his chin. "Three words and a hundred moody stares. Come on then, what did this fellow that we cannot trust properly say exactly?"

Randali listened, and drank, and ate and drank once more. His own predicament and his decision to remain with them was not touched upon again. For his companions, the matter was obviously now closed. He was feeling the effects of the wine now and was becoming emboldened. So much so that when Shak had finished briefing them all he decided to ask Stan a question that had been interesting him for a while.

"Stan," he said finally. "In the tavern you told the Tanarese that you had killed a baron and now drink from his skull. Do you have it with you now? The skull I mean, I would very much like to see it."

Stauncher sniggered as Stan leaned forward and gave the young man a confidential wink. "See my fists?" he waved one a few inches from Randal's face. "Useful weapons, there is much power in them, but believe you me, it is as nothing when compared to the power of bullshit. I look the part you see, so when I speak people believe me. It makes them fearful and a much easier opponent. In truth, I was there at the battle when the baron died, but as to

58

ACT ONE : THE HUNT

how he died, or as to where his skull is, your guess is as good as mine." He tapped his lips with his finger. "Daggers pierce innards, axes split skulls, but words can destroy a man utterly, far more than any edged weapon. Now, where is my wine, and who is starting the singing? How about that one about the nobleman's daughter, what was her name?"

"Roger!" Shak, Stauncher, and Dead Eyes answered as one.

"Aye that it was! Roger the nobleman's daughter..."

Randali drank more wine, he had long since forgotten about the bread, and so he was but little surprised when he passed out shortly after...

****

Oh but the waking! Purple skies, freezing air, and his face breaking the ice in the horse trough he had been hurled into. He thrashed about helplessly, uttering a strangled cry as he saw Stauncher and Stan grinning from ear to ear, delighted with their present handiwork.

"By all the Gods!" Stauncher exclaimed. "You sleep like a dormouse! If you are coming with us you had better move sharpish, we are late enough as it is!"

****

And now, four days later he was here.

The rain kept hitting the leaves above him with a monotonous thud, he tasted bile in his throat and felt his stomach constricting with tension. Sleep was all but impossible, it was too wet, too cold, and his nerves were dancing like a maiden at her first ball. He sat up and looked around him.

The scout Siras, Stan, and Stauncher were all close by and all appeared to be blissfully in the world of dreams. He knew if he opened his eyes one of them would say how important sleep was the night before a mission, how being refreshed and alert was essential for the task ahead. Fine words, but impossible for him to adhere too.

Earlier that night Shak had gone through the plan with them, giving everybody a job to do but leaving his responsibilities to the end. In fact, he had become so impatient he had straight out asked Shak what his role would be.

"To stay with me, and to do as I tell you. Immediately." The tall man had said.

"Nothing more than that? Don't I have a specific job?"

THE FANGS OF THE FEN SNAKE

"It is your first time with us," Shak grinned at him. "If we were at sea you would be called ballast. Not essential but useful to have around. Stay with me Dormouse, and don't fall asleep!"

Asleep, if only...then he came too with a start. He had been nodding off despite it all, his lids had closed, he was almost gone, it was only the hand on his shoulder that had brought him to his senses.

It was Dead Eyes, she had been at the ambush point with Shak, her coming back here could only mean...

"Time to move," she whispered to him, her cloak, cowl, and leathers making her almost invisible even this close up. "They are stirring in the village, ready your weapons and come with us!"

And they were all awake now, and, silent as that hunting owl, it took them but moments to pack, prepare themselves and disappear into the trees, mere tendrils of shadow under the heavy boughs.

ACT ONE : THE HUNT

5

Nico Lasgaart looked up at the strip of grey blue sky framed by the sheer sided ravine he had the misfortune to be standing inside. Past noon already it seemed. Past noon and he was angry, angry, and dreadfully disappointed. Both he and his sister, younger than him by some twelve years, were unusual in family terms insofar as they were both fair haired, indeed his hair was almost snowy blonde and Lasgaarts as a rule were dark, almost saturnine in appearance. And the differences didn't end there for most of the men in the family were wiry and athletic, good jousters and able swordsmen. Nico was far stockier and muscular than the rule, he had little interest in the joust and though his skills with the blade were as proficient as any man, in the thick of combat he often preferred the mace. Yes, it had little finesse and required limited skill to wield but when fighting in the wilderness or at close quarters there was nothing better for denting armour and cracking skulls. He cared little for the opinions of the effete classes when stuck in the middle of nowhere with his life under constant threat.

Yet the threat in this place had long passed. He looked around him, trying to piece together the events that had recently occurred here, then stroked his lantern jaw with a gloved hand. His keen blue eyes expressed regret, regret at his own failings more than anything else. And he was wrong too, the threat here was a constant for he was in the lands of the traitor Fenchard, a man who would relish the prospect of displaying Nico's severed, parboiled, head upon a spike on the Vinoyen bridge.

The smell of the sodden, black earth, churned up by dozens of horse hooves, and the damp, moist, rank odour of the ferns that clad both sides of the ravine stung his nose with their pungency, but, strong as they were they could not overpower that other scent, the scent of blood, blood that still leaked from the dead that lay here. He counted four of them, all men, all this side of the landslip ahead, a slide of shale and soil that had blocked the path completely. He had little doubt that the landslip was deliberate, created by human hand to divide the party riding through the ravine. This was, after all, part of the road to Fenchard's new capital, the town of Tetha Vinoyen and there was no better place for an ambush along its entire length. But had the ambushers claimed the prize they wanted?

ACT ONE : THE HUNT

His horse would not settle; it could sense the anxiety of the humans here. Nico eased himself off the saddle, his boots part sinking into the mud. He patted the beast and said something soothing into its ear. Then he walked up to the rocks, mud, and saplings that formed the landslip. His men and the others from the party he was trying to rescue had been working in these filthy conditions for an hour or more, finally though, they had cleared a space wide enough for a wagon to squeeze through. A gaggle of people were there, his own knights, their silver grey surcoats sometimes showing through their muddy riding cloaks were standing with other grim faced, mail clad men, all of them talking over each other. Nico ignored them though, instead he walked straight past them towards the only woman in the group, cowl of her black cloak lowered to reveal a homely face now stained with tears and mud.

"Lady Iris." He spoke to her, his voice grave as the surroundings. "Are you well? What happened here exactly, who did this to our men? And is E..."

"I am well as can be expected my lord and if my lady is not on your side of the avalanche then I fear..."

"She is not," he said grimly, his worst fears were being realised. "Four men dead, a lot of horse tracks but no horses and that is it."

"The landslide," Iris gasped. "There was no warning. Most of us reared back to safety, I was almost crushed, but my lady was riding up front with her escort. There was a lot of shouting, we could hear cries of pain, but we could do..."

"Do not blame yourself for what happened, the whole thing was carefully planned by people who knew the area..."

"But they had no interest in us at all!" Iris started to weep. "The baggage train, all those precious objects, they made no attempt to take any of it, they just ignored us and attacked those in front, on the other side of this cursed pile of earth."

"There was only one precious object they were interested in." Nico spoke through bloodless lips. "And I fear they have claimed it. Iris, I will be assigning most of my men to escort you and the baggage onwards, hopefully all the way back to Bear Valley. There are loyal ferrymen in villages north of Tetha Vinoyen that will assist in crossing both rivers. Artorus protect you all."

Iris gave Nico a slight bow, one that he reciprocated before returning to his horse where another knight, a true veteran, his hair the colour of wrought iron, his eyes grey and keen, his beard silver as spider silk, was waiting patiently for him.

THE FANGS OF THE FEN SNAKE

"Well Ursus?" Nico asked without smiling. "Any idea where they went? Three of the four dead here were killed by arrows, the fourth was wounded by them but finished off with a cut to the throat. It seems the ambushers waited atop the ravine, started the landslide, and hit the escort with arrows till they were all felled save Eleanor. Presumably one or two of them on horseback then rode into the ravine and took her, the wounded man resisted so they killed him. They were relaxed enough to collect the arrows they had spent, and they must have seen a weakness up there long ago, seen that it would be possible to disturb the earth and affect a landslide. It was probably a plan they were keeping in hand until the right occasion arose, and, Keth curse it, this was just that occasion. The whole operation would have been over very quickly and would only have needed what? Half a dozen men?"

"Half a dozen men who knew what they were doing." Ursus removed one gauntlet, wiping the sweat off his brow with his bare hand. "I followed the trail out of the ravine, noting three distinct hoof patterns. It does seem that they chased a panicked horse, overtook it, stopped for a little while, and then resumed their journey, heading east all the time."

"Did they turn south at any point?"

"Not that I could see, but I didn't follow the tracks that far."

"Mmmm," Nico deliberated. "Who do you think did this?"

"You don't think it was Fenchard?" Ursus sounded surprisingly pleased, though it was more at Nico's thoughtful demeanour than at the events they were both observing.

"Neither of us do my old trainer. If Fenchard had sent his men here, they would have just ridden into the village and kidnapped everybody, bold as a mountain face. He would have sent a lot more men and, knowing the little snot as I do, he would never have ignored the baggage train."

"Sound logic," Ursus said. "Greedy little prick Fenchard. So who are the culprits here?"

Nico shrugged his shoulders. "I am guessing but, if the tracks head east, then that would indicate that they are heading for the river Whiterush, which means the town of Grest, which means they intend to reach a city controlled by Arshuma, which indicates that Fenchard's new masters do not entirely trust their little lap dog. This is of course both good news and bad, for us at least."

"I am struggling to see the good..." Ursus growled.

ACT ONE : THE HUNT

"Fenchard hasn't got her, so I will not be having him as a brother in law any time soon and I can only thank Artorus for that. The bad news is that they have half a day on us and are probably hoping to be at Grest by nightfall tomorrow. If Arshuma get her then I have no idea what will happen next, what they will do with her. All I do know is that it will mean great dishonour for the family, and that is bad enough as it is."

"It will take a demon's own ride for us to catch them now Nico." Ursus put a comforting arm on Nico's shoulder."

"Us?" Nico queried. "Only a lone rider could reach and overtake them from this point on. You and the others are to get everybody back to Bear Valley before Fenchard realises they are here. My sister is my responsibility, and I will be chasing her alone."

"And what will you do when you catch them? Ursus raised a sardonic eye. "Ask them kindly to hand your sister back? The Arshumans have several raiding parties in the disputed territories, they are elite men, been here for years, they know the land as well as we do, they knew this ambush point for example. How can one man stand against them, can you tell me that?"

"Well here they launched a surprise assault against superior numbers, perhaps I can do the same to them. I need to be swift, they will be travelling through the woods today but tomorrow, when they move south the ground is far more open. If I can find them by early in the morning then I have a chance."

"But your tracking skills are non-existent, you have always left such things to others, as soon as night falls you will have to stop or you will lose the trail. Maybe though if you took another with you, you could continue your pursuit a little longer and be that much harder to shake off."

No," Nico shook his head firmly, "you are not coming with me. An old man like you will only slow me down." He had a twinkle in his eye at that last sentence.

"Pah!" Ursus snorted. "I could outride you over open ground anytime, and unhorse you in a joust..."

"Have you been drinking?" Nico was grinning by now.

"I will not dignify that with an answer. If you are to pursue your sister, then I am going with you. Remember how I saved your life as a child, on more than one occasion, so you owe me."

"Oh Artorus sainted beard, not the apple tree thing again..."

"Yes, idiot boy. Only a fool would climb along a branch overhanging a lake when there were perfectly good apples to be had elsewhere..."

"It was the reddest and the biggest."

"Had to fish you out with a stick I did, you were wetter than a fish scale, still I never regretted rescuing you..."

"Well, I am grateful for that at least."

"You were still holding the apple, and I was hungry."

"Oh yes, I had forgotten that you ate the damned thing. Alright, against my better judgement and to stop you from grumbling incessantly about this in the years to come you can come along, bring your bow mind, we might need it. Now, we need to get everybody moving, every second that passes is costing us time and risks bringing Fenchard's men down on our heels."

"Well," Ursus looked thoughtful, "there is at least one positive we can take out of that at least."

Nico set to checking his gear on his horse, prior to mounting it. "Then enlighten me, because I cannot think of a single one."

Ursus put two fingers to his mouth and whistled. Instantly a proud great mare with a white blaze on its forehead started to trot towards him. He took the rein and started to pat the horse on the neck. "Steady Utta, steady, I will have much to ask of you over the next few days. Well Sir Nico." He addressed the mounted man again. "The longer it is before we catch them the longer they have to accommodate the lady Eleanor. I may not know her well, but from what you have told me, the longer they are subjected to her..."

"Singular personality? Mmmm." Nico pondered. "I may have exaggerated a little, but she has a tongue as venomous as any tree viper. Perhaps you are right. Maybe when we do catch up with them they will be only too happy to hand her back to us after all."

****

The flanks of the horses were steaming and white when they finally stopped for a rest. They had reached a higher ridge of ground densely clad in mixed forest, though the trees had shed most of their leaves under the keening wind. It was a good vantage though for Shak and the others to stop, eat, and gauge the extent of any possible pursuit. So, as soon as he was off his horse Shak strolled to the edge of the ridge, peering east and south over the lands beneath them.

Dead Eyes joined him momentarily, gazing at the same places as him,

ACT ONE : THE HUNT

shading her eyes with her hand. "We have done well," she said after her examination. "We can move south from here, spend the night at the edge of the forest then move on at dawn. Things have gone as well as they could have really."

"Apart from Dormouse's wound."

"It is not serious, just a gash on the leg and it will teach him than many men play dead on the battlefield, Stauncher is sorting it out for him now."

"Maybe." Shak sighed and hunched his shoulders. "First Red and now this, perhaps I am losing my touch, or getting complacent, or both."

"These things happen, it is just misfortune, both Red and Dormouse should have had their wits about them. It only takes one slip; we both have enough scars on our bodies to tell us that. This boy will learn, and he killed his attacker in fine style. Blame me if you want to blame anybody, my arrow did not kill as it should have."

"I would never blame you Kal, we go back too far for that, besides you did everything expected of you, felling the men after Stan and Stauncher started the landslip, it made it easy for me and the boy to grab our hostage."

"Well I was not satisfied with myself. Perhaps I am getting complacent too. Everybody is talking about going home after this, perhaps I should as well."

"Home?" Shak turned to her in surprise. "You hardly ever speak of it, or even where you consider your home to be."

"No I don't, but I am getting older now, I am thinking more and more about leaving this life behind me. As for where I consider home to be, well it would still be the lakes, and the mountain forests, it could be nowhere else really."

"But I thought your people were killed or enslaved."

Dead Eyes bit her lip. "Yes they were, but some may still live out there, in the wilder vales. I could find them, put all my new skills to use."

"Killing the men of the Chiran empire?" Shak laughed.

"Surviving. My skills are in survival and there are many ways to survive without killing."

"You would not want vengeance for what happened to you and your people?"

She shook her head. "It is a road that leads nowhere. Now I know that the soldiers of the empire outnumber the raindrops falling from the sky I know that fighting is pointless, avoiding is everything, that is if any of my people still live free of course."

"My hopes are with you." Shak turned away from the edge of the ridge to return to his other companions. "Now the land slopes gently to the east of here, gently enough for the horses. Let's have something to eat and we can move on. The faster we get this done the faster we can all go home."

They started to walk back together but had not gone far before Dead Eyes asked him. "You called me Kal just then, you hardly ever use my real name."

"Not in company," he said. "It is good to keep our names secret at times, but two friends together? That is a different matter."

She nodded in agreement. "Well then Prasiak, let us re-join the others, I am sure Dormouse will want one of us to hold his hand by now."

****

And indeed he did. He half sat, half crouched as Stauncher pored over a shallow, but inches long gash on the upper right thigh. It had been tied and bandaged but the hard ride had kept the wound open, bleeding, and painful.

"Do not move," Stauncher said through gritted teeth. "I will need to stitch it first, then a tourniquet, then a poultice. Stan, can you cut a stave for the young fellow, ash preferably to help the boy keep the pressure off his leg for a couple of days."

"Give me a few moments and he will have the king of walking sticks." Stan had been whetting his axe but now slipped it into a leather thong at his belt and started to look around for a suitable branch. "Siras!" he called to the scout, who was tethering the horses. "Come and watch the girl until I have finished here."

Siras, a swarthy man with a mane of black hair and even less predilection for conversation than Shak had warned them about muttered a simple, "as you wish," before heading to the stout sapling to which the target of their morning raid had been tied.

"Now we will have to get your trousers off." Stauncher cheerfully told his patient. "Stitches and bandage first, then you can put them back on again. What is the problem?"

"I can't possibly do that!" Dormouse could not sound more affronted. "There are ladies present."

"She is blindfolded," Stauncher sighed and nodded in the direction of

ACT ONE : THE HUNT

their captive. "And gagged."

"No not her!" his umbrage was increasing. "Her!" he pointed ahead of him where Shak and Dead Eyes at last re-joined the group.

Stauncher shook his head dismissively. "She doesn't count. She is one of us."

"She is still a woman!"

"Well spotted." Dead Eyes said drily. "So Dormouse, are you saying you have got something worth hiding from me?"

"Yes! Well no. I mean yes!"

"What do you reckon it is?" Stan returned to their clearing with a heavily foliated branch that he proceeded to whittle lustily. "He is a young fellow, so I reckon he has an overly pimply arse."

"Or an embarrassing mole," Stauncher grinned.

"Right in the middle of his cock." Stan laughed as another lopped side branch fell on to the leaf covered soil at his feet.

"No I haven't!" Dormouse protested.

"It is a swollen testicle." Dead Eyes sounded like the voice of wisdom. "All red and angry, with the skin smooth as a baby's cheek."

"Now that is a verifiable condition," Stan confirmed. "Saw a chap in Kitev with it once, his left one looked like a blood orange. They lanced it, leeched it, in the end they had to cut it off."

"Cut it off?" Dormouse whimpered. "You are making it up, I haven't got that...condition anyway."

"Then prove it sweetie." Dead Eyes smiled at him, showing a mouth of perfectly even, white enamelled teeth. "But just to the boys, I will go and stand with the horses with my back to you until you have been...administered too." She started to saunter over to where the horses were tethered. "Oh, and good kill by the way, you did well today."

Dormouse untied his belt and started to painfully lower his breeches. "But I got stabbed! I was rubbish."

"Nonsense." Shak spoke at last. "All of us here are covered in scars, yours was well won. Let Stauncher do his work, his physic is good, the rest of us will just wait and see if you scream like a hungry child."

"Great." Dormouse said miserably. "Wait, Stauncher, you are going to put that giant needle through my skin?"

"Yep." Stauncher sounded bored. "Normally I would put it in fire first, but we cannot light one here, somebody could well be pursuing us so there is

THE FANGS OF THE FEN SNAKE

no need to signpost our presence. But the needle is clean enough anyway. Do you want to bite on some wood?"

Dormouse shook his head.

"Well, have some of this anyway." Stauncher handed him a flask, he took it, sniffed it, and wrinkled his nose in disgust. Stauncher though was looking at him expectantly, so he took a deep breath and swigged it gingerly. It took him a full minute to stop choking after he had swallowed.

"What in the name of Keth was that?" Dormouse was hoarse.

"A bit of home brew. Everybody in my home town made their own booze, a lot of the stuff would make you go blind, this is one of those recipes."

"You mean," Dormouse gagged, "that you gave me something that could make me go blind?"

"No, you big baby. I mean it could, but you would have to drink a lot more of it than that. Now, pour some of it on to your wound to clean it, and be grateful the cut is just a shallow one."

Dormouse did so, wincing as it went into the wound. Stauncher looked on regretfully, as though rueing the loss of such a precious fluid.

"Good man," he said briskly. "Now let's get on, the less you move the quicker I finish, the quicker you get your trousers back on. Now grit your teeth and pray that Meriel is free with her blessings today."

Shak walked past the grimacing boy; he had seen enough of Stauncher at work to know how it would play out. Instead he went up to the prisoner, hands tied behind her with the rope looped around a young tree. Her eyes and mouth were covered in a cloth wrapped tight around her head, she breathed heavily, sucking her gag into and out of her partly opened mouth. She was over a foot shorter than Shak and her headdress had come off in the ride, so, unusually for a noblewoman her straw yellow hair, straggled and whipped by the wind now hung limply almost down to her waist. Her green velvet tunic and dress were both stitched with small gems and spattered with mud, a contrast that made Shak smile. He spoke to Siras first.

"Get back to the horses and ask Dead Eyes to come here."

Siras nodded and left without a sound. Shak now stood directly in front of his hostage, craning his neck towards her ear so that she could hear him clearly. He spoke firmly, precisely, emphasising the importance of every word.

"Eleanor Lasgaart, Lady Eleanor Lasgaart, listen to me and listen carefully. You are our prisoner, you have nowhere to run and no prospect of

ACT ONE : THE HUNT

escape. We are surrounded by wilderness and unless you stay with us you are food for wolves, bears, or even trolls. It is in our interest to keep you safe; for the moment we are your protectors so keep that at the front of your mind. Now, I am going to lower your gag to give you some air, if you have questions then ask them but scream, cry, or swear and the gag is going straight back on. Understood?"

Eleanor nodded.

Shak slowly pulled her gag free.

"You traitorous whoreson dogs! My brother is a knight of the Silver Lances, and he will be hunting you down right this very moment! And when he does find you he will nail you all to these trees and open your stomachs to the sky. And each time a set of your rotten innards spills on to the mud the only sounds you will hear will be your own agonised screams and my ecstatic laughter." She spat at him, hitting his cloak, all Shak did was sigh.

"That may be the case my lady but please don't call us traitorous, surely our accents alone can tell you we are not Fenchard's men."

She hesitated, but only for a moment. "Arshumans. Yellow bellied, garlic munching, snail chewing Arshumans." Her voice was a reptilian hiss.

"That's us," Shak said breezily. "I could call you a Tanarese mud bathing, flea attracting barbarian, but I am sure we can raise ourselves above the level of childish abuse, can we not?"

"Don't try the smooth, reasonable approach with me, you are nothing more than invading brutes, killers, savages…"

"And you took this country from the elves did you not? I am sure they would say the same about you."

"Keth's gizzard, they were just Wych folk, their opinions do not count…"

"Is that so?" Dead Eyes arrived at just that particular moment. "Commander, if we have to kill her can I be given the honour? You have my word I won't do it too quickly."

"Dead Eyes here is an el…I mean a Wych," Shak told Eleanor. "I would apologise if I was you, she has a very long memory."

"I will apologise only after you do the same for abducting me. What do Arshumans want with me anyway, what am I to you. And why haven't you just handed me to Fenchard?"

"You would rather be with Fenchard?"

She shook her head. "That is like choosing to be with an asp or a viper."

He nodded. "Reasonable comment. We are taking you for ransom by the way, our king is trying to agree terms with your Grand Duke, you may well form a part of them. A small part. And we are keeping you from Fenchard because we don't want him marrying you. We are taking you to Grest now and from there to Tantala where we will hand you over to the governor in residence. You will be treated well and will want for nothing but freedom. So, if you behave yourself and don't cause trouble you may only have to keep our company for the next three days or so. Understood?"

"Perfectly. But I will have you know that it is my duty as a Tanarese noblewoman to cause you all as many problems as I possibly can. Now will you do me the courtesy of removing my blindfold, or are all your pretensions to civility mere artifice?"

Dead Eyes sniggered, looking over her shoulder to where Stauncher had just finished applying a bandage to his patient's thigh. "Dormouse is not ready yet, don't tell him I have seen him like he is. The cold never does a man any favours now, does it."

Dormouse yelped. Dead Eyes sniggered again.

"We will take it off once one of our number has had some medical treatment. As yet he is not fit to seen by a lady, Dead Eyes here not really counting in that respect."

The elf gave him a sideways look, and a wry little smile.

"You are talking about the blonde one aren't you, the one that killed Barten aren't you?" Eleanor had returned to her vituperative hiss. "Well at least Barten gave him something to remember him by. Blondie!" she raised her thin voice to a level that was both piercing and extremely irritating. "Hey Blondie! Did the knife cut you to the bone? Is it painful? I bet it is. Careful you don't get gangrene; I hear it stinks something awful. Maybe the leg will rot and will have to be sawn off, maybe all that pus will go to your brain, and you will go mad. If it does I will find it really, really funny. Ha!"

"That is enough," Shak was just beginning to sound weary of her. "Stauncher, are you done with the boy yet?"

"Just finishing up, his trousers are back on anyway, I just need to apply the poultice, that is all."

"Right," Shak said, pulling Eleanor's blindfold down at sufficient speed to make her blink with shock. "Any more out of you and the gag and the blindfold go right back on. Now act like the lady you are supposed to be rather

ACT ONE : THE HUNT

than the way we Arshumans think a Tanarese lady behaves. Understood?"

Eleanor was still blinking at the influx of light. "My brother is coming. Don't you forget that," she said coldly.

"Who is coming?" Stan had arrived to stand next to the two of them, he had evidently handed his stave over and seemed keen to be doing something, he was never one for idleness when in the field.

"My brother. To kill you. To spill your guts onto the cold earth, and, looking at you, they would cover a substantial area. A lot of people could end up slipping on them."

Stan and Shak exchanged amused glances. "She is a funny one isn't she?" Stan came closer, looking her up and down. "Still, if one of the horses goes lame we can throw a saddle on her instead, she certainly looks the part. They say Tanarese nobles have an unhealthy interest in beasts so I would imagine it would be best not to look too closely at her family tree."

"How dare you, churl!" Eleanor's hiss was her loudest yet.

"Oh I dare, you insult me, I insult you, that is the way it works. Still, I have enough hospitality in me to offer you some oatcake. Feel free to refuse, you could do with losing some weight from the look at you."

"You are hectoring me about losing weight? I have a mirror in my saddlebag if you need clarification on who the fattest one around here happens to be."

"All muscle my lady, I keep the muscle, you keep the flab. Now, food or no food?"

Shak and Dead Eyes left the two of them arguing and returned to the others. Dormouse was leaning on his new staff with one hand and chewing oatcake with his other, Dead Eyes went up to him and gave him a reassuring pat on the shoulder.

"This girl of yours, the one you are trying to impress, what is her name?"

"Lady Sandrine of Lakala." Dormouse looked puzzled.

"Well, when Lady Sandrine of Lakala has her wedding night with you, she will not be disappointed in the least." The elf walked away from him leaving him staring open mouthed after her.

"You SAW!" he gasped accusingly.

"Well," Dead Eyes answered, not looking back, "it was so large it was very hard to avoid."

"Oh." For a second he was lost for words. Then though, the slightest of

73

smiles crept over his face. "Oh right. Of course. I knew that all along."

Shak was standing at the western edge of the clearing where Dead Eyes joined him a moment later. "Come with me," he said to her, "I want to see if she was bluffing about her brother, the knight."

Together they retraced their steps through the woods along the animal track they had ridden up earlier until at last the path started to descend toward the lower ground where the trees still sported a good covering of leaves. There they changed direction, with Shak leaving the path and striking northwards, taking a mazy route through the trees until he stood a few steps from a cliff edge. Dead Eyes joined him a moment later, both of them keeping to the shadows.

Below them was a landscape both were very familiar with indeed. An escarpment colossal in scale sloping downwards from right to left, north to south. To their right were the Derannen mountains, their brown and broken heights now tipped with winter snow and reflecting the sanguine hues of a sun beginning to slide into the horizon ahead of them. The lower slopes of the mountains were green with ancient woods, cloud forests changing to pine forests, pine forests to the broadleaved woods they were standing in right now. These woods were marbled by swift watercourses, ranging from slippery brooks to great rivers, the closest and largest of them being the Whiterush, half a day or so behind them to the east. Left of their position the woods broke into a patchwork of fields and copses, level ground dotted with scrub and hillocks. It all used to be farmland, with dirt roads linking sleepy villages, managed hedges criss crossing fields trod by beasts both playful and lumbering. Now though the villages were burnt and abandoned, the hedges overgrown and neglected, the fields reduced to wilderness, and the beasts long consumed by voracious armies. Shak should of course have felt little about the despoiling of the enemy's lands, but he did feel something, and the feeling was not one of pride.

"You keep watching," Dead Eyes broke into his thoughts. "I want to follow the path a little further, if I hear anything coming..."

"Arrow into the air and hide?"

She nodded and slipped away, silent as midnight snow, a silence he could not possibly hope to replicate. He set himself to standing motionless as stone and stared ahead at the blanket of trees and more specifically at the place where he thought the path ran through it.

ACT ONE : THE HUNT

****

Unlike her companions Dead Eyes never felt threatened by woodland, never felt that every standing tree, every fluttering bush, every bank of moss concealed unseen and watching eyes. The woods to her was as natural a place as the city to the others, there was nothing to fear, as long as one kept one's ears pricked and eyes sharp. The city was much more dangerous to her, and its air infinitely more noisome. Her childhood and youth were spent in the woods, she had undergone the ceremony that marked her passage to womanhood in the woods, her wedding day had been in the woods; no, there was nothing to fear, not as long as her wits and senses were sound.

She moved noiselessly down the path, hand on her short bow, eyes scanning the ground, ears scanning the trees for any sounds that did not belong, down the slope she went and then a little further over the level ground. The mud of the track was soft, the hooves of the horses, their horses, for they had ridden along here not an hour ago, was easy to read. Seven horses at a canter, course and direction not altering, if anything was pursuing them they were surely still some distance behind.

Seven horses, course and speed constant. Or was it?

She stopped and crouched on her haunches, free hand touching the tracks in front of her.

Seven horses, and this one.

For here, one set of tracks led off the path and into the trees.

And that was not all, for just at the point the tracks veered off there was something in the mud, at first she thought it was just a stone but as she looked at it, it caught the dappled sun and glinted. She picked it up, peering at it with curiosity. It was a coin shaped disc of polished metal, it could indeed have been a coin not yet minted, perhaps that was its original purpose. Instead it had just been burnished to a very high degree. Almost as if it was designed to be dropped by somebody so that it could be seen by those riding behind. She picked it up, wiped off the mud and placed it carefully in her waist pouch.

She stood again and peered in the direction that these rogue tracks led. No movement. No sound over the trilling of the birds, maybe just the odd snapping twig. Her usual senses were giving her nothing.

So why was her skin tingling, and why was the merest film of sweat coating her fingertips?

THE FANGS OF THE FEN SNAKE

Because she was being watched.

Keeping low she started to follow the tracks, they were easy to follow for the grass was bruised, the odd branch here and there snapped. She examined the broken end of one, the sap was still wet, the breakage was very recent. And now here, a second set of prints meeting the first, this one coming from further up the path, from part of it she hadn't yet explored. A little further on and a third set joined the other two. She stopped when she saw that, it was fruitless going any further, not if she was going to be so outnumbered. As noiselessly as only one of the Wych folk could be she started to back up slowly, only turning round fully when she was a few feet from the path.

So, she thought, there were at least three of them, and they may have passed this way just minutes ago.

Once back on the path she fitted an arrow to her bow and loosed it skyward, then she headed back up the ridge, towards Shak and the others as fast as she could without drawing attention to herself, her dark green cloak and brown leathers melding in perfectly with her surroundings.

She had scoffed earlier at the wariness the city folk had for such places, at their suspicions that unseen eyes and ears were everywhere, following them, threatening them. These wilds rarely concealed the stuff of nightmares, hardly ever cloaked those who would do harm to others.

Yet sometimes, she had to admit, the city folk were right.

ACT ONE : THE HUNT

6

"Well, they have definitely got her." Nico Lasgaart crouched for a moment before standing and stretching to his full height in an effort to ease saddle soreness. In his hand, plucked from the mud and now sporting several earthy smears was a woman's headdress. It was a simple one, a thin silver circlet with a veil and crespine attached, a standard headdress for a young noblewoman. It would have taken a lot of movement and jostling for it to come free, Nico wondered if its owner had pulled it off deliberately.

"Is it definitely Lady Eleanor's?" Ursus asked.

Nico shrugged his shoulders. "No idea, but how many noblewomen ride in this part of the world during a war? The Felmere great hunt has been a thing of the past for a good while now."

"It was not a serious question." Ursus said drily.

Nico ignored him. "We are gaining on them. We know there are six or seven of them and they have a prisoner, there is no way they are riding faster than we are."

"But just how quickly are we gaining I wonder?" Ursus patted his horse, she had ridden like the wind today, if anything it was Nico who was struggling to keep the pace.

"Only time and the Gods can tell. But they will have to strike out over the plains soon and then we will both see what we have to do. If they are headed for Grest we can intercept them part way, we have the better and more powerful horses."

"And when we do intercept them, what then?"

"I grab Eleanor and lead her clear, you keep the rest of them off me."

"What? All of them? All six or seven?"

"They can't all come at you at once."

"They won't form an orderly line either. And you know they won't just let us ride away with her, yes?"

"I know," Nico said grimly. "No need to belabour things, but we are Silver Lances, the bodyguard of the Grand Duke, the knights of Artorus..."

"Yes, yes, we know no fear, even when the odds are insurmountable..."

Nico shook his head. "Sorry to correct you old mentor but only a fool

ACT ONE : THE HUNT

has no fear. What a knight does is overcome fear, his faith and sense of honour and duty carries him across the field, his foes see the light of the Gods in his eyes and scatter like chaff at his coming."

Ursus was laughing silently by now. "Of course, there is nothing foolish about us at all. Our honour is great, our faith unshakeable, if only our punctuality met the same standards."

Nico went back to his horse, tying the headdress to his saddlebag. "A low blow my friend, if we had got to Bear Valley when we promised we would then we could have escorted Eleanor all the way and this kidnap would never have happened. You think I am not reproaching myself with every passing moment?"

Ursus adopted a more sympathetic tone as Nico remounted. "We were delayed by duties unforeseen," he said. "Baron Felmere was keen to use us, so use us he did. We departed as expediently as was possible. It was the decision of the wedding party to leave for the south before our arrival, sometimes the Gods contrive to throw shit in our face, that is all."

"And now we have to wipe it off and clean it up. And if we can't we have to explain to the Spalforths that the erstwhile union between our families is postponed. Dishonour for us and an insult to them. As if there isn't enough going wrong around us."

"Clean it up we may but the smell still lingers. And you sitting here listening to a blathering old fool isn't helping matters. The horses have had a rest, time to push on, your little sister is out there somewhere, and she is relying on you."

Nico kicked his horse's flanks, stirring the beast into a trot. "Maybe. Sister to me she is, but the two of us are hardly close in truth, too many years between us for that."

"And you have so many siblings as it is. Five brothers and five sisters, and don't let me start to count your cousins and uncles."

"If you did start," Nico laughed, "you would still be counting ere dawn. The Lasgaart family tree is labyrinthine indeed and we are connected in some way to all the great families of Tanaren."

"And, dare I say it," Ursus chanced, "quite a few of the great families of Arshuma too. Intermarriage between the countries was commonplace before this war started. Why even you, as a child, was promised to some Arshuman heiress or other."

"Lady Taracine Bectalian, I remember her. I was looking forward to the wedding, their family had sent me a painted miniature of her, she seemed very beautiful to my thirteen-year-old eyes though I suppose she was only about the same age. I was, last time I heard, still technically betrothed to her, all talk of nuptials obviously ended when this war started. I wonder what she is doing now?"

"Married elsewhere no doubt." Ursus shrugged his shoulders as they eased the horses into a canter. "They marry them young over there, even younger than we do here. Must be frightening for these young girls, sent away to a strange place to wed a man she might barely know."

Nico had no sympathy. "They are born to it and have no expectations to the contrary. It is what Eleanor wants and it is our job to see that she gets what she wants. Now, sluggard, I really hope you are not going to hold me up any longer, I would have been in Grest by now if it weren't for you."

With a roar, Ursus spurred his horse on as the canter became a full gallop. He left Nico half a furlong behind before the younger knight could react. Along the animal track they thundered, scattering the birds and the deer, hooves sending up mud and dead leaves, bare branches of the trees sighing at their passing. The knights of the Silver Lance were on the hunt again, and their quarry was getting closer and closer.

****

"So," Stan said in a slow drawl, "we are being watched. And hunted." He scanned the trees around them looking for a suspect shadow. There were dozens of them.

"Well, the girl did say her brother would try and chase us down." Stauncher adjusted his permanently shapeless hat, an adjustment that made no sartorial difference whatsoever.

"My name is Eleanor," she said in cut glass tones. "Eleanor. Not "the girl", not "the prisoner": Eleanor. Or is the concept of correct first names truly beyond all of you?"

Everybody ignored her.

Shak and Dead Eyes had returned to the clearing and in hushed voices explained to all present what had been discovered. Now they were contemplating their next move.

"I do not think the tracks I saw belonged to knights;" Dead Eyes, her arms folded, was shaking her head. "The hoof prints were too small; the horses of knights are so much larger than the norm. And would knights creep

ACT ONE : THE HUNT

around like that? Concealment is not their usual way, is it?" She sounded uncertain.

Shak, however, had no such doubts. "No, they were not knights, they were something else. That is not to say that your brother is not chasing us down also." He looked at the smiling Eleanor. "But it seems there is another party keen to skin our carcass."

"But who?" Stauncher voiced all their thoughts.

"Assassins of some sort, that is all I can think of." Shak looked thoughtful. "It seems they have been following us for a while, so they are not bandits or raiders with robbery on their mind."

"You think they are after you?" Stan asked.

"I am nobility, you know how intrigue works in our homeland, I am just surprised that it has taken this long for them to come for me. Perhaps it is only now that my family has heard that I still live."

"Your family?" Stauncher asked. "Seriously?"

"Who else might want me dead?"

"The king? A rival city?"

"Possibly, but when an Arshuman noble is hunted the first place he looks to find the hunter is amongst his own family. Anyway, that is a question for another time. For now, we just need to work out how to deal with this threat."

He looked at each of them in turn before his gaze fell on Siras the scout, who was still some distance away tending the horses. His eyes remained there awhile before he started to speak again.

"Assassins strike when we are at our most vulnerable, when our backs are turned..."

"Or when we are asleep." Stan finished the sentence.

"Yes," Shak confirmed, "and it will be dark soon. My initial plan was to continue along the path until we reached a hillock at the edge of the woodland that I know of, but even that might be too compromised. We will be at Grest tomorrow night so any attack will have to come tonight or not at all. We need a position that we can defend, that will force them into the open..."

Stan snorted like a bullock. "Tell me you are not thinking what I am thinking..."

"I am, and you know I am."

"Where?" Stauncher asked, brow furrowed like a ploughed field. "What are you lot talking about?"

THE FANGS OF THE FEN SNAKE

"You weren't with us," Stan said. "It would have been about three years ago. We were raiding a secret supply line the Tanarese were operating up here, did well too, ended up closing it down, but we did attract a pack of mercenaries who hounded us like dogs. A running skirmish developed, there were more of them, so we were forced off the path to head north. Suddenly the forest cleared a little and, standing in front of us, next to a stream, was a small, long abandoned manor house..."

"It was more a summer house I reckon," Shak took up the tale. "A place for nobles to escape the smell of the city and enjoy the hunting and the sunshine. It was a ruin back then, Artorus only knows what it is like now. But there were walls and windows we could use as cover and the remnants of an encircling wall too. We holed up there and forced the mercenaries to come at us over open ground, after five of them fell dead they thought better of it, leaving us in search of easier pickings."

"Sounds like the ideal place to go to me," Stauncher said brightly. "So why do you sound so wary?"

"Because it is haunted," Stan said. Dead Eyed snorted derisively and rolled her eyes. "It is, elf girl!" he insisted. "The noises I heard were not natural, I will swear that on the sacred book."

"Haunted?" Dormouse had been quiet up to this point, obsessively examining the dressing on his leg; that one word though summoned him back to the present.

"He heard animals, that was all," Dead Eyes tried to reassure him. "When we walked into the place deer were running around on the ground floor, the corner towers were full of birds and bats, there were mice everywhere, when night fell a thousand creatures stirred around us..."

"And yet," Stan folded his mighty arms, "at the time you could not attribute some of those sounds to any animal that you knew of, and you know all of them."

"Not all." Dead Eyes shook her head and chewed her lip.

"What sort of noises?" Stauncher and Dormouse spoke in unison.

"Scratching and a sort of low moaning, like a strong wind blowing through a cave or tunnel, except that it had a voice of a kind, and I swear to this day that the voice was not human, but not animal either. It spooked me, I was happy when our attackers turned up and I could crack a few heads, there are things out there that defy rational explanation."

Some members of Stan's audience seemed undecided on whether the

ACT ONE : THE HUNT

man was trying to stoke their fears for his own personal amusement, or whether he was speaking in earnest. Stan though was not smiling.

"Well," Shak said breezily, "those of us that have served with you for any length of time will be well used to low moaning and strong wind by now. Time to break things up, we head north, if we push on hard and I remember aright we should get there just before nightfall. Now move, and Stauncher, you have a way with women, you can guard our guest, I can see that she is pining for intelligent company."

Eleanor had been sat staring morosely at the ground for a while; now though she looked up at those talking about her. "The only way I will meet passably intelligent company is if those deer are still there, there certainly is none of it to be found here."

"You only think that because we have yet to talk at any length." Stauncher gave her a toothy smile.

"A healer who puts a poultice on top of a bandage? And who wears such a ridiculous hat? My hopes are not high." She screwed her face up at him.

"The healing power of the poultice is all in its liquid," he explained to her. "The solid part just sticks it in place. Then the liquid slowly seeps through the bandage closing the wound, healing the flesh, and stopping blood loss. Does that make it clear to you?"

Eleanor remained unimpressed. "Well your hat is still stupid. I'll wager you are bald or have an amusingly misshapen head, or something similar."

"Right on both counts." Stauncher lifted his hat up, his gap toothed smile broadening, gold teeth catching the dappled rays of the sinking sun.

He was bald, or at least the crown of his head was, it being fringed by a semicircle of wiry russet hair. His shining pate sported a couple of pitted pox marks but Eleanor barely noticed them for, just off centre from the top of his head ran a deep furrowed scar inches long. It had long healed, a cicatrix of thick, fibrous skin having formed over the initial wound, but what a wound it must have been.

"How didn't that blow kill you?" Eleanor asked in breathy tones.

"Because," Stauncher replaced his hat with a flourish, "as several physicians gleefully told me at the time, I have an abnormally thick skull. Any normal man would have been killed instantly but, as I like to say, it is a good thing not to be normal."

"How did you get it?"

THE FANGS OF THE FEN SNAKE

But Stauncher had little time for conversation. "Maybe I will tell you later, right now we have to move, or it will be dark, and we will be marooned in the forest and vulnerable to people who care as little for your safety as they do mine."

****

Shak rode slightly ahead of the others. They were off the animal track now and the ground was uneven and treacherous, crossed by gnarled tree roots and thickets of brush and tangled ferns. He knew the way; he knew the distance they had to travel but that was not the reason for his current desire for solitude. He was thinking, and he did not want interruptions.

Siras the scout had not joined their little meeting and so, once it was concluded, he went over to relay his instructions. "We are heading north," he told the man, who appeared to live in a state of near permanent apathy.

Not now though, he reacted to those words as if pricked by a needle. "North? But that takes us in the opposite direction to Grest."

"It does," Shak agreed, "but we need a secure place to stay the night and there is one to the north. We are being followed you see; hunters are tracking us and where we are going we should be safe from them."

"But where exactly are we going?" Siras asked him.

"Follow me and you shall find out." Shak smiled and walked away, deliberately leaving the other man shaking his head in bewilderment.

And now Shak was replaying that briefest of conversations over and over in his head. And what he needed to do regarding it.

Now though it was time for his isolation to end. For suddenly his horse broke through the treeline to stand, fetlock deep, in a broad but sluggish watercourse directly crossing their path. Most streams and rivers in this part of the world ran north to south, flowing downwards from the Derannen mountains. This one though was over ten yards wide and ran west to east, the usual southern route being blocked by the ridge Shak had just ridden away from. Soon it would curve again and head southwards once more, but its unorthodox direction afforded them all an opportunity.

He put his arm up, allowing them all to gather close to him. "It is a shallow waterway," he told them. "Ride to the centre then follow its course until I tell you otherwise. That should serve to confuse and delay our pursuers even if it doesn't stop them altogether."

They did as he commanded, horses churning up enough mud to

ACT ONE : THE HUNT

discolour the pristine waters. Out, away from the shelter of the tree line they shivered under the keen, persistent wind of early winter. The pallid, low sunlight was beginning to set behind them and the full throated song of birds at dusk was rather diminished by the splashing hooves of the wearying horses. The wearying humans atop them too were in little mood for conversation, they were just a little too tired, and more than a little too tense. The one elf amongst them though was of a brighter mien, dropping her horse back a little so that she could speak to a rather dejected looking Dormouse, who was not so much riding his horse as slumping on it, his shoulders stooped, his eyes blank as the sky. He looked more like a leather and wool clad jelly than a man basking in the glory of his first combat.

"Hurting?" She asked.

His expression was an answer in itself.

"Look," she said, "when we stop I can do something about the pain. I, or rather my people all have some ability with healing. Just let me lay my hand on your wound and it should help, both with setting the wound and easing the soreness. That is, if you are prepared to have me touching your leg of course."

"I thought the elf healing thing was a myth," he said feebly.

"No. We can also tell when somebody has an illness just by looking at them, some of the time anyway, we have a sense, an instinct for these things. Do you want me to do this for you? I rarely use the ability for it is tiring for me, but for you, as it is your first trip out with us, I will make an exception."

"Thank you, I will take any help on offer."

"You don't mind me touching you?"

"Right now, if it stopped the pain, I would happily be ravished by a black bear."

"Ha!" she laughed. "You are funny. Plenty of bears in these woods, though they must all be thinking of hibernation now. Comb your hair and put on your best shirt and you never know, you might get lucky."

He groaned. "No honour is worth all of this."

"Well we did try to tell you."

He nodded. "So you did. Can I ask you something?"

"Of course."

"You are not from the elf forest to the north are you?"

"No. I am from Chira, from the lakes, from the mountain vales of the Hagasus, many hundreds of miles from here."

"So," conversation appeared to be perking him up, "why are you here?

THE FANGS OF THE FEN SNAKE

This isn't your war and neither us nor the enemy are your people. Why risk your life like this?"

She paused for a moment, wondering how to precis a very long story.

"In short, I am from Chira but am not Chiran. My tribe were forcibly assimilated into the empire. My ability with the bow meant that I ended up working as a scout with the Imperial army. The empire tacitly backs Arshuma in the war and has offered them support troops on an ad hoc basis. And I was one of those support troops. Officially you see the empire doesn't have elves in its army, I was only allowed because I was part of a general's private retinue, but, over time the other commanders raised objections and in the end I was happy to leave, and they were happy to get rid of me. So here I am."

He looked sceptical. "There is more to it isn't there?"

"Yes."

"The empire is not known for its gentle treatment of its elves."

"No it isn't. And with some justification. As I said, I was happy to leave."

"Are you going to tell me the rest?"

"Of course. Maybe tonight, for we appear to be leaving the river now."

And so they were, Shak leading the group onto a shallow part of the north bank that was relatively free of undergrowth. Dormouse spurred his mount slightly to catch up with Dead Eyes, she seemed very keen to be under the trees again; as he did so he passed Siras who seemed, if anything, to be slowing for some reason.

"I don't quite understand why we did this," Dormouse asked the elf. "Do our pursuers have dogs? If they follow our tracks into this water they are bound to guess at what we are doing, surely it won't take them too long to pick up the trail on the other side."

"I saw no evidence of dogs." She had to shield her eyes against the sun which was now so low it was beginning to disappear behind the distant trees. "And you are right, it will not take them long to pick up our trail. Yet it will take time nevertheless, and maybe the sun will be down by the time they realise where we are going. It is highly unlikely that they will follow in darkness, too easy to make a mistake and lose our tracks completely. So, if this works they are not likely to attack us tonight, and a night attack offers them the best hope of success. Now, if we rest up securely and start off at first light we should get to Grest by nightfall tomorrow. So, we are forcing them to come at us in daylight, good for us, bad for them. Anything that might give us an advantage

ACT ONE : THE HUNT

is good; agreed?"

"Very much so." Dormouse climbed up on to the bank, feeling the rise in temperature as he regained the cover of the trees. "How much further is it?"

"We should just get there before the moon rises, hopefully just before the sun dies. We should have just enough time to scout around and find a safe spot in this big house to camp."

Dormouse uttered a "thank you" and set himself to diligently follow everybody else as fast as he could. For they had picked up speed and seemed eager to get this long, tiring, journey over with. Only Siras was behind him now but he had been at the rear for most of the journey, so Dormouse saw nothing untoward in that. After maybe some fifteen minutes of weaving a path between the trees Shak called a halt again.

"Stan, take over, you know the way, I will catch up with you shortly."

"Where are you going?" Stauncher asked in surprise.

"Full bladder, won't be long." And with that Shak peeled his horse away, riding back pretty much the same way they had come.

"Strange," Stauncher mused. "He normally has a bladder of iron."

"Nature's way," Stan's reply was nonchalant. "When you have got to go; you've got to go."

"I need to go as well," Eleanor said sulkily.

"You are not in charge, you will have to hang on, we are almost there, then Dead Eyes can find a secluded spot for you."

"Wait, I have to be escorted?"

"Let me just remind you of something," Stan said cheerily. "This morning, we abducted you. You are our hostage, you do not go anywhere or do anything without an escort, just be grateful we have a woman in our company otherwise you would have to pee in front of me. And believe me when I say that watching such an activity is not high on my list of things to do before I die."

Eleanor glowered at him. "You Arshumans are all perverted."

"Yes we are. We revel in it. Now shut up and ride."

Shak re-joined them maybe another fifteen minutes later, and maybe it was just another five before they cleared the forest once more and saw before them a low, crumbling wall, a broad, heavily overgrown clearing, and the crumbling skeleton of a manor house, the place they were to spend the night and the sight of which reassured Dormouse not one whit.

7

In its day, it must have been a sight that induced sighs of awe, a grand house built on three storeys with a crenelated stone tower at each corner. Flags and wall hangings in crimson (the colour of the now defunct baronetcy of North Whiterush) would have fluttered in the mountain breeze, the fields enclosed by the encircling wall would have supported herbs, crops, and livestock, the joyous song of the foaming stream running along the east side of the house would gladden the hearts of any guest. It was its own little community in the foothills, a retreat for the baron and a place to entertain prestigious visitors, a symbol of the luxury enjoyed by the nobility prior to this war. Now the baron had been dead these nine years, his young heir was living in exile in Tanaren city, and the lands he had a claim to had been disputed, ravaged, and laid waste many times since.

And the house was now little more than a cadaver, a desiccated husk long picked clean of its finery. The glass and lead in the windows were gone, the roof tiles were gone too, much of the wood in the internal walls and floors had rotted and collapsed, a fire had blackened the stonework and scorched the remaining plaster. In the fields the stone outbuildings had crumbled into mossy stumps, the well-tended lawns around the house were now a thicket of briar and tangled grass swallowing the gravel path running up to the main doorway, which itself was now little more than a gaping, dark maw, the doors having long since disappeared. As Dormouse looked at it he was reminded of an aunty of his. He had met her as a young child and thought her the most beautiful woman he had ever seen. Then nearly twenty years elapsed before he saw her again, twenty years that had given her some fifteen pregnancies, three husbands, and a spell in jail for some perceived slight against the king. And the woman he had seen most recently was not ugly as such, rather she looked defeated, beaten down by care and sadness, a testament to neglect and dereliction. Her breath had smelled of sour wine and her eyes, those dark eyes that had so entranced him as a child were no longer the eyes of a living person; she was walking, she was breathing but to all intent she was a dead woman, her spirit sucked into the void. He had felt an overpowering sense of sorrow at what she had become, a feeling that was being replicated now, if perhaps not as strongly.

ACT ONE : THE HUNT

Dusk was well set now, house and surrounding field were clothed in deepening shadow, birds and insects were singing lustily, seizing the few precious minutes remaining before darkness swallowed all before it. To their right, rising above the stream and the shallow cliff beyond it rose a pale winter moon, its rising signifying a drop in temperature that hinted at the possibility of frost by morning, Dormouse sincerely hoped for somewhere secluded to sleep that allowed for the kindling of a fire. Last night he had been wet and cold, tonight it looked like he would be dry and colder, and the cold would not help his wound, right now it was hurting him to distraction, it needed time and rest to heal properly, and he was worried that it would get neither.

Shak led the way, riding up to the shadowed doorway with gusto, Stan followed, Dormouse bringing up a dejected rear. Behind the house lay the rising mountains, snow on the tallest peaks, pines and fir trees, still a verdant green, clinging to the higher foothills. Here and there a silver ribbon of a waterfall would dissect the seemingly endless forest, tumbling over hidden rocks, carving gorges of their own before joining greater rivers further to the south. It was a wild place, far from help, far from aid, here they truly were on their own, the city boy in Dormouse was recoiling in horror at his surroundings.

The doorway, with its absent doors and crumbling supports was easily large enough to ride a horse through, and the room, or rather the shell of the room that they rode into was large enough to accommodate both horse and riders. Shak dismounted, landing onto a floor that was now all grassed over.

"Stan and myself will scout the house, check that it is all secure. Going on memory the corner towers to the north are both crumbled and ruined. The best place for us to stay is the south east tower." He pointed to his left, past a cracked, half ruined wall still sporting fragments of paintwork to where a near intact stone tower reached skywards, it being visible mainly due to the ceiling above them having all but disintegrated. "There," he continued, "the floors are of stone and hopefully still viable and through the windows we have a view of the field that any would be attacker would have to cross to get to us. If we stay on the second floor all we have to defend is the stairway up to it. Siras, stay here and tether the horses, the rest of you can explore the tower and try and get comfortable. We will be with you shortly, and now we are concealed by the wall I will allow a light, if one of you wants to carry one." He nodded to Stan and together the two of them disappeared through another doorless aperture, headed towards the south west tower.

THE FANGS OF THE FEN SNAKE

"Well," Stauncher said with noticeably forced cheeriness. "Shall I light the lamp?"

****

Stan kept a firm grip on the haft of his axe. Ideally a relaxed grip was preferable but there was precious little to be relaxed about at the moment. Shak was carrying his own lamp, a small, hooded affair with a wick powered by oil it was comforting to be close to and yet not really adequate enough to fulfil its role of illumination. All it did was cast shadows upon shadows and attract heavy and drowsy moths that would bump into it from time to time, making Stan start and look wildly around him, expecting to see his studded leather jerkin being pierced by the ghost blade of an assassin.

He assumed that the sun was down now for the darkness was nearly complete. The two of them moved softly from room to room, from small ante rooms to chambers where once a lady may have retired to listen to music, or to be read to by her scribe. Some of the floors still had some of their original tiles, enamel painted in gaudy colours now concealed by fronds of grass or wandering brambles. Spider webs clung to the forgotten corners, field mice scurried unseen over rotten planks, bats were beginning to take silent flight from their roosts in the towers, from the forests close by a night hawk called and, further away, on the bald heights of the mountain valleys the wolves were howling at the incipient moon. They were at the south west tower now, the opposite tower to the one where they planned to spend the night. Its narrow, arched doorway opened onto a flight of broken stone steps, Shak went up to the arch, holding the lamp out, so that its light picked out the moss and lichen clinging to stairs and walls. He stuck his head under the arch before looking up and listening.

"Smells musty," he told Stan, "damp and animal droppings, hopefully the tower we have picked is drier."

Stan exhaled, looking up at the stars flickering wanly above the absent ceiling and long collapsed roof. Something occurred to him then, something he had to share.

"All the ceilings have perished," he said. "Outside of the towers, which are all stone, this house no longer has a second or third floor."

"I know," Shak answered, "it was pretty much the same last time we were here."

"Ah, but it wasn't," came the reply. "Last time we were here the grass,

ACT ONE : THE HUNT

all of the ground floor in fact was strewn with rubble, wood, plaster, stone, broken tiles. As the ceilings got damp and collapsed all of it ended up around our feet. So where is it all now?"

"You have a point," Shak said. "A very good point. It is almost as though someone has been here and..."

"Tidied up?"

Shak gave him a half smile and nodded. "Let's push on."

They did so, going room by room until they were at the north western part of the manor. If Stan remembered correctly the room in the very corner was some sort of larder. The tower next to it had the servant's quarters and an extensive cellar under the room held the wine butteries. There was a double doorway in the external wall to take deliveries and a single doorway allowing for easy access to what Stan believed were once herb gardens, judging from the spacing of the enclosures outside. Go through this room, turn right and they would soon be in the great hall, or rather, what was once the great hall. Now of course it was little more than a cavernous ruin full of whispers and memories. Stan now gripped his axe so tightly his knuckles were white under his gauntlets.

They crept down a narrow passageway, a rare place for both walls and ceiling were mostly extant, then, as Stan remembered correctly, they were in the corner room. He stepped inside to stand next to Shak, had a good look around then exchanged glances with his taller companion. Both men stood still, frozen in place, stunned at what lay before them.

For it appeared that all the missing rubble had been brought here.

This room too still had a partial ceiling, strips of jagged starlight filtering through its gaps. The double doorway to their left was a completely open space, the night breeze blowing through it cooling the sweat on their faces and bringing the scents of damp grass and earth. Dead ahead though, concealing the entrances to the tower, cellar, and herb gardens was a pile of wood, masonry, plaster, and soil. It had been fashioned into a sort of semi-circle about eight to ten feet high, they would have to squeeze past it to get to the eastern doorway that led to the great hall.

"Did bandits do this?" Stan whispered to his companion. "Is it a defensive structure?"

"Maybe. I don't know." Shak took a couple of steps forward to examine it more closely. "All I know is that it definitely wasn't here last time."

He edged forward a little further so that he was now standing next to the open double doorway. "It appears to surround the tower and cellar entrance. I will just have a quick look." He slowly drew his sword with his free hand, buttercream light from the lamp glinting off the blade. A great ruby, the cherry of Mazuras was set into the pommel, the hilt too sparkled with tiny sapphires. He had taken the sword, a great heirloom from his home city when he had fled from it, no brother or nephew was getting his hands on it whilst Shak still lived, for the blade was his birth right, the blade of the heir to the Heron throne.

"What are you doing?" Stan hissed at him. Shak raised his lamp in an appeasing gesture and started to disappear behind the hastily constructed wall. With a look to the heavens and a mouthed. "Artorus keep your eyes on us, from now on I will obey all the high tenets of the faith. Most of the time." He trotted forward to stand next to his leader.

Shak was looking perplexed. Ahead of him should have been a bolted wooden hatchway in the floor that opened on to a flight of steps to the cellar below. Instead, surrounded by the wall of rubble, there was a hole in the ground many times wider than the original entrance. It looked like it had been broadened by an army of men smashing away at stone and earth with sledgehammers, now it looked much more like a jagged entrance to a subterranean cave. Furthermore, a good portion of the spoil produced had buried the steps, meaning that any man trying to descend would have to clamber over a sloping floor of treacherous rubble. The two men stared at it with virtual incomprehension before Shak shaded the lamp with his hand and indicated that they should get out of here, a suggestion that Stan agreed to readily. Moving past the strange structure to get to the eastern doorway Stan suddenly saw the moon glint off something, something in the newly thrown up barricade. He stopped to examine it more closely, Shak coming to stand next to him. Stan touched the object, which was wedged firmly into this bizarre construct, then slowly managed to pull it free of the rubble surrounding it.

It was the thigh bone of an animal, maybe a large stag and it had been shattered at one end by what could only have been teeth. The two men looked at each other before Shak pointed out other parts of the wall that were also sporting fragments of denuded bone. Stan shuddered, then placed the bone he was holding gently on the ground before skipping out of the room as fast and as noiselessly as his feet could manage.

They tiptoed through yet more rooms before finally stepping into the

ACT ONE : THE HUNT

shell of the great hall, a long, rectangular space through which ran a double row of stone pillars, pillars that no longer served any purpose, for they now supported a non-existent ceiling. A lot of their original plasterwork still remained, clean white pillars surmounting a floor of vivid blue and white tiles. Stan tried to picture it as it was, a row of elaborate chandeliers, wax candles reflecting off walls and ceiling, around a dozen great picture windows running along the external wall proffering views of the gardens and the high mountains beyond. A gallery to the right (Stan could see the gap in the wall where it would have run), would have supported a great number of musicians as the great and good of local society laughed and drank and danced till their feet were sore. There would have been a fire, maybe at the halls further end, and trestle tables for feasting. He was standing on the raised dais that all such halls featured, a place where the baron's high table would have stood. If she had been just a few years older their hostage would probably have been invited here at some time, she would have danced and flirted with the knights and accepted food delivered by servants she would have given little or no regard to. Whether it was Tanaren or Arshuma, the elite behaved exactly the same.

And one of them was looking at Stan now. He shook himself free of his thoughts to see Shak regarding him with a quizzical eye. "Tired?" Shak asked him, "well I suppose none of us are getting any younger, especially you."

Stan shook his head. "Just thinking. You know I have to stop doing anything else when my brain starts to work. What did we just see back there? Would bandits really smash up the cellar stairs like that? As far as I can see it serves no purpose. As it was, attackers would have had to come down those steps one at a time, easy to pick off, now they can climb down in their dozens, all that rubble would slow them down for sure but even so...why break up the floor like that? Why build a wall of wood and earth in the room above? Why put bones in it for Keth's sake? What in the name of Artorus did we just see?"

"No idea," Shak replied. "Well you did say this place was haunted."

"Thanks chief," Stan's face was blank. "Thanks. Just for a moment there I thought you were being flippant."

"Well I wasn't lying when I said I had no idea. I couldn't hear anyone moving around in the cellar so I hope it has been long abandoned. Perhaps it was a natural collapse."

"Then who put up the wall?"

"Who indeed. At least that room is at the opposite end of the tower we will be staying in. If any bandits do emerge from the cellar we should hear them coming."

Stan nodded unhappily and they continued their sweep of the manor. There wasn't much left to do in truth, past the great hall were the kitchens, bare rooms in which only the bread ovens still looked relatively intact. The final tower, at the north east point of the manor had collapsed totally, a great, misshapen pyramid of dark stone cloaked in lichen with small mountain plants sprouting through various cracks and fissures. The chill breeze blew over it and into the faces of the two men, Stan could smell earth, and clear water, for the song of the stream was loud here.

Their search done the men returned to the great hall and to a doorway that led south, to the main entrance and, after that, to the tower in which they would spend the night.

Shak turned to Stan, the two men understanding the unspoken meaning of his look.

"Ready?" Shak asked him.

"Yes. I suppose it is time. Just one thing first."

"What is it?"

"Am I killing Siras straight away or are we talking to him first?"

"Talking." Shak answered grimly. "And if, or when he is to be killed afterwards then I will do it. If it wasn't for me being here, these assassins wouldn't be following us in the first place."

****

To the relief of the others, the south east tower was at least habitable. Yes, it smelled of damp and neglect, moss encrusted the internal walls and they had to wave their weapons around to clear the webs away and scare off the mice and spiders but once that was done, they could get about the business of establishing it as a base until the rising of dawn. Stauncher volunteered to do the first watch and so had ascended to the third floor, taking Eleanor with him, leaving Dead Eyes and Dormouse to occupy the second, giving them the responsibility of guarding the stairs and confronting any potential attackers. Each floor held a small, square, room, with a single slit window looking out onto the fields and the front entrance of the house, and a doorway in the right hand wall that would once have opened onto the second or third floors but which now yawned on to an empty space following the disintegration of each storey. The doors had long gone too, leaving them all

ACT ONE : THE HUNT

looking out uncomfortably at empty space, a space which did nothing to make the tower warmer.

Stauncher put out his lamp then spread his bedroll out next to the slit window, where he sat gazing out into the darkness, head on elbow, elbow resting on the embrasure. Eleanor went and sat with her back next to the east wall, her hair had fallen so that it partly covered her face but not to the degree that it masked her scowl, or her overall surliness.

"I am filthy," she said in a bitter tone, "and I have no bedding to sleep on."

Stauncher grabbed the bedroll with his free hand and slid it Eleanor's way. She took it without a word and spread it out, sitting on it and pulling out her dress so that it concealed her legs.

"Are you going to thank me?" Stauncher gave her a sardonic smile.

"No. I do not thank kidnappers."

"Fair point. Try and get some sleep, there will be some hard riding tomorrow."

She lay on her bedroll, twisting and turning as she tried to find a position that approached comfort. It was a fruitless search. She sat up again with a sigh. "It is so cold here."

Stauncher stood this time. Unfastening his cloak, he passed it to her. Again she accepted it without a word, wrapping herself in it so that only her face remained exposed.

Stauncher resumed his watch. "Ever come here?" he asked her. "When it was inhabited? I mean before it was ruined."

"No," she said. "It has obviously been ruined for many years, maybe around the time the war started, and I have little memory of anything before the war."

"Why not? Just how old are you?"

"Sixteen. In a few days. Or weeks."

Stauncher was genuinely taken aback. "Xhenafa take me for a fool, I had you at three or four years older than that."

"We grow up quickly in Tanaren."

"You obviously do. I had no idea we had stolen away a child."

"I am not a child."

Stauncher stroked his chin. "Maybe not to you. But you are in my eyes. I am rather pleased we grabbed you now."

She looked at him for the first time. "Why in Elissa's name would you say that?"

"Well, look at it this way. If we hadn't taken you then in a week or two you would have had your betrothed slobbering over you like a dog with water fever, either that or you would have had this Fenchard fellow doing exactly the same thing."

"Perhaps I want to be slobbered over."

"You are too smart to want that."

"Am I?" She regarded him with curious eyes. "But I very much want to be married, and my betrothed is a good match for me, he is due to inherit a good swathe of land, and several estates as well. What else would I want from life?"

"What else?" he shrugged his shoulders. "If you do not know then there is little point my answering. Ever seen your betrothed?"

"No. Ordinarily I would have done but the war makes travel in this part of the world difficult."

"My fault then." He grinned. "Go on, try and get some sleep. Let me tell you as someone who has spent many years in the wilds, when you get a chance to rest, you take it, because you just don't know when another opportunity will present itself."

"How can I sleep in this damp, slimy hole?"

"I have slept in many worse places, believe you me."

"I believe you. Rats have little choice when it comes to their bedding."

"Ah!" he laughed softly. "Back to the abuse again. Go ahead with it if it makes you feel better. We all know why you do it."

"What do you mean?" her scowl had returned.

"You have spent your life in comfort, surrounded by attendants, maidservants, people who would wipe your arse for you if you so asked them. Now that is all gone, and you are in the hands of rough men, soldiers with little respect for that which you represent. Your natural reaction is hostility, but that hostility is only there to mask the truth."

"What truth?"

"That you are lonely. And very, very frightened."

"Xhenafa take you. Are all Arshumans so utterly ignorant? You do not scare me, not in the slightest. I loathe you, all of you and will celebrate as my brother takes each one of your worthless lives."

Stauncher pulled out his knife, held it up so that the starlight reflected off it, then proceed to absently scrape away some earth clinging to the stone

ACT ONE : THE HUNT

in front of him. "So be it. Now I can tell your age for certain, for you sound exactly like another fifteen-year-old girl of my acquaintance."

"Who?" Eleanor asked tartly. "Pray you do not compare me to some Arshuman peasant girl."

"Peasant girl? Perhaps, perhaps not. It is difficult for a rogue and nobody like me to tell."

"I am sure it must be. Who is she then?"

Stauncher looked out the window, where the moon was beginning to shine onto his craggy, weathered face.

"My daughter," he said finally, "you remind me of my daughter. Now, for the last time, try and get some sleep."

****

Dormouse hunched miserably on his bedroll, shivering, despite being enveloped by his cloak. He pulled off his gauntlets, noticing how white his fingers were, before pulling them back on again with a resigned sigh. His hands felt numb.

"We are all like it you know." Dead Eyes was sat a few feet away checking the string on her bow, she appeared not to be looking at him, yet she seemed all too aware of his discomfiture.

"All like what?" he asked her.

"We all react the same way, after our first kill in the field. You do not feel it at first, your blood is rushing, your head is pounding, your senses are heightened, you feel so much more aware. It is in the quiet time afterwards that you realise what you have done; you are a sensitive soul; it will be bad for you for a while. Your head will replay it many times over. It will pass though, one life may have ended but yours continues on, and you cannot dwell on the past, not if you wish to keep sane."

"He was playing dead," Dormouse recalled. "He surprised me, lunged at me with his knife. I just reacted without thinking."

"And now he is dead, and you are alive. It is a simple life out here; you kill, or you die. Simple, but difficult to learn or to accept. Now, let me see what I can do with your leg. She stood, patted down some unseen dirt off her breeches and crept towards him.

"I haven't got to take anything off have I?" he said guardedly.

She shook her head and flashed him a cheerful smile. He noticed that her hair had grown in just the brief time that he had known her, it was cut severely still but he was certain that it had been the exact length of her collar, now though it was creeping over it. He must be wrong; hair could not grow like that in five days.

"No," she told him," as long as I can get my fingers under the bandage to touch the skin, your honour will remain intact. Now, stretch the leg out a little, like that yes, that is good."

She was as good as her word, working three fingers under the bandage to touch the wound and the stitches holding it together. She shut her eyes and started to whisper softly to herself. He strained to hear exactly what she was saying only to realise there was no chance of that, for she was speaking in elvish. He contented himself with looking out of the empty doorway, up at the stars and the thin, ephemeral layer of cloud under them. Tonight would be colder than the last.

Suddenly though, he realised that this elvish mumbo jumbo was actually working. The pain, the ragged, throbbing pain was easing and his leg, no, his whole body was beginning to feel warm. The average Arshuman would live his entire life without seeing an elf, a lot of them did not believe elves even existed, that they were just strange humans with stranger beliefs, even the aristocracy were not immune to such suppositions. Well, now he knew better, and this elf, this representative of a culture that supposedly despised all humans was showing him a kindness. He thanked her, but she did not respond, her chant still had a distance to go it seemed.

Finally though she sighed and withdrew her hand, dry flakes of blood clinging to her fingertips. He thanked her again, suddenly aware of his proximity to her. He felt her warmth, saw her pale skin glow under the stars, he smelled the leather of her armour, supple leather yet tough, he wondered what beast, or indeed what beasts it had come from.

"Are you alright?" He was suddenly aware that he was staring dumbly at her, he must have looked like a gaping, drooling simpleton. "You…" he fumbled for words, any words. "You smell of leather."

She frowned. "Well, I do wear a lot of it."

"No, I mean, I was expecting to smell something else, but I just got leather, I suppose it is a strong sort of smell, overpowering, it would mask…"

"My natural elfish odour?" she was smiling now.

He put his head in his hands. "No, sorry, I am talking like an imbecile. Just tired I suppose, it has been a very long day."

She gave him a sympathetic stare, her green eyes shining like a cat. He

ACT ONE : THE HUNT

noticed once more the tattoo of the bird with its wings spread that spanned her entire forehead and at last his curiosity found its voice. "Is that symbolic or something?"

She touched her brow, at around the place of the bird's head, and yawned. Surely she was not feeling tired? It would be the first sign of fallibility he had seen in her.

"It is the Culanasi, a mountain eagle from my home. It is red because that is how it appears to us when the sun is strong. I had it at my Userazha, the ceremony that marked me as no longer a child. It symbolises speed, accuracy, and power, an appropriate marking for a hunter."

"Really? That is interesting, I know next to nothing of the ways of your people. Do you have any other tattoos?"

"Yes." She indicated the left side of her body, from shoulder to pelvis. "We all have one here, it is of a tree, the Sylvitrazh, it symbolises our journey through life. We have the tree inscribed on our bodies and then we have other tattoos placed in or around the tree, hunt so many deer and we have its form drawn onto our skin where tree meets earth, become proficient at fishing, then you can have a river winding round the tree, that sort of thing. The tattoo covers my left shoulder, breast, stomach, and goes down the thigh to the top of my foot. I would show you, but I fear you would faint at my lack of decorum. Elves are far less shy about their bodies than humans."

"Oh, your description will suffice, besides, it is too cold for any degree of exposure at the moment."

"And I am not the Lady Sandrine of Lakala."

He laughed for the first time in an age. "No you are not. But what you are is the lady Dead Eyes of the elves and that in itself is something to be proud of."

She smiled and went back to her bedroll. "You do have a good line of patter; I imagine you are very popular at court. A handsome, polite young man like you is, in my experience, a rarity in human society. No wonder the Lady Sandrine lost her heart to you."

"You flatter me."

"I never flatter. That is a human trait. I do not have human traits."

"You have plenty of them."

"Ha! Just as I was beginning to like you. Maybe your lady isn't quite as lucky as I thought."

"I am the lucky one, not her."

THE FANGS OF THE FEN SNAKE

"She is that special? Tell me a little of her."

He seemed to brighten up even more. "Oh, we have known each other for years, we are actually distantly related, I mean, it is not enough to affect anything, if we had children they would not have scales or anything horrible like that. I am just trying to say that we have always been in or around court, we have got to know each other slowly, built up a lasting friendship, but of course that counts for nothing when it comes to the business of marriage. She has similar hair to yours, sable, but it is much longer, she usually has it braided under her head dress, she says it takes an age to prepare. How we really got to know each other though was through music. Nobility like to listen to it but find it beneath them to play, yet her family is a little unconventional in that they tutored her in playing. Anything with strings she is masterful with, you really should hear her. As for me, well I started to accompany her with the tabor, you know, the hand drum. We get the strangest looks from our peers but that makes it all the more exciting somehow. And don't get me started on her singing voice, a nightingale she is, voice as pure as mountain snow. She…."

"And the reason you cannot marry?" Dead Eyes seemed keen to interrupt him.

"It is an odd situation," Dormouse adopted a more disconsolate tone. "If I marry her then I am in truth marrying slightly beneath myself, so my family will not allow it; but, she is such an accomplished court beauty that her family feel they could marry her to somebody far above me, they believe that many men would happily accept a disadvantageous marriage just to possess her, and they are probably right."

"And who is the woman your family want you to marry?"

A look of mild distaste crossed his honest features. "It is politics. The king is from North Arshuma, most of his army is from North Arshuma, South Arshuma has offered only niggardly support for the war so far, so he believes that marriages between north and south should be encouraged and that families that do so will stand highly in his favour. To that end I have been promised to a girl from Draki in the south. Her name is Rosalini, Rosalini Drakistlana to give her full name. I have met her; she is nice enough but very…ordinary, no learning or talents to speak of though I believe she dances passably. And I suppose she is the reason I am here, looking for honour and so far not finding it."

"You did say that just being with us was honour in itself."

"It is yes; I am just not feeling it at the moment."

ACT ONE : THE HUNT

"Well you have your first scar. Show it to her on your wedding night, that should do the trick."

"She will just think what a useless warrior I am to end up so scarred."

"Nonsense," Dead Eyes chirped. "I am scarred here, here and here." She indicated her right shoulder, midriff and pelvis. "Shak has a long, thin scar across his chest and a deeper one on his back, you have seen Stauncher's pride and joy and under his armour Stan resembles a butcher's chopping board, but then I suppose he has been doing this longer than the rest of us. We are not better warriors than most young Dormouse, we have just been luckier, or have been better protected by the Gods, as your human faith believes."

He started a little. "Of course! you are a pagan! It hadn't occurred to me before, blood drinking and orgies under the moon and all that."

She shot him a mischievous look. "Well you are quite lucky then; I am not very thirsty and am far too tired for an orgy tonight. Maybe tomorrow, we shall see."

Dormouse finally felt comfortable enough to stretch out on his bedroll. "One thing I don't understand about you, why they call you Dead Eyes. It seems like a misnomer to me. You are so expressive with them. It just doesn't make any sense."

She shrugged, and, like him, lay back on her bedding, looking up at the shadowed ceiling. "Perhaps, when Shak first met me, I wasn't as I am now, perhaps I was rather more...guarded. It is sometimes best not to express anything when you live around people you do not trust."

He was going to press her further but just then they heard heavy boots on the stairs; Dormouse instinctively pulled out his dagger, but Dead Eyes shook her head at him. "Relax, it is Shak and Stan, I know their footsteps."

And she was correct for, shortly after, the imposing figures of both men emerged at the top of the stairs. Neither of them spoke at first, laying out their bedrolls close by and making themselves as comfortable as they could until Shak finally noted the questioning looks he was getting.

An awkward pause. "I will tell you shortly," he said, "right now I need to think."

Yet, shortly afterwards, he was asleep.

8

Horsehair plumes dancing on a tanzanite sea. The sun, an orb of fierce gold, glittering like a thousand scattered diamonds off the exuberant, effervescent, water. The wind, warm as smouldering coals, supple and strong as a yew tree branch, burnishing exposed skin, basting it to bronze. The taste of salt, the cries of hovering gulls, the school of rising porpoises, sleek, glistening bodies breaking the surface close by, and then the thin, ironwood keel of the Heron of Mazuras, cutting a furrow through the water, swift and sure as a hawk on the hunt. Shak was at sea again, skipping over the pliant ocean with the grace of a maiden dancing at a summer festival. Shak was at sea again, and he was back home, far, so far away.

Unlike the single sailed fishing vessels with their muddy brown sails and broad tub like hulls, who fought the seas, ploughing sluggishly through them as a seal clambers over a shingle beach, the Heron floated over the ocean like a sleeper's breath, light as a cloud, not so much breaking the foamy waves as incising them, as a surgeon's blade slices skin, but without leaving a mark. Its secret was its long, narrow hull and the smaller, equally narrow, stabilising hulls to its left and right, a design copied from elven traders, though in truth the elven ships were far larger and even more elegant than the Heron. Of all the ships in his line of sight this was the only one built solely for pleasure, and for speed. Shak himself took the tiller, standing astern, feeling the squally winds pull at his hair and cool the sweat on his scalp. He did not need to look starboard, for he knew what lay there, the sweeping harbour of the city of Mazuras and the grandiose facades of the palace that dominated it. A series of buildings both square and rectangular, faced in marble, crowned by malachite domes ribbed with gilded metal, opening onto forecourts bearing fountains and fruit trees, it was both home and prison to him and one of the reasons for his love of sailing and the open water.

The other reason was seated daintily on a seat of rosewood lined with red velvet just a few feet ahead of him. Ordinarily, Lady Elspeth Mazuras' hair would be fastened by a thick band of twisted gold from which, hanging like droplets, would be tear shaped precious stones, opals, rubies and chalcedony, the regalia of a married woman. Now though, not wishing to risk such a precious object at sea, she wore her hair loose, an undulating wave of

ACT ONE : THE HUNT

honeyed gold blowing over her back and shoulders. Her dress and cloak were of a lemon velvet, threaded with silver, all the better to protect her from wind and penetrating sun.

He handed the tiller to his captain, who accepted it with both a smile and salute, before going over to crouch next to his lady, the bass timbre of his voice cutting through the noise of the churning waves and the flapping and billowing mainsail.

"Well," he said, his teeth flashing as he smiled. "I have now introduced you to the other lady in my life. What do you think of her? Almost as poised and refined as your good self I feel."

Elspeth's pale grey eyes smiled back at him. "She certainly deals with the conditions better than I do, I had not expected the spray and wind to be so strong!"

"But are you enjoying yourself?"

She nodded. "Very much so, the ship is so fast, it is just…exhilarating."

He could see that she meant it too. There was a bloom to her face, the sort that only a day's hard riding could replicate, and, as he loved to sail so she did love her horses. It reminded him to ask her something.

"How did you find him?" he said to her.

"He has a name now, Klanasto, after my grandfather, and he is probably the finest stallion I have ever ridden. He must have cost half our treasury; I do hope that we still have provision left in our coffers to keep us in our dotage."

"Yes we have, with quite a bit to spare."

"But why buy him for me? There is no real occasion to speak of."

"Yes there is. We are three months married now, surely that is worth celebrating."

Her thin, delicate fingers clasped a hand twice the size of her own. "Of course, call me a fool for forgetting. Three months since the symbols of the heron and the egret, oh and the swordfish, were united under the banners of Mazuras and Arshuma. Now the present of the stallion makes perfect sense, I just wonder what I will be getting for our four month anniversary. A unicorn perhaps?"

"Already ordered, and its horn is tipped with silver."

"And its hooves?"

"Shod in gold."

"I suppose that is adequate for a lady of my standing. Anyway, you have given me a gift, perhaps I can bestow one upon you."

He laughed at that. "A ship that can fly perhaps?"

"Perhaps, or perhaps something a little more mundane."

"I appreciate mundane." He shrugged his shoulders. "The view of the harbour from the picture window in my, I mean our, room, especially at dawn is all that I need. As long as you are with me of course."

"Oh I will be with you my prince of Mazuras, it is just that in the near future we may not be alone. Families grow, do they not?"

It took a few seconds for what she was saying to make sense to him, seconds in which a sudden cross wind tipped the Heron into an angle steep enough for him to put a protective arm around her.

"Is it certain?" he asked once the ship had righted itself.

"Pretty much, all my maidservants and ladies seem convinced. Elissa must have blessed us on our wedding night, and here I was thinking you were too drunk at the time."

"Sap never runs thin in a mighty tree my dear. Well I have to start planning, he will need nurses, attendants, a ceremonial birth dagger..."

"He?" She gave him an arch look. "He?"

"Well, if Elissa sees fit to bless us on the wedding night, she must have surely gone to the trouble of ensuring a son for us. Daughters can come afterwards, as many as you like. Captain! Time to head back to the harbour." He noticed her expression. "You need rest, no more sailing and I am restricting your horse riding. Everything has to be perfect."

"But Shak," she said, eyes wide and soulful, "it already is."

****

"It already is." Shak opened his eyes. It was cold, and it was night, and he was in this tower. To his left, through the doorway without a door he beheld the stars and the sliver of moon that was just creeping into view, moving over the tower and shedding its light on to the floor on which the four of them were lying. He had expected the others to be asleep, but none of them were, Stan indeed appeared to be agitated, scratching his face, running his fingers over his axe, fiddling with the straps on his armour. He noticed that Shak's eyes were open and decided to pre-empt him by answering the question before he could even ask it.

"Can't you hear?" he said. "You need to listen carefully but once you hear it you cannot un-hear it, if you know what I mean."

ACT ONE : THE HUNT

Shak shut his eyes and concentrated. He could hear the wind, soft, it would have been soothing if it wasn't so cold; then there were the surrounding trees, branches sighing, dead leaves rustling on the bare earth, and the stream, shallow mountain water playing over smooth stones. Everything there seemed to indicate peace, a world at rest, but then there were the animal sounds, a screeching owl pouncing on a vole, wolves tearing on the corpse of a deer, mice close by, scurrying over wood and stone, seeking sanctuary before the claws of the hunter struck at them; elsewhere a snake slithered, fish rose and swallowed clumps of low flying insects, a fox broke the neck of a rabbit, yet, underpinning all of it was something else; a deep, sonorous, rumble that seemed to be rising from under the ground. It was very faint, yet very distinctive, for there was a pattern to it, a rise and fall, it would fade and return, fade and return. Stan was right, once the sound had registered it was very difficult to hear anything else.

"Low moaning." Stan said, though he was hardly happy to be proved right. "Just as I said. This place is haunted."

Shak looked over at Dead Eyes, "opinion?"

"I had forgotten," she said. "I did hear it last time, but I just dismissed it."

"Why?"

She shrugged. "It is not an unnatural sound, not like Stan said."

Stan fixed her with a nervous stare. "You are saying that something living is making that noise?"

Dead Eyes nodded.

"Keth's teeth! What?"

"I don't know. Something I have never seen before, something...strange." She was going to say something large but decided to keep the last word back; everyone was spooked enough already. She decided to try and get them all talking about something else.

"Shak, Stan, you still haven't told me, what happened with the scout? Is he dead yet?"

Dormouse started. "Dead! Why? Whatever do you mean?"

Shak ignored him and inhaled deeply. "No."

"Why not? Do you want me to do it? Just tell me what happened."

Shak yawned, putting his hand over his mouth.

Then he told her.

THE FANGS OF THE FEN SNAKE

****

Siras was standing next to the horses, half in a dream, Shak decided to wake him up a little.

"Here, catch." He said, throwing an object at him.

Siras instinctively caught it in his left hand. Then he looked at whatever it was and started.

It was one of the blank discs of metal, one of the sort that Dead Eyes had discovered on the path earlier.

Stan had sidled up to stand next to the scout as Shak spoke to him.

"You might have a hole in your saddle bag because you keep dropping these, though why you have them in the first place is a bit of a mystery is it not? So why don't you tell me?"

Siras started to back away. "I really don't know what you are talking abou..."

He never finished the sentence, for, at that moment Shak slammed his elbow into the face of the shorter man, causing a spray of blood to spurt from his shattered nose. Simultaneously Stan planted a fist into the man's kidney, causing him both to double up and topple backwards.

Stan then immobilised him, putting him in an arm lock whilst Shak pulled Siras knife out of its scabbard, tucking it into his belt.

"Take him to the great hall," he said, "I will fetch the rope."

Stan obeyed, dragging the half stunned, struggling man by the neck through the crumbling corridors and absent doorways to the great hall. There he was placed, in a sitting position next to one of the pillars as the two men, using a rope taken from one of the saddlebags, proceeded to truss him up like a chicken, tight as a vice. That done, they both stood back and regarded their captive who stared back through bleary eyes, blood spattering both face and jerkin.

"Right," Shak spoke in clinical tones. "You are a soldier, you know the way these things work, I ask the questions, you answer them. Depending on those answers we will decide whether to kill you quickly, kill you slowly or even let you go. Understood?"

Siras nodded. Shak rang his tongue over his top lip. In truth he had never killed anyone slowly in his life, torture was an anathema to him, he had only ever authorised it in much more extreme circumstances than this, but it would be self-defeating to mention that now.

ACT ONE : THE HUNT

"Good," Shak said. "Good. Now, who is giving you the orders here, who is following us and what exactly do they want?"

Siras spat at Shak's feet, Shak gave a world weary sigh and nodded to Stan, who knelt and took Siras right hand, bending back the little finger.

"Answer, or this goes snap," he growled in Siras ear.

"We are men in a hurry," Shak told him firmly. "You have been dropping these metal things as what? Warnings? One was dropped before the ridge we climbed, and our pursuers left the path at that point, another, just past the river we crossed, why? Believe me, Stan will break every bone in your body if I tell him to. And I am not interested in your reasons for doing to us what you have, your crippled son or starving wife, each man has his own motivations, and I am not here to judge right from wrong, just talk to us, it will serve you well to do so."

Stan rolled his eyes. Still keeping a tight grip on Siras finger he leaned forward and started to speak quietly in the prisoner's ear, somewhat in the manner of a grandfather imparting sage advice to some errant youngster.

"What Shak is trying to say, "he smiled almost beatifically. "Is that the group of people you are betraying at this moment have been fighting in the wilderness for most of these past five years. Now think of it. Five years surrounded by thousands of people who want to kill you and would without a second's thought if they got the chance. Now, how do you think we have survived this long eh? We have had to use this." He tapped his head with his free hand. "We have had to be smarter than them, smarter, quicker, one step ahead all of the time, and, when the occasion demands it, utterly ruthless. Wounded men slowing you down? Leave them behind, child with a sickle blocking the way to a grain store you have to torch? Well I guess you can imagine. So, what I am trying to tell you is to give the man the answers he needs, because he will get them; whether it is now or in a couple of hours from the pile of pulped, bloody flesh that used to be your body, he will get them, understood? Besides, tell us now and the tiny, tiny chance that you will get through this alive increases a thousand-fold. So, be sensible, just let us know what we need, otherwise hurt you we will. And enjoy it." Stan pulled the finger back even further.

Shak smiled inwardly; the man could be as eloquent as a king's advocate when he wanted to be. They still had to wait though, right up to the point where Shak felt he would have to give Stan the instructions to break a finger; finally, though, the resistance ceased as Siras finally spoke, his voice thick with discomfort.

"They were indicators," he said. "They could follow your tracks easy enough sure, but, in the cases of the discs you found, if they had climbed the ridge they would have ridden straight into you; as for the river, I dropped a marker both before and after we crossed it, whether it has helped them follow you I really don't know."

Shak nodded grimly. "Fair enough. Now, who are you working for?"

Siras did not answer, Stan smacked him in the face with his open palm, the man's lip was beginning to thicken, the blood on his chin beginning to congeal. "Well, let me give you my reasoning," Shak told him. "The best time to ambush us would have been our first night, far less time for us to get wise to your treachery, but they didn't attack. Why? Because we hadn't captured the girl then, so I can only assume that your superior wants her too. This makes him someone who would benefit from her ransom and also from my demise; Ogun is the name that comes to mind, especially as he directed me to you when I spoke to him. If it isn't Ogun, then say so, if it is then keep silent, you don't have to tell me directly if you fear consequences later, if we let you live that is."

Siras was silent, though he did give them the slightest nod.

"Always knew we couldn't trust that little snot further than Dead Eyes could throw him." Stan spat onto the cracked, grassed over tiles.

"But Ogun would be working for someone else." Shak said quietly.

"From Mazuras," blood dribbled from Siras mouth. "The orders come from Mazuras, Ogun stands to profit by your death, I don't know how."

"And the orders were?"

"Kill you and capture the girl. I was to make sure that the people hired to do the job stayed on your trail."

"I see," Shak said thoughtfully. "You know if they had killed me they would probably kill you too, the fewer loose tongues around the better, and they would save on your fee. I bet it was half now, half later, except for you there would be no later. Believe me, I know how politics work in Mazuras."

"You are an idiot man." Stan let go of Siras hand and slowly eased himself on to his feet. "Those that promised you coin probably had a good laugh about it the minute you walked out the door. Now, who are these people sent to kill us? Any ideas?"

Siras had seemed genuinely taken aback by Shak's words, he obviously had not considered himself as expendable before, so his answer came immediately.

"Professionals," he said, "I think they are exotics, or at least some of them are."

"Exotics?" Stan queried.

"Not from Arshuma, from the hot lands in the south, I think I heard the name of Fash being bandied around."

"And you think these "professionals" will find this mansion? Probably tomorrow?" Shak asked, running his hand through his hair.

Siras nodded.

"Then let's give you a choice," he continued. "We can kill you now, quickly, as painlessly as possible, or we can leave you as you are. If your trackers are as good as you say then they should find you tomorrow, they might kill you of course, but that is a chance you'll have to take. If they don't find you, you will linger here till exposure or the wolves claim you, it is your choice entirely. But don't worry, we are reasonable men, we will give you till dawn to decide, you can have all night to think about it. An easy death now, or a small hope of rescue which, if unfulfilled will lead to a lingering, nasty death in days to come; I suspect you will cling to hope, most men do, however misguided that hope might be. Stan, gag him."

Stan did as instructed but, once the gag was in place he stood back with a puzzled frown on his face. "We could just kill him now you know."

"Yes we could."

"But we are not going to."

"Well, I have just made him an offer, given him a choice."

"Yes, but be honest, he is in no position to do anything if you change your mind."

"True, but I would be breaking my word, besides, I know what you are thinking."

"You do?" Stan started to crack his knuckles, a harsh sound in the eerie darkness. "Well I suppose my thoughts are easy enough to read; eat, drink and fight, not much more goes on up there. What am I thinking then?"

"That a couple of years ago I would have killed him without a second thought."

"Well, you would have."

"And that I might be going soft."

Stan clapped his leader on the shoulder. "No, not soft, but I do wonder whether you have the...appetite for this that you used to have."

THE FANGS OF THE FEN SNAKE

Shak pulled Siras knife from his own belt, it was an unremarkable weapon, he had better, but no raider like him threw a weapon away. He replaced it, wondering if Dormouse would want it. "You are right Stan, you are right. I do believe I am getting close to having my fill of this life, killing, burning, in constant mortal peril, and for what?"

"Arshuma?" Stan was grinning now.

"North Arshuma," Shak corrected him, "we are lapdogs for the beggar king."

"Well, we cannot all afford to be disdainful aristocrats like you, most of us have to take work where we find it."

"Your good lady seems to think differently going on what you told me, perhaps she is not alone in wanting a different life."

Stan's face crumpled a little at that. "True."

"Dead Eyes is thinking of drawing things to a close too."

"Is she? Then, if we get this girl to Tantala in a few days it will all be over?"

Shak gave him a wolfish grin. "Not quite, we have to visit Ogun first."

"Ho! Of course, broken bones and mayhem, where we walk, it follows. Come on, leave this fellow here, let's get to this tower before the rest of them steal the best sleeping places."

They strolled back, taking their time, talking softly until they reached the horses.

"The beasts seem unsettled; don't you think?" Shak observed. "You would think they would be exhausted but none of them are trying to sleep. Their ears are pricked, you can see the whites of their eyes, have they smelled something? Something we missed maybe?"

"It is because this place is haunted," Stan insisted. "I am telling you; animals know these things."

Shak cast his eyes to the heavens and spent the rest of the journey gently admonishing his companion over his superstition, yet the horses were restless, and he did wonder if his attitude was just masking deeper fears. Something about this place was not right, he just hoped that, by the time they left at dawn, they still wouldn't know what it was.

****

"You should have killed him," Dead Eyes spluttered. "Stan is right, letting him live is a mistake; he knows us now, if these killers get to him he could tell them many things."

"They will probably kill him before he gets the chance," Shak replied gently.

"Probably? What good is probably? Kill him now and we change the probably to definitely. Besides, what if he gets free of the ropes tonight? He is closer to the horses than us, he could get away with all of them!"

"Stan has tied him up so securely, a smooth snake could not slither free. Do not fear, he is not going anywhere."

She shook her head in irritation. Of the four of them on the second floor only Dormouse was sleeping, his snoring was driving her to distraction as it was, without her leader going soft on them.

"See," Stan told him, "we both think you are wrong."

"Then if I am wrong, I will make sure it is only me that suffers for it. He is cold, his fingers will be numb, he is not escaping, now get some sleep, I will keep an eye on the stairwell."

"Sleep!" Dead Eyes snorted. "If only. Not only is our leader being plagued with delusions of conscience, but we also have to share a floor with this slumbering ox. Hey!" She prodded Dormouse with an angry toe. "Keep it down! If there is one thing that puts me in the mood for murder it is overly extravagant sno...oh by the spirits." She blanched, even in the darkness the two men could see her go pale. "By all the spirits, what are we doing here? We have made a terrible mistake."

"What?" Shak stood, then went and crouched next to her; it was a rare thing to see fear on her delicate features. "What is it? What mistake are you on about? Is it Siras?"

She started a little, as if snapping out of a nasty dream. "Siras? No, not Siras, forget Siras."

"Then what?"

She eased herself on to her knees and met Stan's questioning gaze.

"That noise," she told him. "That deep noise that we can hear, the noise that makes you think this place is haunted. I know what it is."

"Then tell us." Stan said, with no little impatience.

"It is snoring. Something large, something animal, something very close to us, is snoring."

****

Siras too could hear the faint, subterranean drone but it was not the

THE FANGS OF THE FEN SNAKE

thing at the forefront of his mind. For, as Dead Eyes had correctly surmised, he was fervently trying to escape his predicament. He was still dazed, and his back was still throbbing, Shak and Stan had hit him hard as stone and the pain had barely receded since then. Also the cold was showing its wintery teeth and the rope was biting into his limbs with a delicious cruelty, but he was a desperate man with little to lose, it really was escape or die.

He tried wriggling his stiff limbs once more, attempting to prise the tiniest amount of leeway from his bonds. If he could just work a hand free then he could push or pull at the ropes until there was enough room for him to stand. Then it should be easy to work himself free. Easier. After that he would massage legs and arms until the blood started to run through them, get to his horse and be away from here. He had felt a dolt after listening to Shak. Of course Doul and his companions would kill him, why hadn't he thought of it himself, he was a loose end and tidying up loose ends was what they did. So it was stay here and be killed in the morning by Shak, stay here and be left to freeze or starve to death, or stay here until Doul found and killed him. His only real chance lay in getting out of here.

His plan, such as it was, was to ride east, towards the river Whiterush, then follow its course south to the town of Grest. He would then cross the river and be away long before Shak or Doul could get near him. He had no interest in scattering the other horses, his only driver now was self-preservation, the others could stay and kill each other for all he cared, was killing not their job after all?

After that it was time to put his long term plan into action. Although he had only received half his fee for this job the money was still enough for the fresh start he wanted. He would not head for Tantala, would not report to Ogun, he would bypass it and ride into North Arshuma instead, to a small village just outside the King's city of Kitev, the village in which his family resided. Siras the scout was going to desert.

He wriggled again, exerting himself so hard that sweat beaded on his brow and his ragged breath was expelled in frosty, irregular clouds. At last! At last he could move his right hand by the smallest amount, he pulled it up a little until his wrist bone was pressed tight against one of the binding coils; if he could just pull his wrist clear he could change the angle of his hand and, bit by agonising bit, start to work his hand free. His decision to leave this life behind had not been taken lightly, for three exhausting, tiring years he had fought for his country; just weeks ago he had been part of the cavalry

ACT ONE : THE HUNT

contingent riding down the forces of the Tanarese barons at Wolf Plain, he had done his bit, and yet, for his king, his bit would never be enough. Straight after the battle he had been sent into disputed country to harry the Tanarese and prevent them from regrouping, more, more, more, all the time and yet not one serving officer, not one had offered him a single consoling word at his recent loss.

For, some weeks before Wolf Plain the town of Grest had been lost in a terrible battle which had been turned by the powers of an enemy mage. A woman apparently, a woman who could call lightnings from the sky, she had burnt dozens of men into blackened cinders, injured many more and terrified the entire army into a full scale rout. The dead were not counted till afterwards, and one of the dead was his younger brother.

Sirkun had been his name, he was a year younger than Siras, more voluble, more gregarious, he had ten times the friends Siras had; and one little girl. And Siras wanted to take care of both her and his own family. So when Ogun had asked around, offering coin for a slightly dubious service he had volunteered apparently willingly; then though he would exact a double betrayal, first of all he would betray Shak, then he would betray Ogun by deserting the moment he got his full fee. Ogun who had refused him leave after his brother's death, Ogun who was not even aware that he had refused him leave in the first place.

He took a deep breath, readying himself for the effort needed to get his wrist, and then his hand clear. He had a moment of stillness; a moment of calm and it was in that moment that he realised that something was different. He thought for a moment, trying to see through the fog in his mind. Of course! That infernal, repetitive low rumbling noise had stopped. Thank the gods for that, it had not helped his woozy head one little bit, perhaps now he could address his situation with a little more clarity.

So, he would not go to Ogun at all now, he had not the courage to try and bluff his way to his full fee. Instead he would ignore Tantala entirely, crossing the Broken river via the fords to its north. Then to North Arshuma, pick up his wife, his three kids, his sister in law and little niece and be away before anybody noticed. He would head south, then cross Harshafan's Belt, that narrow strip of land between mountains and sea that provided access to South Arshuma. Known for its near total disinterest and half-hearted support for the war it was a favoured refuge for deserters. There, they could all but disappear, he could put his equestrian skills to use, make himself invaluable to some local lord, start anew, both him and his family, it should be easy for both women to find some sort of work.

And yes! His wrist was free, now it was time to work his hand out of the rope, once that was done then escape would change from being a hopeless dream to becoming something altogether more tangible. But these cords were so cruel, his skin was white where they cut into him, the pain was affecting his thinking, but he could not stop now, he had to keep going.

What was that? He ceased struggling for a moment so he could listen all the better. Was it footsteps? No, the sound was too heavy for footsteps. Oh by the Gods do not let it be a bear; the bears here were going into hibernation now and were not known to attack people but it would just be his luck to run into the one exception tonight. He remained still, a dewdrop of thick blood fell from his nose onto his jerkin, silence, the noise had stopped. Now to get his hand free.

It hurt, it cut but half his palm had been freed, now it was just his fingers left, trust him to have thick, chunky fingers, a woman would have been out of here hours ago. He just had to keep going.

But he didn't keep going. Instead he froze. Surely his eyes were lying to him.

Something, some great shadow was moving along the top of the wall ahead and to his left and it was moving with some speed. Then, the moon cleared a cloud and picked it out in greater detail, pallid wraith light reflected off glistening scales and a sleek, sinuous, reptilian body. A baleful yellow eye was looking down into the great hall. Its gaze passed the pillars, moved onward, further onward.

Until it finally stopped at him.

With a sudden spurt of fear induced energy he tore his bruised, aching, numb hand free of the ropes at last. Pain no longer mattered as he pressed down hard on the coils, trying to loosen them so that he could stand, stand, free himself and run to a horse nearby.

Then the thing was no longer on the wall, now it was in the great hall, landing with a soft bump, a far softer landing than a thing of its size warranted, a landing made easier by the spreading of its veined wings, translucent in the moonlight.

And now it was in the great hall with him.

He stood on legs without feeling, his skin torn and bruised, grazed until it bled; this thing was now in the nave between the double row of pillars,

114

ACT ONE : THE HUNT

moving forward on four toed feet, four legs, four toes, bigger than a bear, if only it was a bear.

Down he pushed the ropes, up he pushed himself, his breathing short and sharp, his sweating profuse, he started to drag his dead, unfeeling leg out of the ropes, his mind was too paralyzed to coolly assess his chances. And probably he had the Gods to thank for that.

His leg was over the ropes at last, he planted it on to the grass, his body wracked with cramp, but, as his leg landed another landed right next to it, a leg that was not his own. From this distance he could see that the scales were a dark, burnished silver-grey and the claws digging into the soil were at least six inches long.

Finally, reluctantly, he looked up and beheld the thing standing before him. He wasn't sure if he had soiled himself, he probably had but his legs were still too numb to tell for sure, however, as he looked up it looked right back at him.

It had an arrow shaped head that was about the length of Siras body. As he stood, mouth agape, fingers nerveless, it put out a wet tongue, forked, black under the moonlight, thick saliva dripping onto his feet and legs. It ran that tongue over his face, his chin, and his jerkin, all the places where his blood had clotted and accumulated. Siras thought of Shak's promise to make it quick and painless, he hoped, by the names of all the gods and saints, he hoped more than anything that it would be the case for him now.

And mercifully it was, and it was with one final word in his mind that he died. One final word as he beheld that great, slitted, golden yellow eye for the last time, one final word as the jaws and their jagged teeth closed in around his head and neck and pressed down, Siras skull cracking under a deluge of foetid breath and thick, rheumy spittle.

One final word.

Dragon.

9

Eleanor had, despite the horrible smell, the hard, uneven floor, the damp, the cold, and the sounds of crawling insects in their crawly crawlspaces, she actually had, miraculously, managed to fall asleep. Of course it was not the type of sleep she was used to; it was not her room in the manor in Bear Valley where she always felt safe and secure. It was a more precarious type of sleep altogether and it led to a different type of dream, a fragmentary dream, with glimpses of things half forgotten, disjointed words and phrases, fleeting, unconnected images that induced both happiness and fear. Unbeknownst to her she was twisting and turning on her bedroll, gasping and whimpering incoherently, hands and hair covering her face as Stauncher looked on at her, his smile unreadable, his thoughts unknowable, though on several occasions he came over to her to replace the cloak she had kicked off as she thrashed around in her nocturnal reverie.

She dreamt. She saw her mother's face, her broad, honest, homely face, strands of grey blond hair fluttering free of their pins, "You write beautifully my little Ellie, it is not a womanish pastime that is true but if you enjoy it, then keep doing it." But then her mother faded and disappeared from her sight. "Come back to me!" Eleanor implored her, "come back, come back!" But her mother did not return. Instead the iron hard face of Michalis, the house steward hung before her "I have to tell you my lady that your mother is dead, as you are now an orphan you will become a ward of your uncle the baron."

"Your mother is dead, your mother is dead, your mother is dead." How she remembered that moment, the bone hard delivery of those words, the crisp, forensic way she was told of it. She saw something else then, a small girl, seven years old, clad in black, standing alone in a room lit by a single candle, a room whose walls moved backwards and backwards, expanding outwards until they were no longer visible. The room was now the size of the whole world, and she was at its centre, and she was alone.

"You are twelve now, the age of majority, and I gift you the manor of Bearnside." It was her uncle's voice, no face, just a voice, he was so distant to her she could not remember his face. Although he had never done anything to hurt or reproach her she was still a little frightened of him. And now there it

ACT ONE : THE HUNT

was, the manor, her manor, sitting in a deep, wooded valley close to a walled village and a bridge that crossed a sluggish, slow moving river in three spans. Her heart leapt for joy when she saw it, her manor, hers, when she married she would retain it and visit as often as she could. She had to retain it, had to, had to...

And then she saw it in flames, burning from foundations to roof, but the flames were bright yellow, Arshuman yellow. No, she thought, this hasn't happened, this hasn't happened. Then though the house disappeared and she was standing in a room surrounded by frowning people, no, not just any people, her family. She was reading one of her poems to them, hand shaking as she looked at the parchment that she clasped in a rictus grip of frozen terror. She finished and looked at the faces looking at her. And the people whose approval she was not seeking were smiling at her but the people whose approval she sought so desperately were frowning, grimacing, shaking their heads. Then they started to laugh. Louder and louder the laughter became, mocking, cruel laughter and, as she stood there dissolving in her own tears, their heads floated free from their bodies and started to circle her, laughing, still laughing. And the heads grew in size and the laughter grew in volume until she had to put her hands over her ears. Spinning round her these heads were, faster and faster, louder and louder, crueller and crueller. "No!" she cried. "Go away! Go away!"

And then it was silent again.

She stood, she was in the same room and standing in front of her was Sir Hugh Spalforth, cousin of her betrothed. He was in full armour, a knight of the Silver Lance, there was no light in the room yet the armour shone like a beacon, molten, blinding. She spoke to him, in a voice so small she sounded like a tiny, undernourished mouse. "So please sir knight, tell me of my betrothed? Is he handsome, is he brave?"

"Lady," the knight replied. "He is lame, and he is stupid. All he does is drink and fornicate, there is not a woman in court who has not felt his hand on her arse. He hates poetry, he loves to hunt, all he wants a wife for is to give him an heir, a thousand heirs. You will be his womb, popping out brat after brat as your body decays, becomes loose and flabby, and your hair thins and your teeth fall out until, a dozen or twenty pregnancies later, you die of exhaustion. He will take you for wife, and you will be grateful for it."

"No," she shook her head vigorously. "He did not say that, he said he was quiet and brooding, he said he was respectful, he said I could live the life I wanted. He did not say that. You are not Hugh Spalforth, you are Keth the deceiver and you are lying."

And again, the knight began to laugh, and as his mockery increased in volume his armour grew brighter and brighter until she could no longer see the man inside it. Then finally, the man was gone. In his stead was a pillar of red flame, it was Keth after all. And he reached out with burning arms and grabbed her. She screamed as she was pulled into the flames, she screamed as her skin peeled away, her flesh blackened, her blood sizzled in the heat and her eyeballs vaporised. Dying, she was dying, she had wanted so much from her life, she was consumed with longing for...for what exactly? She didn't really know. She just wanted, as did everybody else, wanting and needing, two phantoms made of air, they could not be grasped yet their mere presence made her want to grasp them. She wanted, and that in itself sufficed for her. But of course it didn't matter now because she was dying anyway, like her brother who fell from his horse a couple of years ago, she was dying, dying, dying...

No she wasn't! She was in that smelly tower, and this was just a stupid nightmare. And what was that? Yuk! Disgusting! She rolled over and sat up, eyes like saucers, face flushed with anger.

"Something just crawled over my face! What sort of stinking hole have you all brought me too! I have a mind..."

She stopped abruptly. A man was behind her, a strong, powerful hand was clasped firmly around her mouth, another pinned her arm to her side, somebody was breathing close to her right cheek.

"Quiet!" Stauncher half whispered; half hissed into her ear. "You will give us away! Something is out there; can't you hear the horses?"

Her heart was hammering fit to explode. Her dream was still vivid in her mind; she could barely breathe. It took a few faltering moments for her to get her bearings, for the blood to stop pumping in her ears so that she could listen properly. Stauncher felt her chest heave and loosened his grip, feeling her relax as she did so. She placed the palms of her hands flat on the grimy floor and listened.

It took little effort to understand what Stauncher meant.

The horses were half whinnying, half screaming in terror, it was a sound to freeze Eleanor's blood in her veins.

Just then a lithe figure appeared at the top of the stairs. Dead Eyes looked at Stauncher, he looked back. Both of them wore expressions that were

ACT ONE : THE HUNT

a mix of confusion and fear. The elf made her way silently to the slit window to look out over the open fields outside, Stauncher and Eleanor inched over to the open doorway overlooking the manor, craning their necks, trying to see past the walls, through the ceiling fragments, trying to see exactly what was going on.

There was something, some shadowy movement going on where the horses were tethered but the moonlight was so weak, the light so poor it was impossible to get any clarity. Sound however was crisp and clear and could travel a great distance through the night air. Hooves were thudding onto earth and rotted floorboards, there was the sounds of a heavier impact as though the horses were bucking against their ropes, the screaming of the beasts cut through the still, freezing air as a sharp knife cuts through flesh, a horrible, harrowing sound. But then there was something else, something deeper, a long, menacing growl that appeared not to belong to this earth at all; it was a primal sound, coming from an older time, a time before men, maybe even a time before elves. Eleanor felt Stauncher tense when he heard it, she was just too numb to react at all.

"What in the name of Zhun was that?" Dead Eyes voice was a frozen whisper. She did not get a reply.

"There they go," Stauncher finally breathed. As Shak and Stan came up to join them the horses it seemed, had finally pulled themselves free. Into darkness they fled, through the doors and into the fields, heading straight for the tree line, heedless of roots and animal burrows they fled, oblivious, reckless, desperate to find the cover of the trees and the safety they perceived was there. For something else was with them, running alongside them.

"The horses!" Stan cried hoarsely. "We need the horses; we have to get them back!" He started to make his way back down the stairs.

"Stan!" Dead Eyes risked raising her voice at last. "The horses are gone. Stay where you are. You cannot pursue them, not in this darkness, not with..."

"Not with what?" Stan asked her, stopping his descent. "Not with what?"

Dead Eyes was looking out of the window. She could see a number of similar sized shadows, that of the horses, hurtling into the distance and, right at their backs, another shape, a much larger shape, and it appeared to be above the ground. Then she saw what appeared to be a small gout of yellow flame in the same area. It briefly provided some light, she saw the backs of the remaining horses, saw their kicking and bucking hindquarters, and, for the most fleeting of moments she saw the other, the pursuer, the predator on their trail. She saw and sat back on her haunches, shaking her head, and gasping softly.

"There is something out there," she said. "Something we do not dare meet. We should stay here till dawn and make no noise at all."

Stan did not answer. Instead he climbed wearily back up the steps and re-joined them. They all found a spot on the floor and made themselves as comfortable as they could. There were no more disturbances that night, but none of them slept a wink until dawn finally rose.

****

They did not emerge from the tower until Dead Eyes was certain, absolutely certain that there was nothing untoward in the vicinity. When they finally did so it was into a manor cloaked in a rolling mountain mist, one not strong enough to hamper vision unduly but still powerful enough to make everything eerie and silent, every shadowy wall and rotting beam a potential lurking monster.

They stopped at the main doorway, where the horses had been tethered. The horses were of course no longer there and the grass and earth where they had stood was torn and bruised, great clods of soil ripped up and scattered hither and thither. Nobody spoke at first, though plenty of looks were exchanged, Dormouse had wandered a little till he stood just outside the manor, and it was he who broke the silence.

"Come here," he said, the merest hint of a tremor in his voice.

They did so and looked at the patch of ground he was indicating, a patch of exposed mud sitting next to the remnants of the gravel path. There, pressed into the earth lay a partial footprint, two toes each longer than a man's arm ending in what appeared to be a sickle shaped claw the length of a soldier's dagger. The company stared out into the mist, over the field, straining to hear anything over the dawn chorus.

There was nothing.

"Well," Shak said at last, "we had better go and see Siras."

Of course Siras was also no longer there. Actually that was not strictly true for parts of him did remain, pieces of viscera scattered around the bloodied coil of rope, fragments of shattered bone thrown about like some morbid seed crop, great gouts of blood sprayed over the ground resembling

ACT ONE : THE HUNT

the overspill of some demonic fountain. Shak knelt, then stood again, he was holding parts of a hand, a hand on which portions of palm and two fingers were missing.

"Messy," Shak said. "It eats like you, Stan."

"But what is "it" exactly?" Stan ignored the joke.

"Whatever it is, I reckon it uses the wine cellar as a lair." Shak then told the others about what he and Stan had found there.

"You mean," Eleanor backed away a little, "it might just be over there somewhere?" She pointed in the direction of the north west tower.

"I do not think it is there now," Dead Eyes said quietly.

"And how do you know?" Eleanor continued to step backwards, eyes widening all the time. Her foot suddenly touched something firm, assuming it was a stone she looked down to see what it was.

It was not a stone.

"God's fire, "she croaked. "That is obscene."

Shak came over and picked the object up.

It was part of the front of a skull. A skull to which a portion of face and hair remained. Siras face. One white eyeball, ribboned with blood still sat in the eye socket, held there by the portion of brain that had not been sucked out by a probing tongue. Slugs crawled over the whole thing, the thing that had once been their scout. The treachery of the man was suddenly forgotten as they stared at what was left of him. Shak threw it as far as he could into the long grass. "We should have killed the poor man," he said in disgust. "We would have spared him this."

"What in the name of the furnace did this to him?" Dormouse echoed all their thoughts.

"Troll?" Stan suggested. "They sometimes come down from the mountains, looking for a change in diet maybe or perhaps they are driven by hunger. When we first invaded this part of the country, that first winter a troll came down on a raid, it could probably smell all the blood and the burning. Attacked a scout patrol it did, according to the survivors it bit a man's head clean off. Had to hunt the thing down, I was included in the party. Elusive bastards they are for all their size, took weeks to find him. Brought him down with arrows and spears in the end, took a hundred arrows at a guess before it fell. Took its head back to camp, and its leather, spent the next week or so drunk as a Fashtani poet. By Artorus the thing stunk, I can remember the smell to this day."

THE FANGS OF THE FEN SNAKE

"Can you smell it now?" Shak asked.

Stan shook his head. "No, no I can't, but not all trolls are the same."

Stauncher was grinning. "Somewhere in the mountains a troll is telling his mates, "avoid the humans lads, they stink out the heavens, especially the big fellow that never shuts up..."

"It is not a troll." Dead Eyes spoke with such assurance that everybody else stopped talking immediately. "I saw it. Besides, trolls do not make lairs, though their eating habits are this disgusting."

"You saw it?" Several people asked at once.

Dead Eyes nodded. "Through the window, in the field, only a brief glimpse but it was enough to tell me that it wasn't a troll."

"Then what did you see?" Stan asked her.

"It was only a glimpse..."

"A glimpse of what?"

She shifted uneasily on her feet. "You will laugh."

Stan's exasperation was clear. "Right now I am finding it difficult to find anything amusing. Just tell us, I promise I will not laugh."

"Very well." Dead Eyes thought again, scanning her memory once more till she was absolutely certain that what she was about to say was as absolute a truth as she could make it. "I think it was a dragon."

Stan laughed. As did Stauncher. Even Dormouse managed an incredulous smile.

Stan stepped forward and tapped Dead Eyes gently on the forehead. "Anyone notice an echo?" he asked his audience. "Like Dead Eyes brain somehow might have rolled out through her ears."

"I," Dead Eyes was defiant, "do not lie."

"I know," Stan said. "I am just suggesting that what you saw and what you thought you saw might be different things."

"Its shape, the way it moved, was reptilian. It could fly. And breathe fire. I saw flame, now tell me what other type of creature can do that?"

Stan was suddenly less certain. "Are you sure? Dragons do not exist, they are beasts from fables, no living man has seen one, how could one materialise out of a story used to scare naughty children and end up here of all places? Besides aren't dragons supposed to be massive, I mean the size of this manor house. Whatever killed Siras seems to be a big animal for sure, but if it is a dragon it is a lot smaller than the tales say."

"Dragons do exist Stan, just because they are exceptionally rare and

ACT ONE : THE HUNT

hardly ever bother human settlements does not mean that they are only tales. As for this one I do not think it was fully grown," Dead Eyes said. "I think it was a juvenile at best. And humans do not understand dragons, they have had barely any dealings with them. My people do."

"Used to worship them didn't they?" Shak asked her.

Dead Eyes nodded. "The chief of the spirits, the oldest are said to be immortal, the first children of Zhun, our god, and no Stan, I do not know why one would be here either."

Eleanor had now backed away far enough that she could only be seen as a shadow to the others. "I cannot believe all of you," she suddenly said. "The Wych is suggesting that we might have a dragon flying around the area, one that could attack at any moment and all you can do is stand around and gossip like a lot of queen's damsels! Is anyone going to suggest getting out of this damned place? I mean a man was eaten alive here just hours ago, do you think it might be a good idea to, you know, move?"

"Stan," Shak said. "Try and retrieve as much of that rope as you can."

Stan nodded and went to the pillar to recover it. "I will try and clean as much of this gore off as possible."

"Fine," Eleanor said. "As you are all ignoring me...again, I am going to escape. As of now. Bye." The mist finally swallowed her up.

"Without horses," Shak continued. "We are stuck. Try and cross the plains and our pursuers will ride us down in an instant. Get your things all of you, we will head directly east, go through the woods, get to the river that way."

"Then what?" Stauncher asked. "It is too wide and deep to cross, and we don't have the time, nor probably the skills or equipment to build a boat or a raft, so what do we do when we get there?"

"Have a chat," Shak said. "See what our options are. Now, let's get moving shall we, oh, and Stauncher."

"Yes chief?"

"Pick up our escapee first, we don't want her breaking a nail, it might bring down the ransom."

"And if she stumbles into a dragon?"

"Then you will have to affect a rescue, that poor old dragon would never survive a tongue lashing from our hostage, I am weary of them already and I have been married."

THE FANGS OF THE FEN SNAKE

****

"Hold there girl, hold, hold, there is no threat here, that is it, there, relax, relax, good girl, good girl."

The horse, which had been tearing through the trees, bereft of saddle and cloaked in sweat at last started to calm a little as the man talked soothingly to her. He kept up the mollifying line of patter, patting the horse's flanks until at last he could finally put a halter on her. Finally, when he judged the time to be right and the beast suitably docile he started to lead her through the woods towards the clearing where both he, and his companions, had set up camp for the night.

He was tall and would have been rakishly thin had he not been clad almost completely in black furs. Even his boots were lined with fur, as were his gloves and his cloak. Only his face was open to the gloomy, fog shrouded dawn and it was the face of a man whose place of birth was a long way from here.

He was young, in his twenties, with skin the colour of ground nutmeg. His eyes were dark, keen, intense, an expression that suited his sharp, angular features. Under his prominent, imposing, nose lay a thin, hard mouth that only ever softened when, as now, he was working with the horses that he loved. Horses were skittish, foolish creatures but to those with the gift of reaching out to them, they could be far more loyal a companion than a human could ever hope to be. However, even as he led the animal onward he gave out the air of a man who spent his entire life walking a tightrope, he was tense, wound like a wire, constantly looking around him as though he perceived a threat to be imminent. Yet somehow this state of agitation never transferred itself to his horses, to them, he was a protector, always putting their interests first, an impression that was invariably the correct one.

He led the horse into a glade open to the sky, where the mist swirled under an intermittent, but cold breeze. Without even looking at his companions he started examining the beast in greater detail. "She has a wound," he said flatly. "Left hind leg, a cut, I will get my poultices."

"What caused it? A thorn?" Doul the assassin had moved to stand at the younger man's shoulder without making a sound, his soft, sibilant tones seemed to belong amidst the fog, the naked trees, and the silence.

"Looks more like an animal, too deep for a thorn, a claw wound, big claw, deep." The man spoke in staccato tones and with a heavy accent that tended to over emphasise the vowel sounds. The language of the Chiran

ACT ONE : THE HUNT

empire, of Tanaren and latterly, Arshuma, was not his own, and he was still wrestling with it all.

"A bear? Inzukanash, you think a bear did this?" The third member of the company had joined them, like the young man Inzukanash she too was clad in thick black furs, with most of her lissom form hidden under a great cloak that reached over the top of her supple leather boots. The cloak was fastened by a gold brooch, studded in emeralds, fashioned in the form of a pouncing leopard, a sign that at some time in her life, she would have enjoyed a lifestyle encompassing a fair degree of opulence. Her looks were striking too, eyes of smoky quartz smouldering under arched brows, hair dark as raven feathers flowing over skin of glowing amber. Her lips and nose, though not nearly as pronounced were similar to those of Inzukanash, hinting at the possibility of a familial relationship. Rather incongruously given their surroundings she wore earrings of gold and black opal, long earrings that hung till they touched her shoulders. In her right hand she was carrying a long, stiletto type knife, the blade of which she had been whetting prior to this most recent interruption. She too spoke with a similar accent to the young man, but, having a lighter pitched voice it was not as strong, or indeed as harsh as his had been. Her grasp of the language too appeared to be far more confident, though it may have been partly due to her age. Her looks were still there, but there were a couple of lines of care on the face and the occasional stray grey hair, indicating that perhaps, the bloom of youth that had given her such notable beauty was beginning to recede. That, however, was an opinion that had never been expressed to her personally, few people would ever have the courage to look into those aloof, imperious eyes and break unhappy news to her without quailing.

"Most bears would be sleeping now." Doul still had all but eyes and nose covered, yet those eyes were colder than the oncoming winter, not a shred of emotion was reflected in them. "Maybe an underfed, dying creature struck out at it yet had not the wit to catch it."

"Not a bear," said Inzukanash. "Single claw wound, bear would rake with full paw. Sister..."

"Yes Zukan," the woman replied.

"Hold the halter whilst I apply poultice."

She nodded and did as requested, stroking the horse as her younger brother went about the business of healing. Doul meanwhile was going through the saddlebags, looking for anything that could be of use to them.

THE FANGS OF THE FEN SNAKE

Suddenly he called over to the woman. "Sirisibali..."

"Siri, Siri will do."

"Siri then. This horse belonged to our man." Doul walked around the horse to show her what he was talking about. In his gloved hand were around a dozen of Siras' metal discs.

"So he is dead then." Was her flat response.

"Dead, or at least discovered."

"Then he will be dead soon anyway."

"Probably." Doul went and replaced his discovery in the saddlebags. "I cannot see him being shown mercy somehow. Still, he served his purpose and Ogun saves on his fees. The tracks lead north, make sure the boy finishes with this horse quickly so we can move. We do not need this beast anyway so there is no point wasting time on it."

"I am not leaving this horse until she stops bleeding," Zukan said defiantly.

"I know brother but be as quick as you can. Patch her up, then we can carry on with the job we were paid to do."

Zukan nodded. Leaving him fussing over the now placid animal both Doul and Siri strolled nonchalantly towards the further end of the glade where their own horses were tethered. Doul kept his voice even lower as he spoke to her, meaning she had to lean over a little to make him audible to her.

"Did you have to bring the boy? I have never worked with him before and I am unsure as to his qualities. His empathy with horses is of little use to us in truth, I know he is your brother but..."

"Yes he is my brother. And he has nowhere else to go. He does whatever I ask without complaining, all the little jobs, all the things that take time. He is also good in a fight when called upon..."

"But there is something...odd about him."

"As there is about you. And me."

Doul gave her a grudging nod. Loosening a strap on his saddle released a leather flap that fell until its top end hung just inches from the ground. Secured to it, and normally protected from the weather were a series of different knives ranging from thin bladed stilettos, to daggers both straight and curved, to blades over a foot in length, the tools of his trade. All were polished and sharpened to murderous perfection. And now he went through them one by one, pulling them free of the leather thongs that secured them, holding them up to what little light there was before running his finger over

ACT ONE : THE HUNT

the edge and sighing with satisfaction. He then slid them back into their strapping with a degree of tenderness normally seen in a mother comforting her grizzling child.

"With Siras no longer able to warn us of any hazards ahead," Doul spoke as he checked each blade. "We will have to proceed with a little more caution. The tracks continue to lead to the north, away from the town of Grest so they obviously know they are being followed and are trying to lay a false trail. The problem for us will be if they double back south and pass us without our noticing."

"North," Siri grumbled, pulling her furs closer around her body. "As if this country isn't cold enough already."

"You have mountains in Fash surely, I know you have, your own home town is halfway up one of them. I am surprised you feel the cold so strongly."

"It is only this cold near the summit of our mountains. Most of the uplands are covered in pines and cedars, and it is warm, and dry, and there are many villages where the rivers and gorges are not so steep, all the houses are painted white to keep them cool. We both come from such a place, our parents harvested olives and grapes and kept a small herd of mountain ibex like so many others. We would drive them up the mountainside to graze during the winter, where the leopards used to hunt, and where the nobles came to hunt the leopards."

"Is that how you were noticed?" Doul sounded interested for once.

"Yes." There was the merest hint of regret in her answer. "Yes. They had stopped to water their beasts, as had we. We were ordered to move out of the way and as I passed them, driving the ibex with my staff I had my hair uncovered, it was too warm for a hood that day. The lord thought my face appealing and so sent his man to my parents with an offer of coin for me. I believe there was some haggling, but the offer was accepted soon enough. I was part of their hunting party the following morning."

"Your parents did not need you for herding the animals?"

"Three brothers and five sisters remained," she shrugged. "So no, there were plenty of hands left to help out and the offer for me was a good one. Zukan was barely walking at the time and does not remember it happening. Anyway, that was how I saw a city for the first time."

"And became a dancer. And a courtesan. And a spy. And an assassin."

"Just a dancer at first. The other skills only follow if you succeed at that and have the aptitude for them. We are all trained for years to be dancers; if we are good at it we are invited to perform privately in many noble houses in the country. Rivals to those nobles see opportunity in this and so a select few of us learn how to spy on the enemies of their patron and even fewer of us learn how to kill in their name. That is what happened to me, I became the favourite of Usabrazanipal, the High Opekun of the city of Csal. And I followed such a path at his command, something I was well rewarded for. For a woman in Fash not of noble blood an Egoulian dancer is pretty much as far as you can go in life; we are revered, perform in all the great palaces, live a life surrounded by riches, we want for nothing in truth. Most of us remain dancers, only a small number become...more than that."

"So why did you flee the country?" Doul asked bluntly. She tutted at his lack of tact before replying.

"I made too many enemies. The killing of one particular magnate was blamed on me and I spent a year avoiding his assassins after my patron was murdered in revenge. I decided to leave my homeland for a while until the furore had abated somewhat. Zukan joined me when I took ship for South Arshuma, he had outgrown the family home and was not married, so I brought him along, seeing some of the world can only help his...ways, don't you think?"

"Well I hope that works. And that the cold does not affect the poisons you have brought..."

"It will not. They will stick to the barbs on my arrows no matter what the weather."

"Good." There was a brief silence before he continued. "You have heard the rumour? About the king acquiring the services of a Kozean assassin?"

"A Strekha?" Siri appeared to shiver at the word. "Yes I have. What of it?"

"Could you kill her if you had to?"

She shook her head. "Unlikely. They are the personal guard of the Kozean Emperor, trained to kill from childhood. They take poisons that augment their abilities and give them some immunities to the poisons I use. I dance, I entertain, I give pleasure to men, those are my primary functions. The other things that I do follow on from that. A Kozean Strekha is there to kill and only to kill, they specialise in one thing, I have abilities in many. They are the best killers in the world, to kill one, you would need an advantage such as surprise, or strength in numbers. In truth, I think they are monsters. Are you

ACT ONE : THE HUNT

suddenly disappointed in your choice of companions, annoyed that you only have second best?"

Doul waved over at Zukan, who started to bring the horse towards them. "Not at all, I have seen you work remember. Of those we hunt only one of them needs to die, if the others also fall then so be it, I do not care either way. But remember, the girl is not to be harmed."

"I can kill or render a quarry unconscious with my arrows and darts. Some poisons can induce sleep not death."

Doul did not answer her, instead he said to Zukan. "We cannot take the horse with us, set her free, I am sure she knows the way home."

Zukan appeared uncertain. His face hardened and he looked over at his sister who just nodded. He stroked the head of the beast and said quietly. "You are feeling better, I can see that. You rest here till you are stronger then go and find your stable, I am sure it is warmer than here."

Doul's eyebrows raised by an infinitesimally small amount. "Right. We will head north, following their tracks. We have to be both swift and wary, for they know we are following and could set a trap for us. At some point they will turn south again, heading for Grest, when they clear the forest and get to the fields then that is the time to strike them hard." He raised his head and sniffed the air.

"My guess is that at some point they will head for the river for it flows directly southwards and following its course will be the fastest route for them, so, when we can we will do the same. If we locate them soon enough we may even be able to get ahead of them and lay an ambush, that would best suit our skills I feel. Get to the river and kill them there, then get the girl to Ogun, after that we can leave this cold, Gods' forsaken place behind. Hopefully for ever."

Both Siri and Zukan seemed cheered by his words. And so the three of them mounted and left the glade, letting the fog hide them, shrouding them in a silence that not even the clopping horses could disturb.

10

If ever a river lived up to its name it was the Whiterush. Stan stood looking over it realising that, because of the high clouds of spray churned up by the swirling rapids, the series of stepped falls that extended both north and south of his position, and the scattered, saw toothed rocks jutting out of the savage depths, he could not actually see the furthest bank. And he was getting soaked too, the exposed skin on his head was coated in a watery film, the damp was penetrating his cloak and leathers, even his feet in their woollen socks felt sodden, though that might have been sweat, it had been a hard walk from the manor house to here. He watched the trunk of a felled tree being carried downriver, branches splayed like a twisted corpse, trunk partway split by impact after impact against the watching stones, those guardians of the river, ready to tear up anything that dared chance the violent, broiling waters. There was no way they would be crossing here.

He sighed and thought of his Aureline and of his last parting from her. He was standing at the door and checking his gear, everything seemed to be in order. Now all he had to do was check his weapons. And it was Aureline who passed them to him for examination and storage.

"Your axe," she said, picking the thing up with an effort and handing it to him.

"Thanks," he said, gripping the haft and running his finger along the blade.

"It is notched," she said, as she saw what he was doing.

"Not seriously, it will do for now, I will get it to a smith on my return."

She placed her hands on her hips. "And how did it get notched exactly?"

"Oh you really don't want to know."

"Don't want or don't need? Really, even after all these years I know so little about you; you spend maybe three months a year with me, the rest of the time I have no idea what you get up to."

"And for that same amount of time I have no idea what you get up to either."

"Oh you do," she harrumphed. "I bring up your children, make sure their stomachs are not empty. So, will you tell me now?"

ACT ONE : THE HUNT

"Tell you what?"

She gave him a playful slap on the shoulder. A none too gentle playful slap. "How your blade got notched, you evasive dolt!"

He rolled his eyes, scratched his scalp, stroked his chin, then rubbed his nose but still her determined stare persisted. "Very well, it was an iron stud on a man's armour, a man who got in my way, swung his weapon at me."

"You kill him?"

He shrugged his shoulders. "I really do not know, he went down, I stepped past him, he was definitely out of the fight, of that I was sure."

"So he might be alive then."

"Meriel may have favoured him but then wounds get infected, blood does not always stop flowing, I have seen shock alone kill a man, even a single punch can be fatal."

"Well you sound sloppy to me, you should have made sure, I am amazed you are still alive."

"As am I."

"Obviously the thought of seeing me again keeps you going."

"That must be it, yes."

She did not answer, choosing instead to pass him another weapon. "Your spare axe."

"Thank you."

"It is in far better condition than your main axe. Why do you never use it?"

"Oh I do sometimes. But it is not as well balanced, the haft is too smooth also, sometimes my fingers slip, especially in warm weather."

"Well you are the expert in such things, I have to defer."

He clapped his forehead. "By all the Gods! A subject I know more than you about. I have waited my entire life for this moment!"

"Now you are being annoying. Your throwing axe?"

"Please."

She handed it to him. He tossed it from hand to hand with a broad grin, knowing she half expected him to drop it onto his toe or something. The appraising look she gave him once he had finished was most satisfying.

"Hunting knife?"

He took it, a broad, clean blade of grey steel a foot long, he ran his finger along the edge and smacked his lips. "Sharper than a whore's tongue." He then shifted awkwardly on his feet, adding. "So I have been told."

THE FANGS OF THE FEN SNAKE

She shook her head and whispered something inaudible. It was time for the next weapon, "Dirk, for your belt."

Watching him slide it into place she decided it an opportune moment to talk a little more. "Stan..."

"Yes?"

"You can tell me you know; the things you do in the field. I know what you are, there is no need to try and protect me, nor the kids for that matter. Just the other day they hung some Tanarese collaborators in the square, we were all there. We didn't know that it was happening, we were just looking for shoes for the winter but once that was done we all stayed and watched. Death does not scare them, if anything children are blasé about such things."

"I know they are, so was I at that age," he stopped and sighed deeply." Look, this is how I do things alright? I go out there," he waved his arm in a vaguely western direction, "and I do what I have to do, then I come here, back here to specifically forget about all that. Do you really want me to regale you with the story of how I cut a man's stomach open and that, as he lay there, whimpering and dying, trying to push his entrails back in he kept calling out the name of a woman? It might have been his wife, his daughter, even his mother, Keth only knows, but when the fight was over I went to him, put my arm around him, held a flask to his lips, so that he could sip the strong stuff, and I did this until he died. Do you really want me to chat about that? I come here, I come home to put all that behind me. It is important. I have known good men, family men who have been unable to separate one life from the other. They bring the battle back with them, the stench and the fear and the pain and it destroys them, either they drink till their liver turns to stone and they spend nights sleeping in a sewer trench, totally oblivious to the piss soaking their hair, or they use their wife as combat practice, beating them till they look barely human. Sometimes they spend their time picking fights with somebody in the street, sometimes they just stay in one room and cry, sometimes they do all of these things. They have stopped distinguishing between war and...and normality, war has become normality for them.

But it will never happen to me, I fight partly for my country but mostly for you, letting this life here be destroyed by the life out there, well, it would be rather self-defeating don't you think. Anyhow, that is why you escape my tedious war stories, actually the exciting bits with battles are outweighed greatly by the nights spent in the pissing rain, rubbing the blisters between my toes, now that is a story I can tell you if I want."

ACT ONE : THE HUNT

She smiled gently, walked over to him, stood on her toes, and kissed him on the cheek. "You are a good man Crastanik."

"I am a thug."

"You can be both a good man and a thug you know; it is always nice to see glimpses of why I chose you in the first place. Small dagger?"

"The one I put in my boot?"

"The very same."

"Hand it over."

She did so.

"Actually," he said, "the leather sheath I slide it inside, some of the stitching has come loose, can you fix it next time I come back, or I can see myself stabbing my foot."

"You can't fix it yourself?"

He shook his head. "Well, I can I suppose, but you would do a better job, I do not have your dextrous fingers."

"To the rescue again is it?"

"As ever."

Next time she spoke her voice took on a more perplexed tone. "Your last items, and I wonder by all the Gods why you need them or if you ever use them."

He took them off her with relish. "Ah, my darts, easy to store and always useful."

"So you do use them then?"

"Hardly ever, but it is always nice to have something to chuck in an enemies face at close range. Breaks their concentration, gives me an edge. Excellent. Now there is just one more thing."

She groaned. "You are not taking them again?"

He plucked the item off her, a slightly curved metal band with four holes of different sizes running through the middle. Slipping the fingers of his right hand through them he formed a fist, brought it up close to his face and smiled fondly. "Ah, my lucky knuckles," he said, "never let me down in my street fighting days, turn a man's jaw to mush if you time the blow correctly..."

"But do you use them now?"

"Aureline," he gave her an exasperated sigh. "They are LUCKY!"

"I thought you were supposed to travel light."

"Three axes, three knives, darts and knuckles, doesn't get much lighter than that, and speaking of travel, I really have to go, a nearby tavern is

133

demanding my presence."

She came over to kiss him but whooped in surprise as he lifted her off her feet so that she lay cradled in his powerful arms. "What are you doing, you Uba touched bonehead!"

"Well," he shrugged, "I have just had a rethink and the tavern's demands aren't THAT pressing."

He started to carry her towards the stairs but stopped at their foot. "Xhenafa take it, but I am getting old. There was a time I could lift you and carry you through the whole city without drawing breath. Now I go a few steps and I can feel a twinge in my back."

"Oh poor you," she affected a sympathetic tone. "What are the pains of childbirth compared to a twinge in your big manly back?"

He started up the stairs. "The problem with childbirth is that you women moan about it so much. Start to push a brat out and all you do is scream like a noble forced to walk and fetch his horse. Have a back twinge like mine and you would know the true meaning of pain. And that lack of sympathy means I am going to throw you onto the bed from here."

"No Stan, no! Don't you dare you great, clumsy bear!"

From the top room of the hovel there came enough shrieking, screaming, laughing, and groaning to attract knowing looks and smiles from the people tramping the smelly, muddy streets outside the window.

****

"You know, just looking at it and giving it your best stare is not going to help us cross the damned river, not unless you can sprout wings." Shak had crept up unheard to stand next to him and now both men were getting a soaking from the great blooms of spray vomited forth by the watery turbulence just beneath them.

"We are in some trouble, aren't we?" Stan said in flat tones.

"Oh, I don't know," Shak's reply was similarly deadbeat. "Trapped this side of the river with no horses, having to walk all the way south to Grest, facing a journey of days rather than hours whilst being pursued all the way by men on horseback who could probably ride us down at will. Things sound fine to me. And of course if Dead Eyes is correct we might even have a dragon to contend with too. Anyway, the choice for you right now is stand here and get drenched or come back with me and help sort out some kind of plan with the others. Coming?"

ACT ONE : THE HUNT

Stan nodded and turned away from the river. "Ordinarily I would say a forced march leaving us some time to set up a defensive position would be our only option. But then we have an additional handicap this time. Has she stopped moaning yet?"

Shak shook his head.

"I imagine the first time she was clasped to the wet nurse's teat she complained about the milk being too warm. Can't we just cut our losses and throw her in the river."

"I fear," Shak sighed, "that even the river would spit her right back at us."

"We are stuck with her then."

"Afraid so. Stauncher seems to find her amusing anyway. But then he has always had an odd sense of humour. Remember his betting thing?"

"Oh yes." Stan flashed a gruff smile. "He used to crash the taverns just to see what people would be prepared to lay a bet on. Once blew all his ready coin on a snail race, his snail was the fastest, it just went in the opposite direction to the finish line. He tried turning it round and it just turned back again, tried putting a leaf in front of it, it just sped right past. Said it was worth losing the money because he hadn't laughed so much in his life."

"Then there were the flies on the latrine wall."

"Now that was serious. I bet on that, mine was definitely the fastest bluebottle till somebody pissed on it. Tanaren is full of cheats."

Shak gave a resigned shake of his head and walked into a clearing in which the remainder of the party were sat in gloomy silence. With one exception. For Lady Eleanor Lasgaart had taken one of her riding boots off and was studiously examining a hole in her stockings and that part of the sole of her foot thus exposed by it.

"Look at it!" She said peevishly. "A blister! I am blistered! You can't seriously expect me to walk after this, not at the pace you were going. You will have to find a horse, or slow down, or..." her eyes flashed mischievously, "you will have to leave me behind altogether."

"No chance," said Shak dismissively, "keep up or get carried like a sack."

"I am NOT a sack!"

"More's the pity. A sack doesn't have a mouth. Now we can't linger here for too long, or the lady Eleanor may get reunited with her family, an outcome for which her family will have my deepest sympathies. However, as such an eventuality will lead to the demise of the rest of us we cannot really let that happen."

"They have horses, we do not," Stauncher said. "They can ride us down at their leisure. All they need do is find us, keep their distance, and pick their moment. Horses against men on foot, it is an uneven struggle, especially if there are knights after us. I have stood against knights before; they can floor a dozen men in a single charge"

"So how did you survive then?" Eleanor said tartly. "Either knights aren't that lethal, or you are making it up. You would run if a knight came within half a league of you."

"And how, Lady Eleanor," Stauncher was not as stung by her words as she had hoped, "do you think I got my head wound?"

"Oh!" Eleanor was surprised. "A knight did that? Well at least you lived."

"My recovery took months, even now I can get terrible headaches. I am in no hurry to face a knight again, especially if one of them is your brother, I doubt he would be particularly merciful to the rest of us."

"No." She pursed her lips, surprised at the emotions such a scenario had stirred in her. "No, he would leave none alive."

"Exactly," Shak said. "We need to neutralise the threat of the horses, or we are just dead flesh."

"And you have an idea don't you," Dead Eyes said quietly.

"I have," Shak admitted. "But you might not like it."

"Well anything is better than dying," Stan voiced all their thoughts; "let's hear it."

"It is a simple enough idea," Shak said. "Our original plan was to follow the river south till we got to Grest and safety. Try that now though and we will end up being trampled into the mud. So, instead of us following the river south we follow it north, go up the mountain till the river is shallow enough to cross on foot. Then we go south along the rivers east bank instead of the west. What do you think?"

The silence was telling. A few heads did turn northward where, even over the close pressing trees, the snowy tips of the mountains, wreathed in burning cloud, glowered back at them.

It was Dormouse who finally asked the next question. "How far do we have to climb before the river can be forded?"

"No idea," Shak said.

ACT ONE : THE HUNT

"You mean; you have never been up there?"

"No," was the honest, if rather deflating answer; "none of us have. The war is not being fought on the lower slopes of the mountains so there has never been any reason to go there. I do know however that the slopes get rather steep quite soon and it will be very difficult, if not impossible for horses to follow us over this broken terrain. If we keep close to the river there are several waterfalls nearby, indicating very steep ground. They will have to leave the horses behind or if they do manage to bring them they will be slowed and probably quite easy to track down or even ambush. If we keep sharp and on our toes the hunters may just become the hunted. They will not, at the very least, be able to ride us down. It won't be easy for us but if I am being honest, I really don't see any other survivable option. I am however prepared to listen if somebody has a better idea."

"I have one, a serious one," Eleanor said. "You go on and leave me here."

There were several surprised looks, but nobody shut her down, so she continued. "My brother is after me, not you. Just go and let me stay here. He will find me and take me to my wedding. You get to keep your lives, I get what...I want. Just leave some food with me, that is all I ask."

Stauncher and a couple of the others looked like they were taking her words seriously. Shak however was dismissive. "We came out here to get you and that we will do. We have faced worse odds than this many times before. Besides, how do you know he will find you, you might end up starving to death out here or ending up as a meal for a wolf pack, or a dragon, if Dead Eyes was right about what she saw."

"I know what I saw," Dead Eyes said defensively. "My people venerate dragons though none alive have ever seen one, they are a large part of our culture. We used to worship dragons and it was a dragon that I saw last night. There are no doubts."

"Besides," Shak continued, "we only have your word Lady Eleanor that your brother is following us, up till now we have seen no signs that he actually is."

"He is." Eleanor's chin set stubbornly.

"Your faith in him is admirable, but do you really want to be left alone in these woods, at night, in the dark, beset by Artorus only knows. And I am not just talking about beasts; brigands and desperate men wander through here too; I dread to think what they would do to you if they found you. Lastly of course we do have some men on our trail, paid assassins after my blood and probably whatever bounty they can get for you. Ironic is it not that your best hope my lady is to stay with us for now."

"So you are saying I could get eaten, raped, or sold for coin?"

Shak nodded. "Or all three, depending on who finds you first," Stan added for good measure.

"But I cannot climb these slopes, I will only slow you down. And you have a man with an injured leg, how will he manage."

"I will be fine," Dormouse interjected, perhaps a little too quickly.

"You will not slow us down," Stauncher told her. "We can handle you; it will not be a problem. Now, we should all have a bite to eat, to give us strength for the climb ahead."

"Agreed," Shak said. "But we must be swift, I want us a good way up these slopes by nightfall, if we do not find a position we can defend then we might as well put our feet up and let them kill us here."

****

"They are heading east, towards the river. First north and now east. And on foot so yes, they have definitely lost the horses. Something has happened to them, something bad…"

"For them maybe, but not for us." Nico Lasgaart clapped his hands together with relish. He stood next to Ursus who was crouched over the ground examining the footsteps of their quarry. Behind them stood the east wall of the skeletal manor house, silhouetted by the cold afternoon sun. Closer, but still behind them the stream plashed its way over its stone lined bed, its song marrying that of the myriad birds perched hungrily in the leaf denuded trees.

Ursus stood and ambled back to the ever patient horses. "They can't be far away now, no doubt they can walk swiftly but their prisoner is, like as not, not as fleet of foot as they might be."

Nico laughed as he remounted his horse. "Never a truer word has passed your lips my friend. Walking is an anathema to Eleanor, if she could be carried to the latrines by divan she would happily do so."

"Yet I wonder what happened to her captors, how they could be so careless as to let their horses flee. The answer probably lies in yonder building but just stepping through the main door and seeing the torn earth, hoof prints, and whatever that other print was…something felt very wrong there,

ACT ONE : THE HUNT

don't you think?"

Nico was happy to agree. "Neither of us were keen to explore the place further, our horses were spooked by something, I am just grateful that we found this trail without having to wander around those derelict rooms. Even now I feel that the building is somehow watching us, let's gain the cover of the trees again, I will feel safer there."

They rode on slowly, following whatever trail was visible to them until they were surrounded by trees once more. For the first time since they had started this pursuit the sense that their quarry was within catching distance kept them both alert, starting at the slightest sound, expecting ambush at every turn. The path wound but little, bearing eastwards all the time, its course leading them inexorably towards the river. Shadows grew longer and, as the crepuscular gloom of approaching evening began to sit heavily on the boles of the trees and under the shadowed places beneath branch and root they finally reached it, and the traces of the camp where Shak had made the decision on where to travel next.

Ursus dismounted and picked up the fragments of a discarded oatmeal cake. "They appear to be well supplied," was his dry comment.

"So when they lost the horses they didn't lose their food." Nico sounded disappointed.

Ursus then spotted the trace of a boot print, then another, and another. "Looks like they have gone north from here." He shook his head. "Why north? And why did they abandon the path to Arshuman territory and ride to the manor house in the first place? They had horses then, it makes no clear sense. Having said that though, I have to say it does support a theory I have had for a while."

"And I take it you are desperate to tell me this theory?" Nico raised a knowing eyebrow.

Ursus returned to his horse, ignoring the younger man's sardonic tone. "I was not that desperate to tell you, not without proof but now you ask me I might as well say something. It is just that there has been a discrepancy at times in the number of horse trails we have been following. Most of the time there have been about six distinct hoof patterns but there have, on occasion, been more than that, maybe ten to a dozen."

"So what are you implying?"

"That maybe these extra tracks weren't made at exactly the same time and that the Arshumans turned north because..."

THE FANGS OF THE FEN SNAKE

Nico was suddenly startled. "You are saying that somebody else is chasing them?"

"Yes, and that they are closer to them than we are right now. The Arshumans got wind that they were being hunted so turned north to shake them off. They stopped off at the ruined house for the night but somehow lost all their horses, perhaps it was these "others" that drove them away."

"But if they had driven the horses off why wait to attack them afterwards? There has been no evidence of a fight even till now, why scare off the horses and just sit back and wait? And who are we talking about anyway, have Fenchard's men got wind of them?"

Ursus shrugged, though he would never admit it both his knee and elbow joints were aching uncomfortably. "His was the first name to come to mind," he growled from under his wiry grey moustache.

Nico patted his steed, a wicked grin crossing his handsome features. "So we have two sets of foes ahead of us, Arshuman yellow bellies and Fenchard's traitors, this day gets better and better, I will need a coal sack to bring back all their severed heads; and they have all gone north, you are sure of that?"

"Yes, headed for the hills and the mountains it seems. It will be difficult for the horses but then, that is probably their intention."

"Then they know they have been cut off and are looking for advantageous ground to force a confrontation." Nico started to ease his mount northwards, back through the trees.

"It appears that way, yes." Ursus was back on his own horse and started to follow his commander who, in turn, looked back at him, his perfect white teeth flashing like pearls in the murk.

"Then let's give them what they want, shall we?

Ursus nodded and was about to reply when, from somewhere directly ahead of them, close enough to hear clearly, yet too far away to identify with any certainty, came a noise. It was a low sound, a deep rumble that seemed to set the earth to shaking whilst dislodging those few leaves left hanging in the trees. Both horses, trained chargers used to the frenzy of battle, stirred uneasily, indeed Ursus needed a stern word or two to stop his from turning tail entirely. Then the rumble came again, louder this time, sending clouds of birds airborne, whirling, and chirruping in fear. Nico eased his mace free of its leather saddle thong, Ursus pulled his own sword noiselessly from its scabbard.

ACT ONE : THE HUNT

Then the air was shredded by a high pitched, animalistic scream.

It was so loud Nico had to put his free hand to his ear before grabbing the rein once more to control his rearing charger. Ursus too was almost thrown as his horse bucked underneath him. The sky was dark with wheeling birds, through the trees a flock of white eyed deer fled past them, oblivious to the knights entirely. There was a crash, the death throes of a falling tree, spinning to the ground, splintering the trunks and branches of its fellows as it fell and then came the sound of something heavy, something large and heavy, ploughing through the forest ahead of them.

Nico gasped. "What in the name of Artorus is that!"

Ursus, like Nico, had control of his mount again. All they could see in front of them were trees and sprawling undergrowth but just behind that, in the darkness that eyes could not penetrate, something was moving. Heavy feet landing and rising, branches broken by sinewy hide, the thrash of a mighty tail, a shadow was moving westwards, away from them.

Then the cry came again.

It spread out like a circular wave, a ripple in a still, restful pond, a deluge of sonic power that flooded the ears and set the brain to throbbing and tearing. The unseen, powerful, puissant body had resumed its crashing progress through the trees but for Ursus and Nico it mattered little, for both had been forced to sheath their weapons to try and take control of their horses. It had become too much for both animals, who, confronted by such a terrifying abstraction of the unknown, had turned away from the source of it and fled, kicking and rearing as they crashed through trees and bracken and with only the most skilled of horsemen being able to bring them to heel without suffering a crushing fall onto the stony earth beneath.

****

Fortunately, both Ursus and Nico were just such horsemen. It took a superhuman effort from both of them, wrestling with the reins for many minutes until the powerful, yet panicky animals had been brought fully under rein once more. All four of them now sat or stood, panting and sweating heavily, steaming flanks and steaming breath clouding the still, dank air. Yet those strange noises had ceased for the moment; apart from the churning, omnipresent roar of the Whiterush close by all was silence again. No birds, no animals, not even a twig stirred in anger, until finally Nico had the breath to speak to his companion once more.

THE FANGS OF THE FEN SNAKE

"I suppose," he said falteringly, taking deep breaths between words. "If I were to ask you what exactly that was in the woods ahead of us you would say, ask Artorus, for no man could ever truly know."

Ursus shot him a bleary look. "That is exactly what I would say, how in the name of the Gods would I know what it was when you do not?"

Nico nodded, smiled to himself and once more, pulled his mace free of its leather fastening. "I suppose I asked for that. Still, shall we try and find out?"

Ursus shook his head and unsheathed his sword. "Say that to an intelligent, rational man and he would tell you exactly where to stick that mace of yours. We however are knights of the Silver Lance and in joining that order we vow to set intelligence and rationality to one side in the pursuit of something called...glory, a rather ephemeral aim for even at my age I have yet to find out exactly what it is."

"You forgot honour my friend," Nico answered with a broad smile," but, given your advanced years I can forgive the oversight and put it down to memory loss. Anyway, you attained both years ago and you know it. Whatever that beast was it is a threat to Tanaren and we are Tanaren's defenders, we need to find out more."

"After you then," Ursus said half-heartedly. "As the senior officer you have the "honour" of going first."

They gently coaxed their steeds forward, returning along the path they had fled so precipitously. Gradually, as they proceeded, the sounds of the forest returned, it was evensong and by the time they entered the glade where the beast must have resided the trees surrounding them had fully erupted in a chorus of avian exultation. It was a beautiful sound to behold but neither Nico or Ursus noticed it, for this woodland glade, that must have been so idyllic under the sun and balmy warmth of summer was now a charnel house, a place soaked entirely in blood.

There was not a tump of earth, a sod of tangled grass, a standing mossy stone onto which the substance had not splashed. Even the surrounding trees were coated with a fine spray of crimson gore, something had imported the great shambles of Tanaren market and placed it here, something had turned a place of serene tranquillity into a theatre of death and slaughter. The horses were stirring uneasily again.

The worst place was in a shallow, bowl shaped dell near the glade's centre. Here the blood had collected into a thick, coagulant pool nearly a

ACT ONE : THE HUNT

thumbnail deep. Nico slid off his horse and approached the awful sight, for the place was already buzzing with those flies that had yet to die off for the winter. "It was a horse," he called over to Ursus, "I see a hoof."

"One of the Arshuman horses?" Ursus replied.

"Seems like a logical thing to assume." Nico knelt down and examined the scene a little more closely. "Pieces of gut, or bowel, or something. What in the name of Keth could carry a horse carcass from the manor up to here?"

"Troll? Bear? Giant?" Ursus conjectured.

"No giants left here. All hunted and killed centuries ago and there is no bear that could do this; besides they are hibernating, or close to hibernating by now. Must be a troll, a very big troll, they do come down from the mountains at times. Hello though, what is this?"

Something was poking out of the edge of the blood pool. Grimacing with distaste Nico extended his arm and, using thumb and forefinger carefully extracted an object that had been breaking the surface of the sticky mass. He gave it a perfunctory clean by rubbing it against a clump of thick grass and held it up for Ursus to see clearly.

"By all the Gods," Ursus breathed, "it looks like a snake scale."

"But what a snake!" Nico said. "It is at least a foot in every direction, and thick, you could fashion a shield from such a thing. The snake in question must be what? Fifty foot long?"

"But could a snake catch a horse and bring it here? Besides snakes swallow their prey whole, this poor beast was…chomped into pieces. Ow!" Ursus clamped his hand to his neck, "Xhenafa take these cursed midges."

"And can a snake ever make the noise we heard earlier?" Nico mused. "But if it is not a snake, what is it? The war has made this country so remote and abandoned, all sorts of life could flourish here, and we would not know a thing about it. Any ideas? Ursus? Ursus?"

But Ursus did not reply. Dropping the scale Nico picked up his mace and ran over to his friend, who was pale as milk and still had his hand to his neck. Nico pulled it away to reveal the black shaft and flight of a small arrow, or dart, the head of which was firmly embedded in Ursus neck.

"It is barbed. And poisoned by the Gods, poisoned!" Ursus spoke thickly, a line of drool spilled from the corner of his lips over his chin as he slowly slid off the horse into Nico's arms. Nico set him down as gently as he could before grabbing his helmet and setting it on his head.

"Where are you, you skulking cowards!" He berated the trees and the

THE FANGS OF THE FEN SNAKE

shadows that they cast. "Come on out and fight like a man. I am Sir Nico of the Silver Lances and if I am to die, I want that death to have a name! And a face!"

He swung his mace at the air expecting a similar dart to fly out of the darkness and strike him at any moment, yet he was confused. Fenchard's men did not use such a weapon and neither, as far as he knew, did the Arshumans. What exactly was he up against here?

And then, some twenty to thirty yards away from him a figure did step into the glade from behind one of the many encircling trees. Tall and slender it appeared, though he was surprised he could tell as the figure was swathed almost wholly in furs. In its gloved hand it held the most extraordinary weapon. It appeared to be a crossbow, for it had stock, trigger, grip, and limb and yet this crossbow was many times smaller than the norm and could seemingly be operated one handed. Now Nico knew what had fired the dart, a sort of hand crossbow, a weapon that, as far as he knew, was very rare and only used by certain professionals in the warm countries to the south.

Professionals that killed for money.

The figure lowered its hood and Nico had yet another surprise on this day of surprises. It was a woman, a tall, dark haired woman, and she was wearing gold in her ears and in a stud through her nose.

"You want a name for death?" she spoke, her accent strong, exotic. "Then call it Siri, for it is my name, and this weapon is ready to use again."

"But it need not be used, not unless you give us a reason." A man now broached the clearing. He spoke softly and was covered in black robes, robes that even masked the lower part of his face. He carried a bow, had fitted an arrow to it but had not yet taken up the strain. It seemed he wanted to talk.

"You have killed my man!" Nico spoke defiantly. "I will spare neither of you, yet alone talk to you first!"

"But he is not dead," the man in black said. It seemed he was attempting to adopt a non-threatening tone, but it was still a very threatening non-threatening tone. "He will come around in time, the drug administered was for sleep only. Now, I wish to talk because I believe we have a common goal and I also believe that, if we work together, we have a better chance of achieving that goal."

Nico was dumbstruck. "You are proposing an alliance? With you?"

"That is exactly what I am proposing. Now, let us leave this place, break bread together and talk. My name is Doul, and I believe we have much we can offer each other."

ACT ONE : THE HUNT

11

Darkness had never felt so reassuring. At last, they were hidden, clothed in velvety night after a walk and climb of some hours, a journey that even the strongest among them found punishing. Shak had led them northwards, always keeping close to the river, always trying to keep under the cover of the trees, always trying not to stand out against sky or stars. As he had predicted the ground soon began to rise steeply for they had reached the point where foothills started to meet the lower shoulders of the Derannen mountains, the difficult ground where horses became more of a burden than a boon. And they eschewed the easier routes, those places further away from the river where the climb was steep but even, choosing instead to keep the river in sight at all times, a path that meant scrambling up sharp rocks, clambering around boulders, finding purchase in the roots of twisting, windswept trees; they were probably following a route that no human had trod before, an arduous path for them, but a far worse one for any who chose to try and hunt them down. The river, unfortunately, was still unnavigable, alternating between a series of churning rapids, to crashing cataracts, constantly violent, constantly dangerous, a crescendo of tortured water that had assailed their ears for so long that they no longer noticed it. Fingers clammy, legs burning, soaked by sweat and spray, Shak had called a halt not a moment too soon.

    They had chosen a rocky pinnacle overlooking the falls behind and the forest ahead. There was only one narrow, scree covered pathway to get to it, noisy to climb and impossible for a horse. The pinnacle was ringed by several skinny, silver barked trees which gave some protection from the prevailing wind, if not from the cold and, at its centre, where they had now camped was a slight, earthy depression which provided a relatively comfortable place to sleep. They spoke little, they were too tired in truth, most of them just laying out their bedrolls and collapsing upon them in near instant slumber.

    Stauncher took the first watch, putting his bedroll near the path they had climbed, a path that overlooked the forest to the west, and then wrapping his cloak tightly around him. Given the concealed nature of their hiding place, Shak had allowed a small fire, but it was too far away from Stauncher to warm him directly. He blew into his hands and stared out over the blue-black firs

ACT ONE : THE HUNT

with pale, reflective eyes, his thoughts and memories preventing sleep from claiming him.

He froze, briefly, at the sound of footsteps. These steps however were not ahead of him, not that of an approaching enemy, but behind him, from the camp. Furthermore, they were light steps, not as light as an elf's but light nevertheless, they could only belong to one person.

"Can't sleep Eleanor?" he asked without looking behind him.

"No," was the monosyllabic response.

"I hope you are not trying to escape."

"Escape? Where?" She was alongside him now. He pulled out his bedroll to make room for her as she crouched down. Once seated she continued to talk. "There is nowhere to go. I have never been in such a remote place in my life before, I can hardly believe this is still Tanaren."

"Well it is," he shrugged, "and looking at the river we still have some way to go before we can cross it."

She did not reply at first, choosing instead to stare glumly in the same direction he was, out over the silent trees. She picked at the bedroll and chewed her lip agitatedly before speaking again. "I, I wanted to thank you...for helping me that is, I could not have got this far without you..."

"Carrying you?" he half smiled.

"No need to sound so smug," she said defensively. "I was just trying to say that I appreciated your help."

"Well you certainly made enough noise about it at first."

"I thought..." she said in clipped, impatient tones, "that you were manhandling me."

"Well I was," he still did not look over at her. "I just wasn't doing it for the reasons you thought."

"No," she admitted, "I did think for a moment that you were..."

"Molesting you?"

She nodded and coloured a little.

"Well I should have forewarned you, lifting you up without telling you was a mistake, so I suppose an apology is in order."

"It is?" she replied. Then, a little more firmly. "Yes it is."

"Well now you have it. I told you I had a daughter your age and just assumed that you would guess that my intentions were honourable. Anyway, you will probably have more of the same tomorrow so maybe it is now a matter we can put to one side."

THE FANGS OF THE FEN SNAKE

She nodded. "You are stronger than you look."

He laughed softly at that and pulled at his hat so that it sat a little more firmly on his head. "Well, I am a soldier; I may not be built like Stan, but I have been out here longer than he has. Necessity and hardship builds strength out here, in more ways than one."

Eleanor's hair was quite wild by now, falling over her face with a monotonous regularity. She brushed it away with some irritation before asking the one pertinent question she had in mind before coming to talk to him.

"What is she like, your daughter, what is her name?"

"Her name is Olivia and, like you, she knows everything."

"Olivia?" Eleanor could not keep the surprise out of her voice. "That is a very Tanarese name, I expected her to be called Olipateiris Kitevlobbodybobbody or something, that is how most Arshuman names sound to me."

"You are right there," he agreed. "We do like our grandiose names, it is why we use different ones out here, Stauncher is easier to shout out on a battlefield than Gremmick Prasticas after all. As for Olivia being Olivia, well, younger folks like you will not know that before this war, Tanaren and Arshuma used to get on fairly well. We are neighbours after all and, growing up in a port, Tanaren city was our main trading partner. There was a small Tanarese community in my home town and Olivia's mother was part of it. So she gave her daughter a Tanarese name."

"But..." Eleanor could have rather an intense manner at times and this often asserted itself in small, rapid hand gestures, something that she was doing now. "When the war started, wouldn't this change things, was there more hostility towards Tanarese people then?"

"Certainly." Stauncher stroked his chin, and the wisps of ginger beard that were beginning to form there. "Fortunately, or rather unfortunately, Olivia's mother died the year before the war started. As you can see from my face, I have survived plague but others, including her, were just not so lucky. And yes, when the war started the small Tanarese quarter was burned. The survivors were permitted to take one of their own vessels and leave but I smuggled Olivia out and left the place for good. It was a nasty incident and spoiled my memories of the town. I took Olivia to Kitev in the north. I have an older sister there and Olivia stayed with her while I joined up to fight. Not that I cared about the war overmuch, but the pay was steady and regular. I sent some of it to pay for Olivia's keep, the rest I kept back and saved. I have always

ACT ONE : THE HUNT

had my eye out for money making opportunities ever since."

"Any reason?" she enquired coolly. "Or is it just greed."

Stauncher then looked at her for the first time, his expression was playful enough, but Eleanor had the distinct impression that her words had hurt him somehow. After all her previous barbs had failed on him, a throwaway remark had apparently done some damage.

"Always easy for a noble to sneer at the attempts of their lessers to better themselves," he said. "The money was put aside for Olivia, on the off chance that she had a talent for something, I wanted her to make the most of it if she could and to do that you need coin."

"I am not so sure," Eleanor fidgeted. "Surely talent will out, no matter the background."

"No," Stauncher said firmly.

"No?" she enquired.

"No. Want an example?"

She nodded.

"Very well," he continued. "I knew a sailor once, could sing like a lark. He would often perform for us when at sea, during a lull in the workload or when the weather was calm. Even the ship's captain would stop to listen to him, and I used to think, "if he was a Fashtani merchant, or from a Chiran military family, no expense would be spared on turning him into someone who could perform for emperors, instead here he is stitching sails and mending nets." Poor fellow ended up lost at sea in a storm, a few of us remember him fondly but ultimately his ability, his beautiful voice was wasted because he was a fisherman, his family were fishermen and all he was expected to do was catch fish. How many geniuses are lost to this world because they have no patronage and have to do the same dreary things as a nobody like me just to keep themselves fed?"

"But maybe, Eleanor said, "just maybe, you are overestimating his innate talent because it supports your beliefs about the unfairness of things. I am not saying you blame the Gods and their caprice or just myself and all nobility, but might it just be that a fisherman is destined to be a fisherman because that is what he is best at. Perhaps his voice just wasn't that good after all."

Eleanor wasn't quite convinced by her own argument so she knew Stauncher wouldn't be. She was expecting a firm rebuke and yet his answer when he gave it was a gentle one, as though he had carefully considered her words before rejecting them.

"You could be right; I am hardly able to judge a great singer though in truth though his voice never failed to move me. Perhaps he wasn't that good after all, however, I do believe that he should have had the opportunity to prove he wasn't that good in the first place. Rejection has a finality that endless speculation can never satisfy."

"Er, yes, I suppose you are right," Eleanor said awkwardly. "Does Olivia have a gift for something then?"

He nodded. "I paid for a tutor to teach her her letters. She then read the holy book herself, all of its thousands of pages and after that she transcribed her own copy, with illustrations too! Because of this, a few years back I managed to get her work as a lay sister of Camille, she does menial work for them, sweeping and cleaning, laundry and the like but she does have quarters in the holy house and receives a good deal of religious instruction. They are scholars the sisters of Camille, they value learning on any subject; Olivia, if she keeps up with her studies could become a full sister in due course, but there is an exam, and a financial donation required, that is why nearly all the sisters hail from wealthy families."

"You would know more than me," she admitted. "The Order of Camille in Tanaren is tiny, little more than one tower in the capital, we tend to prefer Elissa and if a woman wants education outside the home she usually joins the Sisters of Meriel and becomes a healer. Like you I suppose, you are a healer too, except that you are a man of course."

"Of course. Anyway that is what I am doing, and I am nearly there, a job or two more and I can pay off the sisters, the rest will be up to Olivia."

"And I bet," Eleanor gave her nose a sly tap. "That is where the real problem lies."

She seemed to have hit on something because Stauncher gave her a most curious look. "Would you care to elaborate?"

"Certainly. You have told me that I am like her. Then you went on to outline your plans for her, what you want her to do, how you want her life to be. Not once have you said that she agrees with your plans. Now, if I were her, being told by my father that he wants me to spend the rest of my life reading and studying and praying...ugh! It is like seeing the whole world laid out in front of your house and being told to shut the door."

He smiled. "Is that right?"

"You have argued over this haven't you."

ACT ONE : THE HUNT

"Yes," he nodded, "an argument that has lasted for over three years and is still to be resolved."

"It is her life Stauncher. Perhaps she would happily remain a lay sister and be free to marry or something. Sisters of Camille are supposed to be celibate after all, and their lives are very austere. I wouldn't want such a life personally and she has seen it first-hand. Can't you just let her choose for herself?"

"She is better than that," he said stubbornly. "My daughter will make something of herself."

"But it sounds like she is already doing that."

"By all the Gods," Stauncher raised his eyes to the stars. "Two peas from the same pod you are. She is capable of so much more than she believes. Anyway, I am surprised at your interest, you are after all, sincerely wishing that I die in the next few days and if that happens this discussion is irrelevant anyway."

"I am sincerely wishing to be set free, that is all."

"Fair enough," he conceded with a shake of his head. "We have abducted you after all, in your shoes I would be wishing all kinds of evil on my captors. Perhaps that will happen ultimately, the Gods are well known for..." He stiffened suddenly, for something had caught his eye. At first he thought it an after vision brought on by tiredness but after blinking and unblinking several times it was still there, in front of him, though some distance away. He decided to get corroboration.

"Eleanor, your eyesight will be better than mine, follow my arm and tell me what you see, all the way over there, past the near trees, at the top of that dark ridge to the west and north."

She did as he asked, lifting herself into a crouch, all the better to follow the direction he was indicating. The moon shone weakly off the mountainside, reflecting distant falls of snow far above them. Just under the mountains though, over a league away, where the trees huddled nervously against sloping buttresses of rock she did see something. Tiny pinpricks of yellow light, three or four of them, winking in and out like stars that had slipped from the heavens. She told Stauncher just as much and saw him nod affirmatively. "So it is not me going mad then," he said.

"No, I see them too, what exactly are they?"

"Oh," was his airy reply, "they are campfires, several campfires. It seems that there are a large group of people ahead of us and if they were to move just a little to the east they would be placing themselves in just the direction we want to go."

****

Huddled away in the dell just behind them Dormouse was having real trouble getting to sleep. He didn't know why, he was exhausted after all, the climb into the lower reaches of the mountains had exposed him to all new kinds of punishment and keeping the others from knowing how hard he was finding it had been just as difficult for him. And now he could not sleep. He rolled on to his back, sighed, looked up at the stars and the tops of the encircling trees and let the lambent flames of their small fire warm the side of his face.

"Restless?" It was Shak. He had been noticed. Dormouse sat up to face him though Shak still lay on his bedroll.

"I thought you were asleep," Dormouse spoke through clenched teeth; in fact, it was probably only his teeth and fingernails that weren't aching right now.

"I always keep a quarter eye open," Shak replied, "you are all my people after all. Dead Eyes over there is similar, she sleeps lightly, she is probably just ignoring us right now."

"And Stan?" Dormouse nodded to where the big man slumbered, his snores cutting into the night like broken glass scraping over granite.

"That dragon could fly up here, land in this dell and blow fire up his backside and he still wouldn't notice. Would you big man?" Shak sat up and slapped Stan roundly on the thigh. Stan snorted, mumbled something about honeyed oatcakes and resumed his snoring once again.

"He has the right idea though," Shak continued. "You need to sleep when you can. Keeps your strength and energy up. Anyway, how are you feeling? You have been noticeably quiet today."

"Fine," Dormouse partially lied, "I am not a big talker at the best of times."

"Hard climb for you though, especially with your leg, even with that stick to aid you."

"Oh, it has scarred over, no bleeding. Stauncher and Dead Eyes do their work well."

"So it doesn't hurt like metal beaten on Keth's furnace then?" Shak asked playfully.

ACT ONE : THE HUNT

"Well...a bit yes." Dormouse had to admit.

"You should tell me when you are in pain."

"I...I don't want any special treatment."

"And you won't get any either," Shak was making a point. "But Stauncher has things to help with pain. A pain free Dormouse is a much more effective group member than one who is struggling but won't dare say it. Do not be worried about being accused of weakness or anything, we have all been pretty impressed with you so far."

Dormouse was shocked to hear this." You have?"

"Yes, for a green boy fresh from the royal court you have done everything asked of you without complaint. I was expecting to have to drag you along by the earlobe before handing your ashes back to your mother, but you have surprised us all. Whatever happens after today the Lady Sandrine will have plenty to be proud about."

"Oh, thank you, I thought I was being a burden."

"Well you weren't, but you might be if you do not get enough sleep. I will let you off watch tonight, try and take advantage of it."

Dormouse gave his thanks before curling up on his bedroll once more. He had barely laid down his head when, from somewhere in the vast forest below them came a long, drawn out howl, the call of some great beast venting his fury at the skies. Though the sound was too far away for it to be immediately threatening, all that heard it knew exactly what animal was making the call and the danger it presented to them.

As the cry petered out into a thin, cold, wail Stauncher and Eleanor entered the little clearing. They both froze at the eerie sound, looking at each other with fearful eyes before Shak decided to break the uneasy atmosphere.

"It is just an animal, no matter what its size," he told them. "Besides, if you ask me it just sounds rather lonely."

At that Dead Eyes sat up and opened her vivid green eyes. She shook her head at Shak. "No, not lonely, lost. It shouldn't be here, and it knows it."

"Where should it be then?" Stauncher asked her.

"With its mother, wherever she may be. Young dragonlings stay close to their mother for some years, perhaps this one is searching for her."

Shak stood and ambled towards Stauncher. "Well whatever the truth of the matter it is probably best to keep well out of its way. Now Stauncher, was she trying to escape again, was she cunningly thinking that because she is so quiet and demure we would not notice her absence from this little hollow?"

"Ha!" Eleanor was back to her haughty best. "I could walk out of here any time, any time, and none of you would have wits enough to find me." She returned to her bedroll, flinging herself on to it with a snort.

"Feel free to try," Shak told her. "Do you know in what direction your home lies?

Eleanor waved a thin arm in a vaguely western direction. "Over there somewhere."

Shak pretended to look impressed. "Anywhere between Felmere and the sea then. And you could find it wandering through these woods, having no line of sight to your objective?"

"I would follow my heart, I know where my home is by instinct, it is a gift compassionate people have, so you would have no idea about it."

"Quite," was the laconic reply. "Now Stauncher, deserting your post? I assume there is a reason."

"There is," Stauncher said. "Come with me, it is best that you see for yourself."

The two men left the clearing together, Dormouse watching them go. He then looked over the clearing, accidently meeting Eleanor's glare. He was about to smile at her, but she just screwed up her face and threw herself back onto the bedroll again, with even more dramatic intensity than before. Dormouse just sighed and stretched his arms out until he was comfortable. And this time he was asleep before he could realise it.

****

"You came in a little too early there Randali, we will have to resume from the beginning again."

Lady Sandrine of Lakala, black hair wound under a coif of gold, gave him a look of gentle reproof before checking the strings in her Arshuman harp were wound correctly.

Lakala was a small town less than an hour away from the Arshuman capital of Kitev. The estate there sat on a small, rocky plateau and, from the windows of the chamber where Lady Sandrine practiced her music the lights of the much bigger city, and those of the palace of the king just outside it, could be seen very clearly as darkness fell.

Of course, Dormouse dreamed, he was Randali back here, the name Dormouse had not even been invented for him yet. He was thinking back,

ACT ONE : THE HUNT

remembering, staring into the wide brown eyes of Lady Sandrine, dissolving in them, she was so beautiful, and he was so much in love with her, he could feel his chest constricting with it, even in his dream.

He set down the drum he had been playing, badly, for her and came over to where she was sitting, in a wide embrasure seat, back to one of the estates broad windows. He sat next to her, keeping a discreet distance from her. Sandrine's father always made sure that both male and female attendants were present whenever the two of them met, her father didn't really approve of him in truth, and so he was always extra careful when he was a guest in their home.

"I," now he was going to have to broach the reason for his visit. "I have some news, some bad news, it is probably the reason why I am playing so poorly tonight."

"Oh Randali," she smiled sweetly, the smile he always thought she probably gave to her many pet rabbits. "You always play a little bit poorly. You are too tense, the drum requires a relaxed posture, it gets more resonance out of the skins. It is all in the wrist my dear, as I have shown you before."

She always dressed grandly but today she seemed to be even more ostentatiously attired than usual. Her dress was of flame coloured silk into the fabric of which little white gems had been sown, she wore a belt of latticed gold with part of the latticework fashioned into the forms of lions and pumas, the emblems of her country. The sleeves of her dress were of thin, sheer silk, fashioned that way so that the three gold vambraces she wore on each arm, a fashion beloved of Arshuman noblewomen, could fit comfortably. Each vambrace had a ruby set at its centre, red and gold was obviously the theme of the day for even her earrings, threaded gold affairs of such length they extended well past her shoulders, conformed to this type. In truth she was attired well above her station, testament to the fact that her father, who Dormouse always thought redefined the word "doting", seemed to spend every last penny he possessed on his daughter, and with great effect, for there was no more dazzling a beauty in the entire Arshuman court.

"Yes," he admitted shamefacedly, "I should practice with the drum more than I do. Anyway, as I was saying, I have news, it seems my parents have been trying to promise my hand to a Lady Ros..."

"Lord Preiklees!" Sandrine shot to her feet in excitement as the chamber door opened and a very tall, elegantly dressed man entered with a flourish of his cloak. "I thought you were not coming; the table is almost set for the feast, and I expected there to be an empty place next to me." She strode toward the man, who went down on his knee at her approach. "I have to introduce you both; Lord Preiklees, this is Lord Randali Aganistlan, a relative of the king and erstwhile musician, and Randali, this is Lord Preiklees Kitevilli, swordsman of renown, newly arrived from the field of battle where I am sure he vanquished many a smelly Tanarese mudgrubber. I am certain the two of you will get along famously."

The two men gave each other a curt nod, and for the next few hours Dormouse was given the distinct impression that Lady Sandrine was using this fellow in an attempt to make him jealous. Their musical interlude was forgotten immediately as Lady Sandrine ushered both men into the banqueting hall, sitting Preiklees next to her and Dormouse, opposite. As the food was served and the wine swiftly downed Sandrine kept up a constant line of chatter, marvelling at the elegant styling of Preiklees moustache, the muscular curve of his thighs, the shapeliness of his waist, the fine cut of his robes. She made Preiklees give an account of his valorous exploits, something that he seemed more than happy to do and so, for what seemed to be an age everlasting, Dormouse had to endure stories of swordplay, heroism, and the slaughter of countless flea ridden Tanarese barbarians. And he didn't believe a word of it, unlike Lady Sandrine, who hung on every syllable, her mouth agape with wonder.

One thing Dormouse did glean over the course of the long, long, evening was that he may have been a lord by name, but Preiklees was of far humbler birth than both he and Lady Sandrine. True nobility rarely soiled their hands with this grubby little war, fighting just enough to enhance their personal status before returning home to boast of their exploits. Preiklees though had it seemed spent most of the last two or three years at war, all the signs were there of a modestly born man trying desperately to boost his social standing through acts of bravery and demonstrable loyalty to the king. And for him the ploy seemed to be working. All he needed to cement his rise to prominence was a good marriage, and Lady Sandrine for one, seemed to be in awe of him.

The meal finally finished but things barely improved when the dancing started. Although most of it was informal, everybody holding hands and dancing in a circle, whenever Dormouse looked up it was Sandrine and Preiklees clasping each other in a grip of iron with her staring at him as though he was the God Artorus descended to this earth. After the third, lengthy dance

ACT ONE : THE HUNT

he had had enough; although his original plan was to stay here for the night he decided to instead feign some sort of vague illness and ride back to his family's estate in the so called Circle of the Golden Lake back in Kitev.

He did not bother saying his farewells to Sandrine, so enraptured did she appear to be with her current companion, instead he ordered a servant to bring his horse to the front gates so he could get away as swiftly as he could and with as little fuss as possible. And it was while he was standing on the front steps, blowing into his hands, looking at the torch lit path and wondering if travelling by night was such a good idea after all when he heard somebody hailing him from the doorway immediately behind.

He spun round. "Lady Sandrine?" For it was her, her hair still perfectly in place despite her energetic dancing display earlier. She looked a little confused, obviously his decision to leave had wrong footed her.

"Are you not well Randali? You do look a little piqued." She put her hand to his brow, "though I cannot detect a temperature. I suppose though that I am rather warm myself."

He wanted to be icy with her, distant, aloof, all the better to needle her but he just couldn't help himself. Flushing red he was unable to keep his feelings hidden.

"You should read more my Lady. The word "piqued" does not refer to one's state of health, rather it references their temper, or lack of it. And in saying it you have accidentally stumbled on its correct usage. For I am angry, very angry and do not want to spend another moment under this roof!"

"But why?" She looked at him with large, disingenuous eyes. "Is it me? Have I done something to upset you?"

He breathed deeply, inhaling the warm night air, the sweet resins, and floral scents of the estate's formal gardens. "You know you have; you have done nothing but flirt shamelessly with that man all evening."

"What man?" She cooed, "surely you do not mean Lord Preiklees?"

He nodded firmly. "Lord Prickless, yes. I'll wager he purchased his lordship from the king in return for a bag of plundered gold. He is little more than a brigand who has done well in this war, and he is chancing his arm tonight, casting his net in the hope of bagging a very pretty fish indeed. Can't you see that his intentions towards you are not…honourable?"

It was Sandrine's turn to sigh in exasperation. "Oh Randali you are not still fixating on marrying me are you? It will never happen, neither of our parents approve of the match. I value you Randali, but as a friend and only as a friend, my father would need a new head before he changed his mind. He likes you but does not deem you an appropriate suitor for me."

"And Prickless is? I have never heard of him before, what are his family connections? Does anybody know?"

"They are southern gentry, from somewhere near the Belt, or so I have been told. In truth he would ordinarily be a poor match for me, but he enjoys the favour of the king and rumour is that he is to be granted lands in the conquered territories. If that happens then everything changes. Father wanted me to keep him close tonight so that his mettle could be judged, and I think father rather approves of him. Camille may have given me reason, but I have so many suitors by now an entire roll could be filled in the writing of their names. Preiklees is just one of those names, that is all."

"So Prickless is, yet I am not."

Her eyes narrowed. "I suppose so, but please stop deliberately mispronouncing his name, it is rather childish."

"What do you mean?"

"You know exactly what I mean, he is not Prickless."

"And do you have proof of that?"

"Oh!" she exclaimed in frustration. "You can be so petty at times. He is not Prickless because I spent the entire evening gazing at the front of his breeches. Satisfied?"

"No," was his dispirited reply. "So what do I have to do to become eligible in your father's eyes?"

"Why don't you ask him?"

"Because, as you well know, he ignores me. Pah! I know the answer anyway; you have told me yourself. I need to catch the eye of the king, do I not?"

"Yes, that would help," she nodded. "But I fear you have already forgotten your engagement to Lady Rosalini. See, I knew of it already, you know how swiftly gossip travels from court to court. As I said earlier, we have a great future as friends and no future as husband and wife. I have accepted it and so should you."

"Never," he bit down on his lip. Hard. "Weddings get cancelled all the time, mine shall be one of them. And before that happens, I will make sure the king knows of me, and that his favour towards me will be greater than it is towards this lanky...upstart."

"How?" she giggled. "Are you going to expose your genitals to the

ACT ONE : THE HUNT

royal court? Like mad Lord Odiantus did a few years back. People are still talking about it now."

"No. I am going to war, and when I return both your father and the king, and you for that matter will see me all differently."

She was still giggling. "You? In the war? Granted you are no slouch with the sword but, you, in the war? Fighting?"

"Yes. And I will be gone within the week. And when I return I will have more renown, and far more interesting tales to tell than Lord Prickly."

And how will you achieve this...renown?"

"Well..." He hesitated. He had no idea in truth, all of his words so far had been hot air, it was only beginning to dawn on him that they actually meant something. The wine he had imbibed that evening was hurting his head. "According to your father who are the bravest fighters in the war, who are the most glorious?"

"Well the knights," she said without hesitation. "Actually no, not the knights. Father was discussing the war only the other evening and he was full of praise for another group of men entirely."

"Who? What other group of men?"

She gave him a playful dig with her elbow. "It was father, and he was talking about the war, do you think I was listening? He was on about raiders, or marauders or something, people that stay in enemy territory and fight the war there."

Dormouse drew himself up to his full height. "Then I shall join these marauders. I have actually heard of a few of them, and your father is right, they do have a great reputation."

Sandrine's large eyes widened still further as it dawned on her that he might be serious about this. Her reply was choked. "Don't be silly Randali, these are hardened, veteran warriors, you would be at a total loss. Can't you fight with the knights and build things up from there?"

"I do not have the time. My family want my wedding to be in a matter of months. I am riding back to Kitev to put my name forward."

For the first time that evening, Sandrine seemed genuinely concerned. "Look, Randali, can't we talk about this rationally in the morning. I have drunk too much wine and am a little tipsy and, judging from the sweat on your brow you are just the same. In the morning we can talk more soberly."

"If you can fit me in after Prickly."

"Not now," she groaned. "Come on, your room is prepared, it is too dark to ride anyway. Stay here tonight."

Dormouse did not answer.

"Please. I will come and say goodnight. I will be wearing my nightshift."

"Oh very well. But I will be gone at dawn. If this is the only way to win your hand nobody will stop me."

"Oh, if you insist, but come on in, I am getting cold."

He relented, and soon after retired to his room. Sandrine did visit him, wearing a nightshift that appeared to be as large and baggy as an army tent. She wished him a good night, said she would pray for him, said that she would talk him out of it in the morning, after they had breakfasted.

But he was as good as his word, by the first light of dawn, he was gone.

****

And now Dormouse was dreaming of this, one of his last encounters with the Lady Sandrine, as the small fire flickered, and he tossed and turned nervously on his bedroll. And as he dreamed his mind started to play with his perceptions slightly. Maybe it was all that had happened since he had left Kitev, perhaps it was the distance that now separated him from his Lady or perhaps events had changed him as a person, but suddenly, palpably, Lady Sandrine did not seem quite the beauteous, talented, witty, friendly girl he had always thought her to be, and, consequently, a rather nasty realisation started to creep over him.

Perhaps, just perhaps, after all this danger, after all this peril he had put himself through, the glittering prize, the hand of Lady Sandrine was, just perhaps, not worth all this trouble in the first place.

****

Shak crouched next to Stauncher and stared despondently at the campfires the other man had just pointed out to him. After not blinking or moving a muscle for at least a full minute he blew into his hand and shook his head wearily. "Well, what do you think?" he asked.

"Well," Stauncher answered. "At first Lady Eleanor thought it might have been her brother and his knights until I pointed out that they must be the worst trackers in the world as they had somehow got ahead of us and moved a good distance to the west."

ACT ONE : THE HUNT

"And any knights following us would be quite few in number and would not need all those fires. I think we are looking at something else entirely here."

"Bandits? Slavers?" Stauncher suggested.

"Possibly, but there are slim pickings here for either of them. I would suggest that they are a group of people whom we have been fortunate to avoid so far."

"Oh!" Stauncher realised, "Baron Fenchard's men. They are supposed to be our allies now though, yes?"

"On the face of it, yes. Fenchard is a Tanarese traitor through and through, but some of his men might have…misgivings about the open betrayal of their country. Besides, in the shape of Lady Eleanor we have something that Fenchard would like to take possession of. Out here, where there are no witnesses why not kill a few of the old enemy and bring their baron the prize of a potential bride. No, I would rather we avoided them. Where they might be useful though is with regard to our pursuers, if they all run into each other we can happily let them all kill each other. So our plan is unchanged, we keep to the river, if Fenchard's men move in the same direction then it will just be one more group for us to hide from."

"And if we fail and Fenchard's men do run into us?"

"Then we bluff them somehow. Maybe we can we hide the girl and talk our way out of things. If they do see her we pretend she is a prostitute or something."

Stauncher laughed. "Dressed like that? With her accent?"

"I will leave the details to you." Shak patted the other man's shoulder. "You have a much greater talent at deception than I. That is a compliment by the way. Now go and get some sleep, I will relieve you here."

"But it is not yet time…"

"I need to think my friend, and there is no better place or time to do that than during the night watch. Tomorrow will be even harder than today; I just hope we can find a place to ford this damned river or sooner or later we will end up running down a blind alley."

"And if we do?" Stauncher asked, standing and picking up his bedroll.

"We will have to turn and fight, and, against knights, assassins, and soldiers not even an optimist like Stan would rate our chances then."

12

If ever there was a man shaped by the times in which he lived it was Teague of Haslan Falls. It had seemed at one point that the whole course of his life was laid out before him, straight and unerring as the famous Chira-Anmir road. Eldest son of a miller, albeit an unpopular one (mind you, was there ever a miller anywhere who was not disliked?), he had a trade, an income, savings, and a wife with her own little inheritance. But of course the Gods can skew everything on the slightest of whims, and in his case, things were not so much skewed as tipped completely on their head.

He remembered that the sun was in his eyes when they first saw the smoke of the burning villages, and that it was beginning to drift westward when the first of the fleeing folk arrived to tell them that the Arshumans were coming, and they were coming to burn, plunder, and kill. Thus forewarned, his family and possessions were soon on the wagon, but there was not enough time, he drove the horses as fiercely as he could, but a refugee laden wagon could never outpace the Arshuman outriders. They were caught as night fell, their goods taken, the wagon burnt, their food stolen. Mercifully, the womenfolk went unmolested, but both he and his younger brother were beaten unconscious. He came to at first light, nursing several lost teeth, a couple of cracked ribs, a broken nose, and a host of bruises. His brother unfortunately, never came to at all. Despite his considerable pain he managed to get everybody to the river Vinoyen by eventide, using an abandoned fishing boat to cross it. The day after that they reached Fort Axmian, that last unconquered bastion against the invaders. Whilst the womenfolk put themselves to use cleaning armour, tending livestock, washing, brewing, baking, and stitching he joined the force of Baron Clavell Aarlen, Fenchard's father. From that moment on, his life was devoted to the military.

And he was a useful soldier, cunning, strong, and wiry, in no time at all he was leading a band of men defending the fortress walls, he was in the vanguard during the sally from the gates that broke the back of the besiegers. He served Clavell loyally for years for the baron was a good man, brave, wise, and with a degree of compassion rarely found in the heat of battle. His singular fault lay in the overindulgence of his only son, for Fenchard was in many ways the antithesis of everything his father represented. Then, a couple

ACT ONE : THE HUNT

of years ago Clavell died. At first there was no noticeable difference in the way the baronetcy of Haslan falls conducted the war, but these last months, these last months, Teague hung his head as he thought about it.

Prisoners were released and pressed into service, then foreign mercenaries were hired, from West Chira mostly, sour looking fellows who rarely interacted with anybody but their own kind. Then, finally, there was a change at the top, Fenchard employed a new general, Trask the finger slicer, a man with a fearsome reputation. Trask was given a free hand to command, brutally purging the army commanders and replacing them with his own men. Teague actually benefited from this, being made a captain, but it did little to alleviate his unease. And he was right, Trask commanded using both incentives and fear. The old guard, people like Teague were cowed and kept their own counsel, even when Trask told them they were changing sides, that they would be aiding the enemy so that Fenchard could establish his own kingdom here, between Arshuma and Tanaren. Many were appalled, Teague was appalled, but the prisoners, the foreigners, those bought with the prospect of booty and plunder now outnumbered those who thought as he did. Teague, whose brother had been killed by Arshumans, was now aiding the Arshuman cause.

He threw the stick he had been aimlessly whittling on to the ground and looked around at the glowing fires of the camp. These days there was nobody left in this forest, villages were long abandoned, homesteads had crumbled and were being reclaimed by nature; secrecy was no longer important. Setting fires was of little risk so he would rather the men kept warm, there was snow in the air, and he was the only man here that did not want to get home as soon as possible.

He had the best part of forty men in his patrol. Of these, he knew and trusted about a third, he knew and distrusted about a third and a third he didn't know at all and so could hardly trust them either. Although he had been promoted to captain he knew that he too was not entirely trusted by those in power and that there were spies aplenty amongst the men he was commanding. One seditious word, one false utterance and he would be swinging from the nearest tree just like his former commander. He had not been present at the battle of Wolf Plain, when, under Trask, the men of Haslan falls attacked their own troops. Instead he had asked for work patrolling the country, keeping the locals in line and, to his surprise, his request had been grudgingly accepted. Now his job was to patrol the north land between the

THE FANGS OF THE FEN SNAKE

city of Felmere and the river Whiterush, scouring it clean of enemies. He had done this several times, travelling back and forth and finding no one and so was overdue a return to Tetha Vinoyen, Fenchard's new base. He knew an attack on Felmere was being planned and he was due to be part of it. And he didn't want to do it, he did not want to attack his own people. Unfortunately, his patrol knew that, to return to Fenchard would mean that his loyalty would be scrutinised, found wanting, and so his life would hang by a thread, or rather, a noose. He had people here, Mercer, Corder, Wainman, Stresh, these were loyal to him and would stand by him if trouble arose. Others though, led by that sallow mercenary Grobthaak, would cut his throat as soon as look at him. The atmosphere these last days had been tense, almost openly mutinous, but then events had taken a most unexpected turn.

And now they had fallen into line again, because they needed him, they needed him for his role, not as a soldier, but as something else entirely. Over the fire closest to him stood a metal tripod, and from that tripod hung a crucible, and the contents of that crucible would be ready just about...now.

He removed the crucible from the fire using long metal tongs, setting it on the ground for a moment to cool. Nearly everybody was looking at him. "Form a semi-circle, "he said to them, "or leave."

Nobody left. As they obeyed his instructions he went over to his bags, firstly pulling out a necklace of inches long, polished yellow animal teeth that he put over his head and around his neck. Secondly pulling out a single glove, where attached to the top of each finger was an ivory coloured, curved claw, with each claw recently sharpened. Both tasks completed Teague went and stood close to the fire, and to the crucible next to it, and faced his crowd.

He was of average height, the crown of his head was bald, it being surrounded by a fringe of thick frizzy hair that was grey and black in equal part. His brown eyes were flat, unemotional, giving nothing away to potential enemies. His mouth too, was concealed under a bushy moustache of great fecundity, again it seemed to be left to grow that way to keep his feelings hidden. He had a ruddy, weather beaten complexion and wide ears that appeared to be a little too large for his head. He was scarred too, as were a lot of those present, his cheek and neck both bore the evidence of former battles. When he spoke it was again with a flat, unemotional voice, strong enough to carry authority yet devoid of those inflections that may have carried the message that he cared, about anything or indeed anybody. He faced his expectant crowd and gave them the address they were waiting for.

ACT ONE : THE HUNT

"Below us, between the foot of this hill and where the forest becomes plain, lies the beast. We have all heard it, a couple of us have glimpsed it and many of us have either seen its spoor or the remains of that which it has devoured. Some say it is a type of mutated troll, others say it is a gigantic lizard, yet sooner or later, perhaps as soon as tomorrow we have to face it down and kill it. For that we need the strength and protection of the Gods, we need a little of the essence of Mytha, God of war; and it is my duty, as a priest of Mytha, to transfer that essence from him, to you."

He picked up the crucible, which was still hot to the touch despite his gloved hands and moved to the first man in the semi-circle. It was one of the youngsters, a boy named Kellan. He was a local lad, like him he was loyal to Tanaren but was thoroughly cowed by the older heads around him. Teague was taller than he was and had to look down to meet the boy's nervous, watery grey eyes.

"Who is the God of war?" Teague asked him.

"The God of war is Mytha," the boy replied.

"And do you accept the spirit of Mytha into your blood, your skin, your viscera and your soul?"

"I willingly accept him."

"And will you fight with the ferocity of Mytha, never turning your back on the enemy until they lie vanquished and bleeding upon the ground."

"I will High Priest."

"And do you swear?"

"I swear by the name of Artorus, Mytha's brother in blood."

"Then taste of the blood of Mytha, take on the spirit of the bear."

He lifted the crucible up to Kellan's lips, tilting it slightly so that the boy could drink. Kellan sipped the contents, not flinching as his lips touched the hot vessel, Teague was pleased with the young lad.

"I now anoint you with the blood of the bear. Fight with no fear. Fight with ferocity. Fight with the Gods at your side, and never give ground to your enemies."

But who exactly were his enemies? Teague briefly thought as he pressed the palm of the clawed glove against the surface of the dark fluid in the crucible. Then he clasped the top of Kellan's head with the same glove, digging the sharpened claws so that they pricked the boy's skin, drawing droplets of blood of their own. Teague lingered there awhile, exerting enough pressure on to Kellan's skull to make him uncomfortable, making sure the

THE FANGS OF THE FEN SNAKE

blood droplets made by the claws had run into his collar, waiting until the bear's blood soaked into the palm of his glove had stuck to the boy's hair, dripping in rivulets from his forehead. Still Kellan did not move.

Finally, Teague withdrew his hand. "Mytha favours you, for you have proven yourself willing to accept his benison. Fight with courage oh scion of the bear."

Kellan smiled as Teague moved away. He looked pale, swaying unsteadily on his feet. Mercer, Teague's second in command stood behind Kellan, arms wide, waiting. And it only took a moment, the herbs and poisons that laced the blood drunk by the boy did their work swiftly and he fainted into Mercer's arms, Mercer lying him on the ground with surprising tenderness.

Teague grinned and moved to the next man. It was Kellan's first or second ceremony, unsurprising that the blood would affect him like that. For most of the men here though, seasoned veterans that they were, all they would feel would be a little sickness for a while, then a very lightheaded feeling for a longer while, then that feeling would pass. Fainting was for novices only, everybody looked at Kellan with a knowing smile, they had all been there after all.

Teague moved to the next man, then the next. Always the same form of words, always the same replies, always the drinking and drawing of sacred blood. Being a priest of Mytha was not an overly complicated thing, though the sanctification ceremony all priests undergo could sometimes be lethal. The most important job of a priest was to maintain the secrecy of the ceremonies, no one partaking in them was to tell an outsider of what happened in them, should such a confidence be broken, the priests had full sanction to hunt down and kill the miscreant. To break the bond of secrecy was to destroy the power Mytha had given them.

The next man in the line was a burly Chiran mercenary called Yaki by his fellows. He looked uncomfortable, fixing Teague with an accusing stare.

"That is bear's blood, is it not?" he asked gruffly.

Teague had been expecting this, in different parts of the world Mytha was represented by a different animal totem. Chirans did not see Mytha as a bear.

"Yes it is." Teague answered bluntly.

"Mytha is a bull," Yaki asserted. "It is bull's blood that is needed for the ceremony to work."

166

ACT ONE : THE HUNT

"Not in Tanaren." Teague's inscrutability was serving him well. "Here it is the bear that gives Mytha his potency, the God chooses a different animal in different places. You accept this, accept the blood I offer you or you leave the circle. Just remember though that if you do leave, when we hunt the beast the only certainty that you will have is that Mytha is not fighting by your side. Choose the spirit of the god in this form or have no divine protection at all."

Yaki's small, black eyes moved quickly. Uncomfortable with the ceremony he may be, but what soldier went into battle after openly refusing the help of the Gods? The world's sharpest gambler would not take such odds. After a brief, almost confrontational pause, he nodded at Teague who then asked him.

"Who is the God of war?"

****

The ceremony over the group of blood spattered, drugged men split into their disparate groups, huddling together close to the fires, some of them keeping their voices so low Teague had no chance of hearing what they were saying. There would have been a time when this would have bothered him, when he would have made an effort to unite them all under a common cause; now though, it mattered little to him, some of these men wanted him dead, some wanted to replace him, they were welcome to try. These days his own loyalties were so confused he had no clear goals anymore. He was a man from a village close to Haslan Falls. Haslan Falls had always acknowledged the authority of the Baron of Felmere and the Grand Duke of Tanaren. Now they were going to besiege Felmere, attack the forces of the Grand Duke of Tanaren. He could try and desert, but he had seen the way Trask dealt with deserters, human beings reduced to a bloody, pulpy mass before being hacked to pieces and fed to the hunting dogs. After a decade of facing imminent mortal peril he had never been so certain that the end of his life was nearing. If his meeting with Xhenafa was close, he was determined to take a few of his enemies with him.

"Sir." It was his loyal man, Stresh, newly returned from patrol. He had been sent out with some others to check between here and the river for signs of the beast. It appeared he had some news.

"Go on, what is it?" Teague asked with little enthusiasm. Stresh was about to tell him but before he could Grobthaak, another Chiran mercenary and the leader of the malcontents amongst his command approached him, speaking without invitation.

"A few of us have a question sir," he asked. Grobthaak always called him "sir", a more insincere word Teague had never heard in his life before. Grobthaak carried a pair of long hunting knives in cross belts over his chest, something that Teague thought was a pointless affectation though in truth, every single mannerism of this fellow he found irritating. He did give him the nod though, inviting him to speak, after all, the quicker he spoke, the quicker he would leave him alone.

"This beast hunt." Grobthaak always spoke like his mouth was full of spittle. "Will it just be restricted to tomorrow? A couple of the boys are saying that we should be returning to the city, to pick up fresh orders. We are overdue there anyway I believe."

"They are keen to return to base? The wilderness not to their taste?" Or do you just want to return so that I can be replaced? Teague's last question remained unspoken.

"No sir, it is just that our orders..."

"Orders Grobthaak? Orders? The orders given to me were to sweep these lands clean of enemies. That we have as good as done but there is some sort of beast on the prowl, and it is our duty..."

"A beast may indeed be dangerous," Grobthaak said, "but it is not an enemy. If we cannot find it, then the reports of it should be given to Sir Trask. He will decide on what to do next."

"And he will, but we should at least try and ascertain what it is exactly, before we return."

"Begging your pardon sir," It was Stresh; "but I have some possible news on that."

"You have?" Teague was relieved that he could divert his attention to somebody else though again, his voice did not betray this.

"Yes. You remember that old Artoran hermit? The fellow with one arm that a couple of the boys ran into days back?"

Teague did frown at that. "Yes. What of him? He was supposed to be a bit mad I believe."

"Odd. Mad. Uba touched; all of these I suppose. Well some of the lads found him again, heading towards the river. Thought about bringing him here but he was babbling at the boys that found him, they found his talk so wearing that they just let him go."

Teague shrugged. "We would have nowhere to put a holy man

ACT ONE : THE HUNT

anyway, I mean back at Tetha Vinoyen, not since the monastery was burned. Time was there would be dozens of hermits in these woods, seeking solitude, trying to see the faces of the Gods. Now he is probably the only one left, and that is probably because he is a few arrows short of a quiver. What was he going on about anyway?"

"Well that was it sir," Stresh sounded sombre. "The boys that saw him thought he was talking bollocks and let him go, I am not so sure though."

"So sure about what?" Teague almost let impatience seep into his voice.

"Well they asked him why he was going towards the river, and he told them that he was going to find the treasure sir, the dragon's treasure. Said that he had discovered it years ago and wanted to see it again."

"Treasure?" Grobthaak's eyes shone with a mercenary's greed.

Stresh nodded.

"And you let him go?" Teague inquired.

"Not me personally," Stresh sounded sheepish; "but yes, they just thought him deranged." Teague, in truth, probably thought the same, but this hermit had just given him a chance to both keep everybody happy and delay his return home. Only a fool would not take it.

"He might be, but we cannot just let his words pass. A war needs money to fight it. Baron, sorry, King Fenchard would be very pleased if someone was to present him with...treasure. Would he not Grobthaak?"

"And so would Sir Trask," the man admitted, "and he would be even more pleased with those that do the presenting."

"So we are all agreed then. Six to ten men to find this hermit and bring him to camp, two to guard the camp, the rest to chase down the beast, or at least find out...wait a minute Stresh, you said this man called it the dragon's treasure?"

Stresh nodded.

"So is he implying that this beast we are hunting is a dragon then?"

"Draw your own conclusions sir."

At last he betrayed himself, a soft laugh emanating from his shadowed lips. "Well it is something to bear in mind. Dismissed, both of you. We all need sleep to face whatever comes at us tomorrow."

As they left he cast himself flat on his bedroll, looking up at the stars, and the sparks rising from the fire. Putting off his return to look for a dragon's treasure! What a way to unite his patrol behind him, perhaps, out here, it

THE FANGS OF THE FEN SNAKE

wasn't just the one armed Artoran hermit who was mad after all.

****

He could smell vomit. His vomit. And it was close by, maybe right next to his head. And his head! A thousand army drummers had taken residence inside it, pound, pound, pound. And his neck! It felt like somebody had stabbed him in...a pause, and recollection, Sir Ursus remembered it all, the bloody glade, and the poisoned dart. Yet, to his immense surprise, he did not appear to be dead for if he was, the seat of the Gods was nothing like the paradise the priests described, unless paradise was hard, stony, and cold.

He eased himself onto his right elbow. The vomit puddle was there, right next to it. Everything round and about him throbbed and pulsed, his nausea was still hanging around him like a bilious pall but at least now he could survey the scene around him as he drank in draughts of chill night air.

There was a fire. They had risked a small fire. It made sense he supposed, it was getting very cold of an evening, no point in avoiding an ambush if you were already dead from exposure. Two figures sat close to the fire, one was unmistakeably Nico, the other was wreathed in a cloak and scarves that hid all bar his eyes. Behind them were the horses, patient and quiet this time, obviously the great animal that stalked the forest was nowhere near at present. A young man stood with them, tall with dark features he paced back and forth, as restless as the horses were placid. Foreigner, Ursus thought.

He swallowed, the acrid taste of bile still lined his mouth like a coat of fungus over cut bread, he spat into the ground and was about to lever himself onto his feet when he noticed another person. This one was sat much closer and was studying him intently, and it took him several heartbeats to realise that it was a woman. The climate was obviously not to her liking as she wore a great fur cloak that was pulled as closely around her as she could manage. Her face was uncovered though; again, this was somebody from a sunnier part of the world, her dark skin and arched features reminded him of his days as a squire, long, long ago. He had gone when the Silver Lances were sent to Bur in the south to aid the Chiran cause after a succession dispute amongst the princes of Vylanta had escalated into all-out war. As a man, no, a boy in his mid-teens he had found the exotic surroundings overwhelming but it was there that a woman not unlike the one staring at him introduced him to, well, all the wiles a woman can perform on a man. She was not this woman though,

ACT ONE : THE HUNT

first of all he was thinking back almost forty years, secondly, the girl he was recalling had been one of the hundreds of victims of the river palace massacre on what the locals now called the night of the scarlet moon. He remembered cradling her lifeless form in his arms, blood soaking into his tabard mingling with his tears. His first love, his first great loss.

This woman was different, he could see that now, more classically beautiful, yet those wide, dark eyes had none of the softness of his long lost love. This woman was diffident, guarded, and cold yet under all that he felt he detected something, a flame held in check, suppressed, restrained. Something in her life had changed her markedly, another clue to this was the fact that here, in this desolate and cold northern forest almost devoid of people she wore both jewellery and make up, kohl around her eyes, blue shading on her eyelids, more colouring on her lips. Of all the things he expected to see when he recovered somebody like this was just about the last.

Still, questions needed to be asked, he breathed deeply, the chill of night burning his lungs. "Who, in the name of Artorus, are you?"

"You can call me Siri." Her accent brought back more memories, laughter among the cypress trees, sweet figs and fragrant wine, sand between his toes, playful laughter and a soothing sea. "Do not touch your neck, the poultice is still cleaning your wound."

He could feel it, a lump of damp, heavy clay against his wounded neck. "What happened to me? What are you doing here? Are you from Bur?"

"Close to Bur," she replied. "Northern Fash. The man with your fellow by the fire is called Doul, it was he who asked me to drug you rather than kill you."

"Wait." He swayed and swung until he finally managed to stand, his legs still felt like they belonged to someone else. "You did this to me?" he indicated his neck.

She nodded.

"Why you..." He staggered toward her, fumbling for his sword. She looked a little surprised but not alarmed, taking a step backwards and pulling out a thin, slightly curved knife, the blade about a foot long. Things might have taken an unpleasant turn had not Nico spotted his old colleague and run over to see him, Doul being not far behind.

"Steady my friend, steady." Nico was almost laughing. He put out an arm that was both restraining and supporting, Ursus looked like he might topple over at any moment. "These are not our enemies, they only wanted to talk."

"Talk?" Ursus was barely mollified. "By poisoning me?"

"We had to do it." Doul spoke, his voice muffled by his scarf. "You might have tried to kill us on sight, by drugging one of you and having a second dart prepared we were both defending ourselves and avoiding needless fatalities."

"Think about it," Siri told him, "we could have killed you both before either of you had even seen us."

Ursus gave her a grudging nod. "Then can somebody explain what is going on here? Why didn't you kill us? You may never have a better chance."

"How would your deaths serve our purpose?" Doul asked him. "Especially as we both have common cause. Come, sit by the fire, we can speak with a little more comfort there."

Ursus looked at Nico who gave him a silent nod. Together they took their places around the fire, all except the young man with the horses, who remained where he was. Once all were comfortable Doul continued.

"We discovered the feeding place of the...creature before you did. We decided it best not to linger there but, as we withdrew we heard other horses, your horses approaching. So we hid, we watched, we listened. If you had been hostile to our cause, or even merely an obstacle we certainly would have killed you, but, as you talked we decided an alternative course of action would avail us all the better."

"They know about Eleanor," Nico said. "They hunt the leader of the men who snatched her."

"Yes," Doul said. "His name is Prasiak. Prasiak of Mazuras. He is a nobleman who commands a band of raiders who have long been a thorn in the side of your country. There are five or six of them and they are highly competent soldiers, a difficult proposition for two or three of us, but perhaps less so for five, do you not think so?"

"What he means," Nico interceded, "is that these people have their own set of skills; stealth, attacking from a distance, speed, and we have ours, fighting face to face, hand to hand, and that the likelihood of success for all of us is increased by our working together, as opposed to us getting in each other's way. They get to kill this man, we get my sister back, it seems a reasonable proposition, especially with a monster stalking the forest. What do you think?"

"Speaking of which," Ursus looked around nervously. "Is it really such

ACT ONE : THE HUNT

a good idea to light a fire with that thing around? It could be anywhere."

"We have the river just yards away and a ridge of rock and clay lies just through these trees, sheltering us and concealing the flame," Nico said. "Besides, we have no idea how this thing hunts, it might be through smell and hearing alone in which case it has many ways to find us and the fire makes no difference either way." Nico took a swig from his flask and stretched his legs out towards the fire. "As for those we hunt ourselves, our chance meeting has slowed us down today, they are some miles to the north still. But they are within striking distance, have no fear of that."

"To the north?" Ursus sounded intrigued. "They are moving north, upriver?"

Nico nodded.

"And you," he nodded at Doul. "Why would an Arshuman want to help us? I have killed more of your countrymen than I have grey hairs."

"I am from many nations," Doul answered. "Arshuman by birth certainly but I left as a young man and have lived in over a dozen countries over the years. I have no loyalty to their king; I go where the work is and countries at war are always very lucrative for those in my profession. That is the only reason I am here."

Ursus was unimpressed. "A corpse vulture then. Who has hired you to do this "work"?"

Doul was unruffled. "A noble, a direct rival to this Prasiak, from the city I mentioned earlier."

"And these other two?" Ursus growled, indicating Siri with a nod of his head.

"From Fash, in the south," Doul answered. "Siri has worked with me before, Zukan is her brother, and he tends the animals."

Ursus grunted and spat on to the ground, he then stood slowly and put his hands over the fire. "Nico, a word. In private."

Nico nodded at Doul, who nodded back, then the two knights strolled away from the clearing to stand under the nearby trees. As soon as they were out of sight of the fire Ursus grabbed Nico's shoulders and hissed urgently at him.

"Have you lost your senses boy! Do you really trust these people? They are paid killers! They will happily use us as meat shields, send us against this noble then kill us all when they get half a chance. You think they do not know about Eleanor and the money they could make out of her? Uba is playing you like a lute!"

Nico attempted a soothing smile. "You are, of course, right, but ranting and raving at them like you are wont to do will really get us nowhere. Besides, there is some merit in his words, working together makes sense...for now. Once we find Eleanor though this...alliance will be dissolved, and it will not be us that suffer as a result. We make them think they are using us when in truth, we are using them. Finding Eleanor is all that matters, and I would rather do it without having to worry about getting a poisoned dart in the throat. Agreed?"

Ursus paused, thinking, then slowly nodded his head. "Marauders, assassins, and some sort of monster running around, the Gods are getting some sport out of us. Very well, we might as well go back to them and talk, just never let them get behind you and never let the two of us sleep at the same time."

They returned to the fire and resumed their sitting positions, Ursus noting how amused both Doul and Siri appeared to be. He spoke to forestall any questions.

"You know why they are heading north?"

Doul nodded his head. "Well I have a theory."

"Which is?" Siri asked.

"Well they obviously want to remove our advantage regarding the horses. And they have succeeded, we will have to leave the beasts here."

Zukan cried out indignantly, Ursus just ignored him. "If I were them I would keep moving north until the river can be forded, then I would cross it and head south again. The thing is, I doubt that any of them know how the country lies north of here, I do, I have been here before, though it was many years ago."

Doul seemed delighted. "Excellent. Is there a place where they could be ambushed?"

"My recollection isn't that good, but there might be. What I do know is that we keep going, up and up and up, past rapids and falls until, finally we come to a waterfall that will be a real obstacle to them. Known as the Whiterush Maw it is a single sheer cataract far higher than all the others we will pass before it. Its walls will be difficult for them to climb, if we can catch them there it might well be to our advantage."

"And if we don't catch them there?" Nico asked.

"Then we have to climb it ourselves and when we do we will find a

ACT ONE : THE HUNT

change in our surroundings. For we will be walking through a great gorge, carved into the mountains, a strip of land between river and mountains that is narrow and full of pine trees and fallen rocks. The river though continues to be fierce for many more miles until finally we get to another series of falls where the river, finally, becomes shallow enough to wade across. That is where they will end up going."

"And how does this knowledge serve us?" Zukan spoke for the first time, his voice hostile, he was still obviously not reconciled with leaving the horses behind.

"Because," Ursus grimaced, annoyed with the interruption, "I said that the river was fierce before it becomes shallow at the falls, fierce but not uncrossable, because, at some points it becomes very narrow. A man with a rope around him could swim across and secure a line. We could all get over the river that way and be lying in wait for them on the other side when they finally get around to crossing themselves. That is the way to set an ambush."

He stopped then, scanning the faces of all present, pleased to see that they were all suitably intrigued, maybe even impressed. It was Doul that spoke next. "So you think we can either get them at this Whiterush Maw or where the river above it narrows, if we have crossed the river first and they are not expecting us."

"Exactly," Ursus confirmed.

"I like it," Doul said after a few moments thought.

"I like it too," said a smiling Nico. "Every time I think your brain has atrophied you surprise me."

"It sounds reasonable enough," Siri said. "But I have one question."

"As do I," said her brother. The two of them then asked it simultaneously, brother and sister thinking alike, and not for the first time.

"Who gets to swim over the river?"

"Well," Ursus asked, "who amongst us can swim?"

"I can," said Siri.

"But I cannot," said Doul.

"Neither can I," Nico added. Zukan too shook his head before Nico continued. "But I believe that you can Ursus, and you know it is not part of our code to let others accomplish what we can achieve ourselves."

Ursus grunted. "Artorus strike me down as a fool, it appears that I have just built my pyre, added the kindling and doused myself in oil," he admitted. "As if I wasn't feeling sick enough already."

THE FANGS OF THE FEN SNAKE

"But perhaps we will catch them at the Whiterush Maw first," Nico added, obviously feeling the need to ease the bad humour of his companion.

"Perhaps," Ursus said, with little conviction. So, he was shortly about to try and drown himself in the company of those who would slit his throat as soon as look at him. And all this to save a spoiled little brat whose face would crack if she stopped scowling, the knights of the Silver Lance lifelong pursuit of honour could, at times, take very strange forms indeed.

ACT ONE : THE HUNT

13

The sky was ghostly white, scarred only by twisting, wraithlike clouds when Shak and his companions resumed their journey north. They prepared and packed with their usual methodical efficiency, though of course things would not have been fully complete without the by now expected grumble from Lady Eleanor.

She had, as ever, been the last to stir from her bedroll. After stretching extravagantly, sitting up and looking around with bleary eyes she punctured the bustling silence with something close to indissoluble relish.

"Ugh! And was I having such a wonderful dream! I was the wandering maiden from the Tale of the elusive prince and the enchanted forest. I had just laid my head down in a fragrant bower of green leaves and wild flowers constructed by the water fairies. Then I wake up and what is the truth? What sort of bower do I actually have? Mud and twigs and sharp pebbles digging into my back...and more Keth spawned insects! Why are you all ignoring me?"

"We are busy," Dormouse told her with a smile.

"Busy! You are supposed to be looking after me! I am hungry. Where is my breakfast?"

"Later," said Shak. "We need to move immediately, for all we know your brother is just downhill from here, waiting for us."

"Really? Perhaps I should just give him a scream. A really, really, loud scream."

"Stauncher," Shak said wearily. "The gag."

"You wouldn't da..." Shak shot her a look that said he very much would dare, so Eleanor shut up, pursing her lips into an angry scowl. Shak regarded her for a moment.

"Perhaps we should just gag you anyway. Anything for some peace."

He walked away from her, leaving her pouting in frustration. She tried combing her hair, but it was a losing struggle. Slipping the comb back into her waist pouch she spoke again, but this time quietly and only to herself.

"And I smell."

From the same pouch, she pulled a tiny, stoppered, flask. Opening it she poured a miniscule amount of clear liquid onto her finger, which she then began to dab on her throat and behind her ears. Dead Eyes noticed her,

ACT ONE : THE HUNT

enquiring politely as to its nature.

"Rose oil," Eleanor told her defensively. "A nice smell to hide a worse one."

"You do not smell," the elf told her, "the fresh air and the breeze keeps us all smelling clean. It is not like the city where odours cannot be dispersed; besides, in our tales, all dragons are supposed to like roses. The scent attracts them. You are setting yourself up to be a tasty repast for the beast."

"Seriously?" Eleanor looked horrified.

"Oh absolutely." Dead Eyes slung her pack over her shoulder and walked away. She was laughing. Eleanor narrowed her eyes and poked her tongue at her receding back. "Never trust a Wych," she whispered under her breath.

"And never ever trust a Wych that trusts a human!" Dead Eyes called back musically, without turning around.

Eleanor made to stamp her foot, thought better of it and with a frustrated little sigh started to gather up her things.

****

As it transpired no-one was waiting for them as they resumed their journey along the riverbank. They were still climbing steadily, negotiating rocks pitted by spray and lichen, taking a course through wooded gullies, trying to keep it difficult for any pursuers whilst ensuring that they were not being too hampered by the terrain themselves. Slowly they were being forced away from the riverbank as the rocks were becoming larger, more slippery, almost impossible to climb, and taking to the sloping woodlands inland. Here, the forests of oak, birch and ash had all but gone, replaced by conifers and wide brakes of fern browning at the approach of winter. There was no sun, the earth was hard and unforgiving and so nobody was particularly surprised as the first light flurries of snow started to drift between the dark trees.

"Gods bake my bollocks," Stan wiped a flake of it from his face. "This is a wild, desolate place. No place for a man to die."

"It is the loneliness," Stauncher said. "Dying is dying, no place is a good place for that. But dying alone, with no one to remember you or even knowing where you are, that is a sobering thought."

"Can you both stop talking about dying?" Dormouse implored. "Talking about it makes it happen. Everybody knows that."

THE FANGS OF THE FEN SNAKE

Stan stopped and gave Dormouse a look that could only be described as one of evaluation. "For an educated fellow, young Dormouse, you do sometimes talk an impressive heap of cow dung. You are a soldier, my friend, Xhenafa sits at your shoulder at all times, like a great, life sucking, withered...bat."

"Bat?" Stauncher enquired, with a twinkle in his eye.

"There are breeds of bat that suck blood," Dead Eyes pointed out; "two such types lived in my home valley."

"Did they suck your blood?" Dormouse sounded alarmed.

"No," she smiled at him, "I have eaten quite a few of them mind."

"What did they taste like?" Eleanor wrinkled her nose.

"Chicken."

"Disgusting," Eleanor continued, "I could never eat something like that."

"That is because you have never been hungry," Stan corrected her. "I have eaten rats and mice before now."

"I had a slug once," Stauncher said. "I wouldn't recommend it. Or shoe leather, tried that as well. Boiled it first to soften it, still took me a week to swallow it."

"Insects, you should try them," Dead Eyes told him, "beetles especially, they can be surprisingly meaty."

Eleanor and Dormouse were gagging by now. Shak was smiling. "Well that has put us rich folks in our place, moan if the bread is a bit stale, don't we?"

"They are making it up," Dormouse said, "they must be."

Stan shook his head at him, Stauncher just laughed, then they continued on in silence.

Soon after they had the breakfast/lunch Eleanor had been clamouring for, which was little more than dried fruit, oatcake, and a thin strip of salted meat. Shak and Dead Eyes went back to the river, to see if it could possibly be forded soon. It was as wide and fierce as ever.

"We are digging a hole," Shak said. "And if this river doesn't narrow soon we will be throwing ourselves into it."

"It will change," Dead Eyes reassured him. "It is being swollen by tributaries at the moment, we have crossed a couple this morning. When we get past them we will be able to cross."

"True," Shak said, "but WHEN will we get past them? Will the

ACT ONE : THE HUNT

assassins catch up with us first?"

"Maybe," Dead Eyes shrugged. "But they will be as weary as us when they do. And weary people make mistakes."

"As long as those mistakes come from them and not us, I will be happy." Shak turned away from the grey, foam tipped waters into which squally flurries of snowflakes were falling and dying, and disappeared back into the tall, gloomy forest. Dead Eyes lingered a little longer, shielding her eyes as she stared upriver, willing her eyes to penetrate the misty, grey blanket that appeared to be slowly smothering them. Finally, she saw, and heard something, shaking her head as she did so.

"That is not good," she said to herself, before following Shak through the shadowy trees.

****

Snow brings its own silence. Though the conifer woods brooded and sighed at the caresses of the eddying winds, at ground level the inch or two of snow that had settled smothered all intrusive sounds, save the crunch of boots and the deep, irregular breaths of the party as they climbed, steadily climbed, moving from foothills to the skirts of the mountains proper. They all noticed that they were now trudging through a deepening valley, as they climbed uphill, on either side of them, to east and west towering ridges of mud and rock rose high above them, cutting off what little was left of the sun. As they walked they kept going to the riverbank to check that it could now finally be crossed, always with the same discouraging result, and Dead Eyes had news for them, news that their own ears soon corroborated.

"There is a large waterfall ahead," she had told them, "it is much bigger than the rapids we have passed so far, if it is wide, it may be impossible to scale, we might have no choice but to turn back."

There had been a silence for a moment, as everybody digested the news, then Shak had spoken for them all. "Well we have come this far, let us assess things once we get there. If we have to change our plan then that is the will of the Gods, maybe it is a good thing to turn and fight, rather than run all the time."

They continued on, soon the dull, booming, roar was unmistakeable, even to Stauncher's ears, for he was well known for being the deafest of the group. It was beginning to get dark, the merest hint of purple touching the edges of the sky when finally, mercifully, the snowfall finally ceased.

THE FANGS OF THE FEN SNAKE

Encouraged by this Shak called a halt, it was time to dish out some instructions.

"It is late afternoon now, we need to start looking for a place to camp, there is no sign of our pursuers so at least..."

Then though he had to stop, for it seemed his words had tempted fate. As soon as he said there was no sign of pursuit they all heard it, the high pitched call of a man, and the call was from somewhere close, just minutes away, to the west, on the slope of the valley.

Instantly Shak started whispering orders. "Dead Eyes, a wide arc to the north, Stauncher, the same to the south, Stan, you are with me, and Dormouse..."

"Yes sir?" Dormouse asked, forgetting in his excitement that he did not need to use the epithet.

"That ditch over there, behind the fern brake, you stay there with Eleanor, do not let her escape and guard her with your life."

Dormouse nodded, took Eleanor by the hand, and started to lead her away, expertly concealing his disappointment at not being awarded a more significant role. Part of the ditch Shak had alluded to was sheltered by both trees and ferns and was largely free from snow. He directed Eleanor to this dry area and bade her crouch down, which she did, pulling her cloak tightly around her with an angry frown. Dormouse stood over her, sword drawn, mostly in cover, eyes boring through trees and ferns in a vain attempt to see exactly what was going on.

****

They were both big men, Shak and Stan, the former tall and lean, the latter not the equal in height, but greater in muscle and bulk, yet both of them could move swiftly over wild terrain, making little noise as they did so. They headed for the source of that call, keeping behind the cover of the trees, eating up the ground, eyes intense, ears pricked, alert to the tiniest sign of what lay ahead of them. The land ahead was gently rising, making concealment difficult, so, as they started to hear more voices, the voices of several different men, they started to crawl on their bellies, moving from shadow to shadow until finally, hiding behind a cluster of stones split by hard frosts and coated in yellow lichen, they could observe the scene ahead of them.

It was a clearing between the trees, covered in snow kicked up and

ACT ONE : THE HUNT

dirtied by the mailed boots of several men. Both Shak and Stan, experienced raiders and infiltrators counted eight of them, no, nine. The eight were the sort of men that Shak was expecting to see, hard faced, bearded, cloaked, carrying a range of weapons, and wearing armour that was a mix of mail and leather. Shak did notice a shield, fashioned of wood and hide resting against a tree. It bore the device of a waterfall, the insignia of Haslan falls, so Shak knew that he was looking at Baron Fenchard's men. As Shak had told Stauncher the night before, they might be allies now but they were once enemies, and he had no desire to meet them face to face. He would have signalled Stan to withdraw and leave this hard bitten gang to their own devices, if it weren't for the ninth man in the clearing, a man who commanded his complete attention.

It was an old man, no, an ancient man surely into his eighth decade. He was spindly as a winter twig and pale as a waning moon, his wizened face encircled by a mass of wild, untamed hair up top and a bushy, curly beard down below. Both hair and beard were so profuse it was difficult to tell where hair ended and beard began. His eyes were large, deep set, and a hazy blue; and they moved, flitting from place to place with the speed of a bird on the wing. His nose was flat and splayed and his lips so thin they might as well not be there at all. His teeth, at least those teeth that remained were the colour of tannin, jutting out at a myriad of angles from his shrunken gums. Most importantly of all though were his clothes, for he wore the dark grey robes of an Artoran monk and the red belt of a monk that had taken the vow of solitude. He was a hermit, sworn to spend between one and ten years in the wilderness, fasting, praying, trying to commune with the Gods, enduring deliberate privations in the hope that the Gods would actually come to him and give him knowledge of the world and cement the meaning of his faith. Each hermit, if they survived the experience had, upon their return to the monastery, undertaken to write of their experience in the book of isolation, so that all the order could understand the Gods just a little better.

Looking at the man, his robes bulging and billowing over his withered frame, Shak surmised that he was much nearer his tenth year of solitude than his first. His red belt meant that he was to be left alone, not helped, not fed, and not hurt but in truth, in this war, even holy men had suffered at the blades of their enemies. This man was probably from the monastery of Frach Menthon, a place that had been sacked and burned just months before. He probably didn't know that his brothers were dead, unless these men had told him, and Shak got the impression that they were not there to give him news from home. And there was one final thing, his robes were stained and dirty and from the right sleeve protruded the hermit's skinny wrist and long, thin, yellow nailed fingers but from the left sleeve...nothing. The sleeve just hung limply; the man had no arm at least up to his elbow. A strange thing Shak thought, surviving for years out here with just one arm, this tiny old crow was obviously a lot tougher and more resourceful than he looked.

"What do they want with the old fool?" Stan whispered to him, obviously as bemused by the scene as Shak was.

"No idea. Listen. They are talking to him." Shak was straining to hear the words, but they were as close as they could get without giving their presence away. The hiss of the wind, the croak of birds high in the trees, none of these things helped him but finally, with an effort, he began to make out the gist of the conversation.

The hermit was standing close to the centre of the clearing having to field questions from two of the other men. The rest of the group were sitting close by eating or cleaning their weapons, though all were listening intently to proceedings. The first man asking the questions was burly, bearded, cloaked, and he spoke with a West Chiran accent, a mercenary no doubt. The other man was shorter, powerfully built with dark hair and brown eyes. He sounded like a local man, and it was he who was doing the talking right now.

"Now, Father Oswold, you remember me yes? Ham, of the Tanarese army? We met recently and talked, remember?"

The old man nodded. "Yes, Ham, I remember. But who is this...ruffian beside you? A stranger yes, with strange eyes and a strange voice. He does not look a friendly fellow."

"I am not a friendly fellow." The Chiran spoke, his voice hard and impatient." And I have told you a thousand times already that my name is Yaki. Now, when you spoke to Ham before you mentioned treasure. We want to know more about this treasure and where it is. Tell us now and we won't have to drag you back to camp with us. It would be a hard walk for an old man. You may not survive the journey. Understand?"

The old man waved his scrawny arm up at the skies, his eyes looking round wildly, seemingly at nothing. "And Artorus smote the demons of fire, and as their flames were quenched each demon in its destruction cried out in agony untold, for each was once the soul of a man, a man damned to the underworld by a lifetime of iniquity. Beware, o man of threats, beware that such a fate does not befall you!"

ACT ONE : THE HUNT

He spoke with such vehemence in his thin voice that Yaki took a step backwards and looked up to the sky himself, almost as though he was expecting to see a god frowning at him. He let Ham continue the conversation.

"No threats were intended Father Oswold," Ham gave a sideways glance at his companion. "We are just...interested in the things that you told me before. You were heading for the river when we caught up with you just now, were you going anywhere interesting?"

A change of tack from Ham, and it appeared to work. "Where was I going?" Oswold pondered those words for a moment before recollecting. "Why yes, I was going to the cave again, if I can find it. You see I made a terrible mistake, years ago and I was wondering if I could find a way of rectifying it. I thought that though I had made a mistake that there would be no consequences, but there will be you see, there will be, for the beast survived, despite it all it survived. All my fault, Gods forgive me, all my fault."

Ham, not surprisingly, looked confused. "The beast? The creature my fellows are hunting?"

Oswold gave him a wistful look. "The beast yes, the dragon."

Ham and Yaki looked at each other. "You are saying the beast is a dragon?"

"Yes, yes." The old man hopped from foot to foot. "A dragon. I thought that by finding all that wealth in the caves again there might be something there to help it. Such a clever beast does not belong in this forest with winter showing its teeth."

The word "wealth" had pricked their ears. "Is there much of this wealth?" Ham asked, as though the matter was a passing trifle.

Oswold nodded, giving them a gap toothed smile.

"And can you take us to it?"

At this though, Oswold became more guarded, shaking his head vigorously. "No, you could not help me, you would not know what to look for, it is best I go alone."

"Keth's teeth!" Yaki hissed. "How do you know we cannot help you?"

Oswold gave him a look that was both smug and patronising. "Camille has not seen fit to bless you with great wisdom, that is obvious to us all. And yet it is only the wise, or the scholar, that can aid me, for in truth, I do not know what I seek either. A scholar or even one of the Wych peoples from the forest could perhaps aid me, for the answer I seek lies in all probability inside a Wych artefact of some sort."

THE FANGS OF THE FEN SNAKE

Shak and Stan exchanged a glance that said, "well we have one of the Wych peoples with us." Ham, meanwhile, continued to press Oswold.

"Are we talking about Wych gold here? You know of a consignment of Wych treasure?"

But Oswold was wise to them now. "All you want to do is plunder and thieve and steal! Well I will not be a party to it! Camille herself once said that all that shines one day ends up dull and defiled the next. Greed has brought low many great men and many meaner men, the only thing that needs enrichment is the soul..."

"Yes, yes," Ham was now as impatient as Yaki; "but any wealth would not be for our personal gain but to help the war effort. It would go to Baron Fenchard, to aid..."

Oswold shook his head. "No, no, I have heard enough of this. I am going to my bed and shall resume my journey in the morning." He made to walk away from the two men and head in a direction that would have brought him close to Shak and Stan. Yaki though, moved to block his path.

"Sorry old man," the big Chiran said, "but you are leading us to the gold whether you like it or not. Ham, the two boys we sent out earlier, Stresh and the youngster..."

"Kellan." Ham replied. "They should be back soon. They were only going to the river to freshen the water skins and look for Oswold there."

"Yes," Yaki said. "When they return both you and the boy can get back to Teague, tell him to follow us. While you do that both this hermit and the rest of us can make a start for this treasure, you should catch up soon enough."

Ham looked uneasy, two of Teague's loyal men sent away while the mainly mercenary soldiers left were free to do some treasure hunting. Oswold glared at Yaki, tried to pass him before being blocked again, Ham's jaw worked as though he was thinking of a pithy reply to Yaki's suggestion. He never got to speak it though for, at that moment, two men, one tall and slim, the other tall and stocky breezed into the clearing with an air of carefree nonchalance.

"Well hello there," Shak said breezily. "So you have found the hermit have you? Well done, for I have many vexing matters of faith to test him with."

****

As they had watched the conversation progress both Shak and Stan had become increasingly intrigued by what the old man was saying. Sense,

ACT ONE : THE HUNT

and cold, hard logic told them both to stay where they were, to let this war band take the old man and use him to whatever end, but of course they both knew that the "end" would, like as not, be an unhappy one for him. So what? Shak had thought, this was hardly their business after all, but at the same time he was acutely aware that the path these people wanted to take and their own would probably cross soon enough. When the old man tried to leave the clearing he was heading north east, just as they would be doing. Better to get this encounter over and done with before these two other men they had spoken about arrived to bolster their numbers. So, with a nod and a roll of the eyes to each other, both Shak and Stan determined to brazen it out, at least they had Dead Eyes and Stauncher hiding close by if need be.

****

Instantly the men in the clearing leapt to their feet and drew their weapons. The man called Yaki carried a short sword so beloved of most Chirans, Ham had a dagger, amongst the others Shak noted a couple of spiked cudgels, some brutal looking axes and, most worryingly, a fellow at the back of the crowd carrying a bow. Shak hoped that Dead Eyes had taken note of that particular problem or both he and Stan could be dead men before they could swing their weapons in anger. He touched the pommel of his sword, still sheathed, for reassurance. One thing that did please him though was that Oswold had moved to stand alongside them both, it looked like a degree of trust had been established already. Having said that he rather wished that the hermit would move a bit closer to Stan for he was, sadly, a most pungent fellow.

"Who, in the name of the furnace, are you?" Yaki snarled at them bringing his sword up so that it almost tickled Shak's chin. Both he and Stan though kept their weapons at their belts, there were eight of them after all, no point provoking a conflict without need.

"Arshumans!" Ham hissed at them, spitting into the snow.

"You mean, your Arshuman allies," Shak smiled disingenuously, "and we have been looking for this hermit for some days, garrison commander Ogun wishes to talk to him back at Tantala."

"Why?" Yaki had a face like a thunderstorm.

"Why?" Oswold asked, spittle flying from his mouth to hit Shak on the arm.

"Because you are pretty much the only hermit left wandering these woods." Stan continued the narrative. "You know the lie of the land up here better than anyone, Ogun would like a map drawn, a reliable one for a change. Also he has heard of this beast, thought you might know something about it, something to help us."

"I am not leaving the forest." Oswold spoke firmly, bony chin jutting like the prow of a ship.

"Well," Shak shrugged his shoulders, "we were told to take you by force if you refused, but perhaps a compromise can be worked out between us."

"He is not your find Arshuman," Ham growled. "He is ours and he is helping us."

"But surely that is master Oswold's decision." Stan loosened the axe at his belt, making sure that all could see him do so.

"Now lads," Shak tried to strike a diplomatic tone. "We are all on the same side now, remember. Arshuman command wants to speak to the holy man, when they have done so he will be returned here, you will know where to find him."

"I will never be on the same side as you, Arshuman," Ham positively bristled. "And as for the hermit, no doubt you will give him to us once you have found and taken this treasure he keeps talking about. He stays with us."

"Treasure?" Stan laughed then spat on to the dirty snow at his feet. "We have no interest in treasure. Your Baron Fenchard though has been leeching it off the Arshuman coffers for months now. Without our largesse both he, and yourselves for that matter, are all dead men. Show some respect to your benefactors, we know your price after all."

"Why you..." Ham would have struck at Stan had not Yaki put out his arm to stop him. "Arshuman," he said coldly, "you are outnumbered here. Just keep your weapons sheathed and go. We have no interest in you, we just want the old man."

"But as my colleague said earlier," Shak was still trying to sound reasonable, though Yaki's reluctance to fight was interesting, he had obviously noticed how formidable both he and Stan appeared to be, outnumbered or no. "Surely it is Father Oswold's decision as to who he goes with."

"Or if he goes with anybody at all," Oswold sputtered like fat in a hot pan. "I came out here for solitude, for silence, to understand the world shaped by the Gods, not to put up with a mob of angry, armed men. Kill each other if you want to, give Xhenafa all the work he desires, I have somewhere to go and

ACT ONE : THE HUNT

shelter to find before nightfall. Good day to all of you."

He started to shuffle out of the clearing, Ham, Yaki, and Stan too dumbfounded for the moment to stop him. Shak however, had other ideas.

"Pity you are leaving holy man; I could have introduced you to our Wych."

Oswold's bony shoulders stiffened. He stopped walking and slowly turned to look at Shak, the strangest gleam in his eyes.

"You know of a Wych?"

Shak nodded. "A good friend of ours. Care to meet her?"

Oswold scrutinised Shak's face, as though trying to see if he was being deceived. "Are you lying to me?"

"No," Shak said. "Look at Stan here, have you ever seen a more honest face? I am not lying am I Stan?"

"No," Stan said, "we know an elf, I mean, Wych."

Oswold still hesitated. Finally though, a bizarre, gap toothed smile crept over his features. "Very well," he said, "take me to this Wych, then perhaps we can talk."

"Not so fast," Yaki was all belligerence again, his earlier talk of compromise seemingly forgotten. "You were given the chance to leave peaceably, you didn't take it. The two of you can still go now, I will grant you your lives, but if you try and leave with the old man I will hang you from the trees suspended by your own innards." He levelled his blade at Shak, a deadly purpose in his eyes.

Shak nodded to Stan, both men's hands were now firmly on their weapons. Oswold crouched on his knees, hand raised over his head, as though to shield it.

"Artorus spare me from such brutal ingrates," he whined, at nobody but himself.

"The holy man comes with us," Shak said icily. "Go back to your bedroll."

For all the men in the glade there followed a moment of total pellucid stillness. A moment in which nothing moved or stirred. The wind froze in the treetops, the birds held their song in their throats, the distant river stopped churning over rocks and stones. Silence. Stillness. No breathing, no pounding heart, just clammy, anticipatory fear. It seemed to last an age of men, mountains were birthed, reaching up to touch the clouds before being eroded into dust. Rivers burst from the hills, all effusive rapture, flowing ebulliently

THE FANGS OF THE FEN SNAKE

over fields, carving out great tree lined valleys before spilling into deserts and being baked dry by the sun, it felt longer than all these things. Yet of course it wasn't, it was less than the flutter of an eye, yet each man there thought a thousand thoughts in that time, of family, of home, of gold, of joy, of fear, for they all knew what was going to happen next.

The moment was broken by a sound, a sound familiar to them all, a taught bowstring being released, it was followed the soft sucking sound of a projectile streaking through the fragile, crisp air, everybody looked around to try and see it, but nobody did, not till it hit home.

A choking, gargling sound, an expression of white eyed terror, the sole archer amongst Ham and Yaki's retainers let his bow drop from his nerveless, twitching fingers. His companions swivelled rapidly to look at him, what they saw was a man slip to his knees, then crash on to his back, twitching and gasping, clutching at the shaft piercing his throat. It was an arrow, an arrow fletched with iridescent crow feathers. All the human archers Shak knew of used goose feathers in their arrows, only one person to his knowledge used crow, and she was not a human.

"And so the Wych introduces herself," he muttered to Oswold. And after that, the time for words were over.

Fenchard's men, seeing their companion dying on the ground, were distracted for a fraction of a second, time that both Shak and Stan had to use if they were to stay alive.

Shak used it to pull out his sword and crack its glittering guard and pommel against the back of Yaki's head, even now after years of guerrilla fighting he couldn't lower himself to just stab the man in the back. To his surprise Stan was the same, he had slipped on his lucky knuckles and used them to punch Ham viciously in the kidneys before putting an arm around his throat and using his other hand to twist the knife out of Ham's palm, it falling point first to stick into the snow. Yaki meanwhile had recovered and turned to thrust his blade at Shak's chest. Shak batted it away with a clash of ringing steel before using his long legs to kick Yaki in the testicles, that was something he could lower himself to. Mercifully, the man was not armoured there and, as Yaki knelt groaning on the ground Shak raised his sword above the man's head ready to strike a fatal blow. Looking round he saw another axe armed man writhing on the ground with an arrow piercing his leg, Dead Eyes had swiftly struck again.

Seemingly from nowhere Stauncher had appeared to ambush one of

ACT ONE : THE HUNT

the others too, his knife bloody as the man he had attacked pitched face first onto the ground, lacing the dirty brown snow with ribbons of gushing scarlet. Two dead, one wounded, two immobilised and three others backing off with weapons drawn, now the time for words had returned.

"Drop your weapons." Shak gave the order. "You know what will happen to these two if you don't."

Axes, knives, and cudgels were thrown into the snow. Stauncher, who had apparently found a sort of sack amongst the men's belongings, busied himself with picking up the weapons and chucking them in. From the corner of his eye Shak could see that Dead Eyes had emerged from her cover, arrow still fitted to bow.

"There you go, holy man," Shak addressed the cringing Oswold. "The Wych we were talking about. You can have a proper chat once we have sent these fellows on their way."

"My arrows," Dead Eyes reminded him, "I want them back."

Fenchard's men were then grouped together and made to kneel, back to back, with their hands crossed behind them. Stan stood over them, muttering threats whilst Stauncher rifled the camp stores and Dead Eyes first withdrew her arrow from the injured man's leg (whilst casually ignoring the looks of hatred she was getting), before moving over to where the other man lay still, arrow still sticking through his throat.

"He is not dead," she told Shak. "Still breathing." She pulled out her knife to finish him off.

"No," Shak ordered. "Not yet. Stauncher, can you do anything for him?"

Stauncher came over, examined the man carefully before shaking his head at Shak, if there was life there it was barely noticeable and, seemingly, not salvageable.

So Shak gave Dead Eyes the nod.

They moved quickly for darkness was encroaching and the patchy snow was starting to glow with an eerie luminosity. Soon, with the camp stripped of useful items and all weapons stored in the sack they were ready to move.

Shak went up to Yaki. "Move, all of you, out of this valley and back to your main camp in the west, we know it is there, we saw the fires last night. Be grateful that we are supposed to be on the same side, or the wolves would be picking at your bones right now."

THE FANGS OF THE FEN SNAKE

"Same side?" Ham spat extravagantly. "I will never be on the same side as you dogs."

Yaki fixed Shak with a murderous stare. "Be grateful that your little Dregg whore was there to tip the balance this time. You should have killed me. Next time I will not be so unprepared and then," he pointed a finger Shak's way. "I will feed you your own ears before I kill you."

"Get moving," Shak told him, "or I will have our little "Dregg" use all of you for archery practice."

Grumbling, moving slowly, some mouthing curses and promises of vile retribution, they started shuffling uphill, leaving the valley behind. Shak watched them until they had disappeared from view, the others standing with him.

"Dregg," Dead Eyes said flatly. "Haven't been called that in a long time."

"I wonder how many bad names we have for your people," Stan sounded distracted, seemingly more concerned in checking the edge on his axe.

"Not as many as we have for you," she observed brightly. "I don't mind Wych though, sounds like we are there to be feared."

"Well I think there are one more group of men fearing you today," Shak blew into his hands. "Right, we need to move, we have left a feast for crows, wolves, ghouls, or dragons in this clearing, and I don't want to be around when they get peckish."

"Those men will be back," Dead Eyes said. "With reinforcements too, perhaps you should have killed them all here."

"No," Shak corrected her. "That would have been…messy. Now they have to go back and report to their leader, it will delay their return and hopefully we will be over the river by then. Besides, I doubt if father Oswold, being a holy man, could be persuaded to side with a bunch of cold blooded butchers."

"You are right there," Oswold was hovering at Dead Eyes shoulder. "Might I touch you my dear?"

"Why?" Dead Eyes said suspiciously.

"Because I have heard that the skin of a Wych is smooth and waxy, and cold, like you have no blood inside you."

She narrowed her eyes and put out her hand for him. He stroked it tentatively, as though it might be poisonous to the touch.

ACT ONE : THE HUNT

"There is no real difference," she told him.

"No, no." His eyes gleamed as he continued to paw her. "Very similar to humans, but it is smooth, very smooth. Do you have warts?"

"No!" she recoiled in horror.

"Oh," He sounded disappointed; "I have several, you can touch them if you want. They are very lumpy, and quite hard."

"Maybe later," she almost winced.

"Chat later," Shak intervened. "Right now we need to get back to Dormouse, find somewhere to dump those weapons and to make camp, the darkness proceeds apace."

"I can help with that," Oswold said. "There is a hollow tree close by for the weapons."

"And the camp?" Shak asked, eyebrow raised.

"Ha!" Oswold gave a dry, husky laugh. "We hermits, we are a community! We have many caves, many holes, and now I am the only one left I have them all. And when we are safe we can talk; I can talk to the Wych lady. Do you have a name?" he asked her.

"Dead Eyes," she groaned.

"Odd name. Still, I suppose Wych names are."

"It is not my real name."

"You have many names? I must learn them all!"

She groaned again.

"Come on then," Shak chivvied them on. "Father, show us a place to camp, we just have to collect our companions first."

"Yes," Stauncher laughed. "Poor Dormouse. She has probably got him plucking a goose to make her a feather pillow!"

And so they left the clearing to find Dormouse and Eleanor. And, as it transpired, they got to them not a moment too soon.

193

14

Dormouse was cold. Eleanor was cold. Dormouse was stoic about it; Eleanor was rather less so, sitting there, rubbing her hands together, mumbling just loud enough to be heard.

"Abducted, cold, and miserable. Why me? I mean I pray three times a day...sometimes. I never do anything to displease the Gods, I mean I do think about things that would displease them but I never DO anything. Perhaps that is it, I am being punished for my thoughts, but then I cannot control my thoughts, nobody can. Besides, you should be able to think bad thoughts for how can you make moral judgements without considering all possibilities? It is unfair, so unfair. And I bet the ransom I will fetch will be a pittance anyway."

"Lady Lasgaart," Dormouse tried to sound courteous. "Do you not think there is a savage wonder in our surroundings? Look about you, the high trees, the soft, white snow, and the stars are coming out too. And the sounds, the wind, the birds and, oddly enough, the near silence, can you not hear them and yes, out here the absence of sound can be as compelling as sound itself."

Eleanor sniffed, briefly looked around, then put her head in her hands. "You are just telling me to shut up aren't you?"

He smiled. "No. not at all, well maybe just a little."

"You wouldn't be the first," her voice had a maudlin quality. "I may have some status where I come from, but it is not as high as others. I have been told what to do all my life."

"Same here," he agreed, "it is one of the reasons I came out here, to get away. Anyway, where do you come from exactly, my knowledge of Tanarese nobility is a little...threadbare."

He sounded genuinely curious, so she was happy to oblige him. "My family, the Lasgaarts, hold a lot of land just south of these mountains, either side of the river Kada, many miles to the west. Our traditional enemy is not Arshuma but the Vinoyen family who hold the land to the immediate south of us. The boundaries between our territories, which manor, castle or town belongs to whom have been disputed between us for centuries, often bloodily. As for me, about four years ago I was gifted a manor in the valley of the Bear river, which runs into the Kada on its western side, so it is close to the lands

ACT ONE : THE HUNT

over which this war is fought, but not actually in them. It is a safe haven, a refuge, a place where I have been learning how to run my own household, ready for the day I get married, whenever that may be."

"You sound like you like it there."

To his surprise, she seemed to brighten up at his words. She actually smiled and to his even greater surprise, he saw that she had a very pleasant smile.

"Yes," she told him. "It is a beautiful house, surrounded by apple, pear and cherry orchards. The cherry blossom in spring is so beautiful, I love to walk through the orchard then, the smell of the flowers are so sweet, so subtle, if I could turn it into a perfume I would be feted in the Grand Duke's court. And the river sings so! Never angry, always gentle, musical, the sun shines off it and makes it seem like a stream of pure holy light. To sit under the shade of a tree, stare at the water, sipping a light pear cider under the late afternoon sun; life is made for such moments, is it not?"

He nodded. "I think we like different things, but you are good with words, you make it sound like a beautiful place. In happier times I would be glad to visit it."

"And in happier times you would be most welcome." She was still smiling but her voice had resumed its earlier, more forlorn tone.

"Oh!" he put his hand to his mouth, "but you are getting married, so you have to leave it behind. I am so sorry!"

She shook her head. "The manor is part of my dowry, I still intend to spend the best months of the year there, if I can, if my husband permits it." She swallowed before resuming, now there was a doubtful note in her voice too. "Still, my husband has lands in the Marassan chalk hills, and they too are said to be picturesque. I am sure I can adapt to new surroundings."

He gave her a slight bow. "I think you are far more self-reliant than you pretend to be my lady. And tougher too, when the occasion demands."

"Like now you mean? I am not so..."

She had begun to ease herself into a standing position, but froze, her lips slightly parted, for once struck dumb. For, some yards behind Dormouse, two figures were standing. They were little more than shadows to her, covered in the darkness spread by the lower boughs of the trees but their silence was unnerving. She stood finally, still staring at them, till Dormouse understood what was going on. Then he too turned to face them.

And then he drew his sword.

THE FANGS OF THE FEN SNAKE

"Who are you?" he called to them, trying not to sound too nervous; his sword however waved uncertainly in his hand.

One of the men strode forward. A man in his prime, moustached, a warrior, his grip on his sword was much surer than the man he faced. The person behind him was more like Dormouse, young, wavering, happy to let his companion take the lead.

"More to the point," the experienced warrior said, "who exactly are you? Still, if you want introductions you can call me Stresh. My friend here is called Kellan and we are patrolling OUR lands and purging it of enemies. Are you an enemy, boy? Is the girl one too?"

Dormouse did not reply, perhaps his mouth was too dry. Eleanor however stared at the men in apparent confusion. Two men, armed, one of them obviously far more confident and capable than Dormouse, and they were both obviously her countrymen, would she ever get a better opportunity to be rescued than this? But then...Dormouse; what would these men do to him? Yet she was a Tanarese patriot, she could not just stand and let things be decided for her. But what about Dormouse? A pleasant, no, he was nicer than just pleasant, and yet it was her duty to speak, her country was at war and Dormouse had abducted her.

"My name," she spoke as clearly as her nerves, and her guilt allowed, "is Lady Eleanor Lasgaart. I have been abducted by Arshuman renegades; they were taking me to the occupied lands for ransom. I would appreciate being returned to my own family."

Dormouse shot her a look of both panic and anger. The other men moved closer. Eleanor mouthed her next words slowly, to Dormouse, so they were easy to understand.

"Let...me...go."

He bit his lip, sweaty hand on the hilt of his sword, the two other men moved closer still. He looked at them, then he looked at Eleanor, his eyes wide, his pupils large, and he mouthed his reply in a similar fashion.

"I...can't."

Stresh was now only about twenty feet away. "Lady Lasgaart." he had a firm, commanding tone to his voice, as though the young man barring his way was no obstacle at all. "You had better come with us. This boy cannot stop you and if he is stupid enough to try then that will be his last bad decision."

Eleanor was about to speak again but this time Dormouse pushed her backwards, gently but firmly interposing himself between her and Stresh. He

ACT ONE : THE HUNT

raised his sword in a defensive gesture. "She is not yours to take Tanarese man," he said. "Besides, is your loyalty to Tanaren, or to Baron Fenchard and Arshuma? If it is the latter, perhaps you should just leave us be."

Stresh seemed to bristle at the insinuation, a verbal success for Dormouse that left Eleanor a little impressed with the young man. "Fenchard and Arshuma's interests are not necessarily the same," Stresh growled. "We fight a war while our Grand Duke dances and banquets at the Winterfeast ball hundreds of miles away. Perhaps we do not want his overlordship anymore, but neither do we want yours, now let the lady pass if you know what is good for you."

As he was speaking Eleanor glanced at Dormouse's belt. His sword might have been drawn but his dagger just sat there, nestled in its scabbard, she could pull it out it easily, force Dormouse to let her go. That way she could save his life and get free. These men could lead her away and take her home. Except that they wouldn't of course, they would take her to Fenchard, vain, preening, arrogant, cruel, and unmarried Fenchard. She looked down again, her hand was almost on the hilt of the dagger, but it was shaking so, trembling, she couldn't do it, she didn't want to go to Fenchard the traitor, no more than she wanted to go to Arshuma, and, bizarrely enough, she didn't want to threaten Dormouse either. She pulled her hand back to partially cover her face.

Dormouse meanwhile was standing stock still, barring Stresh's path to Eleanor. Stresh, his patience wearing thin started to tap Dormouse's sword with his own. "Do you really want to boy? Or shall I separate your arm from your shoulder? It really wouldn't be that difficult for me."

Dormouse still did not move, Eleanor was about to try and fling herself dramatically between the two men though to what end she hadn't quite worked out yet when Stresh's companion, Kellan, who was still standing some yards behind them, spoke.

"People," he said to Stresh, "someone is coming!"

Stresh took a few steps backward. "Our men?"

"Don't know," Kellan said. "But I thought our people were encamped further up the valley."

Stresh did not reply, he was listening intently. Now they could all hear it, footsteps crunching the snow, quiet, more than one person moving very carefully through the forest, Stresh started to move backwards again, taking Kellan with him. Eleanor looked to her right just as a broad, hulking figure burst through the trees. It was Stan. He saw Dormouse, then ran over to him, his, axe raised just as Shak and the others appeared out of the shadows behind him.

"I heard voices," Stan said breathlessly; "were you having some trouble here young fellow?"

Dormouse nodded. "These men wanted to take her." He pointed at Eleanor who had started to slink away from him, seeking a shadow under which to hide.

"What men?" Stan asked him.

"Well, these…" Dormouse started to raise his sword to indicate where Stresh had been standing but by now both he and his young companion had melted away into the darkness.

****

Night was by now truly encroaching over the snow bound land, fortunately though Oswold did not have far to lead them. They walked to the river, Oswold keeping it close, hopping over wide flat stones and rugged boulders in such a sprightly manner it was difficult to believe how venerable he obviously was. At last though he stopped, breathing heavily, waiting for the others to catch him up. And not a moment too soon for the snow was, once again, softly falling.

He was standing in front of two great shoulders of rock that joined together far above his head. In front of him was another flat stone that Shak soon realised had been propped up against these other rocks to conceal something. He helped the old hermit to move it to one side (otherwise they would have been there all night. Sprightly he may have been but the one armed old man did not seem to possess a huge amount of physical strength), and then he peered through the space thus revealed.

It was an earthy hollow, obviously scooped out over several years, a dark little dell over which the two great boulders arched, serving as a sturdy roof. They all crept inside, bowing their heads, and crouching as they did so (even then it was a very tight squeeze for Stan), replacing the stone cum door once they were inside. As they spread out and sat down they saw that behind them there was a thin gap between the enclosing rocks that looked out over the river and let in a thin sliver of moonlight. Just enough for them to see to light a fire and to act as ventilation for any smoke rising from it. Stauncher set about the task with enthusiasm.

ACT ONE : THE HUNT

Shortly afterwards the bedrolls were out, a small but merry fire was burning, and everybody was helping themselves to the oat cakes and dried meat purloined from the raided camp. Oswold sat next to Shak at the top of the hollow where the ground was slightly raised. Tired, but relieved to be under shelter and warming up slowly, the mood was cheering considerably. The only frisson of icy hostility seemed to exist between Eleanor and Dormouse, they had made a point of avoiding each other ever since Stan had turned up to rescue them; even now they lay down in opposite parts of the hollow making sure they did not look in each other's direction. Whether Shak had noticed the frigidity between them was impossible to tell, now however there were more important matters to deal with, it was time to talk.

"Right then holy man." Shak half lay, half sat on his bedroll with the air of a man holding court in a palace. "It all got pretty confused back there for a while, yet it seems that we both think we can help each other in some way. So, while I shall at first thank you for letting us use your shelter this evening would you like me to tell you how exactly we believe you can aid us? Then you can say how we can help you in return."

Oswold looked up from his oat cake, oats had stuck to his face and were freely scattered over his beard. "Yes. Yes of course I shall, but let me thank you too, they were bullying men, they would have dragged me and beaten me to get what they wanted. They have no love for the Gods, or the God's representatives, it is fairly obvious that Artorus himself sent you to aid me in my distress."

"Quite." Shak seemed happy to let the verbose fellow talk to his heart's content. "Now the only thing we require is for somebody to show us where this river can be safely crossed. Can you do that for us?"

Oswold crunched his oat cake loudly before answering. "Yes. Two to three days upriver and there are plenty of places. The gorge widens you see, the river widens, becomes shallow, though it is still swift."

"Two to three days?" Stan stopped drinking from his water flask and groaned. "As long as that? As you can see we are being hunted. We would like to get across sooner if we could."

"Oh there are places," Oswold dribbled into his beard with enthusiasm. "But the important word that the tall man said was safely. There are some places where the river narrows a little, but the water is swift and deep, and it would be dangerous for you all, especially the young girl."

"I can swim," Eleanor yawned, she appeared to be ready for sleep.

THE FANGS OF THE FEN SNAKE

"Well, a little bit."

"Matters not, matters not," Oswold told her; "fall in and thwooom, carried away to drown, or to be hurled over the falls and dashed into soup. Ha!" he laughed. "And bloody soup at that!"

"Falls?" Shak enquired.

"Yes," Oswold nodded. "A great falls, follow me at dawn and you will see them in the morning. You are worried about being chased yes, about travelling for two days, well the falls will slow them, slow them or even stop them, by all the Gods looking down on us."

"But won't they also stop us?" Shak enquired.

"Yes, maybe yes!" Oswold crouched, bouncing up and down on his haunches. "But as Artorus sent you to me, so did he send me to you. We hermits know a way up, we have a rope, we can climb, we all can climb, even the young lass can climb!" he squeaked excitedly. Eleanor did not reply and shut her eyes in consternation, as Oswold had been bouncing up and down she was sure she had caught a glimpse of his pink, shrivelled genitals. She feared that both the sight and the memory of that sight would never leave her.

"Very well," Shak told him with a smile. "If you are happy to be our guide we will follow you." He put out his hand for Oswold to shake, which he did with some gusto. "Now," Shak continued, "how can we aid you in return?"

"But you see you already are!" Oswold's pale eyes gleamed. "Where the river crossings are and where I want to go are in exactly the same place. There are a series of falls, low and shallow, the water there only reaches up to your knees. You cross there and I can enter the cave, for the cave is right next to the falls. We all help each other! We all help each other! You cross the river and I go into the cave," he tugged excitedly at his unkempt beard. "Oh the Gods surely design these moments for us all. Serendipity is always Artorus handiwork, so many theologians have postulated thus! And who could doubt them now!"

"Why nobody amongst us would dare," Shak said. "So, we cross the river, and you leave us to search for the treasure of this dragon, is that right?"

"Yes," Oswold said with a gleam in his eye, "well, almost."

A few knowing smiles were exchanged amongst the company, Oswold however noticed them and inferred their intent with precision.

"Ah!" He winked knowingly at them. "You are humouring the mad old man. "He has lived out here far too long!" you are thinking "he is

200

hallucinating, eaten too many of the wrong mushrooms," but you are wrong I tell you, wrong!"

"About the mushrooms?" Stan asked.

"About the treasure, muscle man!"

"This treasure being gold and silver and the like?" Stauncher was trying to hide his grin by now.

"No," Oswold said emphatically; "knowledge, objects, gems!"

"And all of it is guarded by a dragon." Stauncher cut off a piece of cured salt beef, it would take an age to chew, but it would certainly stop him smiling.

"No, but the treasure is inside the mountains, and the dragon is inside the mountains, I only saw the smallest portion of it before but there is a vast area of tunnels and caves there, many strange beasts must lurk inside them."

"We had no intention of sounding flippant Father Oswold," Shak told him. "But look at your words from our point of view. Dragons? If they exist nobody has seen one for centuries, well no human anyway." He gave Dead Eyes a sideways look. "Treasure? Dragons and treasure is a terrible cliché found in the worst children's stories. We are not saying we do not believe you, just that your tale is somewhat...incredible."

"Humans do not believe in dragons." Dead Eyes had been listening intently to the conversation and now joined it for the first time. "They are a young people, in this part of the world at least, they see, and they know, they break the branch to see the sap, yet they cannot put the branch back together afterwards. They are clever, but they are not wise and they do not perceive."

"Perceive what?" Dormouse asked her.

"You think that the kestrel in flight looks down at the earth and sees it as you do, but they do not, they can almost touch the clouds yet still spy a rabbit quivering behind a stone. There is but one way for you, the human way, whereas in truth every different people, every bird, every animal tastes this world in a slightly different manner. And this was never more true than with dragons."

"Go on," Shak was intrigued. "Time for some elfy wisdom," Stan baited her.

"My people," she continued, ignoring them both, "the way we learn. Each tribe has at least one lore master and they have at least two apprentices. These people usually have more haraska, erm that is power or magic to you, than the rest of us. They learn the history of the tribe, of our people from their predecessor and once they have that knowledge they teach the children of the tribe. By the time we undertake our ceremony of adulthood there are things we must all have knowledge of, and that includes tales of the dragons of this world, for they form an integral part of our beliefs."

All except the sleeping Eleanor were silent now, rapt with attention as Dead Eyes was speaking, their cynicism weakening by the minute as she continued to talk.

"Zhun is our God, the creator of the world, and when he decided to populate this world the first creatures he made were the dragons. The first was Azhanion, the black dragon, the two headed dragon and as he shed his scales other dragons spawned from each scale. Each was semi divine, immortal, invested with the power of the elements and, over time, they bred, and many dragons moved amongst this world, from its frozen heights to its tropical depths. The children of these first dragons were not immortal, but they lived a span of years beyond understanding, millennia upon millennia. And they were wise creatures, intelligent yet their intelligence was not as elven or human intelligence, they would see us as we see the ant, or the mayfly, however, in order to maintain their huge lifespans, they need to hibernate, a sleep not of a winter, but of many centuries."

She put her hands over the fire to warm them. "To do this obviously they need a lair, a place that could be untouched for a vast period of time. Some found places under the sea, others lay under the soil of a vast forest, more still slept buried under the desert sand, but many too lived in deep mountain caves, sleeping as empires of elves and men rose and fell in the world outside."

She sighed. "Can you imagine being born, raising children, seeing your children having children, knowing that three or four more generations were to follow and yet in all that time all that a dragon might do is twitch a closed eyelid? That is what they are like these animals, to them we are the biting tick, the cloud of gnats to be brushed to one side. Yet they have a divine purpose, they are Zhun's guardians, they protect this world from those that would do it hurt, rising to defeat any danger using flame and frost and poison and lightning. The only reason for a dragon to be amongst us now is if such a threat is detected, unless of course the natural way of things has been interfered with, which, knowing humans, is a distinct possibility, especially as the dragon amongst us now appears to be a juvenile." And with that last remark she gave Oswold such a look as to make the old man squirm.

ACT ONE : THE HUNT

"Yes," he nodded his head sadly. "I was curious, I interfered as you put it, it is my fault that the creature is running free here. For many years I thought it had died and so I did nothing, but it did not die, and I must now do something to rectify my mistake. The dragon needs its mother, I must somehow find her and reunite them both."

"A young dragon spends a long time at its mother's side, it has much to learn from her, right now it is confused and probably frightened, and a frightened animal is a dangerous one. Do you have a real plan on how to bring mother and child together?"

Oswold shook his head ruefully. "No. I have no idea; I was just going to revisit old ground and hopefully find something that can help me." He then appeared to brighten up. "And that is where you can help me too, you have already shown me your knowledge of dragons, if there is something to find, you will find it!"

"But I am crossing the river, not going with you," she frowned.

Oswold started to splutter in consternation, seemingly ready to argue the point, Shak however, started to shake his head. "No Dead Eyes, we cross, you stay with Oswold here. Then, when he has achieved...whatever he wants to achieve, you travel to Grest on your own. It will be safer for you anyway; you are not the one being hunted, without my presence, you are not a target."

He was giving her a familiar look, the one that told her that words and deeds might not match in this case, that he was telling Oswold only what he wanted to hear. So she just nodded and let the matter drop. Oswold, who was still mightily interested in her asked her several questions about her home and her tribe which she answered in a friendly, if guarded manner and then finally the old man curled up to sleep, his whistling snore filling the little cavern within a minute.

Shak then left his bedroll and came up to her, their conversation taking place in a low whisper. "We need the old fellow to help us climb these falls and find the river crossing. When we get there he can disappear into his cave, and you can cross with us. We can invent an excuse later for you not going with him, if we can think of one that doesn't hurt his feelings. I feel bad about doing this to a priest, but this is our lives we are talking about. My duty is to get all of you and our little abductee into Arshuman territory safely. That is all that matters."

"He won't like it," she indicated Oswold, "and what about this dragon...beast?"

THE FANGS OF THE FEN SNAKE

"A problem for another time," he squeezed her shoulder. "We have assassins, knights, and Baron Fenchard's men chasing our tails, I think that is enough on our platter for the moment."

"I told you that I saw these falls earlier," Dead Eyes confided. "From a great distance, when we were at the river. It was just a great cloud of vapour; it seemed a formidable obstacle. So it could buy us some time if we can put it between us and everybody else."

"Which is why we need the priest," Shak affirmed. "It is a gamble; he may be as mad as a witch in a beehive, he may be talking gibberish, but if he is we are no worse off than we would have been without him. And we have this camping spot. And the snow is covering our tracks. Just keep talking about elven things to him, he seems to love that."

Dead Eyes smiled. "As you wish. What about this treasure?"

"You interested?"

"No. But I know what humans are like. The thought of gold can put the strangest gleam in their eyes."

"Well, let me answer like this then. Is there any jewel in this world more precious than our lives?"

Her green eyes shone like jewels themselves. "Not to me," she said, "but I can only reiterate, that is a question for humans to answer."

"Maybe, but as far as this human is concerned, your lives matter more than gold. And again, he might be mad, this treasure is probably just a phantom treasure, it is not worth the trouble chasing an old man's delusions. Now get some sleep, even you elf people get tired sometimes. As I said earlier, at least the latest snowfall will hide our tracks, so there should be no fear of ambush tonight, we are already benefitting from our new alliance."

Shak was right, she was tired, so she turned onto her side and drifted off, her last sight being of Stan and Dormouse sitting close together, it seemed that they were deep in their own conversation too.

"Something is troubling you young Dormouse," Stan was saying to him. "I have not seen you so edgy of a night time, is it your leg, or what happened to you earlier?"

"My leg?" Dormouse replied absently. "No, that is a lot better. I am just replaying things in my mind that is all, wondering what I could have done differently."

"Ah, so it was what happened earlier. Then shall I tell you what I saw as I approached you, I had a pretty good look at things before I came out of the trees you know…"

Dormouse interrupted him. "She was perfectly happy to see me killed by those men, in fact, I think she wanted it. I had not expected her to be so…calculating or callous, it shocked me, disappointed me. I mean I know we shouldn't be friends but…"

Stan adopted a confiding tone. "First of all, you standing up to those men. Impressive even though you would have ended up as crow food. The margins between courage and bone headed idiocy are exceedingly small but I shall ascribe the former value to you, give you the benefit of the doubt. We are fighting shoulder to shoulder after all, and I would not wish to trust my unguarded arm to an idiot. As for the lady and her disregard for your feelings, well, we have kidnapped the poor mare, dragged her miles through trackless, abandoned forest, almost fed her to a dragon and stopped her wedding after all. Not to mention being from the country that has been at war with her own most of her life, probably killed members of her family and occupied her ancestral lands; I think you can forgive her a certain antipathy; don't you think?"

Dormouse ran his hands through his fair hair. "Obviously, everything you say is true. It is just that she has got to know us a little by now…"

"Three days Dormouse, she has been with us three days, I have probably got lice that have been with me longer than that. Three days against a lifetime of hatred. Don't be hard on the girl for that."

The young man gave a weary sigh. "I am just being naïve I suppose."

"Yes. But in more than one way I am afraid. Now it is time to give you some more practical advice, shall I tell you what I witnessed earlier on?"

Dormouse nodded.

"You, facing down two men with the girl stood behind you. Admirable courage as I said earlier. You however were so focussed on those facing you that you forgot something rather important."

"Like what?"

"Your dagger," Stan smiled at him. "Anyone could have pulled it free of the scabbard and stabbed you in the back with it. Especially an enemy standing behind you."

"What are you saying?" Dormouse sounded confused. "That she could have…"

"Her hand went out to take it," Stan said, his voice sounding more fatherly than ever. "She could have done so easily, so intent were you on the foe. Her hand went out, but then she pulled it back, had she not done so then..."

"I would have been crow food?" he suggested.

"Exactly." Stan sounded pleased. "So perhaps, just perhaps, she likes you a little more than you first thought."

****

Outside the snow fell gently, softly, covering rock and tree, hanging heavily in the boughs, nestling silently in nook and dell, glistening and luminous under a yellow moon. Little moved as ice and cold held out its louring fingers, it was a time for shelter, for sanctuary, to let the elements do their worst until the rising of the pallid sun. Little moved on nights like this, little, yet not nothing at all.

Captain Teague, of the retinue of Baron Fenchard, or rather King Fenchard of West Arshuma as he now styled himself, had had a frustrating day. Dividing the men into three teams, having them scour the land within a ten-mile radius of the camp, had produced no sight of the beast at all. They knew of a possible lair inside a derelict manor house, but it wasn't there. They had found evidence of kills, forest glades drenched in blood and splintered bone, but it had long abandoned these places and they had found tracks, four great scaled toes ending in claws like scimitars yet they too all led nowhere, as though this animal had the power to disappear into thin air. Perplexing, frustrating, one more day of fruitless searching and the pressure on him to return to the city of Tetha Vinoyen would increase exponentially. And even with the snow falling, and the men sleeping so close to the fire they risked becoming part of it, the city was the last place he wanted to be.

He still managed to sleep though, and sleep well, a day of constant physical exertion encouraged such sleep even in these barrens. So to be rudely awakened, long before dawn, by a rough shake to the shoulder was never going to put him in anything other than the worst of moods.

"Sir, it is me, Stresh, sorry to wake you but I have got news." Then, a little more forcefully. "Sir!"

Slowly, like a bear stirring from deep hibernation, Teague eased himself to his feet. Stresh, and the young fellow Kellan beside him were amongst those unfailingly loyal to him so he bit back the harsh words forming in his mind and just asked. "What in the name of Artorus is it man?"

"Sir, we have been running most of the night." He was breathing

ACT ONE : THE HUNT

heavily, and Teague noticed the thin sheen of sweat on his face, with Kellan too the breath was being expelled in jagged clouds. "The old hermit sir, Yaki and his boys found him but..."

"But?" Teague enquired.

"They were ambushed sir, and the hermit went with the ambushers. Two men dead, another wounded..."

Teague reacted sharply to this, who would dare attack his men? "Two dead? Who?"

"Kolb and Gravven sir," he was told.

Kolb and Gravven, Teague thought. Two foreign mercenaries, two of Fenchard's men. A loss certainly but at least the dead weren't Tanarese men loyal to him.

"And any idea who did this to them?" Teague was as composed as ever by now.

"Arshuman raiders sir," Stresh answered, his breathing still ragged. "I wasn't with them at the time but there were several of them, one of whom was apparently a Wych."

"A Wych, seriously?"

"And a woman to boot, if Yaki is to be believed. We ran into him about an hour after it happened, he told us then. The thing is though, we had our own, separate encounter with them too, just me and Kellan sir."

"With one of them," Kellan corrected his superior, "and they have a hostage."

"Lady Eleanor Lasgaart, or so she told us." Stresh took lengths to make sure he spoke the name correctly. "We would have grabbed her, but the rest of the warband returned and we had to flee. If she is speaking truth, then the Arshumans have taken a Tanarese noblewoman as hostage."

"For ransom no doubt," Teague mused softly. "And a Lasgaart too, and I bet Fenchard has no idea this is going on under his nose. Where is Yaki now?"

"They took his weapons sir, but when we left him he was going to try and pick up their trail so that, if we send reinforcements, they know where to go."

"And the old priest is with these Arshumans?"

"As far as we know sir, yes."

One day ends in frustration, another begins with hope. A lady to rescue, and a prospect of treasure to tempt the gullible. If he returned to the city with a freed Tanarese noblewoman in tow, then things would change entirely. His loyalty would be unquestioned, and a reward of some sort would surely be in the offing. His position would be secure and his life free from threat, he could look at his options, to desert or remain loyal without fear of spies or a knife in the dark. This new development cast a fresh light on the whole situation. He actually started to feel enthusiastic again.

"Kellan," he ordered. "Spend the night here then travel to Tetha Vinoyen with this news. Say that we are attempting to free this Lasgaart woman from Arshuman captors and that we also wish to free a priest held by the same people, a priest who may have knowledge of hidden gold."

"And the beast sir?" Kellan asked.

"Don't mention the beast, not till we have seen it. Stresh!"

"Yes sir?"

"Time to break camp, we have things to do!"

"Break camp sir? It is not yet dawn?"

"Keth take the dawn! We can travel by torchlight. Mobilise the men, gold to be discovered, a rich Tanarese woman to rescue and Arshumans to kill. Any man that balks at such incentives has no place fighting at my side!"

****

Dead Eyes had untied the fastenings on her sleeve and was examining her forearm by the feeble glow of the fire. There was a tattoo there; it was not like her other tattoos for it had been put there by human hand, it lacked the clarity, the depth of colour, the clean lines, it was a human tattoo and so by its very nature, it was inferior. It depicted a black snake, one single coil, tongue flicking over a couple of long, curved fangs, it was not even anatomically in proportion. The fen snake: Stan, Stauncher and Shak all had one, if Dormouse got back alive then they would make sure he had one too. It was the roughest, worst, tattoo on her body and yet, these days, it meant more than all the others combined.

She had thought everybody was asleep but then realised that their little hollow was missing one particular sound from the choir of gentle breathing and sighing she had so got used to this last hour, Oswold's unique snore. She pulled her sleeve up and started to tie the fastenings, realising as she did so that he had moved, that he was now sitting between herself and Shak, his eyes gleaming by the light of the fire.

"Can I help you?" she asked politely.

ACT ONE : THE HUNT

He pointed a crooked finger. "Your tattoos, I would love to know the story of them, you have more than the one on your face, yes?"

"I do. They are normally hidden by clothing but on some festival days we display them openly, they tell the tale of the person wearing them, and of the tribe they come from."

He sounded surprised. "Do men attend these festivals?"

"Of course. We do not have your ridiculous churlishness when it comes to displaying our bodies. Shak, Stan and Stauncher have all seen them in the past, I can show them to you if you wish; just not now, it is too late for me to start fiddling with these straps."

He was, as she had hoped, horrified. "No, no, I would never ask a lady to do such a thing, just describe them to me, when you have the time."

"Maybe tomorrow then," she said, "now is the time for sleep."

"I agree, may Artorus, or your Gods, keep you safe."

"And may yours do the same for you."

She lay on her side facing away from him, her nose started to wrinkle. She then realised that he had curled up right next to her, his own overpowering odour wafting her way and impossible for her to escape from. She shut her eyes hoping by Zhun and all the spirits that she would get used to it soon.

She did not have to worry about it for long though, for it was close to dawn when he spoke to her, and it was at the rising of dawn that they left their little hole. And then, after travelling for just over an hour, with a fragile sun still poking drowsily over the eastern trees and the river, that they finally beheld the Whiterush Maw.

15

It was summer, she remembered that vividly. A warm periwinkle sky barely scarred by thin streaks of gossamer cloud, the local thyatasis trees with their polished olive green leaves and ripening crimson berries hugging the grotto like an intimate friend. They were hiding, nurturing, keeping the place secret, a hidden place in this high valley, never seen by human eyes, a sanctuary for her people. As for the high, white water cataract that fed the grotto, well her vision of it was somewhat obscured for she was standing directly under it, upon a natural stone plinth onto which the water splashed and crashed, runnels and rivulets transformed to spray by the impact. She spread her arms wide, tilting her head upwards, letting the water invigorate her, luxuriating at the shock of it upon her pale, shivering skin. She was purifying herself, cleansing her pores, freshening her spirit, quickening her blood. It was a tradition in her tribe, all women had to face the ice cold waters, it was an opportunity to reflect on the past and contemplate the future; this, after all, was her wedding day.

She was so much younger then, so much more naïve, and yet so much more optimistic, maybe optimism and naïveté were traits that went hand in hand, in a perverse sort of way she hankered for the return of both. Dozens of watercourses ran into this valley, flowing from the grey peaks of the enclosing mountains and forming countless, crisscrossing brooks and streams that continued to slope through gorge and dell until they finally emptied into the great, circular tarn about thirty miles away. And it was at the opposite end of this tarn, in a town built at the head of the mountain pass, that the humans lived.

She was a scout then, as was Graonic, her husband to be, her job was partly to hunt, and partly to observe. She would often go down to the lake's edge to watch the humans fish in their wide keeled boats; they knew the elves existed, as the elves knew the humans existed, but neither would ever risk encroaching on each other's territory, for bloodshed was nearly always the end result, far safer to leave each other alone. By far the greater threat to her tribe was the other tribe of elves that dwelt in the southern part of the valley. This tribe, the Vistrian, were sometimes friends, friends enough for intermarriage to occur between them, more often though the relationship, as

ACT ONE : THE HUNT

it was at this present time, was both tense and hostile.

"Kalinaga, it is time for you to dress." Her eyes were shut but she knew the voice of the loremaster, and of course, she was Kalinaga then, Dead Eyes did not even exist. So long ago, yet remembered with such clarity, such vibrant colours, such intense sensations. She remembered the warm fragrant breeze raising bumps on her skin as she stepped clear of the torrent and opened her eyes at last.

The loremaster was standing on the grass just a few feet away, with her attendants behind her. She was carrying the sheer robe of flame silk that all new brides wore. It was a precious thing, the worms that spun the silk were rare creatures and all had to die to yield up the material for the dress. And now it was hers. The attendants were carrying the flowers and ribbons for her hair which was not short back then but rather reached down to the small of her back when untied. She could feel the wind drying it already, a glossy blue-black cascade flowing behind her, lifted by the breeze. She stepped into the soft, doeskin moccasins she would wear for the ceremony, they had been intricately stitched with images of valley flowers. A marriage for her people was symbolised by flowers, strength, fertility, and beauty, what else could be better encapsulated by a flower? Children were a rare gift for her tribe, elven fertility was not human fertility and it had already been decided that this very autumn, she would head into the mountains for her meliantele, the ceremony to make her fruitful, maybe in a year or so it would not be her marriage the tribe would be celebrating, but the birth of her first child.

She stood still and let them dress her, silk robes, flowers, ribbons, perfumes, even colouring pigments for her eyelids, lips, and cheeks. For just this one day, she would be the most beautiful elf maiden in her tribe. She was proud of what she was and of the people she belonged to; Kalinaga of the Vavanaskal tribe, a free, independent people, not subject to the humans and their brutal empire. She had never spoken to a human, never wanted to, she did not even know their language.

And, as they finished dressing her and led her along the path to the glade where the ceremony was to occur, she had no idea that this would be the last morning of her life that such a happy unfamiliarity would ever exist.

****

And the Whiterush Maw was nothing like the grotto of her reminisces. There were no colours here outside of grey, white, and the muted sedimentary brown of the water. To look at the falls, Dead Eyes was reminded of a giant letter "U" where the bottom part was the lip over which the great torrent spilt, and the sides represented the mighty gorge hewn out by these waters over years beyond counting. Either side of the river at the top of the falls was a strip of land twixt water and mountainside to which tall trees clung tentatively. Presumably, the western bank was where Oswold was leading them, but how exactly would they get up there?

Because of course they would have to scale the falls first, or rather not the falls but the flat expanse of rock to its immediate right. It looked sheer, glistening almost metallically as it endured the constant soaking from the spray churned up by the thundering waters. Hanging trees, vines and clusters of foliage clung to its recesses, a sheer cliff, a climb of hundreds of feet, surely an impossible climb and surely their pursuers could not be too far behind. Dead Eyes shoulders slumped, she looked at Stauncher to see that he was thinking exactly the same as her.

Oswold however, seemed entirely unperturbed. Keeping the bubbling, muddy water close to his right he skipped over stones, greasy pebbles, and slippery rocks with utter abandon, seemingly oblivious to the fact that he was close to toppling to a watery death on several occasions. Shak and his companions followed rather more circumspectly and for once it wasn't only Eleanor who was shaking their head and muttering to themselves.

They drew closer to the cliff they would have to scale, the roar of the falls increasing in volume, the height of the cliff getting ever more apparent. One good thing though, they could now see that the cliff was not as sheer as it initially appeared, there were ridges, overhangs, protrusions marking it in many places. Dead Eyes could finally see that she might just be able to scramble up somehow but then, how would the young girl manage? And how would a one armed old man?

By now Oswold had reached the base of the cliff. He ran along it for a while, seemingly keen to find a particular spot. When he did find it he started capering around in a sort of impromptu dance, cackling wildly to himself and running his fingers through the tortuous tangle of his beard.

Finally, the others caught up with him, Shak first. Oswold was singing in his thin, tuneless voice, a song in praise of the god Artorus, as befitted a man of faith. Then, however, he saw Shak and stopped, pointing his bony finger at the cliff behind him.

"Here, you see, here!" he squeaked, his voice enthralled. "Faults in the

ACT ONE : THE HUNT

stone, ridges, crevices. We climb along them, up, up, and up again. This ridge intersects with another and then another. We climb all three till we are almost there and then..." He stopped and looked up at the top of the cliff, it was barely visible due to its height and the pall of spray that hung lugubriously over everything, diffusing the weak sunlight into a golden haze that carried little heat.

"And then?" Shak asked him. He could see the ridge, a ledge jutting out from the cliff face, climbing slowly from east to west, it was three feet across at best and its surface was crumbling and uneven and, like as not, the trees and plants clinging to the cliffs probably straddled it in places, creating unwelcome obstacles. Still, if Oswold could do it...

"We shall see, we shall see. I shall show you when we get there." Oswold seemed keen to start, hopping on to the ridge and beckoning the others to follow him.

Stan, however, decided to voice an objection. "You're sure we can't just chop a tree down, hollow it out and float across the river that way? This climb will be difficult and time consuming, surely, surely we can come up with something better than this."

"And fashioning a log boat wouldn't be difficult and time consuming?" Stauncher asked. "Sitting around chopping wood while these assassins, or Baron Fenchard's men creep up on us and say hello?"

"Even if we could," Shak added. "You have seen the river. It is full of falls and rapids; the chances are we would never get across it alive. We have to trust the good hermit in this case."

"Yes," Oswold said, "you have to trust me. Now come along!" He started to climb: scuttling along the ridge in a sort of half crouch, pressing his hand to the stone underfoot from time to time to steady himself.

Shak followed, then Dead Eyes, then Dormouse. Stauncher beckoned to Eleanor to go next but she hesitated, looking at the frowning Stan before starting her climb. "Do you think that Oswold..." she started to ask him, but he already had a reply to hand.

"Mad?" Stan said. "Touched by Uba? Let's just say not so much touched by Uba as given a full, all over body massage by him, with oils and everything. I will go last, if I fall over I do not want to take any of you with me."

"Hey, at least it's not snowing." Stauncher gave a short, bitter laugh, before Eleanor trod gingerly on to the ridge, taking one careful step at a time, and not daring to look down.

THE FANGS OF THE FEN SNAKE

****

The smells of water, wet stone and earth, the sun at its zenith, warmer than the day before, warm enough to melt the snow yet not yet warm enough to keep out the damp, and the pervasive icy chill that permeated the climbers down to the bone. There was a rhythm to their ascent, cautious step after cautious step, only looking a few feet ahead, only looking for a safe purchase for weary feet. They climbed without knowing they had climbed, they progressed without realising thus, without understanding that they were already a third of the way up the cliff face.

Yet soon enough, old Oswold and young Eleanor needed to rest, and it was the hermit who led them to the place where they could sit for a brief while and finally be able to look around them. It was a rocky knoll, a whorl of stone along the ridge that protruded further from the cliff face than the rest of the ledge. A wizened old tree grew there, thin silver branches still sporting a few lime green leaves. They all sat around it, drinking from their flasks and eating the minimum amount needed to satiate their hunger.

Shak peered through the filmy mist. They were well above the tops of the tallest trees now, the snow was melting on the branches but still clung there, doggedly resisting the inevitable, just as a man resists his own death. It was no longer possible to see the distant southern fields, it was just trees, trees, and water. Underneath, to their left, the Whiterush frothed and churned its way through the forest, there was just one wide, bare, stony place between the tree line and the end of the broad, bulbous splash pool hewn out by the falling river, an open expanse of little soil that was too wet for trees to grow. They had crossed it earlier, when Oswold was leading them to the climbing place and so Shak was expecting to see it empty now, a place where no man would willingly want to explore.

Except that it wasn't. For emerging from the trees to stand on this bare expanse Shak saw five tiny figures. Insects from this distance yet they were insects that moved, and walked, as men. It looked like his worst fears were being realised.

"Eleanor, come here and tell me what you see. Stauncher says you have very keen eyes," he asked politely. Eleanor though was sitting with her back to the tree refusing to stare at anything but the cliff face.

"I can't," she said, the fear obvious in her voice. "I can't look down; this height is making me feel sick."

ACT ONE : THE HUNT

He accepted this without argument. "Dormouse, Dead Eyes, you can tell me instead then."

Dormouse did not look too enticed by the prospect either, but he made his way to the cliff edge, shielded his eyes, and saw what Shak meant immediately. "Oh, they must be the people chasing us, or perhaps they are Baron Fenchard's men. Are we going to fight them?"

Eleanor's ears pricked. "Are they knights? Do they have armour? Insignia?"

"They are all cloaked," Dead Eyes told her. "Some are in furs but...maybe. There are white cloaks there and a glint of armour. What shall we do, fight, or run? They will be at the climbing place in moments."

"I sense an impasse," Shak told her. "They will not come too close for we are above them and our arrows have greater range; conversely if we go to meet them we lose that advantage. Both parties will want to maintain space between each other, at least for now. Anyway, we must move, take the rear, and keep your bowstring taut, if we get to a place where we can stop and face them then we will take it. Father Oswold, lead us on again, as fast as your legs can carry you."

They got up without complaining and continued on a little further, each of them painfully aware that the ledge on which they were standing was beginning to narrow alarmingly. Shak was about to ask Oswold if perhaps he had forgotten the route when the old man stopped, turned, cackled in his own inimitable way, and pointed above their heads.

"There, that ledge just above us, that is where we go next!"

"But how do we get on to it?" Dormouse asked guardedly, unsure if he really wanted to hear the answer.

"Oh, well." Oswold seemed uncertain, scratching his beard and tutting under his breath. "That is it! He said finally. "We go up this ledge a little way, see how it levels out there? We go up to that point and then..."

"We jump?" Shak asked, his sardonic tone obvious to all but Oswold.

Oswold nodded, the excitement had caused him to dribble into his beard. The rest of them looked at the leap he was expecting them to make.

It was from one narrow ledge to a slightly higher narrow ledge, the latter one being maybe three to four feet wide. The stone was wet and seemed to have crumbled in places, as for the gap, a tallish man could do it at a stretch, though keeping his footing on landing would not be easy. Eleanor however was already shaking her head.

THE FANGS OF THE FEN SNAKE

"No," she said, and there was cold terror in her voice. "I cannot do that, I will fall. I won't do it, I would rather you killed me now."

Stauncher was next to her. "Eleanor..."

The whites of her eyes were showing. "No! I will not do it! I will fall, you cannot make me."

"The old man has done it," Stauncher said. "Come, we will do it together."

"HAVE you done this before?" Shak asked Oswold.

"Of course, I do not lie!" Oswold retorted. Then though he clapped his hand to his forehead. "Mind you, it was some years ago and...and...and I had both my arms!"

Shak groaned and tried to ignore the sound of Stan slapping his face. "Tell you what," he said, "I will go first, then I can catch you all before you go careering over the edge. Stauncher, you have got Eleanor, yes?"

Stauncher nodded but Eleanor was having none of it. "You cannot make me," she insisted. She started to pull away, looking down at her pursuers who were slowly beginning to climb towards them. "Can't you people just let me go!"

To her surprise, and her later embarrassment, she felt her eyes water and tears trickle down her cheeks. "I cannot do it!" she half sobbed to them.

Stauncher came up to her, putting a confiding arm round her shoulder and speaking quietly, and reassuringly in her ear. "Those people down there," he said, "they want to kill us. At the same time, we would be happy to kill them, yet, both parties have one thing in common. And that is you. Your safety and well-being is of paramount importance to all of us. We would all die rather than risk hurt to you. Now, once the old man and Shak have crossed, you get behind me and wrap your arms around me, I will do the jump, all you have to do is cling on and shut your eyes. I swear by all the gods that if you do that you will come to no harm. Trust me?"

She shook her head but said to him. "I don't, you should really let me go...but you won't though, will you." She looked up at the chasm and covered her face. "Promise you won't drop me..."

"Promise made."

She sniffed and looked down at her feet. "Elissa keep us safe. Oh and now my nose is running."

Stauncher handed her a clean(ish) rag and as she delicately dabbed her septum everybody else watched as Shak prepared to jump the gap ahead.

ACT ONE : THE HUNT

He was the tallest amongst them and had the longest legs so that if he struggled they knew that they all would. As with most things he attempted in life though it went flawlessly, a short run of two steps before a leap and a two footed landing on the further ledge. A couple of loose stone chippings came away to tumble into space, and, for a moment, he swayed a little as he righted himself on landing, but he was over, and over safely. Now for everybody else.

Oswold exhibited no fear whatsoever, in fact he started to laugh as he took a lengthy, exaggerated run before bounding off the ledge and into Shak's arms on the other side. Shak had to move sharply to catch him, if he hadn't had been there it was more than likely that the old man would have toppled to his death, Oswold though seemed completely unperturbed by this fact.

"We must be past halfway to the top now," he said gleefully. "Come everybody, we have need of haste!"

Stauncher looked at Eleanor, his eyes pools of utter calm; her eyes in comparison were still red and tearful, but she did nod at him. "Quicker it is done, quicker we can forget it," she said, her throat as dry as her nose was wet and viscous.

"Hang on." Stauncher told her. She stood close behind him, then she put her arms around him, smelling leather and sweat as she gripped the flaps in his armour with all the strength her small frame could muster. He leaned forward a little, lifting her up and encouraging her to wrap her legs around him too. She felt him tense and shut her eyes, trying to picture the goddess Elissa looking down on her, lifting them up with her gentle hand.

He took two steps then launched himself into emptiness, she felt a rush of cold air play with her hair and sting her hands, it was not comfortable, a sensation of lurching and nausea before a hard, staggering landing. Somebody reached out and held them firm, it had to be Shak; she was yet again shocked at the sense of strength and power in her captors. Then they were still. She could breathe again. And it was only then that she realised she was still screaming.

She felt Stauncher lower her back on to her feet and opened her eyes. "Are we here?"

"Quite safe," Stauncher told her, "and you can let go of me now."

"Oh yes. Sorry." She was embarrassed, letting go and taking a step backwards. "Thank you Stauncher."

"Come on," he said. "Let's start making our way along here, give everyone else room to jump."

THE FANGS OF THE FEN SNAKE

She did so, heart still fluttering like a trapped bird, legs still feeling as though they belonged to somebody else. As she stood back and tried to regain some composure she watched Dormouse jump the gap with assurance, not even needing Shak to steady him on landing. He came and stood next to her wearing a smile of such overweening smugness she had to make a comment, despite the apparent stiffness that existed between them from the previous day.

"Show off," she told him, her nose in the air.

"Well, I have got to be good at something," he replied, his smile still in place. She did not know why, probably her relief at still being alive, but she couldn't stop herself from smiling back; and with that the veneer of coolness between them melted again.

Dormouse might have found the leap easy but a big, heavy man like Stan was far less suited to the task. As he landed his trailing leg slipped off the ledge sending a shower of loose stones into the pall of mist. For a second his eyes blanched with fear, Shak though got both arms around him, hauling him to safety before his own bodyweight carried him to his doom.

Stan stood up, patting fragments of moss and stone off his damp breeches. He was angry at his brief loss of composure. "Keth's burning bollocks, Xhenafa's withered chopper, Artorus giant bloody weapon, Uttu's..."

"You are over master Bectalis." Shak, so deadpan normally, was laughing. "Over and safe. Now come on, we have climbing to do."

"And to where?" Stan continued to grumble. "Following a mad old fool chasing a bag of gold. We will all end up as bones Shak, I am telling you."

"We will indeed all end up as bones Stan," Shak observed. "But, while I am with you, I am determined to keep a healthy distance between that day and this. Let us get off this damned cliff, then we can chat about the old man, agreed?"

Stan nodded and strode past Eleanor and Dormouse. He was still muttering to himself. Shak had barely got himself into position when Dead Eyes jumped, Eleanor had wondered about the elf, who was little bigger than she was, wondered whether she would have the strength and courage to make the leap. She needn't have worried, Dead Eyes sprang over the chasm like a hungry cat, landing on both feet with barely a stagger. They were now all over, another obstacle safely crossed.

Shak looked over the precipice. "They are getting closer," he said to the elf, "and they are not being slowed by an old man and a young girl."

ACT ONE : THE HUNT

"I am not that young," Eleanor piped in.

Shak acknowledged his mistake. "An old man and a youngish girl. Do you think you could trouble them with an arrow?"

Dead Eyes was unimpressed. "Unlikely, the distance and this mist, I would only have a one in ten chance of hitting anything. It would be the waste of a shaft."

"Do not worry about hitting them. Just let them know that we CAN hit them if we want too. That should slow them down a bit. Worth risking a shaft for surely? It certainly wouldn't be wasting one."

She nodded to him and fitted and arrow to her bow. The pursuers were some way below still but had passed the tree where they had lunched earlier. Below and to her left, and the mist covered everything.

The arrow was loosed, they all followed its course (except for Eleanor who still refused to look down). It sped straight and true and, for a while, looked to be hitting the leader of the group full in the face. Then, however, a projecting part of the cliff face intervened, diverting the arrow so that it skipped over the heads of the entire company, the white of their upturned faces visible even at this height. They stopped moving and appeared to be talking furiously amongst themselves.

"Something for them to think about." Shak gave his archer a playful nudge. "Come on, let's put some extra space between them and us, take advantage of their confusion, we can always send another arrow their way if they gain on us again."

The others were already moving on, Oswold leading them at some pace, heedless as ever to the threat of falling and certain death. Eleanor was grateful the wind was not stronger, a strong gust would surely whip at her skirts and carry her over the edge, the thought brought bile to her throat. She did not look at the edge though, concentrating rather on staring ahead of her and keeping her shoulder as close to the damp yet reassuring cliff face as possible. This part of the climb, as it was turning out, was hardly a climb at all being rather a straight traverse from west to east, towards the falls themselves. Shrouded in misty spray as she was she had hardly been able to see them before but now, as they drew closer and closer she could regard them in some detail. A soaring plume of foam, lurching drunkenly over the precipice still high above her head, the constant drumming of tortured water throbbing in her ears, the great, earth brown river spilling its guts over the mountainside, it both terrified and enthralled, appalled and enraptured. Her breathing, already shortened by altitude and exertion almost stopped completely as she contemplated the sheer power of the display unfolding before her.

She had never seen a waterfall before, not a real one, and the savagery of the river, raging in its twisted fury just yards from her was something she thought mere water incapable of. Bear river, even when swollen by late autumn rains was never as furious as this, neither was the nearby river Kada which, though wider than the Whiterush was of a more placid mien altogether, moving sluggishly through its deep valley cloaked with ancient, sweet scented, woods. These sights, these sounds and smells were all new to her, she had travelled so little in her short life, she had so much still to learn. The furthest she had ever journeyed had been to the capital, Tanaren city, a journey she had made on two occasions. A great distance to the south and west of here, the capital was by far the largest of Tanaren's cities, a place like no other in the country. Her first visit there had been when she was about three, before the war had even started. The Emperor of Chira was visiting, and nobles from every part of the country had been invited to witness the rare and historic event. Eleanor remembered little of that time, save being frightened by the endless crowd, a river of humanity she had no idea existed in her little world. The second visit was more recent, less than three years ago, to witness the accession of the new Grand Duke following the death of his father who had seemingly been ailing for decades. This visit she remembered a lot more clearly.

They had travelled westwards before boarding a barge on the river Erskon. Now that was a river, many times wider than even the Whiterush here, so wide in fact it was difficult to see the farther side. It was heavy with boats, cruising the slow, almost black, waters in search of fish, or transporting goods to and from the towns and villages within its locale. Many boats were of course heading in the same direction they were, and, after a journey of some days, they finally reached their destination. And this time, the capital really did dazzle her.

They had stayed at the family estate, high on a hill close to the ducal palace. From there the whole city was spread out before them. It was vast, beyond vast, immense, colossal, gargantuan, the city walls enclosing thousands and thousands of souls, all those hopes, dreams, desires hemmed in, in a stinking, seething broil. And beyond the city, the sea; the sea that she had never seen before, purple-grey, both angry and placid, both restless and

ACT ONE : THE HUNT

peaceful, it possessed all the vices and virtues of a human mind, frustration teetering on the brink of violence, contemplation that could lead to discovery. She had insisted that she saw it close up and so they had taken her, first to the harbour that housed the warships, all tied up with ropes thicker than her arm, then to the pier and fishing harbour, dotted with hundreds of much smaller vessels, at anchor or heading out to sea, gulls following them like a trail of vapour looking for an easy meal. She smelled the salt, the dank, rotting weed, the hot tar and the wet timbers of the boats, the slick, wet shingle of the beach, the sun baked stones on the pier. She thought it wondrous, she would have lingered for hours had not her family and escort chivvied her to leave (it was not a reputable area apparently). The following day she had gone to the Grand Cathedral and ducal palace for the accession ceremony but grand, no spectacular as it was it made far less an impression on her than the sea had done. All she could remember of the occasion was the dress of silk brocade she had to wear that itched her interminably. Seeing the Whiterush Maw right now brought the memory of the sea back to her; she had to see it again one day, even travel on it, if she was bold enough.

"Hey! Dreamer! It is this way!" Stauncher was calling her, she spun round to see him standing by that part of the cliff that heralded the next part of their climb; so drawn had she been by the wonder of the falls she had walked right past it without noticing.

It was another fault in the cliff face, a great crack that had slipped to make a scalable path and it began pretty much right next to the ridge they were currently traversing, so no great jump required this time. The downside was, as she followed its course with her eyes, was that it was a steep climb, rising into the watery mist before levelling out into a regular pathway above her head. A climb. She was definitely going to tell somebody what she thought about this. And Stauncher was the closest.

"I cannot climb that! My legs are burning enough as it is. When I travel anywhere I normally go by carriage, that or I ride. I would never, ever be expected to stagger up that path. I am nobility you know that, surely."

"Don't we all know that," Stauncher rolled his eyes, "shall I carry you again?"

"No," she said firmly. Then she gave an enormous, exaggerated sigh. "Fine. If I drop down dead can you arrange my funeral? And I leave all my worldly goods to my younger sisters, except for my poetry of course."

"And who gets that?"

THE FANGS OF THE FEN SNAKE

"You."

"You hate me that much?"

She nodded and started the long, wearying climb up the cliff face.

And it was a long slog for all of them, even sprightly old Oswold was flagging now, Shak keeping him upright and walking by placing the flat of his hand on the man's back. He was glad he was wearing gloves for Artorus only knew what resided in the folds of the hermit's robes. Dead Eyes brought up the rear but, because this part of the ridge protruded much further from the cliff face than any of those they had climbed so far she could no longer see beneath her and so had no idea where her pursuers were, let alone be able to send an arrow their way. The ridge here was strewn with spindly bushes and clumps of thick, stubborn grass, rudimentary cover if they were surprised somehow, still, they were a lot closer to the top of the cliff now, if this ridge led them there, well, they should still ascend to the top long before the sun went down.

Eleanor meanwhile was doing little more than stare at her feet. Her soles were throbbing and radiating heat, she really and truly would love to dangle them in the icy river awhile, once they had finished their climb, but first they had to finish it. So stare at her feet she did, trudge, trudge, trudge, counting each grinding step, ignoring the pulling on her thighs and calves, trying to breathe without pain, 100 steps, 200, 300, the whole thing seemed as if it would never end. Then her skirt caught on a thorny bush, she stopped and pulled it free only to realise she had forgotten her count and had to start all over again.

She had passed 500 and was on the point of flouncing extravagantly, sitting down on the spot and refusing to go another step when the long, sloping ridge suddenly levelled out into something approaching an even walk. She brushed past the hanging branches of a twisted, spindly tree and sighed with relief. They seemed to be nearly at the end of the climb.

She still did not look down. She dare not. Artorus only knew how far above the ground they now were. The walkway ahead was straight but quite short, it seemed to narrow to the point where it disappeared into the cliff. Yet they were still some thirty or forty feet beneath the summit. What exactly did this mean for them?

She scurried along the path to join Shak and the others who were standing in a group together despite the narrowness of the precipice, listening to Oswold who was as excitable as ever.

ACT ONE : THE HUNT

He was holding something in his hand. "Here it is!" he gabbled; his voice hoarse. "Up this and away, two more days and you will be over the river and on your way home. Artorus rewards the bold just as Camille favours the wise. Now. Who is going first?"

Eleanor groaned inwardly. Oswold was holding a rope. It was a thick rope for certain, maybe a ship's rope that somebody had long ago brought here just for this purpose. Once it would have been pale brown or raffia in colour, now though, after maybe decades sitting here in this mist and spray, exposed to wind and rain, ice and snow, it was black and covered in patches of weed or lichen. It looked wet, slimy, and well beyond treacherous. She was about to raise an objection but was pleased to hear that others had got in before her.

"Climb...that...rope," Stauncher said, pointedly emphasising each word as though hoping it would clarify the absurdity of such a premise.

"Is it secure?" Dormouse asked. "It looks as though it has been there a very long time."

"It was last time I climbed it." Oswold gave them his gap toothed smile.

"And when was this?" Dormouse persisted.

Oswold shrugged. "Time is so difficult to count out here. Some years yes, many years maybe."

"So it might have rotted or come loose since then."

"Only one way to find out," Oswold's smile never left him.

"Might I make a couple of hopefully salient points here?" Stan interjected; he was looking at Shak more than Oswold. Shak gave him the nod.

"Well," Stan continued. "Point one, we don't know what this rope is secured to up there, also it seems to be very greasy. Point two, yon master hermit here may have had no trouble climbing it but there are people here who are considerably heavier than he is, a rotten rope could snap under excess weight no? And point three, we have to get a young girl up there and point four, how can a hermit climb a rope when he has only got one bollocking arm!"

Shak gave him a thin smile, for he already knew Oswold's reply. "Oh when I did this climb last, I had both of them!"

"Then how in the name of the deceiver were you expecting to climb it now!" Stan kept his tone reasonably restrained, but all there could see he was bristling.

223

THE FANGS OF THE FEN SNAKE

"I thought you could help me," was the simple reply. At this point, probably to avoid the prospect of the old man being hurled headlong into the void Shak decided to intervene.

"We cannot go back Stan," he said calmly.

"But why not?" Stan countered. "There are what? Five of them on our tail. We charge back down, surprise them, we would be through them in no time. Then we can get to Grest just as originally planned, along the west bank of the river, with no horsemen to stop us this time."

"Five of us against five of them?" Shak said quietly.

"Why not?" Stan replied. "We have faced worse odds, much worse odds. Better to trust our own sinew and mettle than a dangling piece of rotten twine."

Oswold looked horrified, for Shak was seemingly giving his companions words due consideration. He turned his back to them, grasped the rope with one clawed hand and started to lever himself up off the ledge, with very little success. "Artorus give me strength!" he cried over and over again as the futility of his struggle became ever more apparent to him.

Shak reached up and plucked the old man off the rope, setting him down gently. "We are discussing things holy man, it will not take long, just bear with us."

"So what are we doing then?" Dormouse asked nervously, looking over his shoulder to the tree that marked that point on the ledge where the climb ended, and the level walk began. Any pursuers would appear there first.

Shak shut his eyes wearily. When he opened them again both voice and expression had an air of resignation about them.

"The people following us are assassins, they know how to kill. Even if we charge them and surprise them they will take some of us with them as they die. By trying the rope, we may all yet live. I have also given my word to aid Father Oswold where I can. So I will try the rope with the holy man, he can hold on to me as I climb. If we can get to the top, so can you. If we fall then only one of us is lost. The rest of you will be free to play hazard with the enemy if you wish. My responsibility is to see that you all live, so whilst I breathe it is a responsibility I will discharge and getting up this cliff remains the best prospect for us all. Now stand back, Dead Eyes, guard our rear, Oswold and I have some climbing to do, Stan, that rope in your pack, lash him to me with it."

They did as ordered, though Stan and Shak looked at each other in

ACT ONE : THE HUNT

silence for a long while after Shak's little speech. As Shak placed a gloved hand around the rope, Oswold now lashed firmly to his back, Eleanor made the following observation to Stan, who was closest to her.

"He always says that it is your lives he wants to protect, never his own. Is it an Arshuman thing? Or something else?"

"Something else," Stan replied. "Since coming out here Shak has never cared whether he lived or died. It is what makes him such a good leader."

"But why?" Eleanor persisted. "Why should a man not fear death?"

"For some people there is a point where living, where continuing on, is a worse experience than death ever could be. Most of us never get to that point. I never have. I never want to."

"But what..." Eleanor started to speak, but saw that Stan was in no mood to continue their conversation, Shak was starting his climb.

It was like carrying a heavy sack. A heavy sack with three wildly flailing limbs and a predilection for singing religious songs in a tuneless, high pitched, reedy, voice. A heavy sack that had been left in the rain too long and carried odours of thick mould and the floor of an unswept stable. And, last but not least, a heavy sack with an irritating, tickly beard. Shak looked up at the sky just to see that there were no gods up there laughing at him then started his ascent, arm over arm, slowly, methodically, one pull at a time.

The rope was sometimes sticky, sometimes slippery under his gloved hands. It appeared to be tied securely enough, it remained taut under the weight of the two men but gripping on to it was so difficult, so treacherous. He lost his hold several times and was only his supporting hand that kept him from coming off the rope completely. Oswold, as ever, seemed oblivious to his imminent peril and was on his eighth rendition of "Artorus, o great protector" by the time Shak hauled himself over the clifftop and to safety. His gloves by that point were black and coated with slime.

He wasted no time in untying the rope and setting Oswold free, the old man rolling off him in an ungainly heap before righting himself and capering about wildly. "You did it!" he cried. "You got me up here! Now I can find the tunnels and put right the mistakes of my past! And I can take you to the crossing point. Two days! Two days and we will be there!"

"Two days," Shak said laconically, "then perhaps I can correct my mistakes too."

He threw their rope down to the others, Stauncher catching it one handed. Eleanor looked over to him. "Same as last time?" she asked him.

THE FANGS OF THE FEN SNAKE

Stauncher however looked uncomfortable at the prospect. "What is it?" she enquired.

"The jump over the chasm was a matter of seconds," he said. "This would take some minutes; I don't really want you clinging onto me for that long."

"Well I can't climb that thing on my own," she pouted. "You want to leave me here? Well I am fine with that; I can just wait for these people chasing us to come and get me."

He sounded exasperated. "It is not that. It is just that you are no longer a girl but not yet a woman…"

"I am a woman," she insisted. "I am getting married, remember?"

"I remember."

"You are saying that I am not yet old enough to be able to fulfil all the duties of a wife. Well I can assure you that I can."

"No," he sounded even more exasperated. "That is a private matter for you and your husband. What I am saying is that if you were my daughter and her husband did enforce his rights on her at her age he would be wearing his testicles as earrings by now. No that is not what I am saying, I am saying that I feel awkward carrying a young woman up that rope with me. Don't you feel the same way?"

Her eyes widened as she made her plaintive reply. "Stauncher, all I want is to get through this day alive."

He smiled at her, a sad smile as he tucked his hat into his belt. "Wise words. Well, let's get going then. Dormouse, bring my stuff up when it is your turn to climb, I will have enough baggage of my own. Do you want the rope around your waist Lady Eleanor?"

She shook her head. "I can hang on, besides, if you fall so do I, no rope will help me then."

The two of them made ready, Eleanor hanging on with all her strength. Oddly enough, she no longer felt the cloying fear that had possessed her when they jumped the chasm. It was as though she had passed that point where fear no longer had relevance, the Gods had decided her fate already, how could she possibly change it?

Whereas Shak seemed to make the climb seem effortless, long limbs scaling the cliff like a human spider, Stauncher, shorter and more pugnacious, took longer to get to the top. However, he never faltered, never slipped, or lost his grip like Shak had done, Eleanor felt almost relaxed, she even started a conversation halfway to the top.

She was looking at his head, and its great scar. "That knight must have dealt an incredible blow to you. Did he use a sword?"

"An axe," Stauncher huffed, "and it wasn't a knight."

"Oh," she was surprised. "I am sure you told me…"

"I lie," was the breezy response. "The truth is often so mundane, and I get so bored with the same questions over and over again that I often make the answers more interesting, more in line with what the questioners expect."

"So I ask boring questions then."

"Well it is the second time you have mentioned the scar."

"And it wasn't a knight."

"No."

"So who was it then?"

He strained for breath. "Not now, I need to concentrate and for Keth's sake keep your hands tight to my belt!"

"I am! I dare not do less!"

"Then good. And shut up till we get to the top!"

She did so and minutes later they were there, Stauncher letting Eleanor clamber over him to take Shak's hand before easing himself up safely.

"The rope is well secured," he said to his leader, his words punctuated by heavy breathing.

"Around this tree, and a heavy stone behind it, and finally to a thick metal pole of some sort hammered into the earth," Shak told him, "come see."

Stauncher got to his feet to observe that Shak was telling the truth. He knelt at the metal object, running his fingers over it. "Could be an anchor," he said. "A ship's anchor."

"Yes," Oswold said. "Many seamen have joined our order over the years. Some choose the life of a hermit; I remember a couple heading into the wilderness when I was but a novice. Perhaps they put this there, in a quest to discover a new place of solitude."

They returned to the cliff edge, where Dormouse was now attempting the ascent, Stauncher's heavy pack slung over his shoulder. Like the jump earlier, the young man found little to trouble him, completing the climb in no time at all to be met by Shak and Stauncher, and several appreciative pats on the back.

Stan, who had been out of sorts all day was next. He made the climb, cursing all the way, but close to the summit his hand slipped off the rope completely. In his frantic attempts to compensate his body started to swing wildly, taking the rope with him as he rolled from left to right, right to left, hundreds of feet above ground.

"Just hang on!" Shak implored him. "And stay still!"

Stan's reply was not repeatable.

Finally, he was there, flopping on to the cliff top like a dead fish. Shak helped him stand.

"I have had an absolute dunghill of a day," he said finally.

"Still got all your weapons?" Shak asked him.

A quick check, then Stan gave him an affirmative nod.

"See," Shak told him, "it could have been worse. Your lucky knuckles did it again. We can talk fully afterwards, let's make sure Dead Eyes joins us first."

They returned to the precipice and looked over to see that the elf was already past the halfway point of her climb. She was, as ever, making it look easy.

"She is good at everything," Eleanor observed with a hint of bitterness.

She then noticed that both Shak and Stan were not looking at the elf, but towards the tree on the ridge below, at the point where it levelled out. There were several figures there, a couple of tall men and another man who seemed to be totally clad in black. They had been seen too for one of them put his hand to his mouth and started to shout up at them. And then she started to tremble, for she recognised the voice.

"Eleanor! Eleanor! It is Nico, your brother. I am here with Sir Ursus, and we are coming for you! We say to your captors, let her go! If you wish to live let her come to us! For we will show no mercy when we reach you!"

"Nico!" Eleanor called back excitedly, waving her arm in the air. "I am here, I am here!"

"You have to scale the cliff first, knight," Stan said quietly. "Just try it with us waiting up here."

Shak however did not hear him. He was staring intently at the figures as they hovered around the lone tree, especially the one in black, who they could now see had a scarf wrapped in such a way as to cover most of his face.

"Keth shrivel my skin," he said at length, as Dead Eyes finished her climb and came to join them. "Doul."

ACT ONE : THE HUNT

16

The floors were of white marble, veined with a rich, decadent black that patterned it like an ink droplet diffusing in water. A double row of gilded columns supported a ceiling covered with gaudily painted frescoes, their rich colours illuminated by innumerable picture windows with casements of silver and gold. Shak studied the frescoes for a while, he had seen them pretty much every day of his life yet had rarely truly looked at them before. They depicted many battles, each characterised by a well-known landmark or a particular warrior. He knew all the battles, Cresh ridge, Pyran river, Zantras, Peraderon, Groggari fields and so on. His conclusion? Most of Arshuma's greatest and most glorious battles were against fellow Arshumans. Especially in the south where each city state jealously protected its own interests. To someone from his city of Mazuras, the Arshuman city of Bect could be as fierce a rival, as deadly an enemy, as any foreign army.

His feet echoed off the floor as he strode along the hall, white cloak trailing behind him, sun through the windows glinting off the gold thread of his robes. He stopped and looked through the nearest window, wherefore lay the harbour and the sea, foam tipped breakers toying with the ships and the sailors crewing them. He sighed. He would rather be out there than in here, but in here was where duty lay, in here was where his father lay on his sickbed, and that was where he was headed right now.

Through the doors of carved rosewood and up the spiral stairs of the tower he went, his long limbs fairly skipping up them in his haste. As he climbed and turned circles on the winding stairs the various slit windows in the tower afforded him a panoramic view of the world outside. The ornamental ponds in the courtyard, the trellised walkways latticed with grapevines, the formal gardens, the citrus orchards, to be wealthy in Mazuras was a desirable thing indeed. Of course he knew that to take the road from palace to harbour was to see the other side of the city, the cramped, whitewashed buildings, tenements five or six storeys high, the piles of refuse steaming in the streets, the smells of fish oil and sweat. Then there were the ragged, wide eyed beggar children congregating along the canals, the spice and dye merchants under their crimson awnings looking to fleece the gullible, the armed gangs and their whores clad in cheap gauze touting for business in

ACT ONE : THE HUNT

the shadowed alleyways. All this whilst the city watch counted their bribes and turned a blind eye to a knife in the dark. So many signs that life in this compact, overpopulated, walled city in the marshes could be a lot less than harmonious. To run such a place, to control it, to keep it happy enough to stop blood flowing in the streets was a gargantuan task and one in truth that a man with such limited abilities as his father would never successfully accomplish. And now his father had returned from his hunting trip in the Zantras forest debilitated in some way, though in what way exactly he was yet to find out.

    He entered a much narrower corridor, though it was again marbled, in black this time, as were the thin columns whose role, with their gilded capitals and scrollwork, was more ornamental than practical. Here were the private rooms of many of Mazuras most prominent citizens, or, to put it another way, his family. He passed an ornate, bejewelled golden brazier smoking with woody incense, he passed a doorway of carved mahogany in which lay his wife, recovering well after her third miscarriage, and then he stopped, outside a similar doorway flanked by two guards carrying long ash spears and wearing blue and yellow livery. He was about to go through when he saw a man rise from a nearby bench and come towards him. In some ways he resembled Shak, tall, but not as tall, handsome but not quite as handsome and on his face, covering his lower right cheek and chin, he sported an angry red birthmark which almost glowed under the light of the lamps. He had a slight paunch and a nervous, listless disposition which meant he could never look Shak directly in the eye. Odd really, for this was Shak's younger brother, Ilasko.

    "Father is sleeping," he said in hushed, confidential tones, though the hall was so quiet his voice still fairly echoed off the marble. "It may be best that you don't see him till he wakes."

    "I will see him when I choose," was the cool reply. "Do you know what happened to him exactly?"

    "He was hunting snout boar in the forests when he was struck by an arrow. The hunting party were all close to him and in view, so it didn't come from them. They searched the woods thoroughly after the incident but found nothing."

    "Where was he struck?"

    "In the back, just below the shoulder, they took the arrow out quickly enough and cauterized the wound, but it appears that the arrow was tipped with some sort of poison, a residue of which is still in his system. The healers are trying to counter the poison and the Artoran priest is next to them praying

THE FANGS OF THE FEN SNAKE

for deliverance but as of yet, we do not know exactly what the poison is."

"A poisoned arrow," Shak folded his arms. "A premeditated assassination attempt it seems. I will have my men out in the streets within the hour."

"Mine are out already." Ilasko's reply contained just the right hint of smugness. "I am hoping they can at least find out the type of poison soon. If not..." he opened his arms in a gesture of futility.

"If not?" Shak asked him, being deliberately obtuse.

"Then the city will be yours brother, yours to command. One man's poisoned arrow is another man's golden crown," he quoted an old Arshuman saying. Shak however was frowning.

"Are you suggesting I played a part in this...treason?"

"No brother, no!" Ilasko's fervent denial made up in volume what it lacked in integrity. "All I meant was that the Lady Mazuras needs all the prayers we can give her, the need to produce an heir might be more pressing than we suspected."

"You have two boys Ilasko, the succession is secure, even if my bloodline isn't. When my men return, and yours do the same we will confer. We need names, suspects, the city will want a mass public garrotting for this crime, they will expect a speedy resolution. Artorus only knows the populace are angry enough already, it is barely a week since we put down that last riot"

"There will be heads on display on the city walls within the week, and body parts sent to the subject towns for the same purpose." Ilasko spoke with no little relish. Shak had to smile. "You always had a penchant for excessive bloodlust my brother."

"A family trait," came the smooth reply.

Further conversation was interrupted for at that moment the door opened noiselessly on oiled hinges and a sister of Meriel, in her robe of red and white padded gracefully into the hallway. She was well past middle years with her fine silver hair bound tightly around her head, severe, yet appropriate. She saw them and came over, small beads of sweat on her brow a testament both to the summer heat and the importance of the people she was addressing.

She bowed, going down on one knee before speaking. "My lords, your father sleeps still. His condition appears to have...stabilised; we have taken steps to neutralise the poison and both the priests and healers believe that his life is no longer in immediate danger."

232

ACT ONE : THE HUNT

"Meriel be praised!" Ilasko clapped his hands together with delight and a little too much enthusiasm, almost as though he had to be seen to be happy with the outcome. Shak however was more circumspect in his response.

"The tone of your voice priestess, it is at variance with the optimism of your words. What exactly do you mean by stabilised? Stabilised at what point exactly?"

Her eyes were wary, the sweat on her brow a little more profuse.

"There was a delay of hours before a sister was able to see him and a further delay before the nature of the poison could be determined and an antidote provided. I am afraid that the poison had already done a lot of harm by then. We will not be certain of its full effects till he wakes, but..."

"What has it done to him?" Shak's gaze was steely, impossible to turn away from.

"My lords," The sister blurted out, "I fear your father has lost his sight. I fear also that many of his internal organs have been attacked, he may be unable to properly digest food for example and even simple things such as walking may be difficult or even impossible for him. I am sorry, we have done our best."

"Neither of us doubt that sister." Shak and Ilasko exchanged a telling glance, a glance that told of little trust between the siblings. Shak just had one more thing to ask.

"The poison, sister, what exactly was it?"

"A compound harvested from the bracts of the skullweed plant, that thrives in the remote marshes of the country of Mothravia. We used a clay based antidote, mixed with milk, honey and several powerful herbs. He will need more treatment obviously, maybe for many months, maybe for the rest of his life."

"Then we have detained you too long already, it is best you return to your patient, I will be in to see him shortly." Shak gave her a courteous half bow; she responded with a curtsey and left the two of them alone.

"A professional job," Shak said to his brother, "organised by someone who knew he was planning to go on a hunt. How many people did know I wonder?"

"Well there was us two," Ilasko said brightly. "Then his inner circle, their spouses, and retainers, it was hardly a secret, it must be at least fifty people."

THE FANGS OF THE FEN SNAKE

"But not all of them have the wherewithal to hire an assassin for the job. Few of them cultivate such connections, just the political players, like us. Which assassin was daring enough to try this? Brakaro maybe? Brakaro of Lentisi? He has the flamboyance and the arrogance for this job and has many "talented" people on his payroll."

Ilasko shook his head. "He is a man on the wane, it happens with such people, the more they become known, the less effective they become. It could be a local man, someone like Threshen the dagger…"

"The same Threshen the dagger found face down in the north canal not five days ago. I suppose his ghost could have done it," Shak was silent for a moment. "What about that new fellow, from Crallbok, he uses a bow."

Ilasko frowned, it looked like he needed further prompting. "You know," Shak said, "supposed to have killed that magistrate a month or so back. Wears black, keeps his face covered because he was scarred as a child."

"Oh!" Ilasko understood at last. "He was a young boy caught stealing apples. The stall holder is supposed to have said something like, "if you are so greedy you need a bigger mouth" before slashing him cheek to cheek with a butcher's knife."

"That's him," Shak snapped his fingers. "Uses an alias, no one is sure of his real name…"

"Doul," Ilasko said, "he is known as Doul."

"Doul," Shak nodded. "I will send my men out to look for him now, he has many questions to answer."

"He has," Ilasko agreed. "Ten gold herons say my men will find him first."

****

"Stauncher, Dormouse, try pulling that rope up. It is wet and heavy but the two of you should manage it. Stan, come with me, it seems that this knight is happy to parley."

Shak gave his orders and went to stand as close to the cliff edge as he dared. On the ledge beneath figures hovered just behind the lone tree where the ridge began to slope downwards, including the one he suspected was Doul. The two knights, if that was what they were, were much bolder, strolling towards him along the ledge, looking directly up at him, exhibiting no traces of fear at all.

"We want to talk," the knight called Nico shouted up to him. "See, my

ACT ONE : THE HUNT

sword is sheathed, as is Sir Ursus' next to me. Your archer could slay us both easily and you know it. A brief truce, a chance to parley, then it is up to you."

"Come closer then, all the better for me to hear you," Shak replied. "As you can see, my archer is not with me, and I will not call her whilst this "truce" holds. So talk, you have my word as a nobleman that my reply will consist of words only, not arrows."

Nico was now standing directly under Shak and Stan. "First of all," he said, "the Lady Eleanor, I have heard her, now I would like to see her, to see that she is well."

"She is," Shak replied. "Her voice, especially, is thriving, but if you want confirmation then you shall have it."

Stan disappeared briefly, before returning shortly after holding Eleanor by the waist. She waved down at her brother. "Nico! I am here, what a mess we have found ourselves in!"

"Are you well sister?"

"Well apart from all the walking, the lack of clean clothes, the bland food, no decent latrine, no hope of a bath..."

"But are you well?"

"Oh!" She put her hand to her mouth. "Yes, they treat me better than they treat themselves. Does my husband know what has happened?"

Nico frowned. "No. We will keep this between us for as long as we can. It ill serves the family honour that one of our own should be held by the enemy."

Eleanor pulled a face. "Are you saying that I am bringing dishonour to the family?"

Nico, realising his harsh tone sounded inappropriate tried to be a little more mollifying. "It is not your fault; we should have got to you before you were taken. Still, perhaps this matter can be resolved here and now, if your captors are amenable to reason."

"And what reason would that be?" Shak enquired.

Nico stood tall, the pallid sun piercing the smoky haze to gleam off his armour. "The proposal I make is a simple one. Send Eleanor down. Send Eleanor down and we will leave you alone. Send Eleanor down and your lives will be your own again."

Shak nodded ironically. "And what do your "allies" think of this proposal? I know for a fact they are after more than just the lady, our heads would bring them good reward from their employers."

THE FANGS OF THE FEN SNAKE

"You are right of course. What they do is their own concern. But Ursus and I will abandon them. There will just be three of them against what, five or six of you. And you have the high ground. All you need do is wait for them to make a move and your archer can do the rest."

Shak laughed. "I see you are a man of honour, but you need to educate yourself as to your new friends. Not everybody fights the way you do."

"But you have the rope," Nico seemed genuinely surprised. "You are pulling it up as we speak. All of the advantages are yours."

"At least one of those with you has many tricks up his sleeve. Poisons, flash bombs, fire arrows, burning oils, he has used them all. He would wait till nightfall and attack us in whatever way suits him best. While he is with you, none of us are safe. And if you think they will let you ride off with the lady, well you are naïve. I trust you Sir Nico, but not your associates. Eleanor stays with us."

Eleanor looked resigned, Ursus groaned, Stan bit his lip. "So be it," was all Nico said. Ursus though finally found his voice.

"Then we have no choice than to take her by force," his voice was gravelly, commanding, "and any of you that try to prevent us from fulfilling our duty will suffer for it. I am Sir Ursus, we are the bodyguard of the Grand Duke, we have sworn an oath, and the Gods are with us."

Bold words, and enough to prick one of the listeners. Stan took his hand off Eleanor's waist, noting that she was ruefully shaking her head. "Your name is Ursus?" he said, "then have mine. It is Crastanik Bectalis of South Arshuma. I have faced many of your knights in battle and look! I am still here! I remain unkilled! Your armour is no defence against my axe and your courage is counterfeit! I only ever recognise a knight of the Silver Lance from looking at his back, when he is running away from me and leaving behind a streaky trail of his own liquid shit! Pursue us and you will never return home again!"

Nico stood, his jaw clenching at the insult. Ursus coloured, drew his sword, and pointed it at Stan. "When the time comes sir, I will seek you out in the field, that is another oath I will take gladly."

"And I Sir Ursus, will not hide from you. But I urge haste on your part for I can see infirmity sitting on your shoulder like a bitter old crow. Hurry old man, lest you have to meet our assignation by being carried there in a chair!"

Ursus laughed at that. "Your arrogance will be no shield against my blade. And I see that you are closer to me in years than you would dare admit.

ACT ONE : THE HUNT

I sense a fear in you, that the day is near when a younger man will supplant you. Well fear not, I will remove such concerns by taking your head!"

Stan stuck his neck out, over the cliff. "Here it is old man, have you the reach? Or the skill?"

It was time to cut this short. "Our deliberations are over," Shak said to all, "we have our duty, you have yours. You are both men of honour, in happier times I would be glad to count you as friends and allies. But our paths are set, you know where we are, try and stop us and let us see what transpires."

The rope had been pulled up. Shak turned and disappeared from the cliff top, Stan leading Eleanor the same way a moment later. They had gone, and Nico was left with the roar of the falls and a cliff face he had no idea how to scale.

****

"They saw you," Nico said. Doul had now joined him, leaving the cover of the tree behind. Siri and Zukan too were on their way. "The leader recognised you, they were never going to release Eleanor after that."

"Pity," Doul hissed. "I was complacent; I was not expecting to be in full view so quickly. Well you did what you could, it is not your fault your sister is not with you now. Though your pledge to abandon us was an interesting one."

"A bluff, no more. Anyway, how does he know you exactly?" Ursus spoke abruptly, he was still ill at ease with his new companions and in no mood to deal with awkward insinuations.

Doul though took no offence at the brusqueness of the question. "He is South Arshuman nobility. It is a given that such men have connections with those in my profession. In South Arshuma the city states are all antagonistic to each other and within each city all the prominent families seek pre-eminence, often at the expense of their supposed allies. For a man with no money and no prospects, as I was, the art of murder is an easy path to riches. Many try it, most of them expire soon enough, but the best, the very best, can command the lifestyle of kings."

"Which is why you are here of course, freezing your gold coins off in the wilderness," Ursus was unimpressed.

"It is precisely why I am here," Doul sounded almost happy. "To maintain such a lifestyle I have to take on one or two jobs like this a year. I do not work solely in Arshuma for regrettably, a man such as I has many enemies, stay too long in one place and they tend to be drawn to me, like parasites on a prize buffalo. So I work in the Chiran empire, Arshuma, and in southern countries like Mothravia and Fash. It helps me keep my anonymity and my enemies guessing."

"So it was in Fash that you met your companions?" Nico asked, for Siri and Zukan had joined them by now, Siri being occupied in a close scrutiny of the cliff face. She had pulled off her gloves and was touching it with her bare hands.

"No," Doul replied. "They had fled from Fash when I met them. We worked together on a job in Arshuma, our talents complemented each other, so, when I took this job I had a mind to bring them along."

"You mean bring Siri along," Zukan sulked. "I was just an afterthought."

"Nonsense," Doul corrected him, though he was staring at Siri as he replied. "You have already proven your worth. And you will again."

Zukan did not look placated, he continued staring gloomily into the mist. Ursus was looking over the ledge at the distant ground below. He spat into the space, watching gloomily as the spittle disappeared into the rolling cloud of spray. "One of the reasons our enemies cited for not giving Eleanor to us was that they suspected that you have the capacity to attack them at night. When it was suggested that all they had to do was wait at the clifftop for us to come to them, then pick us off with arrows they were not convinced, they thought you had the capacity to overwhelm them even from here, even where they appear to hold all the cards."

"Poisons, flash bombs, fire arrows and burning oils, he suspected you had all of these things." Nico remembered what he had been told, word for word. "Was he correct?"

Doul looked over at one of the heavy packs Zukan had been carrying for him. "He was. We have the capability to deliver all of these things."

"What are flash bombs?" Nico asked.

"Metallic spheres, purchased at great cost from characters even more disreputable than me." Nico guessed that Doul was smiling behind his scarf. "A burning wick ignites the contents. Some explode with a white flash that stun the victim and leave them deafened, others just explode in a ball of flame sending hot metal shards flying everywhere. Imprecise, but effective. We have further spheres, delicate ones that shatter and emit a poisonous cloud, they are kept in a velvet lined box and are the most expensive of all."

"Impressive," Ursus spoke in a distinctly unimpressed tone. "But I

238

ACT ONE : THE HUNT

would hardly call it war."

"It is not war," Doul enthused, "it is art."

The two knights looked at each other, but kept their silence, at least until they saw Siri removing her heavy fur cloak. "What are you doing?" Nico asked. "Is it too hot for you?"

"No," Siri narrowed her eyes. "Two hundred miles south of here is still too cold for me."

"Then why...?" Nico stopped and stared. Zukan was in the process of tying a rope around his sister's waist, under her furs she wore a white linen tunic and breeches, like a man. When he had done that he tied the other end around his own.

"Sir knights, perhaps I should tell you a little more about our previous collaboration." Doul still sounded immensely pleased with himself. "A wealthy Arshuman merchant was our mark. He knew though that people were after him, so he converted a cave into a defensive sanctuary. All his luxurious furnishings were moved there, all his wealth, all his gold, all his guards. There were several chambers in the cave and seemingly the only way to access them was through a tunnel that had at least a dozen guards manning it at any one time. I was thinking of using bombs to clear the tunnel, but it was a risky enterprise. Besides, reinforcements were housed in a chamber nearby and they would have swarmed me soon afterwards. It was then I realised there might be another way in."

Zukan handed the rope to Ursus. After a brief moment of confusion Ursus started to tie it around his waist as Zukan had done. Then Ursus handed it to Nico who started to do the same. Siri meanwhile was placing the flat of her hands against the cliff. Doul continued.

"You see there was another entrance, one that ventilated the caves, a narrow opening of about four feet at its widest point. The problem was that it was in a cliff face that opened out onto the sea, hundreds of feet above a narrow shingle beach. I put out the word but had little hope of finding the person I needed, then someone put me in touch with Siri. Siri you see may be a professional dancer but one of the other things she excels at is..."

At that moment Siri put her foot into a stirrup formed by the crouching Zukan's hands and with little warning launched herself against the cliff face. To the surprise of both Nico and Ursus her fingers found a purchase, a tiny crevice in the rock only the keenest eyes would notice.

"Climbing." Doul finished his sentence. For the next few minutes, the men stood in silence as Siri, splaying her legs and fingers like a lizard in the sun slowly started to move upwards, her feet sure, her fingers strong. Even Ursus looked slightly awed at her heretofore unknown talent.

"So she climbed this cliff for me, took her hours, then she let down a rope for me to follow. The merchant died that night, along with the two guards at his door. Nobody else even knew we were there, not till the morning when they found the bodies and a goodly proportion of gold missing. Sirisibali has more courage in her fingertips than a dozen normal men have in their entire bodies."

She was already a third of the way up, feeling her way then hauling her lissom, athletic form a few inches closer to her goal. Nico had to smile. "If she keeps this up then lets the rope down for the rest of us we should be off this cursed cliff before nightfall. The Gods surprise us all. Again."

"Siri is not a goddess," Zukan put him in his place, "she is my sister."

Doul was now thinking ahead. "Prasiak and his men will be making haste right now, they know that this cliff will not defeat us and that soon we will be hard on their trail. What they will not be expecting however, is for us to cross the river and be lying in wait to intercept them in a few days' time. We are working as a team, Siri gets us up the cliff and you, Sir Ursus, will be getting us over the river."

"Either that or I will be sailing down that waterfall head first," Ursus grumbled.

"No," Doul said emphatically. "The Gods have brought us together for a purpose. Keep your weapons keen and your eyes as sharp as your blades. You will be needing both in the days to come."

ACT ONE : THE HUNT

17

It was twilight in the great gorge and nary a breath stirred in the tall trees. In this deepest of valleys, they lined the lower slopes, gaunt, skeletal, guardians of a wilderness where man had seldom ever set foot. The river still ploughed inexorably southwards, its eerie roar echoing off high mountainsides that gleamed a pale icy blue in the light of the emerging moon. Cascading in frothy plumes down their nameless heights poured the Whiterush tributaries. Never too wide to cross the narrowest of them had started to freeze in the teeth of strengthening winter, Dormouse had already cracked the ice on one when he had inadvertently trodden on it earlier. Little grass grew here and the brakes of fern and heather that they passed were brown, dead, and dry. The narrow gorge, for the landscape appeared identical the other side of the river also, acted like a funnel for cold airs, for a chill breeze had been burning their faces and watering their eyes from the moment they had started their journey in this shadowy, little known, wilderness. Above them a great eagle soared on the bitter winds, silhouetted by the moon, feathers splayed like human fingers, eyes keen as a lance, scouring the broken ground for a furtive meal. Dormouse stopped a moment to look at it and it seemed to notice him for at that moment it called out, a piercing, shivering cry, a lonely, isolated call that slowly faded into the spectral wind. At least it could just fly across the river Dormouse thought, if only they could do the same.

Nobody had spoken for an age, they had been walking for some hours and all of them had seemingly adopted the same sense of alertness, or perhaps a better description would be paranoia for all of them were doing little but listen out for signs of pursuit. But there had been nothing; the odd cracked twig, the occasional snickering animal or loose sliding stone had given them pause, but no, the silence and the echoing mountains amplified these noises, gave them a presence, a threat that they didn't truly deserve. The river was a constant, the mountains were a constant, the sense of claustrophobia was a constant but there had been no feeling of threat for a good while.

Dormouse felt the need to say something, a few words to lift the spirits but inspiration deserted him. Instead, he settled on a question. He half knew the answer, he had heard many people, far removed from the conflict discuss the topic many times over the years. But it was one thing to hear

ACT ONE : THE HUNT

louche gossip from half cut courtiers and another to hear the opinions of men who had been embroiled in this conflict for a long, long time.

"All I have seen these last days is wasteland and wilderness," he said, in a voice that sounded very small. "It makes you wonder what this war is for in the first place. There is nothing here, nothing worth seizing, nothing worth possessing and certainly nothing worth dying for. Why did our king commit so much in such a futile enterprise? If I did not know him better I would almost accuse him of being rash."

Shak laughed at the last statement. "If you had said that at court there would be a wall spike somewhere specifically tailored to fit your perfectly excised head. Just woods, fields, and mountains you might think but the woods are fruitful, the fields are fertile and the mountains…"

"What can mountains possibly provide?" Dormouse asked innocently though again, he half knew the answer.

"These mountains?" Shak answered. "The Western Derannen mountains are famous for their gem mines. They are far richer than the mountains that encircle our country. Why have so many hard bitten, cynical men bought into father Oswold's tale of treasure? It is because these mountains have a reputation, common folk are said to climb up them carrying nothing but a pickaxe, but to come back down being carried on a golden litter borne by a dozen servants. Much of all this is a myth of course, but people catch gold fever easily it seems, even kings can fall for such talk just as our own beggar king has done."

"Why do you call him the beggar king?" Eleanor asked.

"Because he is descended from common stock, unlike us southern Arshuman princes who can trace their ancestry back to before the time Arshuma was even founded. You appear to be limping slightly my lady, are you feeling footsore?"

She was, and she seemed grateful that somebody had finally noticed. "All this walking, my soles are throbbing a bit, I hope there is not much further to go."

"Not far, not far," Oswold, who seemed unaffected by cold or fatigue, answered. "A bit of an uphill climb in a moment then we get to a cave. It is hidden behind some boulders, a good place to hide. You can rest your feet then."

"I might be able to help you, Eleanor," Stauncher told her. "I have a flask of liniment that can be rubbed into the sore areas. Will toughen your skin though, turn it into shoe leather, or cow hide, great for walking long distances, not so good for..."

"A girl about to be married?" Eleanor pulled some hair from her face to reveal a suitably glum expression. "A woman in a noble marriage should be soft and pliant, delicate and pleasing to the eye. She should not be a bedraggled vagabond that smells like an ox that has pulled a plough all day with feet you couldn't push a darning needle through!"

"Last time I was in this cave there was a pool," Oswold smiled at her, a most disconcerting spectacle. "One you can wash in; it is in a small chamber that provides some privacy."

Eleanor perked up. "Really father, I can bathe? By Elissa let it be so. Did you wash in it yourself then?"

"Oh, I never wash," Oswold said proudly, "you find when you live alone that it is a most taxing diversion, time wasted when you should be thinking of the Gods and your place in their grand creation. And the Gods provide anyway, your own skin secretes an oil that cleanses the body."

"I know," Eleanor answered flatly, "it is called sweat. The first thing a man asks when he is told of his bride to be is "Oh I do hope she sweats a lot; I like a girl that is clean"."

"You jest of course," Oswold replied. "Men rarely exhibit such wisdom. Ah! Those rocks up there, that is our route, soon we may sup and sleep...and wash too if that is your inclination."

The moon was strengthening and so provided some illumination as Oswold led them up the silvery, rubble strewn mountainside to a series of larger boulders, obviously evidence of an avalanche many years ago. Ducking behind these boulders revealed a cave mouth that was little more than a narrow gash, so tight that Stan had to breathe in sharply to squeeze through. Once in, he immediately volunteered to take the first watch and squeezed straight back outside again.

It was almost as narrow inside, more of a crevice than a cave, and it was dark though fortunately the previous occupier, another hermit presumably, had left brushwood, flint, tinder, and oil near the entrance. Once they had a fire going Dead Eyes and Eleanor slipped through a side passageway, to where Oswold told them that the pool would be.

Shak found a corner, sat, and stretched out his long legs before saying to Oswold "Presumably the water in that pool is runoff from the mountain above, melted snow and ice and the like..."

ACT ONE : THE HUNT

Oswold nodded.

"So it is probably quite cold."

"Oh without a doubt."

Shortly afterwards a loud splash, followed immediately by a high pitched shriek gave him all the confirmation he needed.

****

She was clean. She was dressed. She was beginning to warm up at last and Dead Eyes was sat behind her combing her hair. Water dripped into the little pool in front of her, a pool whose depth had surprised her, the water reaching up to her shoulders after she had jumped in. After the shock of the cold, she realised that Dead Eyes had got in next to her. They had a little water fight, throwing handfuls of the freezing stuff over each other, she was sure the elf had started it. It was fun, she had laughed. And now Dead Eyes was combing her hair by the feeble glow of the lighted taper they had brought with them.

"You are not like I had expected a Wych to be," Eleanor said, unsure if she had used the correct grammar. "We have an... image of your people and you don't really conform to it at all."

"I don't?" Dead Eyes sounded amused. "What exactly is this image that you speak of? Remember that I am not from here and have never been to the elf forest on the other side of these mountains. What am I supposed to be like then?"

Eleanor frowned, now the question had been asked she realised that she didn't really know the answer. "Oh, sort of aloof, haughty, slightly superior. You do not talk much and are very hostile to humans. Some people even say you use human blood in your pagan rituals."

"Which we conduct naked, and which invariably ends in an orgy, I have heard such stories too. Alas my tribe never indulged in them, they sound like fun, better than singing songs about the properties of flowers that last all morning, which is one of the worst things I remember from my childhood." Dead Eyes put down the comb and started teasing Eleanor's hair with her fingers. "The truth is that some of us are aloof and haughty and some of us laugh merrily from dawn to dusk. We have as many different personalities as humans but, when we have to face you we are nervous and guarded. It is understandable when given our past histories, but such reticence can easily be misconstrued as haughtiness I suppose. I have been the same around humans in the past."

"Yes, that makes sense," Eleanor sounded thoughtful, "and I suppose us Tanarese are even more paranoid about you as we have thousands of you living in an impenetrable forest right on our borders. So what do elves think of humans? Do they have similar misapprehensions?"

"You are hairy, you don't wash, your speech is barbarous, you have a predilection towards mindless savagery, and you have weird attitudes towards sex." Dead Eyes handed Eleanor back her comb. "So no, I think we have judged you pretty accurately and no elf has been closer to humans these last years as I have."

"Weird attitudes to sex?" Eleanor was laughing now. "How so?"

"You dislike it so; you have so many rules about it. I had a partner, a man I was going to marry, but that marriage never took place in the end. The human response when I tell them this is one of pity, insofar in that we never got to... what is your word? Consummate the relationship. When I tell them that we were sharing each other for years before the wedding they are shocked. But why? What is wrong with that? I put it down to human fertility, children are far easier to come by for you, so you fear the process by which they are created. Yet there are ways to avoid such an outcome, you just never seem to take them. My theory is that if you shared your bodies with each other more, your desire for war and domination would decrease markedly, you may even end up believing in peaceful coexistence. Anyway, enough nonsense talk from me, it sounds like the others have a fire going and where there is fire there is food. And I am hungry, and your stomach rumbles like a rolling boulder."

Eleanor put her hand on the offending organ, she had hoped that Dead Eyes hadn't noticed. Easing herself to her feet she made ready to join the others. "It doesn't help that your people are perfect," she moaned. "You climb, jump, hunt and fight like it is no effort at all. And your stomach never rumbles. I really do not know how we defeated you in war."

"Numbers," Dead Eyes said. "A hundred humans to one elf, there is only one outcome. Oh, and you humans never know when you are beaten, a defeat and you merely redouble your efforts. You are resourceful and determined and you do not compromise, so as you can see, there are human qualities that I do seriously admire. Others however, such as an inability to share food I have nothing but disdain for, if we do not move now there will be nothing left for us!"

ACT ONE : THE HUNT

They re-joined the others, sitting round their little fire and finding that, in fact, food had been left ready for them. Dead Eyes tucked in ravenously, Eleanor was rather more circumspect, one oat cake after all did taste much like all the others. She noticed that Dormouse was already asleep, that Shak and Oswold were sitting next to each other like old friends and that Stauncher was holding an open flask and giving her a playful look. She suddenly knew why.

"How are your feet?" he asked her.

"The cold bath helped," she replied, "but they are still a little tender."

"Throbbing?"

She nodded.

"Right, slip your boots off, Dead Eyes can rub this stuff in for you, once she has finished stuffing her face that is."

Eleanor eased them off slowly, grateful that she hadn't put her stockings back on. "Will it sting?" she asked. "Phew, I can smell the stuff from here."

"The stronger the smell the better the medicine," Stauncher smiled; "first thing you learn as a healer." He handed the flask to Dead Eyes, who, for someone so precise and fastidious in movement and actions had, rather incongruously, some oaty flakes adhering to her chin.

Eleanor stretched and put her feet out, allowing the elf to administer the medicine. It did not sting nearly as much as expected and, before she allowed weariness to overcome her, decided to ask an inflammatory question.

"So, let's just say you manage to get me wherever you are taking me, without my brother snatching me back or me escaping (she ignored Stauncher's snigger). What happens if nobody pays the ransom? Which one of you is going to kill me?"

As she suspected, they all seemed rather more amused than offended. "Your faith in your family is overwhelming," Shak told her.

"It is a hypothetical question," she replied.

"Then the hypothetical answer is none of us." Shak picked up a strip of dried meat, thought better of it and had some dried fruit instead. "When we get to Tantala we hand you over to those in charge there and our responsibility for you ends. It would be one of the commander's thugs who would do the deed. However, this war has been running for a decade, many hostages have been taken and to my knowledge none of them have ever been killed. Think of yourself as a bag of gold with legs, you don't just throw it away.

THE FANGS OF THE FEN SNAKE

Even if the ransom remains unpaid you would have other uses. Say the war goes badly for us, you could be a useful bargaining tool, let us return home unmolested and you can have the noblewoman back, I can see Ogun doing that, if he survives our next meeting that is. Or failing that you could just get married off. The war has to end sometime and being married to a Tanarese noble could give somebody some leverage; you must have some land or property in your name after all. So in short, all of us are far more likely to be killed than you, so stop worrying about it. Your future may be uncertain, but it is likely to be a longer one than any of ours."

"Well I consider myself comforted," Eleanor stuck her chin out. "A bag of gold with legs married to some Arshuman chancer who probably reeks of garlic."

"At least you would be alive," Shak pointed out to her. "Many thousands of people have been denied a future at all."

"And who's fault is that?" she pouted.

"A simple question with a complex answer," Shak said. "But remember, a great many Arshuman people have little reason to love the beggar king any more than you do. This is his war, and his subjects have little choice but to abide by his will."

"So, if he is that unpopular why don't you stop him then?"

There was a certain plaintive innocence about the question that made both Shak and Stauncher smile. "Are you asking me to delineate the current political situation in Arshuma?" Shak asked her.

She, in truth, was not that interested. But now she had asked the question..." Well, you seem determined to be my hosts for a good while longer, so perhaps I should make an effort at understanding, yes?"

"Very well," Shak said. "The current king is a paranoid and suspicious man. He keeps himself at a goodly distance from the populace in his palace on top of a hill outside the city limits. His food is tasted, he regularly purges his generals and advisors to prevent them building up power bases of their own. In short, he is a difficult man to reach, let alone kill.

You have heard of the antagonism between north and south, but the truth is we can unite; we can follow a common cause that we all believe in. All this king has done though is foment the distrust we have for each other.

This war you see was started because he wanted to increase northern power to the extent that it would far eclipse us in the south. He wanted to render us irrelevant, a rump no longer capable of asserting its own

ACT ONE : THE HUNT

independence. The south did not want this war, his southern advisors warned him against it. His response was to publicly execute the most vocal of them. And, to begin with it was all going well for him. The army made vast gains and were over the river Vinoyen in weeks. He expected you to sue for peace, lest his men march on your capital city, which looked an achievable goal at the time. Of course he totally misjudged the spirit of the Tanarese people, their stubbornness, their pride, even their love of a good fight; a spirit, if I may say so Lady Eleanor, that you fully embody."

Eleanor blushed a little, she had not expected the compliment. Shak did not notice in the gloom though and carried on.

"So slowly we were forced back, positions became entrenched, the king was spending money he didn't have just to maintain the status quo. He needed aid, so who did he turn to? Us in the south naturally. He can hardly have been surprised at the niggardly nature of our response. We sent men yes, we sent aid, but we sent no more than the minimum we could get away with. Even the mage college, which is based in the mountains not too far from my home city, started to withhold its obligations. All the mages they had already sent to the war had been killed so when reinforcements were called for it is said that they paid people to ambush and rob them so that they could claim that the roads were too dangerous."

"It was also said," Stauncher gave Shak a knowing smile. "That they were paying certain nobles to organise the raids to ensure that the attacks were not too savage. And as Mazuras is close to the college the likelihood was that their nobles were involved somehow. Is that not true, Shak?"

Shak shrugged. "Do not ask me, to admit to such a thing is tantamount to treason."

"So," Eleanor frowned, "you want the king to fail?"

"Not fail," Shak corrected her. "We just want him diminished so that the balance of power in Arshuma swings southwards once more. It is felt that this last gamble, paying a Tanarese baron to turn his coat is indeed his final one. If it does not succeed, then his time on the throne is probably limited. Extremely limited."

"The other thing that keeps him there is Chiran support," Dormouse had woken by now; they were discussing a topic that interested him. "It is secret, tacit, money and mages..."

"And me," Dead Eyes piped in.

"Of course. And you. In court circles it is well known that Chira supports him and that when that support ends, so will he. But..." he added confidentially, "some say that he is casting his net wider, that he is courting the Kozean empire in the south, Chira's greatest enemy. If he is, then that is a balancing act that would tax the greatest of politicians."

"And he is not one of them," Shak interrupted. "Koze, well, I didn't know that. Sorry Dormouse but any sensible gambling man would say that if the king cannot keep hold of his recent gains then the north is going to implode. Allying with Koze would anger Chira and cause him to lose a lot of internal support. We in the south need only be patient and wait, our time will come soon enough."

"Are you manoeuvring to become king?" Dormouse asked in a voice that said that his question was wholly genuine. "You are heir to a southern fiefdom and a hero of the war, you would have a lot of support, especially if the country descends into chaos, as you seem to think," he added sadly.

"I abandoned my city to my brother," Shak intoned seriously. "I have regrets about that now and have thoughts about returning and wresting control back. But they are just thoughts at the moment. And I have no interest in becoming king, I have seen too many pretenders publicly garrotted for that."

"But why did you leave in the first place?" Eleanor asked, noticing the shaking heads of Shak's close companions.

"Several reasons," Shak told her. "All personal and requiring a lengthy explanation that I will not give right now. Another time maybe, when I am less tired. You ask searching questions though Lady Eleanor, I will give you that."

At this point Oswold joined the conversation, his expressed spittle sizzling in the fire as he spoke. "You keep things close o lord of Arshuma, I had not realised your importance in the country you have so much disdain for yet fight so fiercely for too!"

"It is complicated, as I said earlier," Shak said wearily. "I both love my country and hate it, these people I fight with out here though, they mean more to me than my entire dynasty ever could, saving my first wife that is. Anyway hermit, we know far less about you than you do about us. What drove you to this lengthy exile? Why choose seclusion over a monastic life? Was there too much discipline there for you, you do not seem the sort of person who likes rules."

An interesting deflection, Eleanor thought. There was almost a tremor in Shak's voice when he mentioned his first wife, she made a point of

ACT ONE : THE HUNT

remembering that as Oswold began to speak at length.

"Oh I was always in trouble," he admitted, "I suppose in my younger days I was a bit strange (he either didn't notice or ignored the raised eyebrows of the listeners). I didn't become a hermit for those reasons though, let us just say I was, with some others, "advised" to leave the monastery for a while."

"And why was that?" Shak asked him.

"There was a dispute, over a point of doctrine. I and my companions wanted the monastery to debate a theory raised by a Chiran brother, those in charge of the monastery wanted the matter suppressed. But suppression does not stifle thought, only open debate, yet open debate was paradoxically the only way to destroy this particularly theory, or any theory for that matter. Theories can only be defeated with words. Swords cannot do it, silence cannot do it, a more powerful counter theory can. But alas the debate never happened, a mistake in my opinion. Shall I continue?"

They all nodded, with varying degrees of enthusiasm.

"It was a humble Artoran priest called Bonbobulus of Leir. Now Leir is located at pretty much the most southerly point of the Chiran empire, close to the Isthmus of Gurdo. Every morning he would walk the seashore looking at the hordes of birds feeding and wading in the shallows. He used to watch the way they all fed and, over time, realised that they all fed in a different way. Some birds had long, thin, curved beaks that were used to probe the sand for worms or shellfish, others had wider beaks that they dragged through the water, filtering out food that way, there was even a bird with a bill the shape of a spoon, which, unsurprisingly, scooped up food the same way wealthy folks would use a spoon. Amazing don't you think. So, he wondered, why had the Gods gifted them in such subtly different ways? He concluded that the reason was that they were each adapted by the Gods for survival, to feed on a slightly different food source to all the other birds, thus establishing a harmonious equilibrium between them. A perfect resolution don't you think?

But then he took things further, studying many different types of animals to see what made them unique. And he saw that every animal was slightly different, even the great mixed herds of wild horse and cattle that live on the great plains of the empire. And he had a thought. We often assume that we are the chosen of the Gods, raised above the humble beast so that we can see their wonder and try and divine their purpose. Our intelligence is the key, just think of all the things that have been borne of this?" Here he tapped his head with his long, bony forefinger. "But, what if our intelligence is merely our unique gift, nothing more than our adaptation for survival. What if the reason the Gods gifted us in such a way was so that we could learn to hunt, make fire, build shelters, co-operate, master the basic traits we need to ultimately survive? And so, what if everything else about us, culturally, creatively, artistically, is just a by-product of the Gods' gift."

Eleanor sat up; her face appalled. "Wait, you are comparing us to mere beasts?"

"That is a bit much, Father," Dormouse frowned unhappily.

"But why?" Oswold had the gleam of the zealot in his eye. "There is so much about us that we share with beasts. We eat the same way, drink the same way, pass waste the same way, though I have to admit I am having a bit of a problem with that at the moment, I probably need more oats. We even reproduce using the same processes as beasts. On those criteria alone we have to class ourselves as animals."

"No, no, no," Eleanor was not having this at all. "What about marriage for example, animals do not marry."

"But," Oswold countered, "you can have children without being married, and there are many animals that pair for life."

"Well, what about, say, the Grand Cathedral?" Eleanor was not giving up. "If you put a herd of pigs together with a pile of stone blocks you will not end up with the Grand Cathedral, you will end up with a pile of stone blocks."

"Covered in pig shit," Stauncher added. Oswold however had a reply to hand.

"You will not get the Grand Cathedral because a pig lacks the intelligence and skills to build, that is not its gift, it is a pig after all, but, my lady, can you sniff for truffles?"

Eleanor looked cross, she had not expected this mad old man capable of formulating an argument, let alone giving plausibility to such an absurd one as this.

"But you are dismissing centuries of cultural progress and achievement with a wave of your hand," Shak spoke this time. "We, as people, are not where we were a thousand years ago. We have moved forward, developed in dozens of different ways whereas a pig snuffling in the dirt a thousand years ago is still doing pretty much the same now. At one time we were not capable of building a grand cathedral, but, through centuries of learning and collaboration, one was finally built, and if the Tanarese can do it, any nation can."

ACT ONE : THE HUNT

"And yet the ability to collaborate and construct wonders is not a solely human gift," Oswold said. "In some arid southern countries ants build great nests that can be ten foot high. That is like a human building something the size of this mountain! And again you are missing my point, that the reason we do collaborate and build or paint or write wondrous things is because of our intelligence. That gift from the Gods again; Bonbobulus postulated that once we had conquered the basic challenges of life, food, warmth, shelter, our minds started to cast around for other things to fill it; and that was how culture was born. It is not necessary; we do not NEED it as such wondrous though it is. It is like that portion of a crop put aside for the church, nine tenths of the crop we need to survive, the remainder we can give away, and our culture involves that part of our intelligence that we can give away."

There was a very brief, but uncomfortable, silence. Then though Stauncher adjusted his hat and spoke. "But Father, this excess crop, this surfeit of intelligence as you put it. Without that, the ability to sit and think, then we would never have come to an understanding of the Gods in the first place. If we had never learned to work together in such a way as to leave us this...thinking time, then the Gods, the houses of Artorus, the books, the monasteries, and all that would never have come into being. The Gods would remain as much a mystery to us as they do to these pigs everyone keeps talking about."

"And that," Oswold said triumphantly, "is why the Gods gave us more intelligence than we actually needed."

"So you are saying we are special then," Eleanor was still frowning. "That our gift was given in excess because the Gods chose us to be aware of them."

"Of course we are special," Oswold told her, "but we are still animals nonetheless."

"There are many types of animals though," Shak observed. "Comparisons with cats or pigs or something I can just about see but what about fleas or ticks or worms; you cannot liken a person to a worm, unless perhaps you are talking about my nephew."

"Very true," Oswold said. "As you can see Bonbobulus treatise opened up a whole new way of thinking. Do animals have souls, do they get judged by the Gods, do they sit at the Gods' side or get condemned to labour on the furnace? And what constitutes an animal? Does a flea eat and pass waste as we do? Are we, if the Gods see us as animals, similar to say, the great apes of the southern jungles? I am sure some of you have seen illustrations of them. It was a treatise that angered the church but one I felt should be debated in the monastery. I have never said that I believed everything that the man said, but that the issues raised should be discussed. Anyway, it never was, events overtook my request, and I was told to head into the wilderness to avoid repercussions."

"What events?" Several of them said at once.

Oswold shook his head sadly. "It turned out that many monasteries wanted the issue raised as I did. We were all called agitators at best, heretics at worst. Then one day as Bonbobulus took his morning walk many of the brothers from the monastery followed him, all of them carrying ash staves. They surrounded him and beat him to death, throwing his bloodied corpse into the water. His treatise was burnt and some of those in other monasteries that had championed the treatise were executed as heretics. None were in my monastery at Frach Menthon, but those deemed to be troublemakers were kicked out. And here I am now, that is why I became a hermit. My faith in the Gods has always been solid, it has just not always taken the path that those in authority would approve of."

"Oh!" Eleanor looked suddenly distraught. "It had not occurred to me that you were from the monastery. You probably have not heard the terrible news."

"Terrible news?" Oswold asked.

"Yes, about the monastery. It was attacked. By mercenary renegades looking for plunder. A lot of it was burned and nearly all the monks killed. The survivors are trying to rebuild, and Baron Felmere has vowed to hound the perpetrators to the death...but Baron Felmere is dead now too. I don't know what is happening anymore. I am sorry."

"God's help us all," Oswold breathed softly. "Burning the monastery, has this war really been that savage, that mindless?"

"More so," Shak concurred. "I have seen enough to think that your comparing us to beasts is not as fanciful as some here think. From what I have heard the mercenaries in question had been dismissed for being unreliable, they got drunk and attacked the first target they came across. We are all here truly sorry for the death of your brothers. Arshuma had nothing to do with the attack."

Oswold shrugged. "Does that matter?"

There was a sad, contemplative silence. Eleanor wiggled her toes;

ACT ONE : THE HUNT

Dead Eyes had finished with the liniment and the soles of her feet were tingling pleasantly. She lay back on her bedroll, not bothering to put her boots back on. There was an itch in her scalp, and she scratched it and shook her head. Stauncher leaned forward and whispered confidentially in her ear.

"Careful. If that was a flea you may have just killed one of your cousins."

She giggled, lifting the mood just a tad. Then, a moment later, Stan came bustling in busily patting his sides with his hands. He scanned the glum faces in front of him and snorted loudly.

"Bah! I was going to lower your spirits by telling you that it is snowing lightly outside but to the furnace with that, you miserable buggers need cheering up. How about a song? Who wants to sing "O wizard, stop waving your wand around"? I nominate Eleanor, she looks the sort to be at home with a dirty ballad. Hope you can sing as lustily as you moan."

"I can." Eleanor was blushing inside, not so much at the fact that Stan was teasing her but rather because she actually knew the words of the song in question. She knew that idly listening to stable boys in the courtyard of her manor would benefit her one day. She cleared her throat, asked all the Gods (especially Elissa) to forgive her, and began...

****

Conversation was keeping the cold at bay elsewhere too. Where a rocky shelf curved to form a sheltering elbow, under a tarpaulin rigged to keep the snow flurries at bay, flickered the crimson embers of a small fire. And, huddled around it, those sworn to hunt down Shak and his companions had made camp. They were some miles from their quarry, but yet not as many miles as they probably thought. Hunched close together to share body heat they sat and they talked with only Ursus noticing how keen Nico had been to sit next to Siri. And it was Nico who was speaking now.

"I have barely left Tanaren in my entire life, yet I did not know that such a bleak and remote place existed in my own country. Was that rope there when you came here before Ursus? If it wasn't, how in the name of Artorus did you get up here?"

"It wasn't there no," Ursus told him. "I came here with three other squires chasing bandits who had been raiding and burning local villages for some time. And we climbed, just as the lady did earlier. The weather was a lot warmer then, but windier, which brought its own problems. It took us a long time, but we all got up in the end."

"You...climbed?" Nico asked in disbelief.

"I was a lot younger, and a lot thinner," Ursus answered. "Younger than you are now, about the age of Zukan here. And I had no fear, for you don't at that age. We climbed, rested, crossed the river and ambushed the bandits a day or two later, just as we are planning to do now."

"And the outcome of your ambush?" Doul looked directly at Ursus. He had pale eyes, expressionless eyes, if eyes were a reflection of the soul then this man's soul was hollow as a gourd. He rarely blinked, he just gazed, gazed at the sky, at the landscape, at his companions, regarding all of them with the same, predatory stare. It was the stare of a dead creature, of a creature incapable of feeling, of empathy, compassion, or sympathy, a creature to which joy, love, laughter, or happiness were unknown concepts. Few could hold his gaze for long, it was like staring at some, strange, alien species, unnerving, unsettling, a lifeless stare to make the spine shiver, the innards recoil. And Ursus was playing none of this man's games, he had no intention of locking eyes with this fish man, he looked away from him immediately before replying.

"They did no more raiding after that day, though we too lost one of our own."

"Then you did well," Doul said quietly.

"We did. We all were confirmed as knights of the Silver Lance upon our return. It was one of the proudest moments of my life."

At that moment, a swirling wind sent a scattering of light snowflakes under the tarpaulin to strike several of them in the face and set the fire to hissing as they turned to water under Its heat. Ursus shook his head. "Enough of stories about this place," he blustered, "I want to hear tales of warmer climes and of happier moments. Young Zukan, day or night, you barely utter a word, tell me of your homeland, tell me of Fash, tell me of sunshine and skies bereft of clouds. If I am to freeze to death I want to be found with a smile on my face."

"I say little because I have little to say." Zukan devoured a piece of hard bread before putting his hands out to warm over the fire. "Also I do not have the ease with your language that my sister has. But if you want a tale...Siri and I come from a simple village in the foothills, there is no main road running through it, to trade we must go elsewhere. It is a forgotten place where time moves little, where years are only counted by the distance the

ACT ONE : THE HUNT

vines and bougainvillea have climbed up the walls of its buildings. Of my brothers and sisters I was the least popular; I liked to dream rather than work, what joy is there in the driving of cattle and the picking of fruit?"

"You have to eat to experience joy, so there is a purpose to such mundane pursuits," Nico told him.

"Yes," Zukan said, "but I was young, always in trouble, always being beaten by father. The only sister that cared for me," he looked at Siri, "had been sold. I was alone. I wanted to be alone. One day I had taken the ibex up into the hills to graze. I sat with them all day, watched them nibble the tips of the tough grasses, noticing what peaceful, placid creatures they were. But the shadows were lengthening, and it was time to return. I led them along the coastal path for a while. It ran across the top of cliffs hundreds of feet high, staring down at a sea the colour of the pale, blue flowers that sprout from the scimitar thorn. The sea was deep there, but so clear you could almost see the sands at the bottom. The air was warm, the breeze tempted me towards sleep, but it was then that I saw them.

"I had seen ships before, ocean going merchant vessels in the harbour of Fohila, yet these were larger still and they were not ships but living, breathing creatures. They were whales, creatures that many spoke of, but few ever saw and there were maybe six of them right beneath me. At first I thought them all black in colour, but as they swam they sometimes rolled in the water exposing white patches on fin and underbelly. Their tails slapped the water sending up fountains taller than a red mountain pine. They moved slowly, sometimes coming close to the cliffs, sometimes moving further away, four great adults and two little ones, though those little ones could easily sink a ship just by ramming it. I stood there, unable to move with the wonder of it all, until finally they headed back out into the deepest waters.

"Then though, as I was about to turn away one of them broke the water, head and body, all bar the tail emerging from the sea before crashing back into it with a splash that deafened, even at this great distance. Then another did the same, and another, others just thrashed the waters with their tails. And I shall swear by the Gods that they did this not for hunting purposes, not for display, but with a sense of sheer joy, almost as if they were playing, revelling in their power, that strength that could shatter stone. How small and ugly are people in comparison. I waited till they were gone for certain, till the cicadas started to sing in the bushes behind me and the leaves rattled in the mountain winds. I had lost half the flock and had a beating such as I had never had before, but I would go through it all again, and much worse than that, to witness such a sight once more."

Zukan finished, his dark eyes mournful. Siri took his hand and squeezed it, a smile was briefly exchanged, then she gazed out into the night.

"It has stopped snowing," she said, "if we were tracking them then all footprints would now be covered."

"But we are not tracking them," Ursus said. "I have the honour of crossing a freezing river tomorrow to put us ahead of them. If I survive of course."

"I am sure you have survived worse," Siri said.

"I know he has," Nico confirmed. "Even now, at his age, when he should be in the capital, mentoring squires and the sons of gentlefolk he prefers to test his mettle in war. Sir Ursus is the epitome of what a knight should be. I would never tell him this of course," he grinned at Siri and Doul, "it would make him quite insufferable."

"I thought I was always insufferable," Ursus told him.

Nico nodded, indicating that Ursus had a point. "And you have been to Fash of course, so you know something of their homeland."

"Fash mares kanzalo, ste tutta lakbali," Ursus said. Both Siri and Zukan looked up in surprise.

"Stata honrosa ima glanto bistilli," Siri answered with a bow of her head.

Ursus noticed Nico's questioning look. "I told them that Fash was the jewel of the sea, that its countrymen are always blessed. The reply was that those that recognise such beauty will always have honour. It is a traditional formal exchange for outsiders meeting the people of Fash for the first time. The fact that you have taken time and trouble to learn the greeting will guarantee a warm welcome. You are then invited into their home; your feet are washed, and bread and dates are shared. I was unfortunately there, in Bur and Fash, during a time of strife, but even then there was still much beauty in evidence. I even, briefly, visited the island of Egol, where the Egoulian dancers are first trained."

Siri's eyes widened in surprise. "You have been there?" she asked hoarsely.

He smiled, "probably before you were born. I was the least important member of a delegation of Silver Lances invited to watch your company perform. I remember sitting on cushions being served bread and fruit on silver

ACT ONE : THE HUNT

platters in a hall that was all marble, columns and incense burners. Your troupe danced, I think it was something like, "Blood in the forest of golden leaves." Is it an old Fashtani legend or something?"

Siri's defensive reserve was pricked momentarily, she smiled, a generous, open smile that, for the first time, hinted at the beauty and charisma that the dancers were famous for. "Blood fell like rain in the forest of golden leaves", she corrected him. "A tale of a princess on a pilgrimage set upon by spirits of the forest who are secretly in thrall to the princess's uncle. She is almost killed but then a lion appears who drives the spirits away. It turns out that the lion was once a man, changed into animal form by this same uncle many years ago because he was the genuine heir to the castle this uncle had usurped. Anyway, lots of things happen, the lion kills the uncle, becomes human again and he and the princess marry. It is a very dramatic production, lots of colour and emotion. Very demanding to perform."

"You have performed it?" Nico asked.

"Oh yes. I have been a forest spirit, the princess, and of course, the wicked uncle. That last part was the most fun, it soon becomes obvious to all performers that the villains are the most interesting roles."

"Yes," Ursus said reflectively. "As a young man it made a big impression. The performance lasted the whole evening, I got very drunk and, to my shame, had to be carried back to my quarters. I remember several very beautiful young women covered in dye and smelling of jasmine laughing hysterically as I was being dragged across the floor. I saw all of the performance though, I remember the wedding at the end, I must have passed out shortly after." He gave a short laugh. "Actually the whole thing was fantastic, one of the best nights of my life, puts Tanarese theatre to shame. Love, death, passion, and half naked girls. What more could a man wish for? I will have to take you there Nico, once all this mess is over, it would be good to see the sun again. And, by Mytha, those animals in the courtyard."

"Elephants," Siri said.

"Elephants yes, massive beasts, with tusks that were capped in gold. Why they were there I do not know, you would have loved them young Zukan..."

"I have seen them yes," Zukan told him. "They always seemed so very sad."

"They are used in some performances, though only a couple of outdoor venues can accommodate them," Siri told them. "Animals of other kinds are used too, birds especially. We can use their feathers too, when they shed them."

"So," Nico frowned and scratched his head, "you perform in a troupe re-enacting tales and myths from your own history. I thought you just danced on a stage or something."

"Well, in its most basic form we do," Siri said. "We train for years to do just that. But of course there are many other aspects to our performance, we would not have a fame that crosses boundaries if there were not. I, and many others, specialise in dancing whilst wielding blades for example, ones that strike sparks when they clash. I also perform with venomous snakes, in a ritual dance that has since been stolen by our enemies in Kudrey. I have danced whilst draped head to foot in gold or painted in dye, I have performed whilst climbing up ropes or pillars, in full animal costume, wearing voluminous silks and wearing nothing but jewellery. I can portray a man, woman or child, a murderer, or a symbol of holy purity. Each dance we do is different, taking all of them together there are maybe a thousand characters we end up portraying in our career. It is a good life for a woman, better than weaving baskets or pressing grapes or olives."

"But how did you end up here?" Nico's frown had only deepened. "It is a big step from dancing to, well, killing."

"It is." Her enthusiasm seemed to wane a little. "The Egoulian dancers do not just perform on the island. They do commissioned performances, maybe a dozen a year, moving from city to city, palace to palace. They bring great prestige to those who host a performance. But, for maybe two to three months a year our time is our own. Sir Ursus described Egol as an island but that is not quite true. It is joined to the mainland by a permanent causeway and, in the town at the end of the causeway many of us have homes. It is not an isolated life, we can be approached, and we can be susceptible to the blandishments of wealthy men. We can take private commissions, just one or a handful of us performing for a group of rich men, eager to throw money at us for going a little further than…" she paused and sighed.

"So you can see that these private performances are usually of a more…lascivious nature than our official engagements. And if news is leaked to a rival of the person we are performing for then we can be approached by them too. To spy, or even yes, to kill. We often acquire secret patrons, who pay us great sums when we perform in the houses of enemies for purposes that well, should not be scrutinised too closely. That is what happened to me.

ACT ONE : THE HUNT

Many poor girls are selected, and their training paid for by such a man. One of the first lessons you are taught is diction, a dancer with a rustic accent earns a lot less and is suspected of being a spy immediately, an obviously poor girl must be a spy, yes? If the Egoulian dancers found that we were working and spying on the side we would lose our position, but money changes hands there too, many an eye is wilfully blind to our activities."

"So your patron financed your training." Nico was obviously finding this very interesting.

"Yes. His name was Brazan, he was a ruler of a city called Csal. He died, I lost his connections and friends, so it was flee or meet the same fate as my patron."

"Did you love him?" Ursus started at Nico's bluntness.

"No. I liked him. He was rich. He rewarded me well. He had a wife and five children. I would see him four or five times a year. Sometimes he would give me work. That was all there was to it. Are you married Sir Nico?"

"No, I have been promised to many, but delivered to no one. There is a war on, I could die tomorrow, marriage is best left for more stable times, do you not think?"

"Life is uncertain in both times of war and times of peace. If you can marry, then do so," Siri answered, her earlier animation now having disappeared.

"But you are not married," Nico said. "So you are hardly following your own advice."

"Our circumstances are hardly the same," Siri answered tersely. "You are a knight, you have every advantage, I am a woman from a poor family, I have used what few gifts I have to acquire wealth and some status. Marriage at this time could jeopardize all of that. When I return home I will collect the wealth I have hidden there and, well, I will see. If Fash is safe I will retire from dancing and set myself and Zukan up as best I can. If that means finding a good marriage at a future date, then so be it."

"And if Fash isn't safe for you?" Doul had been staring into space for so long it was easy to think he wasn't there.

"Then I will have to live somewhere else. Arshuma maybe, or Mothravia if I can put up with the ticks and swamp fever. Too many things have to happen before I can decide. For us both brother, if you wish to stay with me."

"I do," Zukan said, "I do not want to go home again."

261

THE FANGS OF THE FEN SNAKE

The fire crackled, the awning flapped, the silence settled awhile. It was Nico who spoke next.

"So, Doul, we have heard a little from Zukan and Siri, of their life and the things that make them happy, but what of you? What is it in life that gives you the most pleasure?"

Those dead eyes, and the scarf that hid half his face made the man almost impossible to read. The timbre of his voice though seemed almost playful. "A job well done gives me all the satisfaction I require. What greater thrill can there be than to hold the power of life and death twixt thumb and forefinger? Why it is almost to be a god, meting out divine justice to those deemed unworthy. There is surely nothing that can exceed the feeling of one's own omniscience."

"Your "divine justice" though always has the same outcome," Ursus pointed out.

"Then call me Xhenafa, the bringer of death, for I am such to those I hunt."

"But "Xhenafa" has to live somewhere, has to spend his money on something," Nico said.

"I live in the Derannen mountains," Doul said. "At the top of a mountain valley, in a house that can only be approached by a single narrow path. I have guards, men who I have risen up and who will stand with me and fall with me. I spend my money on sculpture and on my courtyard, on the pool at the centre and the hanging baskets that surround it. It is cloistered, the pool is open to the sky and I spend many hours there, sitting, thinking, listening to the fountain and the birds. It is a good place to plan my next...project."

"Sounds quite lonely," Nico was unimpressed. "Does your gold buy you women?"

"No."

"Men?"

"No."

"Sheep? You know what we say in Tanaren about Arshumans and their sheep."

The playful tone had gone. "No. And I should tell you that I allow one insult to my person, but never two."

Things had become tense; Ursus moved swiftly to try and calm things a little. "What my brother knight has a tendency to forget is that humour does not always transcend different cultures. What we here in Tanaren see as little

ACT ONE : THE HUNT

more than broad humour could easily be construed elsewhere as a slight on one's personal honour. He was jesting, that is all, an ill judged, thoughtless jest maybe," he gave Nico a sideways look, "but a jest all the same. No insult was intended; you have my word."

"And mine," Nico added. "I see that was passes as ribaldry amongst knights may not be viewed in the same manner elsewhere. You have my apologies, master Doul."

Doul relaxed, slightly. "Then the matter is forgotten. A man once abused me to my face in front of his family. He was given the opportunity to withdraw the insult, he declined. It was a sweet arrow that burst his eyeball and skewered his arrogant little brain. He died twitching with his daughter weeping over his body. You wanted to know the moments in my life that gave me the greatest pleasure; well that was one of them."

"Then I am doubly apologetic for my crass behaviour." The lack of sincerity in Nico's words set Ursus' teeth on edge. "And shall take my contrition to my bed with me."

"And look," Siri said, having watched the exchange between the men with bemused amusement. "The weather has changed again. It is sleet now, wet, it will disperse much of the snow if it continues."

"And turn the mud on the riverbanks into a quagmire," Ursus moaned. "Tomorrow will be a test for us all, I am getting some sleep. If it is to be the last sleep of my life then by Artorus, I want it to be a good one."

And so they slowly settled down, pressing into each other, letting sleep slowly overcome them. All except for Doul, who continued to stare into the fire as though he wanted to freeze it with his eyes.

18

It was just past noon, a ghost of a sun struggled for prominence in a thin, grey, sky and Ursus' sleep had been anything but a good one. It wasn't quite freezing, as the sporadic sleet showers felt wet on his face, but the wind in the gorge was savage as a boning knife and here, on the riverbank, away from the trees, there was no protection from it.

The river was brown and swift, churning like milk, frothing like newly poured ale. Fed by a thousand joyful tributaries, gorged with mountain silt, it cut exuberantly through its own valley, keen as an arrow in flight, deadly as a diving hawk, it was a beast as destructive as a hunting dragon. Only a fool would even chance dipping a trembling foot into it.

Let alone swim in it.

So what kind of madman would contemplate such folly?

Ursus smiled to himself.

For there truly was no fool like an old fool.

He looked downriver; there the banks narrowed somewhat, they were raised, supported by large rocks, rocks that could crush a man's skull like desiccated parchment, yet that was the place he was headed. Climb out of the river the other side and secure a line over it, a rope the others could cross with their equipment. They would not find it easy; the wind and a swaying rope made the whole enterprise perilous, but at least they would stay dry.

Unlike him.

He checked the rope around his waist. It was as secure as it had been the last time he looked at it. Nico and Zukan were holding the other end, his life would truly be in their hands. He took a step forward, a trickle of water spilled over the tip of his boot.

"Ursus." Nico's voice. He looked behind him.

"Artorus keep you safe," the younger knight said to him. He looked nervous Ursus thought, but why not? Ursus had mentored him, then fought alongside him these fifteen years. Nico was his superior now, but he was still like a second son to him. Ursus acknowledged him with a nod.

"Gods give you power," Siri was standing next to Nico. Ursus realised that, against his better judgement, he quite liked the woman, and her strange brother. They had both revealed a little of themselves last night and he had

ACT ONE : THE HUNT

been surprised at the passion they had displayed as they talked. Fashtani people were known for their hot blood and fervent emotions, he had thought of the two of them as frigid anomalies, runners against the wind, but they were not. They were just damaged by circumstance, sad, but these days there were few people who weren't damaged by circumstance, Doul being the most extreme example of all.

"I like that," he told Siri.

Then he planted his right foot fully into the water.

He kept going forward, soon it was up to his waist and by the Gods was it freezing. The current was getting stronger all the time, dragging him, pulling him. He had to retain control, dive in at a moment of his choosing and not be swept away. Rope or no, if the water overwhelmed him he would drown like an unwanted cur.

One more staggering step, up to his midriff now, water sprayed into his face, it tasted of earth and clean gravel. He took a deep breath of air that was so cold it burned his lungs.

Then he dived fully into the water.

****

"Hold that rope Zukan! No matter how strong the pull, hold it!" there was an edge of panic in Nico's command.

"He is being pulled downriver far too swiftly," Siri demurred, "he will end up coming out on the same bank we are...no, by all the Gods no, he has made the mid channel. He must have the strength of Mytha."

"He has." Nico was lantern jawed; his face grim as the mountains. "Doul! Help us! Take some of this rope!"

"As you wish," Doul seemed almost disinterested. He picked up the rope yet was hardly bending his back into it.

"Now, Zukan, feed a little more rope out, he will need it, he is gaining the farther shore."

And Nico was right. Slowly, surely, the grey bearded old man was defying his years once more. Siri had been confounded, she had expected his death or his humiliation. For once in her life, it felt good to be wrong...

****

The shutters were open, and the screeching of the ornamental lorikeets in the formal gardens below drifted up on torpid and woozy airs, over the balcony and into her faineant ears.

The mattress was firm, the bolsters were of goose feathers, the sheet was of silk. She lay face down, sheet up to her waist, feeling the sun warm that side of her face open to the blue skies of a hot summer morning. She had danced for them till it was close to dawn and then had let Opekun Brazan use her for a further hour after that. She would rest till noon, if permitted, then be on her way with her payment.

She did not open her eyes; she did not need to to know Brazan was still in the room with her. He was shuffling around looking for his clothes, soon he would give up and call upon his servants to dress him, which they would in an ante chamber, well away from her. A ruler of a city, commander of its garrison, controller of its treasury, a man who couldn't even dress himself unassisted.

And he would have to dress soon, and dress magnificently, for his wife would be here this afternoon, the main reason that Siri had to depart when she should. He would often do this, arrive at one of his houses a day before her, to make sure it was well run he would say. But it meant he had a night free, a night for her to perform for him and, as it was last night, his friends. He liked to show her off did Brazan, his own Egoulian dancer, her role was to inflame them and incite their jealousy, a task that she had, so far, never failed at. She could see them, arms outstretched, spittle clinging to their chins, desperate to get their hands on her smoke smooth flesh, but they could not, for Brazan was her patron, her master, and she was as much his possession as the robes of gold latticed silk he was searching for now.

"Siri," he was speaking to her; she would have to open her eyes now. She did so, turning her head slightly, half expecting to see him standing close by with his genitals pressed close to her face, as tended to be his wont. That was something else that confounded her, the assumption that no woman could witness the male reproductive organ up close without being consumed with desire, that it was somehow his most attractive feature. For Siri, the first thing she looked at in assessing a man in that way was to look at the eyes. They usually told her all she needed to know. Personally, she was drawn to eyes that expressed a certain delicacy of taste, a degree of sensitivity, curiosity, sympathy, interest in anything but her own body, interest in her. What she did not like were those eyes that displayed hunger, greed, cravings of the more animalistic kind, desire for power, domination, those that saw her as a dancer, and only as a dancer. Naturally, the former of the two types, when

ACT ONE : THE HUNT

regarding her, usually ran a mile. So she was stuck with the latter sort, like Brazan, although to be fair to him he had tended to become more interested in her the longer they had been together, he could easily have cast her off by now, but he hadn't. Then again, she was useful to him.

And, though he was naked it did seem that he wanted to talk. He was holding something, a small wooden box, its lid secured by a clasp. It was a dark wood, oiled, expensive, she sat up, pulling the sheet around her, he had made her curious.

"What is it, Opekun Brazan?" she addressed him formally; lover or not he was still vastly her superior and clung to his status as a strangle vine clings to the trunk of a tree.

"You are performing for Opek Kandrassus three weeks from now, at his villa overlooking Lake Csalna."

"I am yes, myself and three other girls. I was not aware I had told you Opekun." She hadn't told him, she knew it, but she was giving him an opportunity to boast, flattering his intelligence had often proved lucrative in the past.

"You did not. I have my own ways of finding things out, especially as I helped get you the commission in the first place."

"You did Opekun?" She was at least a little surprised by this. "I thought the commission was given to Merisatsi; it was she that asked me to join her."

"She was offered the commission on the grounds that you joined her. You pleasingly complied."

"So you wish for me to spy on somebody?" Down to business then, what was the job and what did it pay.

"No." His tone was curt, he was tense, almost nervous. She sat up and put a consoling arm on his shoulder. He shook it off. "Kandrassus tried to have me killed last week, I was mobbed on the streets, it was supposed to look like a robbery gone wrong, but a knife was thrust at my heart in the confusion. Fortunately, my personal guard was wise to the situation, the assassin was caught and gave us Kandrassus' name before he died. Ambitious young man, Kandrassus."

She was not liking the sound of this. "So Opekun, what do you want me to do?"

"Kandrassus has a weakness. He loves his wine; he has a personal vintner in Sessithulo from whom he imports a vintage that only he is allowed to drink. I want you to find his cellar and where this wine is stored, and I want you to put this in it." He flipped open the box, inside was a small metal vial sealed by a stopper. "A few drops should be enough for the task."

She shrank back in horror. "Opekun, you want me to poison this man?"

"Not out loud Siri, but yes, it is regrettable, but necessary."

She shook her head defiantly, this was not her at all, was it? "I have spied and listened for you for years now, but you have never ordered me to kill before. I am no murderer; it is one step beyond that which I am willing to take."

"Why?" the man asked. "What is he to you?"

"Nothing Opekun, but he is a man."

Brazan left her for a moment, her heart rearing in her chest, her pulse hammering, her breath short and sharp. He returned presently, this time carrying something wrapped in cloth. "You have a choice then, decline me, leave my service and keep your already compromised principles intact, or add some drops of liquid to the drink of a man you do not know and get this as reward." He opened the cloth up and lifted its contents high for her to see.

It was a necklace. It was a necklace, just as the great snow leopard of the Derannen mountains was just a cat. It was fashioned in gold and from its circlet hung at least a dozen fine golden threads, each acting as housings for countless tiny white gems flowing from the main band like rivers of weeping tears. The one exception was at the centre point of the necklace where sat a ruby the size of a cat's eye. Brazan turned and held it up against the block of sunlight flooding in from the balcony. Each gem glittered, a hundred tiny prisms, all the colours of the rainbow shining on to her awed face. He was offering her this?

She looked down where his genitals were now silhouetted against the light of the day. Neither up nor down, neither night nor day, she was reminded of a weed on a cracked stone path, once strong but now wilting under the heat of the noon sun. She knew how to change that situation.

"It is an heirloom," he said. "I have many better, but it is still a pretty thing no? And if you don't like it you can melt down the gold and sell the gems. I would have offered you mere coin, but I do know how you like such trinkets. It could keep you in some style, could it not?"

He was offering it to her. She reached out to touch it, but he pulled it away. He was offering it to her, but there was always a price with Brazan.

ACT ONE : THE HUNT

All she had to do was kill a man.
All she had to do was kill a man.
All she had to do...

Outside the city walls, far away from the great buildings at its vibrant heart was a deep pit into which the people dumped all their refuse. In the heat of the summer the whole thing steamed, and the reek hung in the air till the rains came. Everything was piled into it, from unwanted pots and pans to rotten food to dead animals to stillborn babies, or babies that were unwanted or could not be fed, left to die from exposure. Brazan might look grand in his robes of silk and gold, his purple cloak trailing behind him as he climbed the marble stairs to the Palace of Justice, but he was just as much trash as that which filled the pit outside the city. And she was decrying him, but she was the same as he, a different kind of trash maybe but her heart was as black and rotten as the man standing before her. She knew what he wanted, and she was going to give it to him.

She let the sheet slide to the floor.

He beamed as she pulled her hair clear of her neck allowing him to affix the necklace around it. "You see, my beautiful, beautiful dancer," he crowed. "I have a theory. It is that the accumulation of wealth is a thing in itself, a goal, a life's pursuit. Though coin may be acquired initially for food, for shelter or clothing, once these goals have been achieved and such acquisitiveness is no longer necessary, we carry on, we have to carry on. Avarice has supplanted our basic needs and has become that thing that drives one's sense of purpose. I have never wanted for anything; neither I hazard, do you anymore and yet we always want more, do we not? We always want more."

And he wanted more now. His desire for her was never stronger than when she wore nothing but his jewellery, she always kept her golden anklets on for him for that reason. She looked down, below his navel and saw her suspicions confirmed. She climbed back onto the bed, top end low on the pillow, other end as high in the air as she could manage. He moved into position behind her. The bed lowered, the gems on her necklace, for it was hers now, chimed together musically, like a set of ringing glass bells. The lorikeets still squawked incessantly. Soon she would be joining them in their cacophony. She took a deep breath, planted her hands palms down on the mattress and prepared to start moaning, simulating the sort of unbridled ecstasy he thought he always incited in her.

THE FANGS OF THE FEN SNAKE

****

He was alive! He wanted to roar at the Gods. He was alive! He was alive! Ursus staggered onto the stony bank dripping like a gutted corpse. He was alive, Artorus be praised, he was alive. The rope had done its job, it had stopped him from being carried between the narrow channel with the great boulders where the water frothed and foamed like a rabid animal, if he had gone through there then they would be picking up pieces of him till it grew dark. That though was the point where he was headed now he had made landfall, a high narrow channel, secure the rope between trees on either bank and the rest of the group, and the equipment could come over that way.

He got there, tied the rope securely around a gnarled tree trunk next to the channel, then leant forward and inhaled deeply. The air was cold enough to stab at his lungs.

He was alive.

He was alive, but he was freezing, and soaking wet, and there was blood on his clothes. The exultant rush that greeted his climbing on to dry land had gone, he was shivering, and there was a little pain. His arm was cut, and there was a gash on his leg, some sharp stones had found a mark then. He had not felt it, the water had seemingly numbed his senses. He leant forward again and vomited water onto the cratered mud at his feet. To survive drowning but to freeze to death afterwards, how amusing, the Gods were too clever for him by half.

The first person was crossing on the rope, secured to it by some kind of improvised loop harness. He had expected Nico but it was the woman, Siri. She had quite a bit of baggage with her too. At his end he pulled the rope down a little, so the trajectory would be in her favour. After her climbing antics of the previous day he had expected this part of the journey to hold few terrors for her. And he was right. A minute or so later she was standing next to him, examining the baggage, and breathing heavily.

She pulled something from a pack and handed it to him. It was a flask. "Drink," she told him.

"What is it?" he asked suspiciously.

"A cordial. You are freezing. It will warm you till we camp and can have fire. You doubt me?"

His hand went to his still sore neck. "I already have some experience of what your poisons can do." He made no attempt to keep the resentment

ACT ONE : THE HUNT

out of his voice.

"Of course." There was a smile. Beautiful teeth, generous mouth, she was a Fashtani woman after all. "But this will do you nothing but good, I promise."

So he took the flask and drank. It tasted bitter, though he suspected that some honey had been added in an attempt to make it barely palatable. He swallowed and felt it burn his empty stomach, nasty. A moment later though he felt a pleasant heat radiating out to his fingers and toes. And the bitter taste had gone. He stopped shivering for a moment. He acknowledged Siri as she threw a thick cloak over his shoulders, patting his stomach to show the drink was benefitting him. "You are cut," she noted, "we will camp shortly, and I will see to it."

"I have had worse." He tried to be nonchalant, but it was difficult when water was still dripping freely from his beard. "Much worse."

Siri looked at him blankly for a moment. Then she loosened the clasp on her own cloak and put it around him too. "Anyway," he added, "I appreciate your concern." His nonchalance was replaced with sarcasm for he still felt that all his new "allies" had little or no concern for his or Nico's welfare. If she noticed it though, she gave no indication.

"You are a courageous man," she told him, "when you mentioned swimming the river before I had no idea it was as wide or fierce as this. Your bravery impresses me."

"When I did this before it was a dry summer, I had no idea it would be as wide or fierce as this either; not to mention the thirty-year gap between this crossing and the last. My conclusion? I am an idiot with no concept of the passage of time or the inclemency of the season."

"But you crossed, nevertheless. It was an act well done."

There was a brief silence as they watched Nico prepare for his crossing. Then Siri asked him a question he found a little surprising. "You are not married then?"

He saw no reason to lie though. "A widower, my wife has been dead these last ten years."

"Children?"

"One. A son, Ludo. He is a squire in the same knightly order as me. Doing well but needs to toughen up."

"You are proud of him?"

"Yes, he is a good boy."

THE FANGS OF THE FEN SNAKE

Another brief silence. Then it was Siri again. "If you have not remarried you must want for female companionship. Ten years is a long time."

He laughed. Then choked, coughing up a little more water. "I am not sure if I would remember what to do with a woman if ever the chance arose. This war keeps me busy enough, I am getting too old for further complications."

"Pity," she shrugged her shoulders. "I am looking for a new patron. You seemed an option worth exploring."

He was utterly flabbergasted. "What! You jest, surely?"

"I am being serious. I have little understanding of Tanarese humour."

"But I am twenty years older than you at least. Mind you, the cynic in me might suggest that to a younger woman, marriage to an old man has its advantages. You may have to care for him in his infirmity, but you will inherit all his lands and titles once Xhenafa claims him."

She sounded hurt. "There is nothing cynical about such an arrangement, it happens all the time. It makes total sense. And, as you know, if the man in question lingers for too long in his dotage, before the pain and infirmity becomes too much, I have the poison to send him to Xhenafa peacefully."

Ursus spluttered. "You make the prospect more and more enticing."

She smiled. "And that, Sir Ursus, shows that you have little understanding of Fashtani humour. You are not interested then?"

"I am still too dumbstruck to answer either way. What about Nico?" he nodded at the knight, who was beginning to make his way along the rope, hanging underneath it like an engorged fruit about to drop from a tree. "He is rather taken with you it seems."

"I can judge men quickly," was her airy response. "Just from their eyes. Sir Nico is of the type I usually end up with; you are not; you are a thousand times more intriguing."

"And he is a hundred times richer than I am."

She chewed her lip a little. "Pity," she said quietly. Then she inhaled deeply before adding. "I have wealth enough, hidden, back home. If Fash is safe for me, we could return there together. You seem to like what you saw of my country."

"Oh I did, I did," he admitted, "but my place with the knights, your brother..."

"Are any of these issues insurmountable?"

272

ACT ONE : THE HUNT

"But I barely know you."

"And I barely know you. And people marry who have never met each other. Think about it, there is no hurry for an answer."

"I will," he found himself saying. His fingers were numb again but this time the cause was not the cold. He could not help but feel that she was playing a game with him; was she trying to inveigle her way into his favour? Did she want him to gaze into her eyes whilst her knife slid into his belly? She was devious, manipulative, and he still liked her. "What about Doul?" he said finally.

She did laugh this time; her reply was incredulous. "Doul? He is neither man nor beast, but a statue that walks and talks. There is not a jot of passion in him, he is colder than these mountain peaks. Besides, you know about his wounds?"

"What? The scarf over the face? Not really, no."

She told him.

"Well, that gives me a little understanding of why he is what he is."

"But there is more," she spoke in a low voice, the volume of rushing water made it impossible to hear a conversation on the further bank, but she still did not want to take chances. "When I was going to work with him for the first time I did some research, spoke to a man who knew him as a child. He knew about the scarring incident but told me there was more to it than that."

"More to it?" Ursus' bushy eyebrows were raised. "Go on."

"He said that the man who attacked him was known for his violence and his temper, and that after he cut Doul's mouth his blood lust was still heavy on him. So he mutilated him... elsewhere. I have no idea of the degree of mutilation or even if this man was lying, but, there you have it."

"Elsewhere?" Ursus asked.

"Well, have you ever seen the man urinate?"

"No." Ursus was silent for a moment. "Artorus blood, you are saying that..."

"That when he sends an arrow into the heart of a mark, it is the only release that he can have."

****

They were all over. Sometimes nervously, sometimes comedically, but they had finally made it. Nico's attempt to cross, hanging under the rope, swinging wildly, moving with all the grace of a crab with its claws tied had

THE FANGS OF THE FEN SNAKE

made Ursus laugh so much he briefly forgot his chilled, soggy state, though the two men embraced enthusiastically once Nico was standing shakily on his feet again. Zukan went next and seemed to be negotiating the rope with ease, but, at the midway point, hanging with the broiling spume just a few feet beneath him, he dared to look down. Inevitably he received a faceful of spray and this unnerved him to such a degree that he froze, hanging there, unable to move forward or back. Ursus noted Siri's reaction with interest, the sight of her brother's plight seemed to genuinely distress her. She had to crouch at the water's edge, getting herself quite soaked in the process, shouting words of reassurance and encouragement, patiently urging him towards her. Even then, though he was visibly heartened by her presence, it was an age before he got moving again and the embrace they finally shared was just as heartfelt as the one between Nico and Ursus. The rest of the baggage came next and finally it was Doul's turn. Ursus was beginning to wonder if ice rather than blood coursed through his veins, and this belief was strengthened by the nerveless, methodical manner of his crossing. Once over he went immediately for his bow and then started rummaging through his arrows, seemingly searching for one in particular.

Now they were all together Ursus decided to lay out the next course of action, it would stop his teeth chattering at least.

"The safe crossing point of this river, that is to say the point where they will be crossing with Eleanor lies at the bottom of a series of shallow falls that start to climb up the mountain like terraces. The river is very wide there and the water is dispersed and shallow before a series of tributaries emptying into it give it momentum again. Now on this bank, the east bank, the area where a man fording the river would make land is almost completely clear of trees. It is a bare area, before the forest thickens again and a perfect place to catch someone in an ambush. You see, where the land slopes upwards there is a ridge and a number of rocks that provide cover. Perfect for bowmen and bow women. My suggestion is that we hide up there, you then scatter them with arrows and myself and Nico will move down into the forest to catch them as they flee. Sound good?"

"Yes," Nico nodded, the others too seemed happy with this plan, Doul however, despite being engaged with fitting an arrow to his bow, had one observation to make.

"They are ahead of us; they will be over the river and past the ambush point before we can even get there."

ACT ONE : THE HUNT

"You are right," Ursus told him. "Unless we rest for a little while now, eat, get warm and dry in my case, and then march through the night."

"The night?" Nico asked. "We cannot use torches; they would see them."

"We will have to use the moon," Siri suggested. "It looks like the skies are clearing, if that is the case tonight it should give us just enough light to move by. We will reach this place before dawn yes?"

"Yes," Ursus said, "from what I remember. And we should do it with a little time to spare, we may even get to rest a little before the bloodletting starts."

"Then we shouldn't tarry here," Nico told them. "The woods give us more shelter than this riverbank. It is a pity we have to leave the rope behind; it could have been useful."

As he finished speaking there was a hiss and a whiff of sulphur. Nico looked around to see that Doul was poised to release his arrow which, just behind its sharp head, was burning with a yellow flame. As the rest of them stood wondering the arrow was loosed, speeding across the river to strike the rope at the far bank, next to the tree it was tied too. The arrow, thus diverted, sped into a mound of snowy mud where its flame was extinguished. The rope however, started to burn.

"Get ready to pull the rope," Doul said, "any moment...now."

As he spoke the burning rope separated from that part encircling the tree and fell to the ground. Nico started to pull it over the river, the burning end falling into it where the flame went out with a hiss that they heard even over the roar of the water.

Nico examined the burned tip of the rope. "Well we have lost about a quarter of it, and the end is frayed," he looked over at Doul, "but it is better than no rope at all."

"It is," Ursus said. "Well done, assassin."

Doul walked past them, tapping his head as he passed Nico, before disappearing into the woods, Nico and Zukan untied the knot around the tree, whilst Siri and Ursus exchanged a look that said that they trusted the assassin even less than they trusted each other.

****

As the pursuers were crossing the river and landing on the east bank, over on the west bank, some miles to the north, Oswold the hermit was

THE FANGS OF THE FEN SNAKE

eulogising on the wonder of the Gods with his usual wearying enthusiasm.

He stood on a ridge which overlooked the gorge and the river which, to the others, looked as swift, dangerous, and uncrossable as ever.

"Behold!" Oswold declared, his high, thin voice almost whipped away by the wind. "Here as nowhere else can you see the handiwork of the Gods! See how the open hand of Artorus has cloven the mountains in twain, allowing the river to pour through its lowest point. See how he has cast the seeds into the air, blowing them hence to land as trees on this almost inaccessible ground. Artorus, we stand in awe at your creation, we humble ourselves at your unbridled might, we abase ourselves at your omniscience! We...."

"How much further do we have to go?" Shak finally found the will to interrupt the man.

"It will be as the Gods will it, time can never be exactly quantified in the wilderness."

"I am sorry?" Stauncher asked.

"Tomorrow morning." Oswold told him.

"Will we be sleeping out in the open?" Eleanor asked whilst rubbing her arms. "It is rather cold."

"Any night sleeping in camp with you is one too many," Stauncher grinned at her. "By all the gods, the snoring!"

"I do not snore!" Eleanor was appalled.

"Forget the snoring," Stan was shaking his head, "what about the flatulence? Artorus strike me down, but I could swear I was sleeping with a ruminating ox!"

"Now you are definitely going too far," Eleanor pouted. "The ladies that attend on me have never complained about.... such things."

"Then they are probably worse than you." Stan affected the air of a man weary with the world. Eleanor for once had nothing to say, she just looked on aghast.

"They are just teasing you," Dormouse had to put her out of her misery. "They are far more the experts in such matters than you are. Seriously though Father, is there a place we can shelter up tonight? It would be nice to be dry at least."

"Yes," Oswold said. "Not quite a cave but a sheltered cleft in the rocks up yonder. It is close to the crossing place; we should be there at the ford well before noon tomorrow. And the passageway that I seek is next to one of the

ACT ONE : THE HUNT

falls at that point, you will be able to see it before you cross the river."

"Any chance of us getting there tonight?" Shak asked.

"Possibly," Oswold said. "But I know both myself and the girl slow you down. With both of us with you like as not you would arrive there in the dead of night. Not a good time to attempt a river crossing, even if the water there is relatively benign."

Shak looked around the company, especially at Dead Eyes who was standing there fingering her bow with her lips pursed. "I have seen and heard nothing as yet," she said, "but they cannot be far away."

"They are going to catch us sometime," Stan said. There was a brief silence as they became occupied with their own thoughts before Oswold piped in.

"Then you do not want to be caught at night, the camp site I have in mind is on rock, so no tracks, there is also an unobstructed view down the mountain. If you keep a watch you will see them before they see you."

Shak gave a weary sigh. "Very well Father Oswold, we are in your hands, please lead the way."

Stan shook his head unhappily, but Oswold did not notice. "Excellent!" was all he said, before going up to the nearest tree, lifting up his robe and tucking it under his chin. It appeared he was about to urinate.

"Ugh!" Eleanor audibly choked; Dead Eyes cleared her throat as loudly as she could. Oswold stopped before he could begin the act, looked around and put his hand to his face. "Apologies," he said. "I am so unused to company, especially female company. I will find a private place." He scratched his head. "Actually, I can feel my bowels loosening at last, I had better move." And with that he scurried behind the cover of the trees.

Shak waited till he was well out of sight before speaking. "Right then Stan, do you want to tell me why you disagree with this plan? And while you are at it can you tell me the cause of your bad humour these last two days?"

Stan was more than happy to oblige. "Isn't it quite obvious? He might be a loveable old fellow, after a fashion at least but he is madder than a flea on spirit grass! Why do you keep listening to him?"

"He has got us this far," Shak told him. But Stan just shook his head. "No," he said. "No. Our plan was to follow the river northwards anyway. With or without him we would still be here, or even ahead of here because he does slow us down."

"He got us up the cliff."

THE FANGS OF THE FEN SNAKE

"We would have done that anyway!"

"But not as quickly, we would have had to look around, and sure as Artorus leads the Gods we would have been ambushed back there, Doul's arrows rarely miss. He has also led us to some excellent camp sites. We may have lost some speed in taking him, but we have gained in several other ways."

Stan was utterly exasperated. "And what is he doing up here anyway? Righting a wrong he says, what wrong? And what about this supposed "treasure" Fenchard's boys are hunting him for? What treasure? He is making it all up, I can tell you that for sure."

Shak put his hand on the big man's shoulder. "I think the old man is much smarter than his "idiosyncrasies" make us believe. We have trusted him thus far and we will be parting ways tomorrow anyway. Stay with me for this, we all need each other right now."

Stan sighed and shrugged resignedly. "Of course I am with you Shak; always will be. It is just that the guy is barmy...."

Shak laughed. "He is not...." He started to say before they were interrupted by Oswold himself, who first howled in apparent pleasure before raising his voice to the Gods from his place of concealment.

"You have made it happen O great Gods! O Artorus, O Meriel, praise to you both for loosening my humble bowels. Bless this pile of excrement, let it feed the creatures of the forest and make new life happen. My dung is yours O Artorus, as am I!"

Stan gave Shak a look that was in equal part supercilious, world weary, and appraising. Shak stopped the inevitable reprimand with a raised finger.

"Not.... a.... word."

Eleanor was giggling, actually they all were as Oswold finally returned to them, adjusting the belt on his robe in a busy fashion.

"Ready?" Shak smiled at him.

"Well I would be," Oswold said. "But the half giant, master Stan, he has some questions, no?"

"You heard me?" Stan said in surprise.

"Old. Yes. Mad. Maybe. Deaf. No. You want to know of the wrong I have committed?"

"If you are willing to tell." Stan told him.

"I will tell you a little." Oswold replied, he seemed rather affronted that the company should have doubts about him. "The dragon. He is here

ACT ONE : THE HUNT

because of me. I brought him to this place as a hatchling. I should have left him where he was, to find his mother perhaps but I was selfish, I was curious. And now he has grown, and he is lost. I want to find his mother or find a way to send him to his mother. I wish to atone for my mistake. That is all I shall say at the present."

"You brought the dragon here?" Dead Eyes whispered. "What possessed you? Perhaps you are mad after all. But no, humans are always wont to meddle with that they do not understand."

"Yes, yes." Oswold nodded sagely. "But I am sorry more than anything else. Sorry for mistreating and confusing the creature, sorry for the lives it must have taken in its years here. Now, as to the other matter, the treasure I must have conjured up in my fevered mind, well, look at this."

He had several pouches tied around his belt and started fumbling with one, dextrously loosening it with his only hand. He passed it to Shak, who took it and loosened the string. "Something quite heavy inside, several objects, rattling." He said before emptying the contents into his free hand.

"Artorus bones," Stauncher breathed, "uncut gems."

There were six of them in Shak's palm. They were irregular, dull, unpolished, but they were gems alright. "Rubies?" Shak asked.

"Rubies." Oswold confirmed.

Stan and Stauncher whistled as Shak put them back in the pouch, tied the string and handed them back to Oswold. Oswold regarded the pouch coolly for a moment before suddenly dashing forward, free of the trees and hurling the pouch high in the air, where it seemed to hang for an eternity, before plummeting to the ground, disappearing amongst a cluster of rocks close to the riverbank.

Oswold turned, looked at their shocked faces and beamed in delight.

"All that?" he squealed. "Not a hundredth part, no, not a thousandth part of that which I found under that mountain yonder." He pointed to where, ahead of them to the north, the mountain climbed skywards, the river they were following ascending its southern flank before vanishing under its hulking shoulder in a pall of thin cloud. "I can show you." He continued. "But you would have to come with me to see it. Cross the river or delve into the passage under the mountain? You have a dilemma now, do you not? Perhaps it is Oswold who is the sane one and all of you who are the fools!" He cackled to himself before starting to walk into the trees to their west. Before he vanished completely he turned back to see them all standing stock still.

THE FANGS OF THE FEN SNAKE

"Well, do you want to get to the camping spot, or would you rather stay here to be killed by those who hunt you? You have told me how important time is, perhaps you should start to take account of it!"

Shak nodded and started to follow the old man, the rest of the company traipsing behind, all of them (except perhaps for Dead Eyes) wondering how they could deliver Eleanor, find this treasure and stay alive all at the same time.

ACT ONE : THE HUNT

19

He arrived at the crashing waterfall whilst the night was at its zenith, the moon at its apex reflecting lustily in the shimmering lake where the plummeting waters were disgorged. It was cold, the fragile air having teeth of its own; thin needle like shards that pierced hide and scale, blood and bone. It was a ruinous cold for one such as he, it compelled him to sleep, he wanted to sleep but there was a barrier there, something indefinable preventing him from setting down his head, an irritant that had to be scratched or burned before the rest of ages could overtake him.

He stood at the bottom of the cliff next to the falls, a cliff that glistened darkly by the light of the moon. Something lay at its foot, something dead, something that had leaked precious blood which now lay in coagulant black ribbons around the stiffened corpse. Things, small creatures of fur and feather had been feeding upon it, flesh was torn, and exposed, blue grey skin showed marks of beak and tooth, but those hungry creatures were not here now, they had seen him approach, they had fled, they were regarding him hungrily from the cover of the trees, waiting for him to leave, waiting to resume their grisly little feast.

He sniffed the cliff face. Nothing. He moved away from the corpse and sniffed elsewhere. A hint, the merest hint. He tried another place and then another. And there it finally was, the scent from his memory, the same one from the forest clearing he had visited earlier, the clearing where two more, similar to the body lying here, lay dead and half consumed. This was the scent he had been searching for, it was partway up the cliff, it must have climbed the cliff and was in the gorge at the top, no mean climb for such a puny creature.

He looked up at the cliff top, beheld its frowning visage, for most creatures of this world it would be an insurmountable obstacle. The only thing that could get from where he was standing up to the top of this cliff would be a bird.

Or any other creature that had wings.

And so it was time to unfurl his own.

They were getting stronger all the time, the veins running through them were widening, hardening, pumping blood faster and faster and yet, like the rest of him, they still had a long way to go before full maturity was

ACT ONE : THE HUNT

reached. He was strong but not invincible, formidable but not unmatchable, he could kill yes, but he still could be killed in return. His wings could not as yet carry him across continents, but they were more than sufficient for the current task in hand.

Four, five, six great sweeps of those wings and he was there, alighting on the cliff top with an impact that set the trees to shaking and great boulders to hurtling and crashing to the ground below. Forest creatures squealed in terror, birds abandoned their lofty branches and took to the air, this was no longer a haven for them.

For the dragon was finally in the gorge.

He sniffed around, the sparse forest ahead smelled strongly of humans, many humans. If it came to it he could face them, send them burning and screaming to the trees, but humans were no ordinary foe, they could hurt him too and he would rather avoid the risk of a needless confrontation.

So, to the river he went instead, spray from the plashing water at the bank giving his scales a glassy, metallic sheen. He would follow the river, keep to its fringes and taste the air with his tongue, smell it with his nose until he finally had that scent again, the scent of the only human that could possibly assuage his curiosity and answer the one question that never left his thoughts.

Would it ever be possible for him to find his mother?

****

The roar of the water seemed only to be enhanced by the coming of dawn, a dawn that arrived with a swirling wind and a spat of snow flurries. The noise of the sheltering tarpaulin flapping and tugging at its ropes woke Nico less than two hours after he had slipped into an exhausted slumber. He sat up, reaching out for the mace he had placed next to him before he slept. Still there. He felt a strange relief at that. He had fallen asleep with Ursus on one side of him and Zukan on the other, Ursus was still there, Zukan had gone. Siri was still lying on Ursus other side, she had seemed keen to be next to the old man once they had set up camp, he obviously still had something appealing about him. Doul was at the further end, awake, but then Nico doubted that the man ever slept in the first place.

He eased himself out of their little bivouac, located as it was next to a ring of stone that had acted as a buffer to the winds that seemed to assail this treeless space at all hours. Further boulders lay strewn about this low mountain slope, a hazardous spot, prone to avalanches, but one that provided

THE FANGS OF THE FEN SNAKE

excellent cover and a perfect view of the ford over the river.

His boots crunched in the fingers' depth of snow that had settled around and about him. He saw Zukan at last, standing a little clear of one of those covering boulders, hand at his brow, sheltering his eyes as he gazed at the layout of the valley beneath. Nico had not seen it in the daylight so he went to stand alongside the young man, all the better to assess the landscape below him, the ground where their ambush was to take place.

Ursus probably had more years on him than Nico and Zukan combined but his memory was obviously as sharp as it had ever been, for the view was exactly as the veteran knight had described it. It was maybe a quarter of a league between their hiding place and the river, and the river here was broader than it had been so far in this gorge; broader, cleaner and, most importantly, shallower. The mountain slope to the north was a relatively gentle one and the river ran merrily down it, gaining the level ground at its foot via a series of broad, sharp falls over which it frothed and tumbled joyfully before finally spilling over the final cataract, its water clear as glass, onto a bed of loose stone chippings, the depth of that water, maybe two feet at the most.

The crossing place, that part of the river that little sister Eleanor should soon be traversing, the place where they could finally assail her captors, Nico's hand closed around the haft of his mace, his free hand touched the hilt of his sword, he may well need both before the day was out.

Across the river the landscape seemed to be quite similar, a belt of thick trees, then a clearing leading down to the water's edge. The main difference appeared to be the extent of the downhill slope. On this side of the river it was shallow and gentle but on the west bank the slope from trees to river was much steeper and would take a little care to negotiate without turning an ankle.

Zukan gave him a curt little nod before resuming his vigil. "Siri says I have the keenest eyes amongst us and that I should keep a watch and let you know when something happens. So that is what I shall do."

Nico noticed the sword at the young man's side, a short blade, slightly curved in the manner of most Fashtan weapons, he had no idea as to how proficient Zukan was with it. "Have you used that often?" he asked.

"Now and then." Nico was well used by now to Zukan's economy with words, so he had another question ready and waiting.

"Do you always do what your sister tells you?"

ACT ONE : THE HUNT

Zukan shrugged. "Usually. She is clever. She looks after me. She knows what to do."

"You are close to her, aren't you?"

"Yes. You find it strange?"

"No," Nico answered. "Why do you say that?"

Zukan's dark eyes glittered. "Because you are not close to yours," he said, stating it as a fact rather than an opinion. There was something accusatory in the younger man's eyes that Nico found a little unsettling.

"Well I have many siblings," he said defensively, "and there are a lot of years between myself and Eleanor. Also the war has meant that I have spent a long time with the knights and not much with my family. Eleanor was a little girl when it all started, I was a young man of fighting age, things were never going to be close between us when you look at it that way."

Zukan nodded, as though he accepted the points made. "So, what do you think of her then?"

"What? Eleanor?" Nico realised that none of his opinions of his sister were that strong. "Well…. she is not the prettiest of her sisters, she can be a bit moody, she is not one for company. She has an opinion on everything rather like many young women about her age…"

"Anything about her that you like?"

"Plenty of things!" he blustered. "She is clever, she likes writing things, she can be quite funny, in an acerbic sort of way. She is a good girl, sound, an important part of the family and a good marriage prospect. Satisfied?"

"Yes," Zukan said, "you know her little and are more concerned with the stain she casts on the family honour than her own personal welfare."

"Now, you just wait a…." Nico started to bristle, but Zukan just carried on talking, oblivious to any offence caused.

"My sister was sold to a rich man. I was quite young at the time. I cried when I heard about it, cried for days, father bought a dozen ibex with the money. He was pleased."

"And your mother?" Nico asked.

"Obeyed him in all things. Still does, though he is ailing now. He will die soon, maybe he already has. I am happy I am not there."

There was a noise behind them, the rest of the company were all up and about, Doul came over to speak to Nico.

"Those rocks just below us." He said, indicating a lower ridge of stones similar to the ones they had camped behind. "Siri and I will wait there, with our weapons prepared. Zukan will stay with us, act as a watch and guard for us both."

"And, when the time comes." Nico added. "Ursus and I will move down into the trees and catch them as they flee there. How many do you think you can kill, before they react?"

"I will kill Shak first." Doul was matter of fact. "With their leader dead they should panic. Siri will target the archer. That leaves three of them, all of them the sort you should be able to deal with. Still, I will keep the arrows coming at them, it may be that by the time you move into the forest none of them will be left alive."

"The sort of fight I like," Ursus said behind him. Nico just grunted. If Doul and Siri made all the kills, where was his glory, it was his sister after all. He bit his lip and swore to himself that, in the fight to come, he would be more than just a passive observer.

****

The smell of the humans was not as strong now, and the scent was getting stale, he was no longer sure that he was heading in the right direction. And it was cold by the river. His claws were coated in mud and his blood was chilled in his veins. He felt sluggish, he still wanted to sleep, perhaps it was time to give up the chase and find a new spot to hibernate. This land of snow and sleet would never be a true home to him, he belonged in warmer climes, or underground, why wasn't he underground? He stopped, raising his neck as high as he could he sniffed the breeze above the river, then he flicked out his tongue, he needed to taste the air too, he needed all his senses right now, it was so, so cold.

And there it was, the tiniest hint of something, but not here, further up the mountainside, somewhere amongst the trees. He left the river, thrashing the water with his tail as he did so and, keeping his head low, began to navigate a path between lichen covered trunks, trailing beds of ferns, and boulders green with spongy moss. If a bush got in the way, it was squashed, if a tree trunk, it was shivered, high branches rattling and sending down a light dusting of snow to moisten his scales. Birds rose startled into the sharp grey skies calling out in fear and anger. He ignored their alarums for the scent was getting stronger now.

He now stood in a clearing, a clearing trodden by human boots and heavy with human scent. His head swung this way then that way before

ACT ONE : THE HUNT

pushing past the encircling trees and stopping where the scent was strongest. He edged out of the clearing before stopping again at one tree in particular. There it was. The human that had shaped his earliest memories had been here.

Some patted down leaves and twigs, a pile of human waste. What hold did this human have on him? Why was he trying to find him after his long hibernation? He did not really know, but at least now he had a trail to follow.

He moved on. This human had carried him, protected him, fed him, kept him alive when he was at his most vulnerable. At the time he had thought the human to be his parent, now of course he knew this to be untrue, but the human had nurtured him, had established a bond and now he thought that by seeing him again the human could direct him properly, show him the correct way, lead him on the path that every instinct in his powerful body told him to follow.

The path that led to his mother.

****

Ordinarily, with the prospect of combat looming, Nico would be looking to his mace, checking its balance, making sure its spikes were clean and sharp, that the haft was smooth and the grip firm, but not now. Now he felt that with his enemies being as experienced and proficient in battle as he was a different approach was needed. Which was why, sitting with his back propped against one of the sheltering stones, he had taken to whetting his sword.

He swept the whetstone back and forth, back and forth with fluid, graceful movements, checking the sharpness of the edge from time to time with his finger. Now and then the sapphire set in the pommel would catch the rays of the nascent sun, glittering with the sort of unabashed brio that seemed out of place in this sad, mournful mountain gorge. In this place colours were so muted and washed out, in thrall to a winter that was extending its long, gnarled fingers, clutching the landscape from river to sky in a grip of merciless iron. A radiant jewel such as this belonged in a brighter, happier world.

Ursus' blade was honed already and now he was standing slightly clear of the others, limbering up by sweeping both sword and limbs rhythmically, blocking imaginary thrusts, feinting, parrying, before landing the killer blow. He needed to exercise more than the others, his limbs were always stiff and cold of a morning, and out here in the wilderness, after spending a good while immersed in near freezing water, the need to be physically prepared was paramount. He felt younger when he exercised, it kept the spectre of age and infirmity a little further away, yet the spectre was growing all the time and what use was a man who could no longer defend himself and those he cared for?

Both he and Nico though had one eye free to watch Siri and Doul. They were both sitting a little farther away, still behind the cover of the rocks and they were both engrossed in preparing their instruments of war. Nico reckoned that Doul's bow was probably the biggest he had ever seen, the strength required to pull the drawstring back must be immense. Doul had checked the string a few moments earlier. Satisfied with the tension he turned to his arrows that he had laid out on the ground in front of him. Most were regular enough, though even these humdrum ones were beautifully crafted but there were others with small bundles secured just behind the head, presumably they were like the burning arrow Doul had loosed the previous day. Finally, there were three wooden boxes, one of black, secured by clasps and a lock. Doul was lavishing particular attention on these when he caught Nico looking at him.

"My bombs," he said proudly; "they probably cost more than that gem in your sword." He picked up the black box, inserted a tiny key into the lock, flipped it open and held it out for Nico to see.

The box was lined with a lush velvet. Nestling against that velvet in their own perfectly fitted housings were two small, glass spheres. They were held within a protective frame of ribbed metal and inside the glass something swirled, almost like smoke. The difference here though was that the "smoke" was a noxious, viscous green, the colour of rot, putrescence, and decay. Nico could not see but rather sensed Doul's lascivious grin as he took out one of the globes, pulled off one half of the metal frame (it appeared to be divided into equal halves, like a protective egg casing) and gave Nico an unobstructed view of the sphere within.

"Inhale just a little of the poison inside and soon your lungs will start to blister, and you will be spitting blood," Doul explained. "Inhale more and you will die soon enough, drowned by your own body fluids." He shut the iron casing and tenderly, almost lovingly replaced the globe back where it belonged in the box. Then he shut the box and locked it slipping the key back into a fold in his robes. "The fire, smoke, and stun bombs are in the other boxes. They each cost much gold, but it is the poison ones that are the most

ACT ONE : THE HUNT

expensive of all. There is a craftsman on the Isle of Pratugan who makes them specially for me. Pratugan is an island just off the coast of Fash, he lives on a high peak on that island. He is a man who likes his privacy."

"Why am I not surprised?" was Nico's wry response. "I take it he is a wealthy man?"

"A very wealthy man, and he keeps his secrets close."

"Because if he let those secrets slip you would kill him and take over his business?"

Doul did not reply, a small shake of the head sufficed in itself.

Nico turned his attention to Siri. She had discarded her smaller crossbow, the one that Ursus was painfully familiar with and was instead examining a full sized model. Yet, it was not like any crossbow Nico had seen before for its parts, stock, barrel, limb, and stirrup seemed to be fashioned entirely of metal. It also appeared to have a sight, two metal pins just above the groove where the bolt fitted. In addition, there was a mechanism, some small wheels and a handle, for pulling the string back, without such an aid after all, only the strongest of men could accomplish such a task. With such a device Siri could set the string swiftly and with little effort, negating the usual inefficiencies inherent in such a weapon. The whole thing looked light, deadly, and just as expensive as anything Doul had in his possession. "Where did you get that?" Nico asked her.

"Like Doul's weapons, this was made specially for me," she told him. "My patron paid for it, he needed…. a job done and such a weapon was most suited to the task. The bolts are regular enough, they will not need poison, if they strike a vital part of the body then its possessor is a dead man regardless. For the range we are covering here, it is a perfect weapon. Zukan will guard my person while I use the bow. If both Doul and I are accurate enough, two of their people will be dead before they even know they are under attack."

"That is of course," Ursus pointed out, "if they haven't already crossed the river without us knowing about it and we somehow passed each other during the night."

"Well if that is the case," Nico replied, "they will be in Grest before we can get near them. And it was dark last night, we could have passed each other easily." Ursus words had doubt rearing in his mind like a bear threatened with fire. "Keth take it, we were in such haste, they could have got past us easily!"

"But they didn't." It was Zukan, still standing next to the rocks, still peering languidly at the river.

"And how exactly do you know that?" Nico asked.

Zukan pointed. "There. Over the river, the ridge close by the trees. Very small figures are standing there, just come out of the forest."

"What! How many?"

Zukan squinted. "Half a dozen maybe, difficult to be sure from here, the river mist obscures things."

Nico clapped Ursus on the shoulder. "Time my friend. Into the trees and watch, our chance is coming."

Zukan had drawn his sword and, still watching the gorge, had half crouched next to his sister. Both Siri and Doul had sprung into action like cats pouncing on a landed salmon, Siri resting her weapon on the rocks, Doul fitting an arrow to the bow, though he had not yet drawn it, plenty of time for that later.

Nico and Ursus were already making their way to the trees. "Do you need a signal?" Doul called out to them.

Nico stopped. "No. We will be watching. You do what you have to do, and we will do the same."

Just a minute later they were amongst the trees, running downhill, kicking up flurries of snow and mud as they went. "Ursus!" Nico said. "Stop! I need a word."

Ursus looked up at him expectantly. "Eleanor," Nico told him, "when we see her, we go out and get her, whether she is among the trees our out there, on the rocks, understood? I will not skulk around like some common bandit, and I do not fear their blades"

To his surprise, Ursus looked up at the heavens, his face was colouring. "Don't be a fool boy!" he admonished him. "Their blades? Have an eye for our own! Doul wants the bounty on Eleanor too. You leave the trees to get her, and he will stick you with so many arrows you will look like a spiny hedgehog!"

Nico inhaled sharply, embarrassed by his naivety. "Artorus breath, I never saw it. Siri too?"

"Siri too," Ursus said. "They do not have honour, remember? All they care about is coin. Let Eleanor gain the trees, finish her guards if she has any, then maybe the three of us can disappear before Doul has any inkling we have gone. We need not see the three of them again, if the Gods are with us."

"Then let us pray that they are," Nico said. "Come, a little further and

ACT ONE : THE HUNT

we will be halfway between Doul and the river. There we can wait, and then we shall see exactly what the Gods have in store for us."

****

All their weapons were drawn; nerves were once again frayed to breaking. Shak stood atop the ridge along with his company, regarding the lie of the land with a watchful eye.

The ground ahead sloped downwards quite sharply both to the east, where lay the river; and to the north, where it dipped into a narrow, boulder strewn gully before rising again as part of the mountainside, scattered pines clinging precariously to its jagged heights. But it was to the river on their right where most of their attention lay, for here was a waterfall, but a waterfall quite unlike the Whiterush Maw. The falls here extended back up the mountain for many furlongs, water slipping downhill via a series of short, shallow ledges, clear water here, frothing as it fell, until finally over the last and highest lip it dropped, landing on the level riverbed with a joyful and voluble splash. The river at that point whirled and eddied as it encircled sharp stones and broad, flat pebbles. A fine spray lingered in the air here, testament to the velocity of the water and, more importantly, its shallowness. It seemed that they had finally arrived at Oswold's ford. And Oswold was pleased to corroborate the fact.

"There you are," he pointed at the riverbed. "Your crossing, just the briefest of walks away. I have fulfilled my part of my agreement in leading you here, have I not?" he seemed very pleased with himself.

"You have indeed holy man." Shak spoke as though distracted. He looked around once more. "Where are they, where are our pursuers?" he said, half aloud and with just enough volume so that all could hear him.

Nobody replied. Apart from the constant thrum of churning water there was no noise here. No birds, no animals, no sighing trees, even the snow and sleet had stopped falling as rare streaks of sunlight penetrated the high cloud. Near silence pervaded, and silence had never felt so threatening.

"We should get off this ridge," Stan advised, "we are standing out against the sky like a gibbet on a hill."

"Yes," Oswold agreed; "because before you cross the river I have to show you the tunnel. Part of our agreement yes? Part of our agreement."

Shak duly nodded. The time to tell the old hermit that Dead Eyes was not going with him was almost here. Before he could say anything though

THE FANGS OF THE FEN SNAKE

Oswold had scampered off, heading down into the northern gully, right next to the falls.

"Well there is little point just standing here," Shak told everybody else. "Follow the man, keep your weapons readied and your eyes and ears open. And be wary of anything that might be behind these larger rocks! Dormouse, stay with Eleanor, Dead Eyes, keep to the rear, I will lead us for now."

They all fell into place as Shak scrambled down the steep slope, sword drawn, senses keen as his blade. Not for the first time Eleanor was grudgingly impressed by the way they all went about their business, professional soldiers who knew each other's strengths and weaknesses, gelling like a finely tuned machine, seeing everything as they moved, prepared for anything that might be thrown at them. The presence of Oswold however, rather threatened to undo their clinical efficiency.

Cackling and capering as he went, leading the way by some considerable distance, he bounded down the slope raising wet dust with every footfall, as enthusiastic as a small child opening a Winterfeast present. He was at the bottom of the gully now, the shadows there covering all but his snowy head which bobbed around like some manic will of the wisp, never settling in one spot for more than a second. His feet slipped constantly on a thick ribbon of ice that threaded along the gully's bottom but, as ever, he seemed to have no concept of personal safety, coming close to falling flat on his face several times before he started to climb up the gully's further, northern side.

Shak laboured after him, trying to keep tabs on the man whilst simultaneously looking everywhere else for possible danger. Fortunately, the climb back up the gully was not a long one for, after losing Oswold completely for a brief moment he came to a rock formation that caused him to stop in surprise.

It was a block of stone about ten feet high and maybe three or four times wider than that, sitting where the rise of the gully stopped temporarily and the ground became level. It was heavily eroded and covered in lichen and colourful, cold resistant mountain flowers but it was still obvious that it had been worked by some long forgotten army of stone masons. Its shape, its lines were too geometrically perfect for it to be some boulder fallen from the mountain top, it had been placed there, seemingly eons ago, by.... somebody, somebody with skill. Shak moved to stand next to it and realised that, what he had taken for pits and scars in the rock face were actually carvings, though they had been so worn by time and the elements it was impossible to say

ACT ONE : THE HUNT

what they were carvings of.

"Interesting no?" Oswold's head peeked out from the rock's other side. Shak realised that he had been so distracted by his discovery he could have been attacked and killed before he could react. Oswold did not appear to notice Shak's anger with himself. "Just come around here and see some more."

Shak followed him behind the rock and then saw that it was probable that the ground here had been artificially levelled. This was because, though the gully started to rise sharply again at the point almost directly behind the rock the rise was almost vertical. And in this vertical cliff face sat the opening to a cave.

He approached it, Oswold next to him, Stauncher, Dormouse and Eleanor just behind, all of them reacting to the rock in exactly the same manner he had. It was soon obvious that the cave mouth had also been worked by hand, the surround was a cunningly fashioned arch though, Shak noticed, it was an arch without a keystone. It was also not that high, a man such as he would have to stoop to enter it, though of course, entering it was the last thing on his mind.

"Here at last," Oswold said wistfully. "Here at last."

"You are going in there?" Stauncher asked him. "Into that dark hole? Artorus beard but you have more curiosity than me old man. Caves are for bats and snakes dripping venom, not men."

"Yet you have sheltered in such places these last days," Oswold observed; "and through there lies so much more than a mere cave."

"Those gems." Stauncher said.

Oswold nodded. "And so much more than that too."

"Who built this all the way out here though?" Dormouse asked. "And when? The Tanarese have been here about seven centuries, but this looks even older than that."

"It was not the Tanarese," Oswold said, "this was here long before us."

"Then who?" said Eleanor. Oswold merely shrugged. Shak though knew that questions or no questions, spending time here was an ill afforded luxury.

"Well master hermit," he said bluntly. "it is time for us to part ways. You have led us to the ford, we have led you to your tunnel. I wish you all the good fortune the Gods can afford but we really have to cross the river now. Fare thee well, man of Artorus."

He was waiting for it, and it came. "Gods benison upon you all; and now it is time for you to say farewell to your elf companion, she is to come with me after all, it was part of our agreement if you remember."

Shak noted that neither Dead Eyes nor Stan had joined them yet, the former maybe out of reasons of prudence, the latter, well he did not know. And not knowing the whereabouts of his companions concerned him. Oswold though drew the wrong inference from his perplexed silence even though his following words were undeniably correct.

"Aha!" he croaked. "Betrayed at the last! You never intended that the elf leave your side! For all your…."

"Quiet good father!" Shak shushed him with a gesture. He was listening, somebody was calling out from some distance away. And who could they be calling out to but him and his men?

Stan finally appeared, though he stopped just this side of the sheltering stone.

"Shak," he said. "This way. We are being hailed."

Quick as he could Shak went over to Stan, his sword briefly catching the rays of the late morning sun, which was finally finding larger gaps in the unrelenting cloud. Together the two men left the sheltering stone and scrambled part way down the side of the gully where Dead Eyes was waiting, arrow fitted and bow half drawn. Shak looked ahead and saw.

On the ridge, atop the other side of the gully, the same ridge they themselves had been standing upon not so long ago was a line of nine men, widely spaced, all holding weapons. It was the man at the very centre who was shouting at them.

"You! The tall bastard, and the big man with the incontinent mouth! Do you think we have forgotten you? Did you not think that we would seek vengeance? Well now it is you who are surprised! There are no hidden archers or knifemen to come to your aid now! You have no choice but to face us like men. Pray that we kill you quickly, any that we capture will face hours under Ham's boning knife before Xhenafa comes for them. Face us! And face your end!"

Shak nodded to Stan, who nodded to Dead Eyes. None of them had quite expected this, had expected that Yaki and Ham would pursue them so relentlessly. They had committed that most egregious of mistakes for a warrior, they had underestimated the enemy. And there was still no sign of Doul.

ACT ONE : THE HUNT

THE FANGS OF THE FEN SNAKE

20

Yaki and Ham, men in the service of King Fenchard, one a soldier of fortune from a distant country, the other a loyal Tanarese fighter disconcerted by his master's change of loyalties, were both hard-bitten by years in the field. They were capable men, proud, and were never likely to let a slight to their personal honour such as the one Shak and his companions had inflicted, pass without response. After finding the weapons Shak had hidden from them they had sent to Teague for aid. He had responded by sending them two bowmen and had let them remain the vanguard of the pursuers, for Teague and his men had also scaled the cliffs at the Whiterush maw, albeit for the loss of one life, a young fellow who had dared looked down whilst just short of the summit. Teague was still some hours behind them, so Yaki and Ham at last had the chance to claim the vengeance they felt was their due.

Since scaling the cliffs they had found the trail then lost it, found the trail then lost it, before stumbling upon it again just after dawn. They had, of course, known all along that their quarry had an old man and young girl in tow and this gave their heels wings. The Arshumans could not move as fast as they could and, sooner or later, they knew that they would wear the distance between them down. And now, at last, after gaining the ridge, they saw them, clambering up the other side of the gully. There was nowhere for their enemy to escape to, no advantage of surprise for their foe, no advantage in archery; if they ran westwards they would end up next to sheer cliffs, if they ran east they would end up in the river, if they continued to climb northwards up the slope they would just be giving the archers target practice. Yaki looked at Ham, the two men exchanged a wolfish smile, it had taken some days, but this next hour would reward them a hundredfold.

They had them at their mercy.

****

"There are more men up there, just come out of the trees!" Zukan was standing now, having little regard for keeping to their cover. This was a development none of them had prepared for.

"Those campfires," Doul growled. "The ones we saw before climbing the cliff. We knew it had to be a patrol, they must have caught the trail and

ACT ONE : THE HUNT

followed."

"Looks like some sort of confrontation," Zukan pondered.

"Maybe. Shak already has many enemies; he would not be averse to making new ones." Doul spoke the words with some kind of perverse relish, as though he saw somebody with multiple adversaries as some kind of kindred spirit. Siri however was more concerned with the here and now.

"Whatever is going on, we are on the wrong side of the river for it. Can we do anything but watch? Are we totally impotent here?"

"Cross the river and they will see us, and we will be stranded with no cover," Doul said. "So yes, there is nothing we can do aside from seeing how this plays out."

"And if they kill this Shak and take the girl? What happens to our money then?"

"You are making suppositions Siri," Doul softly upbraided her. "If Shak is killed we can still claim the bounty, we just cross the river when it is safe and take his sword or the family ring, or his head, if the body has been looted. The girl is a little more problematic, but she is not our chief target. Let the knights worry about her, we will receive our asking price just for producing evidence of Shak's death. That is all that should concern us at the moment."

"So our alliance with the knights is over?" Zukan asked. "Pity, I liked them, they are honest at least."

"Honest compared to us?" Doul sounded amused. "So are most people, but then, most people do not do what we do and do not have the wealth we have accumulated from our endeavours. Our alliance might end now, but then again it might not. Might I suggest that the two of you just watch and see what happens?"

Siri nodded grudgingly. "Zukan, your eyes are stronger than any of ours, keep telling us what you see. She took her crossbow from its vantage point on the covering rock, removed the bolt then set it on the floor behind her. "There is nothing worse than watching events unfold over which we have no control."

Doul followed Siri's example, placing his bow safely on the ground. "There have been many times in my life when things have not happened in the way they have been planned for. The important thing is to adapt, assess the situation and reassert authority as soon as possible. We will sit, watch, then we will regain control."

"Are you sure?" Zukan was sceptical, "have you ever lost control and never regained it?"

"Never," Doul was emphatic. "If that had ever happened, I would not be here now."

****

Dormouse stood behind the sheltering stone, his face a picture of uncertainty. Oswold had disappeared into the tunnel ahead of them, Eleanor was standing stock still, eyes wide, thumb in her mouth, a reflex action that Dormouse thought quite endearing. She soon realised what she had done though, and that Dormouse was watching her, she pulled her thumb out swiftly, her face crimson, her expression both angry and embarrassed. "What are you going to do then?" She asked him testily.

He did not know, aside from realising that Oswold was no longer his responsibility. "Come with me," he told her, "I want to see what is happening."

She followed, meekly, until getting to the edge of the sheltering stone where Dormouse gestured for her to stop. He was standing just clear of the stone where he had a clear view of the unfolding situation.

Shak, Stan, and Dead Eyes were stood some twenty yards beneath him, grouped quite close together. Stauncher was closer, just a few yards downhill. He heard Dormouse, turned and put his hand out, telling him to stop. Dormouse did so, then looked at the ridge opposite the gully. The tops of the trees behind it reached up to the sky as if to touch it, as, in the first time in days, it was now streaked with cold blue. Nearer to hand though, on the ridge itself, stood a line of men, a good distance away, silhouetted like the trees, their presence radiating threat. The tension in the air was a force potent enough to induce thin rivulets of sweat to run down Dormouse's back. He heard a sound, a whistling, singing sort of sound, something was moving through the air very quickly and the sound was getting louder.

The arrow skipped over the rocks some fifteen feet to Stan's left. He looked at Shak and Dead Eyes. "Archers," being his laconic comment.

Dead Eyes shook her head. "Two of them, either end of the line, their bows outmatch mine when it comes to range. If we stay here, they will just pick us off piecemeal."

"We will have to get behind that stone," Stan said.

"But then what?" Dead Eyes asked. "It covers the front but not our flanks, they just move one archer to the right, one to the left and do just the same as they are doing now."

ACT ONE : THE HUNT

"Isn't there a tunnel behind that rock?" Stan asked. "Can't we use that?"

"We will just be trapped in there, they will just pin us inside and loose off arrow after arrow, or send in fire or smoke or something. We go in there and we lose what little chance we have." Dead Eyes turned her bejewelled green eyes on to Shak. "Any suggestions commander?"

Shak remained silent. Another arrow came close, sticking in a soft area of mud just below their feet. "At least they have no proficiency with their weapons." The elf observed drily.

"Dormouse!" Shak spoke at last, his voice commanding and clear.

"Yes Sir!"

"Get a torch burning and take Eleanor and Oswold into the tunnel!"

"Oswold is already inside sir."

"Then join him. And guard Eleanor with your life!"

"I will sir!" Dormouse disappeared behind the stone.

Another arrow, this one closer still, Shak spoke to the remainder of the company. "Back behind the stone!" he told them. "But slowly and keep your faces to the enemy!"

They obeyed immediately, Stan moving back about ten feet before asking his leader. "What shall we do then?"

"No idea," Shak replied. "But taking her into the tunnel will keep the girl safe and buy me time to think of something."

"And if none of us think of anything?"

"We will," Shak said; "we always do. And if we don't we just make sure we take as many of those bastards with us as we can."

They continued to inch backwards, but as they did they saw their enemy starting to make their way down the slope, keeping the distance between them all constant. The only exceptions were Yaki and Ham who stayed where they were, on top of the ridge, all the better to see their impending triumph Shak thought. One of the archers stopped, he was preparing another arrow, sooner or later they would find their range, find their mark. He was beginning to think a sudden rushed attack down one of the flanks would be the best, if riskiest option, he would tell them all once he was behind the sheltering stone.

But then everything changed, the Gods in their caprice had decided to shake things up it seemed, for, from somewhere in the trees behind their attackers a great beast called out to the sky, a beast rarely, if ever seen in

THE FANGS OF THE FEN SNAKE
Tanaren during the age of men.

****

It was something between a high screech and a shivering howl and it echoed off the mountain side, a reverberating, piercing sound that seemed to hit Shak and his companions in waves. Everybody froze where they stood, save for Yaki and Ham, who were nearest the source of the noise, they turned in place trying to see exactly what had caused it, their body language transformed from easy self-confidence to rigid mortification in a trice.

The trees, those high firs still clad in green, their lower boughs heavy with melting snow started to shake. A great shower of pine needles started to cascade to the ground like a swirling smoke. A branch cracked like a whip strike, mighty tree trunks, decades old, groaned under immeasurable strain, flocks of birds took to the wing, their harsh, croaking calls thick with panic. A heavy shape was moving through the treetops, it was getting larger, closer, Shak slid his sword back into its scabbard, he suddenly felt that it would play no part in the events to come.

Then he saw that it wasn't climbing, it was flying, great bat like wings beating sonorously and rhythmically, finally visible as it cleared the last of the trees. It was a clumsy, awkward flyer, its body rolling as it splintered the treetops, its feet pulled up underneath its powerful sinuous body. It landed with a great crash, sending up a spray of stones, snow, and mud, folding its dry wings behind it as its stabilised itself. It was standing on the ridge, just yards from Yaki, its right flank facing Shak, who at last had a clear view of the beast they had first encountered at the derelict manor house, seemingly so long ago.

It was most like a winged lizard in form, its skin being covered in polished scales that were mainly grey in colour, tinged with a delicate shell pink. Even from where he was standing, Shak could see the thick blocks of muscle rippling under those scales, from the long, snaking neck, to the tree trunk thick legs. Its tail it held high, the thin webbing that ran along it like a fin translucent in the pale light of day, a fin that carried on along the body, up the neck to the mighty head. And it was the head that most drew Shak's attention. It was wedge shaped, triangular, like an arrowhead. Running from one pit like ear to the other was a high crest of horn and scale, ribbed with bone that extended above the crest, each rib ending in a sharp point. For some reason the smaller scales that covered the head appeared to be more polished,

ACT ONE : THE HUNT

glittering like quartz as the head moved left to right, tasting the air with a flickering black tongue thicker than a man's arm. Its mouth was slightly open as the tongue worked, ivory, dagger like teeth running its entire length and then, above the mouth, the eye. The eye of yellow agate, slitted like a snake, the baleful, cold, killers' eye, so unheeding of the men close to it, so unconcerned with their hopes, dreams and ambitions. The eye that spoke of an intelligence far removed in kind to that of man, yet intelligent it undoubtedly was, regarding the puny beings close to it in the same manner as a cat regards a mouse, curiosity without empathy, interest without compassion, whether the man so frozen in terror before it felt pain or fear was a matter of no consequence to it whatsoever. It withdrew its tongue, men were flying hither and thither around it but not this man, not Yaki, this man was standing his ground.

One quick jerk of the head of the beast, faster than quicksilver, swifter than an arrow in flight left Yaki still standing there, still frozen for a brief moment more. Yet, the figure could no longer be truly called Yaki, for it was a figure without a head, blood spurting fiercely from that space atop the shoulders where it used to be. The arms jerked violently, almost as if trying to stop such a gross violation to its person, then Yaki's body slowly toppled backwards, crashing onto the ground in a heap of flailing limbs and spraying blood.

Now Shak could see how Siras had died, now Shak could see how easily a dragon could kill.

A dragon. Just as Oswold and Dead Eyes had told them. And this was supposedly a young one.

Fenchard's men had abandoned their attack plan completely and now were solely bent on survival, running away from the fearsome creature. Whether, like Ham, it took him back towards the woods, or, like many others it took them towards the bottom of the gully and closer to Shak did not matter, putting as much distance as possible between themselves and the beast did. One brave archer chanced an arrow at the creature, it glanced off the scales on its back and lodged itself in a wing, arrowhead punching through the membrane and staying there. The dragon gave its screeching cry once more yet seemed uncertain as to which of the men to pursue unto death, so many there were, and so scattered their flight. Shak had seen enough by now, there was really only one option open to them. He turned to Stan and Dead Eyes.

THE FANGS OF THE FEN SNAKE

"Into the tunnel. Now!"

He didn't really need to say it, both of them were on their heels before he finished the words. The dragon made its piercing, shrieking call once more and, by the time its long, drawn out wail had died in the air Shak was level with the sheltering stone again.

All of his companions were ahead of him; indeed, Eleanor and Dormouse had already disappeared into the tunnel entirely, Dormouse having to stoop a little as he went inside. One person though had other ideas and was moving in the other direction, passing Shak so that he could view the ridge and the gully before stopping.

Oswold held a burning torch high with his lone hand, his eyes wide, utterly enraptured by the sight of the dragon before him.

"Gods fill my eyes with wonder!" he breathed in awe struck tones. "My friend, I cannot believe how much you have grown!"

And the dragon appeared to hear him. It stopped calling and turned its gaze to the sheltering stone and those standing next to it. Shak saw it look at Oswold, then felt its eyes burn into him before looking back at Oswold again.

Then it lifted its head up high, unfurled its wings, flapped them several times before calling out and leaping into the sky, heading directly for the sheltering stone, for Oswold, and for Shak.

****

Zukan no longer cared about hiding, no longer worried about the shattered fragments of their original plan. He stood tall, eyes blazing, stumbling awkwardly down the slope leading to the river, utterly enraptured by the sight before him. But it was too far away, too far away. He needed to get closer, he needed to SEE.

"So magnificent," he muttered to himself, in his own language. "That is no mere beast, it is a demigod. Such a thing is sullied by having to live on this unworthy earth."

He continued to clamber down the slope, stumbling over loose stones because his eyes never left the awe inspiring sight immediately across the river. He was blind and dumb to everything else, including the voice of his sister, imploring him to return to their hiding place. The river was getting closer all the time, if he had deigned to look at it he would see that he was close enough to see the froth churned up by the falls spilling over the

ACT ONE : THE HUNT

riverbank.

Closer he got, close enough to see the roseate tinge on the beast's scales, his breathing became shallow as his excitement rose. His trance was increasing its grip upon him, he was unaware of any of his surroundings, it would take actual physical force to break it.

And that was what Siri had to resort to. After her pleading was ignored she had no choice but to break cover and run down after him. Flushed with exertion she grabbed him by the shoulders, shaking him violently until at last the glazed expression in his eyes started to clear.

"Zukan, what are you doing! You endanger us all!" She repeated the words over and over again until at last they started to register with him. He looked at her panic stricken face, put his hand to his heart, waiting for his agitation to ease before replying.

"But surely you can see...."

"I can see very well," was her pointed reply. "It is the possibility of it seeing us that scares me so much. We need to get under the cover of the trees, then make our way back up the mountain."

She took his hand and started to lead him into the woods, he followed limply, his attention going back over the river once more. "It must be a god, a god descended to this earth. It is surely divine Kudrassos, the snake god. Its scales are impervious to weapon or fire, its teeth can cut diamond and its blood can revivify the dead. I have to get closer, prostrate myself, do homage, get its divine blessing." He started to pull against her; "you must let me go! I have to cross the river!"

"Do that and you could bring it here!" She was pleading to him. "If you think it a god then you know I have done many bad things, do you want it to judge me? Do you want it to kill me?"

He stopped then, temporarily struck dumb. He ran his hand through his crow black hair, then rubbed his brow before admitting, almost reluctantly. "No."

She finally dragged him under the trees, the calls of the beast still ringing in their ears. "If the creature...."

"The god," he corrected her.

"Alright, if the god returns to us in the future then I promise I will not restrain you from doing.... whatever it is you wish to do with it. But right now there are other things at stake."

"Like what?" he asked her.

THE FANGS OF THE FEN SNAKE

"Our futures!" Was her exasperated reply. "We need the money from this job if we are to return home! We cannot throw it all away by chasing that.... thing! Let us secure our bounty first then I swear I will let you do what you feel you must."

"But if I never see it again!"

"It is a god is it not? If it wants you to see it again then that is what will happen. Let me guide you in this, have I ever proven false to you? Did I not let father beat me rather than you when you pilfered the spun sugar cakes for the Haruan feast? I swear I will always have your best interests at heart. So will you heed my words now, am I not your older sister?"

His shoulders sagged a little. "Of course," he said, "you are the only one who cares for me."

She smiled, relieved at finally having got through to him. "Come on then Inzukanash, herder of ibex, we can watch what goes on from the safety of the rocks above."

Suddenly there was a noise close by, a heavy boot crunching branch and snow. She drew her dagger, a curved blade edged in the white metal so favoured by Fashtan warriors, then relaxed her defensive stance as Nico walked clear of the trees to stand with them, Ursus following just behind.

"What sort of gibberish were you two talking just then?" he asked. He sounded jocular but kept his voice low, even he was aware of the dragon it seemed.

"It was Fashtan, our home language," she informed him. "My brother broke cover, he wanted a better view of the dragon."

"The god," Zukan corrected her. Siri just nodded at him.

"Well," Ursus said bluntly, "I have the eyesight of a mole with the white eye, can you, or your brother enlighten me as to exactly what is going on over there?"

So, as they climbed back up to the rocks where Doul was waiting, the two of them told him.

****

Shak no longer cared about having to stoop, he followed the rest of his companions into the tunnel with all the alacrity he could muster. The dolorous wingbeats of the great monster were growing louder all the time as it drew closer and closer to their position. Oswold however was not so convinced that flight was entirely necessary.

ACT ONE : THE HUNT

"It wants me," he said as Shak tried to propel him down the tunnel. "It remembers that it was I that brought it here, it probably thinks that I can aid it now. If I go to it perhaps I can do something, it probably thinks that you are trying to keep me away from it, if I go, it might just leave you alone."

The wingbeats were a cacophony now, a great thudding sound fit to induce a pounding head. "And how could you help it exactly?" Shak asked.

They were well inside the tunnel now, Oswold's torch reflecting off polished black rock. Dormouse was in the lead, he had a torch burning too, Shak tried speeding up to get closer to it, but Oswold was still resisting. "Well I am not sure that I could help it," he admitted. "That was why I was coming here, to see if I could find something, in the dragon cave further in."

"Then don't you think that seeing it now would be pointless? Get down the tunnel, find whatever you think you can find, then seek out the creature on your return. Is that an agreeable sequence to you?"

"Yes." Oswold nodded.

"Then, in the name of Artorus, and all the Gods you hold so dear, move!"

From behind them, just outside the tunnel, came the almightiest impact. Like a great boulder hurled down a mountainside by an angry frost giant, the dragon landed in a shower of snow, mud and shale. The shuddering crash reverberated through the narrow confines of the tunnel causing Shak to stop and look behind him, whilst his companions put their hands over their ears. And there it was, the dragon. Shak's view was restricted to the triangle of light at the tunnel's entrance, but it seemed that the great beast had its hind legs and tail resting on the sheltering wall outside with the front end at a lower level between the wall and cave entrance. Its head though was twisting and turning, trying to squeeze through the mouth of the tunnel, but the narrowness of the aperture was defeating it. It settled for turning its head side on to the entrance, peering into the darkness through one glimmering yellow eye.

Shak resumed his loping run down the shaft but, in his keenness to get away from his reptilian onlooker, he stumbled into Oswold, eliciting a curse from himself and the mild imprecation "Artorus tangled beard!" from Oswold. It was barely a whisper from the old man, but the tunnel amplified his voice and sent it echoing forth, straight to the ear of the dragon.

Its reaction was explosive, an ear shattering screech fit to curdle the blood and send the stoutest heart quaking. The ground above and around

THE FANGS OF THE FEN SNAKE

them started to shake as though riven by many blows, it was only by stopping momentarily again that Shak could see that the dragon was wheeling around, hammering at the mountain side with great beats of its thick, muscular tail. A shower of fine dust went up Shak's nose and coated his hair.

"By the Gods!" he heard Stan say. "It is going to bring the entire mountain down on top of us!"

Shak's mind though was heading down another, equally worrying road. As Stan uttered those words the dragon desisted from thrashing at bare rock with his tail and, though Shak could see but little of it now, having travelled so far along this passage, it appeared to be lowering its head and inhaling somewhat, as though preparing to do something that would cost it no little effort. Shak wondered just how far they would have to run before stumbling into a dead end, he suddenly hoped that this, obviously artificial structure extended a good way yet.

"Oswold," he asked. "This dragon. Can it breathe fire?"

"Oh!" Oswold spoke as though reminiscing in front of his grandchildren, feet poking towards the hearth. "It did used to try, puffing its little sides out then releasing naught but air. Now though, at that size I do not doubt that it can achieve such a task."

"God's teeth!" Shak hissed. "Move! Everybody run! As fast as you possibly can!"

He saw Stauncher scoop Eleanor up in his arms as everybody put on a sudden, desperate spurt, perhaps they did not know why, but their leader had given the order. He saw Dormouse's torch bobbing ahead of him, this way and that, before, surprisingly, getting lower and then disappearing altogether. He was about to call out, asking if Dormouse was alright when suddenly the ground disappeared underneath him. He stumbled onto his knees before rolling onto his side, the impact was hard, jarring, as he continued to roll over and over, seemingly descending as he did so.

Stairs, he was tumbling down a series of stairs.

And the sides of the passage appeared to be widening as down the stairs he fell. He saw Oswold crouching over, him, Stan too had stopped to help him arrest his fall. They were all well below the original height of the passage, a descent that was about to save all their lives.

For, at that precise moment, the dragon breathed its plume of fire.

Shak had rolled onto his back by now and was tasting blood at the back of his throat, he had hit his nose in the fall, and this was the inevitable

ACT ONE : THE HUNT

result. He felt the blanket of searing, oppressive heat, before he saw the river of fire licking at the roof of the passageway. For the most fleeting of moments it illuminated all, Shak saw great black slabs supporting the walls, skulls, or carvings of skulls within alcoves in those slabs and, in the walls ahead, gigantic stone reliefs of figures, stout figures holding double handed weapons high above their heads. He got the impression of space, that, wherever these stairs ended a great black gulf still lay ahead of them. Just how vast was this complex that Oswold had brought them into? Then the dragons fire started to recede, tongues of flame withering and smoking into nothingness above. He had an acrid, sulphurous smell stinging his nose, mingling with the blood in his mouth, the heat that had brought sweat to his brow and curled his hair dissipated.

Then all was darkness once more.

****

"There must be a cave or something, it is trying to squeeze its head inside." Zukan frowned in puzzlement, they really were too far away to see clearly.

"And where is my sister?" Nico asked. "And those that have taken her."

"In the cave, Kudrassos is trying to get to them."

"Kud…. who?" Nico failed to disguise his impatience.

It was Siri who answered. "Kudrassos. It is a pagan god, a snake god. Our blood enemies the Kudreyans have the snake as their symbol. Zukan thinks that that…. thing is an earthly manifestation of the god."

"And what do you think?" Nico asked her.

"My mind is open," was her rather circumspect reply. "In Fash you would consider our faith…unusual. It is a blend of Artoran beliefs mixed with the old gods we used to worship in earlier times. Many of my countrymen would think as Zukan does and see its purpose here being to separate the worthy from the unworthy, with the unworthy meeting death at its claws. Personally I am thinking of my patron goddess Thyasi. I believe she is Artoran but few outside of Fash have heard of her."

"You are right there," Nico said, "it is a new name on me."

"The Goddess of misfortune," Ursus told him. "A partner of Xhenafa, she is said to be there when death strikes suddenly and unexpectedly."

"The assassin's Goddess," Siri said; "but she has worked against us this time." She slipped her hand under her clothes and pulled out a small gold disc attached to a chain around her neck. She held it out for Nico and Ursus to see.

"A representation."

The figure carved onto the disc had long hair, a prominent nose, high cheekbones and long lashes. It looked like a typical Fashtani woman. Nico remarked as such.

"Fair enough," was her dry reply. "I suppose all Fashtani women look the same to you."

"I did not mean…. " Nico started to reply, only to be interrupted by an excited whoop from Zukan. Doul too was on his feet and shielding his eyes.

"I think it has breathed fire." He sounded none too pleased, presumably because his mark may have just been toasted. "Directly into the cave, can you see the smoke billowing out of it?"

"Eleanor!" Nico forgot all discussion of foreign gods and peoples. His mace was in his hand, and he was on the point of bounding down the hill towards the river before Ursus stopped him, having to throw both arms around the younger man to do so.

"Do not stop me Ursus!" Nico cried. "My sister is in that cave, and I have to get her out, I swear by Mytha's claws I will strike down anyone who gets in my way, even you old friend, even you!"

"Hear me out Nico!" Ursus forced the red faced young knight to look at him, to look at his steely grey eyes. "If the fire has killed her then we are already too late!"

"Not too late to strike the beast down, to avenge myself by taking its head!" Nico's fury persisted.

"And if it comes to that then I will stand alongside you, I will fight it and accept whatever end the Gods decide for me. But we do not know the outcome, she may still be alive in there. Her captors will value her life more than their own and they will protect her in just such a manner. What we need to do is to wait for that animal to get bored and leave, then we can move across the river and see exactly what has happened. And I swear that if the worst, and Elissa not let it be so, but if the worst outcome has occurred then I will not take one day of rest until that creature has been hunted down and killed, with its head presented to your family as recompense. We serve no purpose in rushing down there, giving the creature ample notice of our approach then being fried while standing mid river. When we hunt it down it will be on our terms I promise you that, and it will have no advantage, nor will it receive any mercy from me."

ACT ONE : THE HUNT

Nico listened to Ursus' calm, measured tones, the redness of his face cooling as he did so. He pushed Ursus arms off him and replaced his mace in the thong over his back. "Very well," he said thickly. "Very well, just so long as honour is served."

"It will be," Ursus told him. "Now all we can do is sit, watch and wait."

Nico took his seat again, but did not look over the rocks, preferring rather to listen to Zukan's running commentary, which mainly involved the creature hammering away at the cave mouth with claw and tail. There was no more fire, but the wait was a long one and the stars were beginning to poke out from behind the clouds by the time the dragon left the cave mouth behind.

****

The heavy impacts of the dragon tearing at the rock outside sounded duller and echoed far more sonorously now Shak had reached the bottom of the stairs. He could still hear the rattling of falling stones and dust in the tunnel they had just passed yet the feeling of imminent peril he had felt before falling down the stairs was passing. The dragon, for all its fury, could not reach them here, wherever here might actually be. And that of course constituted their next problem.

"You ok?" Stauncher was peering at him by the light of Dormouse's torch. There was blood on his face and his shoulder ached but aside from that he was fine.

"Yes," he said. "Just a bloody nose, nothing more. So where are we?"

Stauncher shrugged. "Inside a mountain?"

"Inside a mountain," Dormouse concurred; "and inside some sort of hallway inside that mountain. Seen the figures on the walls?"

"A little," Shak said. "Hold the torch close to them, I want a better look."

Dormouse did so. Shak could now see that this hallway was far roomier than the tunnel that had preceded it, maybe as much as twenty feet high and almost as wide. The ceiling still had traces of plasterwork, it appeared that there had once been some sort of frieze up there judging from the colourful tiny fragments that remained. As for the figures on the walls both the altitude and cold seemed to have left them better preserved, though there were almost entirely clothed in red and ochre coloured lichens that greatly obscured their features. The one he was looking at was a stout fellow, bearded, armoured in some sort of mail and was wielding a weapon that appeared to have a wooden stock affixed to a number of small chains each ending in a round, spiked metal ball.

"A soldier of some sort?" Dormouse surmised.

Oswold, who had been further down the hallway, return to join them, flames from his torch licking worryingly close to his hair and beard. "Yes, they all are here. The hall of the warriors I call this place. The stonework is cracked and sagging in places but to have stood here for so long and still be in this condition is nothing short of remarkable."

"But how long?" Shak wondered. Who were these people? And where did they go?"

Oswold sucked on his lip, then started chewing it. "I read things, as a young man in the monastery, stories of the mountain men, peoples who lived here long before Tanaren was founded. I am guessing that we are looking at work that is at least a millennium old, maybe even much older than that."

"Mountain men?" Shak said. "We have nothing about them in our history and Arshuma is older than Tanaren by some centuries. Perhaps they were as the name implies, reclusive people who never strayed far from remote places like this one. Still doesn't explain why they are not here anymore though."

Eleanor had been standing next to Dormouse for a while, her shoulders hunched, unsettled by the whispering darkness. She was glad for an opportunity to talk. "I have read a little," she said. "There are accounts of them in the universities in the capital, so they say but they are kept secret, only a few have been allowed to see them, the Grand Dukes dislike the notion that we were not the first here. There are stories about them though, they are supposed to have lived both over and under the mountains and, to adapt to the thin air and cold they were shorter and more muscular than normal men. Indeed, some say that they were not men at all, no more than the Wych folk are, sorry Dead Eyes."

"No need," the elf said, "I am happy the distinction is made. And these people were known to us as the Derreg or the Dirg. They farmed and herded goats above ground but lived below it, in places like these. And they loved war. Before you humans came along they were our greatest enemies, our war with them was said to have lasted over two thousand years. Then, one day they left this part of the world in a great migration, heading east and north, why I do not know. We let them go and they disappeared from our tales. And yes, we

ACT ONE : THE HUNT

did think of them as different from humans, though, having never met one, I cannot confirm the truth either way."

"Is there anything you don't know?" Eleanor asked, now that her attempt to show off and boast about her knowledge had been so comprehensively quashed.

"Yes. That is all I know of the Derg for example. We learned a couple of songs about them as a child, I have given you the gist of them. Apart from their obsessive ancestor worship and their offering of hearts to their gods that is about it."

"Hearts to their gods?" Eleanor licked her lips in distaste. "Like I didn't want to get out of here already. Has the dragon gone yet?"

An echoing shriek from the world outside gave them their answer. "Do you want to pass the time looking around?" Oswold asked.

"Might as well," Shak said, with little enthusiasm.

"Come with me then," he said, "there is not much more to this hall."

They let him lead, hollow footsteps echoing off brooding stone. Shak noted the figures as they passed them, all were striking similar poses, legs braced, weapons readied to strike. There were maces, hammers, flails, and great double handed axes, most of the figures were bearded but not all, which led Shak to believe that these were not some abstract representations of the warrior ideal but genuine depictions of real people, people who had once lived here, who had once defended this realm of darkness. If these people did venerate their ancestors as Dead Eyes had intimated then that would make sense, what better way to venerate them than to look upon them each time this hallway was trod?

For maybe five whole minutes they slowly crept forward, even Oswold seemed happy to slow his gait to accommodate their apprehension, blabbering on about how many figures there were, what weapons they carried, his theory that the frieze overhead would once have depicted their pagan gods looking down from the skies. Then though, he stopped dead, because he had something important to say.

"Well," he looked back at them, trying to gauge their response. "We are here."

They could go no further. They had arrived at a dead end. Oswold and Dormouse passed their torches over the edifice that barred their way. It was a face of level stone, part encrusted in lichen though it seemed that in some places the lichen had been cleared, Shak concluding correctly that Oswold was probably the culprit in this case. Loose stones, some quite substantial, lay scattered around their feet, Stauncher almost stumbling over one with a stifled curse. The lichen free parts of the wall lay on either side and across the top and the carvings exposed consisted of a row of leering skulls at the top, their sinister aspect enhanced many times over by the orange glow of the dancing torch flame, it was not just Eleanor that shuddered nervously as they gazed at them. More bizarrely the carvings on either side were of splayed hands; they were concave as though the handprints had been pressed into the rock when it was soft, there were over a dozen of them on either side.

But the lichen had not formed in another place too. Right at the centre, running from top to bottom was a thick groove, clumps of lichen had encrusted close by but had left the groove clear. Shak almost laughed at his stupidity, as he finally understood what he had been looking at all along.

"Artorus great beard!" He breathed. "It is a door."

"Of course!" Oswold squeaked in excitement. "A door it is. But what lies beyond that do you wonder, what lies beyond?"

Several of them spoke at once. "The dragon cave?"

Oswold nodded sagely, his aura of worldly wisdom slightly diminished by the dribble that ran from mouth to beard. "Yes," he said, his voice serious for once. "The dragon cave."

ACT ONE : THE HUNT

END OF ACT ONE

THE FANGS OF THE FEN SNAKE

Printed in Great Britain
by Amazon